Que Ell One

A War Satire

Skip E. Lee

iUniverse, Inc.
New York   Bloomington

Que Ell One
A War Satire

This is a work of fiction. All of the characters, names, incidents, organizations, and dialogue in this novel are either the products of the author's imagination or are used fictitiously.

iUniverse books may be ordered through booksellers or by contacting:

iUniverse
1663 Liberty Drive
Bloomington, IN 47403
www.iuniverse.com
1-800-Authors (1-800-288-4677)

ISBN: 978-1-4401-7978-5 (pbk)
ISBN: 978-1-4401-7980-8 (cloth)
ISBN: 978-1-4401-7979-2 (ebook)

Printed in the United States of America

iUniverse rev. date: 10/20/09

PART THE FIRST

Our Young Hero Goes To Vietnam

═══ Chapter One ═══

"We are all going to die."

A young man heard the voice but knew not from whence it came.

The 707 jet plane finished its taxiway maneuvers on the runway of an air force base near Sunnyvale, California. It was raining cats, mice and dogs.

At the end of the runway, the aging chartered aircraft began to spool up its engines, which coughed, hesitated and sputtered, until they seemed to catch some vestige of power. Jammed inside the aircraft were 180 soldiers six abreast. The plane had been loaded front to rear according to rank. A superannuated general sat in the front, just behind the locked door to the pilot's cabin. At the back hunched a highly forlorn 18-year-old private draftee. In the middle of this panoply of ranks were the middle level officers, the company grade commissioned types, captains and lieutenants.

A thin reedy voice came over the cabin intercom to announce with an obvious Pakistani accent, "Thank you so very muchly for flying Air Guami. We are now leaving sunny California. After a brief layover in scenic Anchorage, Alaska, and a short stop in beautiful Yokohama Mama, Japan, we shall deliver you to the garden spot of Southeast Asia, gorgeous Saigon. We hope ever so muchly that you enjoy your flight and that you enjoy your splendid vacation in Vietnam."

The jet plane then shuddered forward. An ominous belch of blue smoke blew from a starboard engine. The ill maintained aircraft lurched forward, stumbled slightly and then flapped uncertainly into the rain-pelted air.

"We are all going to die," Remphelmann heard from somewhere.

Second Lieutenant Ronald Reagan Remphelmann, newly minted Lieutenant Remphelmann, newly ensconced in the ordnance corps as a mechanical maintenance officer, was a motor pool functionary. Remphelmann sat back with satisfaction as the airplane lurched itself bloatedly into the sky. For Remphelmann this seemed like the beginning of a great and historic adventure. The dreary past of a inconspicuous youth in Keokuk, Iowa, the faceless young life on the corn fed plains of the American middle-west were blown away as the uncertain trumpet of ill maintained jet engines launched him into the unknown.

Remphelmann settled back. He was a tall yet scrawny young man, who still sported an occasional pimple. He stroked his peach fuzz moustache, which he fancied made him look older than his nineteen years. He adjusted his army issue clumsy black-framed spectacles. His thick coke bottle lenses obscured his dark gray pupils, but in his own mind's eye he could see the true look of incipient glory standing before his gaze. He waited to go forth to make the world safe for democracy. The heroic speech newly issued from the late great John Fitzgerald Kennedy reverberated though his mind.

"Ask not what your country can do for you,
Ask what you can do for you country!
We will pay any price, bear any burden,
Meet any hardship, support any friend,
Oppose any foe, to assure the survival

And the success of liberty."

"We are all going to die," Remphelmann heard again. It was a whiney little almost infantile whisper. Remphelmann scanned discretely for the source of the voice.

Lieutenant Remphelmann looked at his seat passenger. That was the source of the noise. Next to him sat a fat pudgy pasty-faced captain. The captain lurched forward, fumbled for a plastic lined brown bag in the seat pocket before him. The captain hurriedly vomited into the convenient bag, a sick sack, a barf bag, as it was popularly known.

"We are all going to die," the bloated captain intoned sotto voce to Remphelmann.

Remphelmann could not overcome his recent etiquette training at an impromptu officers school. "Begging the captain's pardon," he proffered, "we are on to our way to the sovereign Republic of Vietnam, to offer assistance to the heroic South Vietnamese in their struggle against the horrible menace of communism. We shall prevail and return victorious."

The bloated captain retched again. "We are all going to die." The fatso repeated this phrase in an even more child-like voice.

"Begging the captain's pardon, again," said Remphelmann, as he tried to approximate the stylized language he had imbibed in his brief military career. "I am Lieutenant Ronald Reagan Remphelmann, but I haven't the pleasure of the captain's name."

The captain puked again into the plasticized bag, and wired it uncertainly shut. "Captain Roscoe Arbuckle Falstaff Manteca III, quartermaster corps, at your service, you little twerp." He attempted a retch again. Remphelmann rummaged his military decorum for a fit answer but found only a thankful silence.

Unbeknownst to Remphelmann, Captain Manteca was on the lam from a bigamy charge, absconding from a slam dunk court-martial for officers club petty cash theft, misappropriation of Red Cross funds, not to mention a rather odd near arrest at a transvestite bar outside Fort Ord, California, his home base. Vietnam was his only escape. Captain Manteca again reached forward into the elastic pocket of the seat before him and fumbled for another barf bag. There was none. Manteca cadged another from the pocket in front of Remphelmann.

"Abandon all hope, ye who enter here," Manteca intoned. The literary reference was lost on Remphelmann.

The ill tuned 707 landed in Anchorage, Alaska, with the starboard outboard engine spewing hydraulic fluid in gushes and gurts and gaily onto the ground. The hapless passengers waited four hours in the confines of the airplane while ground mechanics attempted to repair the engine. Nonetheless the engine dribbled. When the onboard toilets were full beyond overflowing, some brilliant ground control genius in his infinite wisdom directed the plane to a nearby terminal. The 707 was greatly dripping fluid and urine as it wheezed itself to a boarding ramp.

The occupants lunged for the exit. There they were met by a bevy of military police, MP's, armed with holstered pistols, telling them that they were quarantined to the immediate boarding area. There somebody or something opened a decrepit hamburger stand. Soldiers flocked to wait in line for any sight of civilian food only to find grease burger on sale, for the immense price of three dollars apiece, a half-day's pay for a private soldier.

Other soldiers, intent only on seeking relief from full bladders and noisome bowels, headed to the toilets. The toilet rooms, labeled men and women, were declared open to all sexes, although nobody but men were present on the flight. They entered to find the toilets overflowing, no running water from the faucets and the stench of turpentine solvent disinfectant stinking the air.

Some of the men, searching for some way out of the glass encapsulated terminal, found a way that was open to an observation deck. There they were assailed by the usual swarms of mosquitoes, called the national bird of Alaska due to their immense size, and such a bevy of gnats that the insects ran up their noses, despite the smell of pine solvent and septic odor from the toilets that lingered in their nostrils.

An hour later the drips of hydraulic fluid were staunched

beneath the right hand engine. The military police gleefully, sadistically, ordered the victims back aboard the aluminum coffin of the aircraft. A gruff MP voice barked, "Re-board, re-board." Back on the airplane Remphelmann found himself reseated next to the feckless Captain Manteca. Manteca groaned again his fore bemoaned moan. "We are all going to die."

Remphelmann dismissed the captain by silently affirming, "Here I enter the paths of glory."

The voice of the Pakistani pilot of the plane came again over the intercom, "Thank you for re-boarding Air India, uh, Contract Air Kodiaki. Your next destination is the glorious Yokohama Mama airport, where we shall pause only muchly briefly for fuel and then on to the beautiful tourist paradise, Tan Son Nhut, Vietnam. We hope you have a wonderful flight and will fly Air Paki again. Fasten your seatbelts."

The hapless fat man had turned green. He attempted to retch again, but only achieved a profitless dry heave. Remphelmann sniffed and snorted silently at the gutless quartermaster. Little did either know that their paths would, sooner than later, meet again on Que Ell One.

══ Chapter Two ══

The airplane began its descent into Tan Son Nhut.

The pilot's voice came over the intercom. "Due to the risk of enemy ground fire as we approach beautiful Saigon, my esteemed passengers may notice that our angle of approach is only slightly different than one would expect on a normal tourist flight. Please to all occupants to most kindly fasten your seat belts and cinch the belt down tight, as the negative gravity force may be disconcerting to the un-re-initiated."

At this point the jet abruptly nosed into a very steep, extremely steep, totally suicidal dive. The starboard engine, which had given so many problems earlier, began to wail uncontrollably as it again spewed horrendous volumes of blue smoke.

Lieutenant Remphelmann was unconcerned. This was part of the adventure. Captain Manteca, on the other hand, no longer having any thing on the floor of his stomach to hurl, clasped to the hand holds of his seat and muttered in that same strange little boy voice, "We are all going to die. Hail Mary, full of grace. We are all going to die. The Lord is with you. We are all going to die. Holy Mary, Mother of God, pray for us sinners, we are all going to die."

At the last conceivable moment the aircraft flared out through the heavy mist. The runway appeared to those brave enough to look out the windows. The ground rushed up in a dizzy crazy quilt of rice paddy, jungle water hazards, small buildings and asphalt. At the end of its tether the airplane snapped up to the horizontal like a dog jerked on its leash and smacked against the runway. The starboard engine erupted in a mass of flames. The port set of landing gears poured forth a volume of black smoke as the tires blew out. The 707 lurched and dithered down the runway. At some juncture the plane settled down and came to an ignominious finish at the end of the runway. Somehow it turned onto a taxiway and limped to a building that had some simulacric resemblance of a terminal.

The cheerful south Asian voice came over the enunciator. "Ladies and Gentleman, we have make a successful landing here at the very muchly high techno golly airport at Tan Son Nhut. In a very muchly few moments we will arrive at the terminal. All ladies and gentleperson men are to keep their seat-less belts securely fastened until we arrive at the mushily desired point of debarkation."

The amazing landing thrilled Lieutenant Remphelmann. It exceeded any roller coaster ride he had ever experienced at the Cook County fair. He turned to Captain Manteca in a burst of youthful enthusiasm. "Begging the captain's pardon, sir, that was one heck of a landing!"

Manteca, on the other hand, was less than impressed. Manteca's voice changed from a whimper into something of a growl. "You little piece of shit, we are on the ground in Vietnam and not only are we all going to die, we are going to die a horrible death."

Remphelmann tried to dispel the negative thought train of the esteemed captain. "Sir, Captain Manteca, sir, we are here to win a glorious victory for the forces of freedom. JFK's speech..."

Manteca stormed, "Idiot, holy mother of god, we are going to die." Then again in a voice that reverted to a child-like whimper,

Manteca said more to himself rather than the lieutenant. "Why in god's name am I invoking Catholic prayers and phrases? I'm not only not Catholic, I'm an atheist. Our father who art, hail mary, pass deep into the end zone, please."

The invalid aircraft made a clumsy zigzag onto another taxiway. The blown out tires on the port side thumped and bumped. The cloud of blue smoke from the starboard engine and acrid smell of burnt rubber tires made its way into the air conditioning system. Men passed out. The 707 collapsed to an ignominious halt in front of the terminal. Out of the mist two boarding stairs appeared. They were marked Air France and Bon Voyage.

The hapless passengers bailed for the exits and the stairs, hoping for a gasp of fresh air. There they were met by a blast of superheated air and the most intense humidity a human could imagine. It was like walking into a steam engine exhaust. The soldiers stumbled down onto the tarmac. Captain Manteca immediately disappeared into the vapor and gathering sundown.

"Good riddance to bad rubbish," Remphelmann relished. "The fat slob is a disgrace to the officer corps."

An air force sergeant with a bullhorn was repeating over and over again to all concerned. "You guys go straight into the terminal. Sit on the frigging floor. When your frigging duffle bags appear on the baggage line, grab your luggage. Look on your frigging boarding pass. There is a two-digit alphanumerical code there. When you get your frigging duffel bag go out the frigging blue door at the end of the terminal and you'll find a frigging bus. On the side of the frigging bus, you guys will see a chalked alphanumeric code scribbled on the side of the frigging bus. Alpha–numeric to you frigging jarheads and you frigging ground-pounders means just that. If your boarding pass is marked A-1 that means go to bus alpha-one. If your boarding pass is marked C-3 then go to the bus chalked up charlie-three. Can I make any simpler to you frigging idiots?" The air force sergeant's voice instantly changed. "However to our esteemed officers, would you gentlemen please retrieve your luggage and kindly exit out the red door? There are there waiting for you three buses chalked up O-1 through O-3. Your ground transportation awaits. You will be whisked away to your bachelor officers quarters awaiting assignment. Now for you frigging jarheads and ground-pounders, I frigging repeat..." The man with the bullhorn did repeat.

Remphelmann dutifully did as instructed. He retrieved his 80-pound duffel bag and trudged out the red door. He checked his boarding pass and maneuvered himself and his luggage onto bus oscar-three. The bus was a cramped vehicle of Japanese make, painted a glorious olive drab. What amazed him was that the windows of the bus were covered with expanded metal mesh. A rather dispirited major struggled in and sat silently next to Remphelmann. The young lieutenant could not remember his military courtesy but he tried.

"Begging the major's pardon," he began.

The major instantly cut him short. "Cut the military courtesy crap short, lieutenant. This is my second tour and I've seen shave tails like you before. Can it!"

Initially Remphelmann did put his thoughts back in the can. However as the bus filled up he could not restrain his errant question. "Begging the major's..." he stopped in mid–sentence, and re-began. "Uh, major, this bus has metal mesh welded on all of the windows. It's like a prison bus."

The major sighed. "The mesh is not to keep us in, it's there to keep the Viet Cong from throwing hand grenades through the windows and disturbing our peace."

Remphelmann waited a long pause. "But sir, we are at Tan Son Nhut, isn't that safe?

The major sighed. "No, lieutenant, Tan Son Nhut is air force, we have to go to Long Bien, which is army. That means we get to drive through Saigon to the army base on the other side of town."

"I don't really understand," said Remphelmann.

"You will soon enough," said the major, who laced his fingers together and clamped them over his eyes and proceeded to take a nap.

Presently an air force airman came into the bus and started the engine. The three officer buses maneuvered into a tight formation and two air police jeeps appeared. Both jeeps sported a M-60 machine gun mounted on a steel post in the back seat with nervous looking men driving and manning the guns. The two jeeps sandwiched the buses and they moved out. The little convoy moved slowly at first, but when they came to the edge of the air base, they picked up speed. They careened through a chicane of concrete obstacles and a maze of coiled barbed wire. Suddenly they were on the streets of Saigon. Remphelmann watched with intensive interest. He had an image of grass huts and bamboo barns but what he saw as the convoy moved through the streets reminded him more of a National Geographic picture of southern France. Block after block of two story buildings loomed up and fell away. He noted with great interest the architecture, which seemed to his inexperienced eye that of New Orleans, whitewashed stone, iron balconies on the second floors, tight metal clad doorways. The sun was already down and the people of the town were scurrying indoors. There was yet another curfew in effect and the bustle of mopeds, motorcycles, pedestrian folks and the occasional ancient cars were pulling into their nighttime places. The little convoy gathered speed as it came into a congested area. The front running AP jeep turned on a siren. The buses seemed to bunch together and took turns as such a rate of speed that they leaned and tottered outward from the centrifugal force. The few Vietnamese on the sidewalks ignored them. Finally they hit an open stretch of road and entered another set of concertina wire and concrete obstacles. The lead jeep squelched its siren. They passed though a heavy steel gate that was opened only long enough for them to pass through. MP's stared down over their machine guns from the two high sand bag bunkers that flanked the entrance. The two jeeps peeled off and the three buses slowed and made their way through an endless maze of what seemed to be sheet metal industrial buildings or hangers. The buses squealed to a stop in front of one of the massive structures. The driver of Remphelmann's bus slammed open the lever that controlled the door, turned on the interior lights, grabbed a comic book and kicked back in his seat with aplomb.

The tired officers grappled with their duffels and filed off into a gaping doorway of the hanger. A sour looking private sat at a desk repeating endlessly, "Travel orders, boarding passes, travel orders, boarding passes." The officers queued before the almighty private, who showed no military courtesy to his superiors. The private took the proffered papers, put the boarding passes through a time-date machine, scribbled a number on each and flipped it into an inbox. He wrote the same number on the margin of each officers travel orders. "Bunk 23, chow hall closed. Chow hall opens five AM. Next." Remphelmann waited his turn. The private droned on as he processed the paper. "Bunk 34, chow hall closed. Chow hall opens five AM. Next."

Remphelmann's four eyes had adjusted to the cavernous dimness. The entire hanger floor had been laid out with yellow marking lines. Hundreds of bunks were lined neatly up and down the lines. A crude sign stenciled with yellow numbers was wired to the foot of each bunk. Remphelmann got the hint, hefted up his duffle and found number 34. He dropped his bag and sat on the narrow cot. 'This is not a bachelor officers quarters,' he mused to himself, 'this like a prison dormitory.' He looked up at the few lights that were still lit in the high roofline.

The humidity and pervasive heat simmered in the gloom as if a cloud had encamped against the rafters. All the other officers were silent, exhausted, hungry and to Remphelmann's mind, strangely dispirited at what was obviously the advent of a great quest for glory and adventure. The officers silently stripped to their shorts, pulled the olive drab blankets from the pre-made bunks and hung them on the foot bar. They shook out the white top sheet and fell in bed. It was so hot that everybody was sweating. Remphelmann looked around and saw that earlier arrivals were perspiring to the point that sweat had soaked every man, sheet and mattress into a soggy mass.

'When in Rome, do as the Romans,' he thought. It was too dim to read the paperback book he had stuffed in his bag. So he stripped, fluffed out his top sheet and stuffed his massively thick peepers under his pillow. The sheet instantly sopped the water pouring from his skin and he felt as if he had fallen into quicksand. However, he did suddenly realize how tired he was. He thought briefly of the Great Game before him, with sugar plum visions of heroic deeds in the offing. Soon though, he was in a soggy exhausted sleep just like everyone else.

Chapter Three

If dawn cracked, Remphelmann did not hear it. All he heard in the darkness was the groan of two hundred company grade officers, captains and lieutenants, moaning and swearing the most god-forsaken oaths. He awoke to find that someone had switched on the overhead lights. A cloud of fog hovered near the ceiling of the warehouse. He rolled slightly, only to discover he was dripping wet. His sheets, pillow and mattress were like a horrible wet sponge. Somebody was yelling, "4:45 hours, wake up, rise and shine, officers mess open in fifteen minutes."

Officers were attempting to extricate themselves from their clammy sheets. Remphelmann realized he had a tremendous urinary and bowel overload. "Where's the latrine," he gasped to nobody in particular. Somebody pointed. Remphelmann could not see and remembered he had forgotten his spectacles under the pillow. He fished them out, oriented himself, and double-timed to the toilet. He found fifty other men relieving themselves into trough like pissoirs, and another twenty evacuating their bowels into a military parade line of twenty crappers without the dignity of stall dividers. Having done his earthly business he looked up to see everybody else attempting to shave at something that looked like a hog slop. He hustled back to bunk 34, dressed, grabbed his shaving kit from his duffel and skedaddled back to scrape the blondish peach fuzz from his face. No sooner than he had finished his ablutions than somebody else yelled, "Officer mess open, orange door to the west." He had no idea where west was but as this gaggle of America's best and brightest was herding themselves in a certain direction, he followed. "Line up asshole to bellybutton and grab a tray," the same anonymous voice barked again. Remphelmann looked around to find this famous somebody else's voice that was barking orders but could find no man to fit the orders. However, he did as told.

He stood in line, grabbed a brown melamine tray from a greasy stack and advanced. Introduced in to the august hall of the so-called officers mess, he was met by a long stainless steel steam table. Behind the gutter were filthy cooks in besmirched jungle fatigues ladling out what passed for breakfast. Step one, two slices of cardboard toast, step two, a gummy ladle full of reconstituted scrambled eggs, step three, the piece de resistance of every American soldier's food life, the famous chipped beef and white gravy was slopped on the toast. This concoction is better known as SOS, or shit on a shingle. Step four, two more slices of army bread. At the end of the feeding trough there was a slimy set of knife, fork and spoon wrapped in the cheapest of paper napkins. Beyond that was a table with carafes of heroic tepid army coffee with fly-infested bowls of sugar and something that passed as non-dairy creamer and something else that ersatzed for pats of margarine. Remphelmann finished assembling his repast. His own mother of sainted memory had never gotten past the skim milk, corn flake and wonder bread toast phase. So the young man thought this breakfast most delicious. He wolfed it down.

The same ethereal yet commanding voice yelled again. "Return to your bunks. Wait for an orderly to direct you to a replacement officer." Remphelmann returned to his bed. He had a sudden urge to go back to the latrine but thought better of the idea. He corked himself up. Almost instantly a specialist appeared and spoke in the most unctuous terms, "Second Lieutenant Remphelmann, Ronald Reagan, follow me and bring your travel orders." Remphelmann followed. They went out yet another colored door and into a smaller hanger.

There at three small metal desks sat sad looking sallow faced officers who would have graced an accountant's office. The cadaverous captain at the first desk motioned Remphelmann. He looked briefly at the young lieutenant's travel orders.

"Second Lieutenant, Remphelmann, Ronald Reagan. ordnance corps. military occupation specialty, 4815, mechanical maintenance. Motor pool officer." The ghostly captain looked up and for the first time observed Remphelmann. "My god, how old are you?" he gasped.

"Nineteen, sir, actually nineteen and a half." Remphelmann was actually proud that he was six months older than his dog tags stated.

The personnel captain did a double take at Remphelmann and his travel orders. "My holy goodness, you look like you are fourteen."

The young man did not know what to say, so he said, "Begging the captain's pardon, thank you, sir."

"Where did you get this crappy 'begging the captain's pardon' line?'" the interrogator snapped.

"United States Army Officer Candidate School, Ordnance Corps, Aberdeen Proving Ground, Maryland, sir. Six months of strict discipline, sir. Begging the captain's pardon, sir."

"For god's sake, stop the begging the general's ass crap, this is the real army."

"Begging the captain's pardon, sir, yes sir."

"Six months at the officer candidate school, my ass. You are still a ninety-day wonder to me." The interrogator continued. "What in jumping jehosaphat! What am I going to do with a little drip like you?" The tired officer consulted a badly typed list of available postings.

"Begging the..." Remphelmann wised up. "Excuse me, sir,

17

I am a Vietnam volunteer, and I gladly offered myself for the most dangerous assignments. John Fitzgerald Kennedy, at his inaugural address, said,

'We shall go anywhere, bear any burden...'"

The interviewer cut him short. "Can the crap. JFK got his brains blown out in Dallas for rhetoric like that. What am I to do with you?" The functionary looked at the posting list. "Hundred and First Air Mobile, Big Red One, Fourth Infantry Ivy Leaf's," he mused.

"Yes, yes and yes." Remphelmann chimed in.

"Shut your pimply little lips," snorted the captain. I can't send you up a real combat outfit. They would kick you back inside of 72 hours, with nasty note that would ruin my career. The only hope for a loser like you is to send you to a rear echelon mother friggers unit, a REMF backwater." The captain laughed to himself, "How poetic, I get to send a lieutenant named Remphelmann to the REMF's." The captain chuckled at first and then the captain cackled.

"Sir," Remphelmann tried to interject.

The godlike man behind the desk said, "This posting sheet says there is a need in Cam Ranh Bay for a 4815. Your original orders assigned you to the replacement depot at Qui Nonh, but with a whisk of my ballpoint pen you are instantly reassigned to the 1369th, Cam Ranh Bay, the 1369th Rear Echelon Maintenance Force. The 1369th REMF's. Deed done, I affix my time and date stamp and my signature." The captain laughed diabolically.

Remphelmann tried to interject but he was at a complete loss. "Sir, begging the... sir! I don't understand... I mean begging the..." Remphelmann stopped.

"Shut up, twerp, you get what you deserve." The godlike officer motioned to a waiting specialist. "Cam Ranh, next flight." The captain motioned him away with an easy brush of the hand. "Next!"

The flunky took Remphelmann's travel orders, made a cryptic note or two in the margin, made the same obscure notes on a pad, and announced "Sir, Second Lieutenant Remphelmann. Would the lieutenant please be kind enough to go back to the cattle barn, and hang out around your bunk, bunk 34." He handed back to a confused young man the travel orders. "Out the purple door, back to your bunk and your duffel, sir. Then wait."

Remphelmann staggered back to his stall in the barn, dazed. 'What's happening,' he pondered to himself. 'I volunteered for Vietnam to be part of an heroic fighting outfit, and this captain sends me to some obscure outfit I never heard of. And what's this joke about REMF's, rear echelon mother friggers? Is my name some kind of a curse?'

No sooner than Remphelmann hit his bunk, than another specialist came flying up. The specialist had a blond surfer boy haircut and dreamy, almost drug like eyes. "Wow, groovy!" the soldier blurted. "Lieutenant Remphelmann, sir?"

"Yes," the lieutenant answered.

"Wow, man, you are in luck. There's a bus pulling up right now, it's going to take you the army airfield for a quick flight to Cam Ranh Bay. Go out the yellow door and there will be a bus chalked up Cam Ranh. Hop the bus. They'll take you straight to the friendly skies. In no time you'll be at the bay. They tell me sugar white sand beaches, tubular swells, and currents running straight on the beach. I'm envious, sir, I'm stuck here inland and you get posted to surfer's paradise!"

Remphelmann, being from Keokuk, didn't understand. He didn't know the difference between a surfboard and a moldboard plow. Nonetheless he muttered, "Surf's up, dude."

The specialist pointed to the door. "Right on! I'm jealous as hell, sir. I'm stuck here in the rice paddies and you get the groovy post. You officers get all the luck." Remphelmann hoisted his duffel and aimed toward the yellow door. As he lumbered away, he could hear the blond soldier sing.

'Surf is running, just up the coast
Throw your board in the woody; you'll be there first.

Don't you worry, don't you fret.
You'll soon be surfing and you won't get wet.
Cam Ranh shoreline, Cam Ranh Beach
Cam Ranh girls are sugar sweet.'"

Remphelmann exited the yellow door. Sure enough there was a Japanese olive drab bus chalked up Cam Ranh. He huffed his duffel to the bus door and entered. A young black private soldier with beady eyes and razor cut hair-do was behind the wheel and eyed him as he got aboard. The baby-faced officer looked down the bus and spied an empty seat in the back of the bus. He began to struggle to the spot. The driver of the bus immediately stood up and yelled at Remphelmann. "Sir, stop there!"

"What?" Remphelmann said.

"Sir, you are an officer, officers got to sit in the front of the bus so they can lead, sir."

Remphelmann was non-plussed. "That's all right, private, I see an empty seat back there."

"No, sir," you got to be in the front, army regulations, sir."

"But," interjected Remphelmann.

"But, my butt, sir," replied the driver. The driver turned around and spied an immense man, a black man of three hundred pounds of solid muscle, wearing the collar insignia of an infantryman. "Hey you, yes you, private, get your raggedy black ass up and move back. Let the officer have your seat."

The immense man sat immobile. "I don't give my bus seat up to nobody!"

"I'm telling you officers to the front, enlisted to the rear."

"I won't move."

"Who the hell you think you are, Rosa Parks? Get your muscular fanny to the rear and let this officer have your seat."

The large man slowly rose. Not only was he 300 pounds of lean flesh, he was at least six and half feet tall. "I'll give up this here seat to an officer, you razor cut little monkey, but if I get you off-post I'll wail your scrawny black ass into the asphalt."

Remphelmann, corn flake skim milk boy from a white neighborhood, was baffled by this interchange of words. He felt for a fleeting moment that he had an instigated a black intra-racial riot. He was totally ignorant that the fore-going interchange of banter between refugees from America's inner cities was simply par for the course.

The driver checked his head count and closed the door. Then he took off at breakneck speed. He careened out of the jumble of warehouses and presently arrived on the taxiway of Long Bien's abbreviated runway. There waited an immense C-130 cargo aircraft with its back ramp down. The aircraft, known as a 'Hercules,' already had its four propellers slowly twirling. "Out, out of my bus," the razor cut yelled. "Get on the tarmac and listen to the airman."

The airman, known as a cargo master who was responsible for loading the huge plane, was an aging air force sergeant with a red neck and redder face. He began to yell at the assembled gaggle of forty men who had dragged themselves and their bags out of the bus. "Look he-yah, you dirt kissing grunt-faces." The cargo master finally noticed Remphelmann. "Sir, excepting the exalted lieutenant, sir." The airman snapped a quick salute and continued. "Look he-yah, assholes, what we have he-yah is a C-130 aircraft that is going to fly you to the beautiful beach city of Cam Ranh Bay, the mother of all paradises for surfers and rear echelon mother friggers. When ye-all get on the aircraft, ye-all will observe that there are no cushy seats. Here in my aircraft, of which I am the load-master and god almighty lord, ye-all will find a huge cargo net which is secured forward, aft, left and right to the airframe. Ye-all will move forward en mass, spread your fat asses evenly across the cargo deck and entwine your worthless butts and your duffel bags into the aforesaid cargo net. That's in case we crash on take-off, crash from the air, or crash on landing, your worthless corpses all won't slide to the front of my aircraft and upset the load balance. That is, of course, all except the brilliant young officer who stands before me, who may do as an officer and gentleman may please." The cargo master threw a perfunctory salute at Remphelmann, and continued. "If any of ye-all got to piss, shit or barf, ye-all get to do the deed now. Onboard we have no stewardesses, no toilets and no ass wipe. Do it now, or forever hold your bowels." The loadmaster paused. "Ye-all got five minutes"

As if on cue, the formation broke. Of the forty, twenty unbuttoned their flies and peed on the runway. A few unfortunate sons scrambled a decent distance, dropped trousers and crapped on the tarmac. No body barfed.

Five minutes later the loadmaster screamed. "Line up assholes, time to get on the magic carpet." The passengers crowded together at the rear-loading ramp. "I have explained, in the most intelligent air force terms, how ye-all mud crawlers have to get on this aircraft. Is there any asshole that has a question?"

The immense 300-pound infantryman, known to Remphelmann from the bus, piped up. "Say hey, sarge, does I got to sit in the back of this here bus?"

The loadmaster rolled his eyes. "Look here, you fat ass colored fellow, this isn't Birmingham, you can sit any where you choose as long as you don't upset my load balance. Who the hell you think you are, Rosa Parks?"

The gaggle filed up the back ramp into the airplane. They entangled themselves in the immense cargo net as instructed. Remphelmann, in a fit of democratic fervor, chose to situate himself in the middle. The draftees surrounding him did not notice. Perhaps they had other thoughts.

The back ramp on the aircraft whined up with a great noise of hydraulics and screw jacks. Seconds later the aircraft, turbines and propellers screaming mightily, lifted itself into the steamy air. The plane took a heroic trajectory of forty-five degrees and climbed to altitude.

Remphelmann could not see anything. There was no window to look out. After only a few minutes the Hercules nose-dived again at another forty-five degree angle. Outside the casket like aluminum shell of the C-130 he could hear the screech of tires on pavement. Sooner than he could comprehend the airplane came to a stop. The back ramp whined down. The men disentwined themselves and their baggage from the spider's web of the cargo net. They all stumbled down the ramp into the muggy daylight.

The boisterous loadmaster began to scream again, "Ye-all get off! Off my aircraft, get off, you cannon fodder asses! Off of my cargo deck!"

Remphelmann followed orders. He piled out just like everybody else. He didn't know what to do. The enlisted were hurried to waiting two and half ton trucks. Miraculously there was a jeep parked there. An unguent and oily driver, replete with duck ass haircut slicked back with brilliantine, scanned the arrivers and made a beeline for Remphelmann.

"Lieutenant Remphelmann, sir?" Remphelmann nodded assent. His ears were so buzzy from the whine of propellers and turbines, he could hardly hear. "Sir, most worthy and exalted sir, I'm told to pick you up and deliver your august presence to the 1369[Th] Rear Echelon Maintenance Force. Begging the second lieutenant's butt, but just how old are you?"

"I'm nineteen, actually nineteen and a half." Remphelmann found the words coming mechanically from his mouth.

The grease ball let the lieutenant place his own bag in the back of the jeep. "No matter," said the jeep driver. "I'm not much older. Off to the 1369th and, as the skinny already says, off to Que Ell One."

The jeep driver put the little car into gear and drove away from the Hercules, the tarmac and into oblivion. Remphelmann again did not understand. 'What was Que Ell One?'

═══ Chapter Four ═══

Cam Ranh Bay is beautiful. It is a long inlet of the South China
Sea and stretches a thin twenty miles from north to south. It is
considered the best deep-water port in all of Indochina. Ocean
going ships can safely dock inside its glassy expanse. The deep
anchorages range from one to five miles over its east to west breadth.
On the landward side, the Central Highlands launch themselves
from sea level. In the distance is the promise of mountains, teak
forests and tea plantations. Rubber tree plantations, a legacy
of Michelin's involvement in the colonization of the area, lay
scattered about. On the eastern side of the calm bay the Cam
Ranh peninsula dangles down. It is like a thin gourd angling
southward, its neck firmly joined to the mainland by a stem a
mere mile wide at the north. At its lower end it swells into a
bulbous low mountain range. The Vietnamese always knew it
was there. It is their home turf. However from the time of the
Portuguese explorers to the time of the British sea merchants
to the French colonizers, the bay held promise. During World
War Two the Japanese navy held it as a crown jewel for their
southward expansion.

On the westward side of this peninsula the waters of Cam

Ranh Bay lay smooth and unruffled. The Vietnamese for a thousand generations have angled this water. Pulling bounties of shrimp, sardine and herring from its calm surface, they found a fisherman's bounty. On the eastern side of this thin stretch of land, the unforgiving South China Sea pounds against the peninsula. Rolling daily waves, augmented by the yearly monsoons and typhoons, smash up against the approaches. The result is a long expanse of rocky shoreline, interspersed with beaches of pure white coral sand. It is not a surfer's paradise. The fierce undertow and suddenly changing wave patterns make for hazardous swimming. However the surging sea and its crashing surf tempts the inexperienced.

The strategic significance of the place was not lost on any aggressor. The bay and its safe haven for sailors was a sea given fact. The peninsula at its northern choke point is only a mile wide. Put a small infantry force at the north and the whole gourd like mass of land would be effectively severed from the mainland. Below the stem is a sprawling mass of real estate that can hold docks for ocean going craft, petroleum stores, oil tanks, ammunition dumps and room for a large airport. Alfred Thayer Mahon would smile in his grave at such a prize. This fact was not lost on the Portuguese, the British, the French, the Japanese, the French again, or the Americans. None of these seafaring powers bothered to ask the locals who owned the land or bay and adjacent sea. In short, Cam Ranh has everything to please a military logistician, a deep-water anchorage, room for jet length runways, security for military forces, recreation beaches and a Never-Never Land separation from the reality of mainland Vietnam.

The pomaded little soldier who was driving Remphelmann down the road attempted to describe his environment to the young officer. "You see here sir, as we leave the environs of the air base that we are going south down the bayside road. Up there, back up there up north, we got a Demilitarized Zone about a mile wide, a DMZ, with about a thousand machine guns and thousand artillery pieces cutting off the neck of the peninsula. Why do they call it a DMZ when it isn't de-militarized?"

Remphelmann had no answer.

"So we go down this road to the army base. And turn inland. Over there across the neck of this penis-olla, about two miles away to the west is that South China Sea with the surf and white beaches that the surfer types claim is so cool. I don't understand that part. I'm from Jersey and the only thing I ever surfed was the New York City subway and women's thighs. Youse a surfer?"

Remphelmann had no answer.

The jersey greaser turned off the main road and headed inland. They came over a slight rise in the sand dunes and as they crested, Remphelmann could see a sprawling army camp. Before him he could see army barracks, long low wooden buildings called hootches, and company streets. On a rise to one side sat a city block of Quonset huts. Farther in the distance there seemed to be an industrial area with row after row of large warehouses. Next to that was spotted an immense tank farm that would grace any oil refinery, a hundred steel shells holding gasoline, diesel and jet fuel. Beyond that was the unmistakable ammunition dump, with artillery shells packed in wooden cartons row on row, and humped concrete igloo like ammunition bunkers protecting the devil knew what.

The driver had a habit that intrigued Remphelmann. The driver had formed the bill of his army baseball cap into a cylindrical scoop. As he drove along he would clasp the hat and with a flourish wipe it back over his duck ass hairdo with its amazing load of brilliantine. Having re-plastered his hair, he would re-perch the filthy cap back over his forehead. Remphelmann had the distinct feeling that the private had neither bathed nor shampooed his pompadour since leaving the States. The lieutenant thought briefly about remonstrating with the private about the joys of personal hygiene, but a small still voice entered his mind, whispering the age old military advice,

'Don't mess with the troops, and the troops won't mess with you.' Remphelmann held a discrete silence.

The driver slowed to a crawl as he entered the company streets. "Gotta go slow," the grease ball explained. "Otherwise the frigging military police will haul up and give me a speeding ticket. They hide out behind the hootches and then sneak up on you."

Hootch is a time-honored bit of military slang. The term derives from the American army experience in the late great lamented Korean War. The word stems from the average soldier's usually bungled pronunciation of the Korean word, hon-cho, meaning a small insignificant building of ramshackle construction. Thus anything from a grass hut, bamboo lean-to, to the military's temporary construction got nicknamed hootch. In Vietnam the standard army engineer temporary building consisted of a cement slab exactly 24 feet wide and precisely 40 feet long. A thin framework of 2X4's was erected at the cheapest cost. A thinner framework of trusses was flipped on top of that and precariously above that, a minimal roof of corrugated galvanized metal sheets was nailed. The sides of the military hootch was then clapboarded a height of four feet. The balance had wire screen stapled up to the roofline in a vain attempt to keep out mosquitoes and flies. Around these glorious mansions a thick double row of green sand bags was stacked waist high, with the great hope that if there was an artillery barrage, or mortar attack, the sand bags would deflect some small portion of the ensuing blast and shrapnel. On this particular row of company streets the military hootches stood in a sad cookie cutter parade. The hootches were two each facing the street, followed by six each behind them, followed by two more. The front two held a company headquarters, and a supply room that doubled as sergeant's quarters. Behind that the six hootches had the barracks for up to 240 enlisted men, crammed forty men to a building, and behind that, two buildings holding the latrines, which were architecturally and artistically designed to hold facilities for the urinary, defecatory, shaving and showering needs of 240 men. The water taps, when they worked, if they worked at all, spouted glorious steams of cold muddy water.

The greaser picked up speed as he left the company street area. Presently he turned off the patchy asphalt road onto a gravel way that lead uphill to the Quonset huts. "Lieutenant, here you see Executive Row, where all the bigwigs hang out to conduct the finer details of this heroic war. Let us reason together and find the frigging 1369ᵀʰ." After a tad of looking the oily young man stopped at a one of the half moon shaped steel buildings. Planted in front of the Quonset was a neatly painted sign that proclaimed:

1369ᵗʰ Rear Echelon Maintenance Force

The oleaginous young driver announced, "Well, sir, uncork your little virgin state side ass here, grab your duffel bag and go in that door. Isn't that unit number a dilly? 1369? You know that joke about the worst outfit in the army? 13 as in unlucky 13, and 69 as in sex pre-vision, you know 69 as to double suck weenies? The 13ᵗʰ 69ᵗʰ Unlucky Cough Suckers!" The lieutenant followed the private's joke and the private's directions. As Remphelmann unlimbered himself from the vehicle, the private added, "By the way, sir, if you ever survive this, and I survive this, look me up in Jersey City because that's my home town. Oliva's the name, women's my game." Remphelmann was about to thank the driver for his solicitude when the brill-creamed man added, "Because if I ever catch youse officer asshole on my sidewalk, I'll kick it from Jersey City to Trenton and back. Besides, the skinny is, youse gets Que Ell One!" With a laugh New Jersey's finest slipped the jeep into gear and roared away with a boiling commingled cloud of coral dust, red clay particles and sand dune grains in his wake. Remphelmann stood, duffle bag at the ready, in front of the Quonset hut and the sign that proclaimed

1369ᵀᴴ REMF

28

He screwed his courage to the sticking point, and advanced heroically to the door. Again that still small voice came to him, asking, 'What is Que Ell One?'

Chapter Five

With some trepidation Remphelmann lugged his baggage through the screen door of the Quonset. Inside there were ten metal army desks arranged in two rows. Down the center aisle way a nifty sign artist had crafted signs that hung by flimsy chain from the ceiling. The signs with pointing arrows proclaimed:

S-1

Officer Clerk

S-2

Officer Clerk

S-3

Officer Clerk

S-4

Officer Clerk

Executive Officer

Officer Clerk

Behind this was a door to another room, over which another sign announced:

Lieutenant Colonel
Horatio Alger Slick
Ordnance Corps
Commanding

In time honored military tradition, each commanding officer from the grade of lieutenant colonel, from battalion up to the most ethereal reaches of high command, is entitled to four staff officers to whom the commander may delegate various tasks. In the army these men are called staff officers or 'S'. The S-1 is in charge of personnel, the S-2 is tasked with divining intelligence, the S-3 oversees operations and the S-4 bears the burden of supply. The executive officer acts as the commanding officers second-in-command.

At this particular headquarters three 'S' captains, one major, and four clerks were laboring away under the influence of heavy floor fans that were blowing the horrendously humid Vietnamese air about. In a mechanical unison each lifted a document out of an in-box, scanned it briefly, took each paper, time and date stamped, initialed it, and deposited it in an out-box. The S-2 row was conspicuous in its absence of officer or clerk. The desks were squeaky clean. Evidently at this headquarters there was no need for intelligence.

Remphelmann stood for an uncomfortably long time. He politely harrumphed. At this signal the S-1 clerk looked up from his automatic routine and yelled over the fans to the S-1 officer. "Hey, Captain Dunghill, here's your next piece of meat." The clerk, without a lost beat, went back to his numbing paperwork shuffle.

Captain Dunghill looked up from his automaton blur of forms and cast a gimlet eye upon the new arrival. Dunghill was an amazing scrawny assemblage of fatless sinew. He had a red face, a redder neck, and red blood-shot eye whites. Despite his carmine complexion he flushed white.

"Hell and horse shit," the captain muttered under his breath.

Then he added with a wave of his middle finger, "Mister Christian, come here!"

Remphelmann took this opportunity to smartly move front and center to the captain's desk. In best military fashion he stood at full attention, presented a salute and proudly said. "Sir, Second Lieutenant Ronald Reagan Remphelmann reports for duty as ordered, sir!"

"Hell and horse shit," the red man muttered again as he returned Remphelmann's salute with a desultory wave of his hand. "Why me?" He motioned again with his hand. "Travel orders." The lieutenant produced his mimeographed papers, which were bleeding government issue ink in the wet heat. Dunghill took the orders and perused them with the same mechanical technique that he used to weed his in-box and out-box papers. "It's that same repo depot idiot at Long Bien! That ass-hole delights in sending me the bottom of barrel every time." He flipped the assignment orders from stapled page to following page. He looked up again and did a head snap. "Hell and horse shit, lieutenant, how old are you?"

"Nineteen, sir, actually nineteen and a half."

"Hell and horse..." The redneck caught himself. "And just what is that on your lip?"

"Sir?"

"What is that on your upper lip, dirt? Chocolate milk?"

Remphelmann got the hint. "Oh, my moustache, sir. I admit it's rather thin, sir."

Dunghill groaned. "And just what is that on your nose?" Remphelmann first thought was that he had popped a pimple on the flight over. "Sir, begging the captain's pardon, sir, I do suffer from the occasional outbreak of blackheads."

"No, damn it, that thing on your nose, that through which you are seeing."

Remphelmann got the hint. "Oh, my spectacles, sir. I admit I'm a tad nearsighted, sir."

"Nearsighted my rosy red ass, I've seen coke bottle bottoms that got less glass than what you see through."

Remphelmann tried not to sound offended. "Sir, God gave me these eyes, I have to live with them."

Dunghill placed his elbows on his desk and buried his forehead in his palms. After a long moment, he resurfaced and sighed. "Lieutenant Remphelmann, behind you is a bench. About face and sit on that bench while I inform the colonel of your presence."

"Sir, yes sir." The young man turned and stepped with precision to the bench and sat. The captain lugubriously raised himself from his sweaty seat, turned and headed back between the rows of desks and disappeared though the door and the sign that said 'Officer Commanding'.

The S-1 clerk, a snooty little sour face, did not even bother to look up or otherwise acknowledge Remphelmann's presence. He simply let drop his mindless routine of paper shuffling. He pulled some forms and carbon sheets from his desk and rolled them into a typewriter. He mumbled to himself, "I'll get the jump on this one, supplemental orders for Que Ell One."

Chapter Six

Presently Captain Dunghill reappeared from behind the colonel's door. He seemed to be swimming in the humidity. He confronted Remphelmann. "The colonel will see you now." The scrawny officer led the way. Remphelmann smartly sprang up and tagged behind. As he navigated the rows of desks, no one bothered to look up from their robotic routine of paper shuffling. The captain opened the door and strode in. The lieutenant followed. "For christ's-sake, close the door, you're letting the cold air out," Dunghill snapped. Remphelmann promptly closed the portal and was met by a most rigorous blast of icy air. He glanced over to see a decidedly unmilitary air conditioning unit set in the wall. It was spewing out mega watts of refrigeration.

"Stand at attention before the colonel's desk," the captain snapped again. The lieutenant did as he was told. However, there was no one sitting behind the desk. Out of the corner of his eye he caught a glimpse of a self-important figure in immaculate starched jungle fatigues. The figure was concentrating on an astro-turf putting green and was methodically plunking golf balls towards a target with a gold-plated putter. Remphelmann waited.

Presently the colonel moved into Remphelmann's line of vision. Rather than seating himself at the desk the colonel moved to something of a side stand, a mirror and shelf arrangement. The colonel began to primp his obviously gray short and curly hair. He turned thus and so, and inspected his visage from every angle. Then he took a comb, hair pick and brush and meticulously re-adjusted every conceivable spot of his scalp. Having thus satisfied his desiring eye, he plucked a spray can of hair fixative from the toilette and sprayed his hair. He cast a few askance glances to insure perfection. Thus contented, he regally turned and seated himself at his armor-plated desk.

Remphelmann was well aware of a cartoon character of the time, Colonel Canyon, a square jawed hunk of a man, an air force pilot of supreme skill and bravery with prematurely gray crew cut hair. Colonel Canyon, brave, fearless, always master of the situation, always the cartoon hero, was equal to Superman, or Batman or Dick Tracy, plus he had a curvaceous girlfriend that always seemed to show up in the hour of the hero's personal needs. Colonel Canyon ruled the comic pages. As this simulacrum of Colonel Canyon majestically deposited himself on the colonel's chair, Remphelmann flinched back in awe.

"Well, what have we here?" the colonel commented. He took up Remphelmann's greasy travel orders and flipped insolently though them. The lieutenant noticed the colonel's pink pristine fingers, with obvious manicured nails and a hint of nail buff, as the august one fingered through the papers. "Captain Dunghill here has apprised me of the situation concerning you. We, in the obvious necessity of finding the right posting for you, have looked both at your qualifications and the needs of the battalion. Thus I need to inquire about some of your less than obvious shortcomings and obvious strengths." The colonel looked up from the mimeographed notes. "My god, how old are you?"

Nineteen, sir. Actually nineteen and a half."

"So," the silver haired one continued. "A few basic questions. First, sex. You like to screw skuzzy little Asiatic pussy?"

Remphelmann rocked back on his heels. "Sir, begging the colonel's question, sir?"

"You like sex with whores?" the coiffed colonel asked again.

"Uh, sir," Remphelmann stammered. "I'm nineteen sir, and I mean, I've thought about saving myself for marriage, sir." Remphelmann immediately knew he said the wrong thing. Out the back of his head he heard Captain Dunghill gagging.

"And your drinking habits?" the colonel queried again.

"Sir?"

"Scotch, bourbon or gin?"

"Actually sir, milk, chocolate milk or the occasional cola, sir." Remphelmann immediately knew he said the wrong thing. From behind him came a kind of retching sound from Dunghill. "Begging the colonel's pardon, sir," Remphelmann stammered. "I don't really get the drift of the colonel's line of questioning. I am a fully qualified military occupation specialty 4815, mechanical maintenance officer, and I had hoped the colonel would be questioning me about that and not my personal habits. I mean JKF's speech, doing my patriotic duty, begging the colonel's pardon, sir."

Colonel Slick summoned up his most regal McArthur-like condescending stare. "Look, lieutenant, we don't care about all that. You are, to us, merely a nineteen-year-old shave tail with no experience in the real army. You're supposed training at officers school bears no relationship to the facts on the ground. I have to arrange a posting that does me, err, the battalion, the best good."

"Sir, begging the colonel's pardon, yes sir, sir."

The colonel began to show annoyance. "Where did you get this 'begging the colonel's pardon' shit?" Remphelmann started to stammer and answer but the Colonel Canyon look-a-like waved his hand for silence.

"My immediate concern is that your initial posting will reflect upon you, me and the honor of the United States Army, an assignment that will benefit all to the maximum."

"Sir, yes sir, but beg..."

"Shut up with that 'begging the... crap', lieutenant!" Colonel Slick sat back with a snap. "Captain Dunghill, inform the lieutenant to retire out of this office, while we discuss the tactical situation."

Captain Dunghill played the perfect part of a lackey. "Second Lieutenant Remphelmann. Do an about face, exit the colonel's door, go to the outer office, and sit on the bench from which you came!"

"Sir, yes sir!" responded the young man. He, as ordered, snapped left-about, went to the door and started to exit.

"And close that hatchway smartly, young sir, or you'll let the cold air out."

Remphelmann went out the door, and slammed the door behind him. There a wall of humid and steamy heat met him. He groped his way to the bench and sat down. His head swam from both climate and confusion.

Meanwhile, back in the colonel's office, a scathing scene unfolded. Colonel Slick's demeanor changed from officer-like decorum to one of rage. He stiffened himself back in his chair and railed at his helpless stooge. "God damn you, Dunghill, where do you come up with these shit head excuses for officers? You're my S-1, you're my personnel staff officer!"

Dunghill attempted to explain. "Colonel Slick, it's that replacement depot assignment officer down at Long Bien. Ever since you screwed his girlfriend back at Fort Devans, he's had the ups on you. Now that he's at Long Bien and you are here in Cam Ranh, what he does is send all the competent officers off to the real combat units, and send the losers to us. For example, think of Captain McSweeney!"

Colonel Slick flew back in his chair in a white heat. "Shut up about McSweeney, damn it!" The silver haired one leaped up. He first went to his impromptu putting green and kicked the golf balls about. Then he went to the massive civilian air conditioning unit and stuck his hairdo into it. When he had cooled sufficiently, he went to his back-bar toilette and began to re-primp his silver hair. He picked and combed and hair sprayed for a long time until he re-gathered his composure. Then he regally re-seated himself behind his bulletproof desk.

"A frigging nineteen year old virgin shave tail that drinks chocolate milk! Crap and damn! I've spent seventeen years in this man's army, doing my damndest to feather my nest, to smooth my career, to get myself the cushiest postings! Then the pentagon ships me to this hellhole! Now as I enter what is supposed to be the golden years of my service, I'm expected to do grunt duty! No golf course, no blond snatch, no officers club worthy of the name! Now look at the nin-com-poops they send to service my needs. S-1's like you, idiots like McSweeney, and now twelve-year-old twerps with milk mustaches! Where have I gone wrong?" Colonel Slick paused in his lamentation.

The red-necked Captain Dunghill stroked his lobster chin. "Well, sir, we need a mechanical maintenance officer here in Cam Ranh with the heavy repair company."

"No, damn it, no! I've got to save that slot for someone who can do me some good. I need that position to fill with somebody useful, that can double up as officers mess liaison, so I can get decent cuisine from the cretins that run the officers club. I need that posting so I can slip in somebody that can co-ordinate my R and R's, my rest and recuperation leaves to Sydney, or Singapore, or Kuala Lumpur, that can find the best hotels and the best pimps. And what do you bring me? An adolescent turkey with no useable skills." The colonel moaned to himself in a pitiable tone. "I ask for competent officers, and you present me with doo-doo."

"You've said the magic word, sir," offered Dunghill in a servile tone. "Doo-doo and Major Dufuss."

"Major Dufuss! The combat forward support area! The FSA! Landing Zone Bozo! Phan Theit! The god forsaken Que Ell One! You've outdone yourself, Dunghill!" The colonel paused from his exclamatory outbursts.

Captain Dunghill patted himself on the back. "I'm only here to assist your excellency."

"But can I cover my ass on this one, Dunghill? Is there an opening at the Forward Support Area? What if higher headquarters gets wind I'm dumping the little shit? My god, people actually get killed down there. I have to cover my tracks before we dump this jerk."

"No problem, sir, we have an opening down there at that disgusting fishing village for a motor pool officer. There's nothing at Landing Zone Bozo, no real officers club, no bar, no running water, nothing but tents and hootches and incoming mortar fire. But there is a legitimate slot for a 4815 at Bozo and Phan Thiet. Your ass is covered. My ass is covered."

"Excellent, excellent, most excellent! Call that little ninety day wonder back in. We'll have him out of my hair within hours. When in doubt, ship 'em out!" This reference to hair reminded Colonel Slick that his hair needed checking. He propelled himself out of his chair and leaped to his barber stand where he again began to smarten his short silver locks and artfully rearrange his hair-do.

Instantaneously Captain Dunghill was out the door and back with Remphelmann again planted square in front of the colonel's desk. Dunghill himself was careful to snap the door closed so that none of the precious refrigerated air left the colonel's presence. The young officer again stared in rapt attention at the commander's empty chair until Slick reappeared in it. Remphelmann saluted again, and the colonel kindly returned the salute with his pink buffed fingernails.

The colonel was now calm and supremely self-composed. He intertwined his clean fingers in a pensive manner and touched his knuckles to his tan-less chin. "Second Lieutenant Ronald Reagan Remphelmann. You do not know why I interrogated you so abruptly about your sexual and alcoholic habits, now do you?"

"Sir, no sir."

"That is because we have a tradition in the army officer corps to weed out the spiritually unfit and morally weak amongst our midst. We must carefully interview officers to ascertain that they meet only the highest standards which will only reflect brilliantly upon our most cherished gentlemanly traditions."

Remphelmann immediately demurred. "Yes, sir, I understand, sir." Behind him was the unmistakable sound of Captain Dunghill swallowing back his own puke.

"We have, after the most calm deliberation," the colonel continued, "decided to post you down to the picturesque fishing village of Phan Thiet, which is about forty miles south of here at Cam Ranh Bay. There are two landing zones, LZ's as we call them, just south of the port village. One, LZ Betty, is home to helicopter infantry, and the other, LZ Bozo, is the home of a combat forward support area, an FSA, which provides essential rear echelon mother forces to LZ Betty. There is a posting open there for a young ordnance motor pool type such as you. I have to warn you, that there are none of the usual amenities available to officer types. There is no officers club, there is no air conditioning, and there are no BOQ'S, bachelor officer quarters with hot and cold running maids. By god, there aren't even flush toilets. Just diesel fuel shit burning privies. Disgusting. What I mean is, Phan Thiet, LZ Betty, LZ Bozo and environs are rough. There's a lot of lead flying around down there, and we want to send you there to get, ah, seasoned. Then later, we can bring you back and make something useful of you, a mess officer, or an R&R officer or a hooker house liaison. You know, something useful."

"I think I understand," said Remphelmann, without an ounce of understanding.

"Now on an organizational point, and perhaps on a political note. First of all there are two landing zones down there. LZ Betty and LZ Bozo. LZ Betty is home to the 1st battalion of the 999th Air Mobile Infantry. The battalion commander is Lieutenant Colonel BeLay, who has a nasty reputation as a cruel dude, one who suffers no fools gladly, especially rear echelon mother friggers, I mean rear echelon support units. We are after all 'in the rear with the gear'. These infantry types, these brainless grunts, seem to think they are better than the rest of us, since they have a death wish mentality to go out and close with the enemy. That whole line of thinking boggles my sense of self-preservation. 'Discretion is the better part of valor', as they say. After all, how can you do your twenty years and retire to a golf course subdivision in Scottsdale if you go out in some god damned rice paddy and get your legs blown off? Consider that there are very few 5 over par retired officers in wheelchairs."

"That is something to consider, sir," Remphelmann offered.

"To continue on organization," the colonel continued, "There has been a change of over all command down there. The whole of Que Ell One was under the command of Brigadier General Slurpfannie, who sadly was just cashiered for gross negligence, incompetence and malfeasance. He is a friend of mine and close to my brotherly heart."

Remphelmann tried to interrupt. "Colonel, what is this Que Ell One?"

"Shut up, you little snot, you'll find out soon enough."

"Thank you, sir."

"To continue the continuation of organization. Brigadier General Kegresse, who as the higher officer skinny goes, is worse, has replaced General Slurpfannie, of fond memory. When you get down to Phan Thiet, avoid LZ Betty like the plague. Do the minimal to get by. Don't go onto the foot slogging infantry's turf. After all, you are risking my career." Slick looked down his aquiline pink nose with a withering glare. "Understand?"

"Yes sir."

"Excellent. Now to finalize organization. Landing Zone Bozo. LZ Bozo is directly across the airstrip from LZ Betty. There is a compound there that houses the Combat Forward Support Area Bozo. The table of organization is thus. Commanding is a dreadful loser, Major Dufuss. Beneath him are four platoons, a quartermaster platoon, currently leaderless, a transportation platoon, mere truck drivers, led by the world's worst uppity nigger." Slick paused. "Captain Dunghill, what's that coon's fancy name?"

From behind Remphelmann came the unctuous voice of Dunghill. "First Lieutenant Pierre Toussaint Gustave Duvalier, sir."

"Makes me want to regurge, that name," rejoined Colonel Slick. "Uppity coon officers that don't know their place. However, where was I?"

"The maintenance platoon," offered Dunghill's voice.

"Ah, yes, the third element of Combat FSA Bozo is a tracked vehicle and wheeled vehicle repair detachment. You, Lieutenant Remphelmann, will command that detachment. But you will not under any circumstances take orders from that blithering idiot, Major Dufuss. No matter how insignificant a matter, you will only take orders from me. If Major Dufuss were to order you to take a piss, you will first telephone me and then I and I only will give you orders on where to aim. Understood?"

"Oh, wow!" blurted Remphelmann in an adolescent burst of enthusiasm, "I get to command a front line unit!" From behind Remphelmann came the obvious sound of Dunghill cutting an earth shaking fart.

Colonel Slick looked past Remphelmann. "Thank you for your comment, Captain Dunghill. However I need to recapitulate the lieutenant's orders. Uno, Remphelmann, you are being posted to Combat Forward Support Area Bozo, in support of Phan Thiet and LZ Betty, to command the maintenance repair platoon. Dos, you will not, I repeat will not, interface with the grunt butt infantry at LZ Betty. Tres, you will ignore any attempted orders from that sleaze ball, Major Dufuss, who would not know a par from a Jack Parr, nor will you take any advice or instructions from that miscegenated Chicago colored boy, Duvalier. Quattro, I repeat, you are not to take orders from Major Dufuss. He is not in your direct chain of command. If you need advice or guidance or clarification, no matter how small, even if you are undecided to wipe your ass back to front or front to back, you are to call me on the telephone, or telex me or radio me. I and I alone am your superior officer. Understand?"

Remphelmann gave a slight quiver of comprehension. "Sir, I understand, sir."

"Lastly, cinco, there is another abomination down there, a jew boy lieutenant in charge of the military police road convoy platoon. Shinebaum by name. Beware!"

Slick's hand flew up in a gesture of finality. "Then these proceedings are closed. Captain Dunghill, get this drip out of my sight."

"Remphelmann, about face and out the door," Dunghill barked. Out went the young man with the crab skinned officer directly behind. Dunghill was prescient enough to close the door smartly so as to avoid any of the colonel's precious cold air from escaping.

Remphelmann made a beeline through the blast of muggy air to the bench and sat. The S-1 was on his heels, but the S-1 clerk stopped the officer short by waving triplicate travel supplementaries at him.

"I beat you to the punch again, sir. I'm a god damned psychic. Travel supps for the lieutenant. I called the helipad and the afternoon huey helicopter for Bozo and Betty is due to leave in twenty minutes. I called the motor pool and a jeep will be here in a moment." Indeed, at that very moment the same jeep and same duck ass driver that had originally transported Remphelmann from the air base came to a dusty halt in front of the Quonset.

"You are a regular wonder, Private Zerk!" marveled the personnel captain. What would I do without you?"

"Just remember captain, get me that unauthorized R&R to Hong Kong next week, and I'll kiss your ass from hell to breakfast. As the saying goes, 'I'll scratch your back if you scratch mine!'"

"It's the army way," exulted the captain.

Dunghill grabbed the papers and advanced on Remphelmann. He thrust the papers at the lieutenant. "Grab your duffle and follow me." They scurried out into a mid day sun that only a mad dog or an Englishman would enjoy. "Throw your bag back there, get in, and get gone. When you get to LZ Bozo Sergeant Shortarm will meet you. Shortarm is the platoon sergeant of the maintenance repair platoon down there and he will teach your little shave tail fanny the ropes. Listen to him. He is about the only swinging richard down there at Bozo with any common sense." Dunghill jerked his thumb to the duck ass driver. "Get lieutenant poop pants out of here!"

The driver said nothing to Remphelmann. Remphelmann for his part had nothing to say. He was still trying to digest the whirlwind of events that had swept him up. The jeep geared downhill onto a flat where a helipad lay. The driver began to sing to himself in a repetitive way, a chant that only a New Jerseyite would understand,

"Do wop a doo doo doo.

Wop dop a wah wah wah.

Wap yop a doo wop yeah."

When they got to the helipad the rotor blades on the Iroquois helicopter, affectionately called a 'huey,' were already twirling. Only then did the driver speak up, "Lieutenant, show your travel supps to the loadmaster, that's the guy next to the chopper with green football helmet. Toss your bag in the chopper. Your chariot awaits."

Remphelmann dutifully followed the instructions. As he dragged his goods out of the back seat, the driver leaned over and shouted at the officer over the gathering momentum of noise and wind as the helicopter turbine spooled up. "Say hey, lieutenant, I figure you get the prize for turn-around. You haven't been here in Surf City Cam Ranh but two hours and they sausage grindered you in and out, out to the boonies. And not only just the boondocks, but smack dab to Que Ell One!" With that the driver threw his head back a let loose a maniacal laugh. He shifted the jeep into gear and away from the helipad while he engaged in another jerseyism,

"Down in the boondocks,

Wah diddly dun dun dun.
Out to the boondocks,
Straight to Que Ell One!"

Chapter Seven

Remphelmann had never been in a helicopter before. The loadmaster threw the young man's duffel bag toward the center of the cargo floor and pointed to an outboard seating place on the backbench of the huey. The ground crew hurled in cardboard boxes and wooden containers that made up the bulk of the cargo. The loadmaster had some sort of a checklist, which he kept consulting. At some point he yelled over the reverberations of the twirling blades to one of the ground crew, "Two hundred pounds over! Two hundred!" He cast about the cabin floor and unceremoniously kicked a wooden box out of the aircraft. It tumbled over the door edge, bounced off of the landing skid and thumped down on the packed clay of the helipad. Thus satisfied, he plugged a headset cord into a receptacle on the bulkhead that separated the cargo cabin from the forward space where the two pilots sat. He sat on a small jump seat on the bulkhead facing backwards. Next to him, hanging on a pedestal mount over the cabin door was an M-60 machine gun complete with a box of belted ammunition.

The loadmaster rechecked everything with an experienced eye. He made a sharp finger point at Remphelmann's belly and made a motion of 'seat belt'. Remphelmann felt about and found that he was plopped atop the loose ends of a lap harness. He fished around, located the ends, and snapped himself in. The loadmaster gave him an 'OK' sign, re-scanned the load, and nodded assent. Then he reached around into the pilot's space and gave a thumb's up while he said something into the microphone of his green helmet. One of the pilots reached down to a large lever next to his seat, twisted a throttle and the whine of the turbine and blades increased dramatically. Then he pulled the lever, the gyrating blades bit the air, and the helicopter was up and away.

Remphelmann was not disconcerted or disappointed nor even nauseous at the flight. In fact, he was exhilarated. With his outboard seat he had a beautiful vantage view as the huey made a long lazy circle in the air to gain altitude. The helipad and the army base shrank to miniatures. As the helicopter gained even more attitude Remphelmann could see the outlines of the Cam Ranh peninsula. To the east ammunition dumps and petroleum tanks dotted a road that extended to the beaches facing the South China Sea. The beaches were indeed sugar white with rolling surf crashing down on them.

The huey continued to spiral up as if it was an eagle riding a thermal. The bay itself came into view. Anchored along its length were huge oil tankers and cargo ships. The sun glinted off the smooth waters. Northward over the inland sea, up the bay, there was a causeway and bridge arrangement that connected the peninsula with the mainland. On the west side of the causeway was a neatly laid out town of single and double story typical Vietnamese architecture, made of whitewashed stone and concrete walls, which reminded Remphelmann of the Cote d'Azur houses he had seen in travel books. On the peninsula to the north of the causeway he could see the runway of the air force base running due east and west. Beyond that, where the peninsula narrowed to its small stem, there was a huge scar bulldozed clean across the narrowest part. It was the so-called DMZ. He was too far away to see any details but he imagined a great swath of bunkers bristling with guns, barbed wire and anti-tank ditches filling the exposed red clay ground.

Presently the helicopter gained sufficient altitude and winged off the south. The flight path kept a healthy two-mile distance from the shoreline and the Iroquois droned steadily on. The sight intrigued the lieutenant. Over to his left there was nothing but the ocean, rolling, stretching to the horizon. But on the landward side, he saw an amazing crazy quilt of rice paddies hugging any which way to the numerous waterways that led to the sea, intersected with rubber tree plantations To Remphelmann's practiced Iowa farmer's heritage eye, he knew that the rubber plantations contained thousands of acres each. The young officer was keenly interested in the lay of the land. One of the few things he had excelled in at officers school was map reading and topography. He soaked in the view. He was of dirt digger descent, yeoman farmer stock, and the land reverberated in his heart.

The terrain the helicopter paralleled rose gently out of the sea on a coastal plain a mile deep. Inland of that, a piedmont or bench 500 feet above the coastal flat went another mile inland. After that the mountains of the Central Highlands thrust abruptly up and marched in cadence off to the far horizon. The littoral and the piedmont were intricately fitted together in an jig-saw of rice paddies, honed through the millennia to take the best advantage of the land, both as to crop yield and the intricate networks of canals and irrigation ditches that fed them. The rubber plantations, in contra distinction, were laid out in geometrically straight rows. He intuitively understood this. He could image his great grandfather combing over every inch of a prairie creek bottom with a single gangplow hitched mule to maximize the acreage and minimize run-off. He could imagine a Vietnamese farmer doing the same. As the piedmont gave way to the mountains, he saw that hardwood forests, stands of teak, rolled away underfoot. Interspersed with the teak were cultivated patches of land in the narrow valleys that were tea plantations.

He interrupted his agricultural musings to look at the roads. He could see that the Vietnamese had followed every contour of the land to make an organic almost spider web network of farm lanes and bullock paths and even foot ways that economically, effortlessly wound from sea to mountain.

Superimposed on this was the legacy of the French road builders. Remphelmann could see the spare narrow French roads intersecting with the patterns of the true owners of the land. The Gallic roads were narrow cobblestone affairs, snaking geometrically amongst the primordial tracks on levees between the rice paddies, with vaulting cut-stone roman archways over the water hazards. Remphelmann marveled also at the economy of those roads. The French they are a frugal folk. However down on the coastal plain there was something new. It was a wide asphalt highway built to American standards. It seemed to sweep headstrong southwards, ignoring the curves and undulations of the primordial landscape. The road brushed aside the ancient land. It pushed itself through ancient villes and more ancient farmland. It leaped on concrete bridges over the many rivulets that wended their way to the sea. It was an inexorable drive of modern engineering. To Remphelmann it was not of its self ugly, it was a road that would easily grace the Sioux River on its way to Des Moines, but it seemed somehow out of place and time. What was it about that road that disconcerted him so much? The helicopter continued to parallel the American asphalt.

After a too short a tourist flight, at least to Remphelmann's mind, the huey began to edge inland. The loadmaster of the helicopter, who here-to-fore had been lounging with his forearm draped languidly on his machine gun, nonetheless had been extremely vigilant. He condescended to get up from his jump seat. He threaded his way past the cargo to Remphelmann and shouted in the officer's ear as he simultaneously pointed down. "Sir, sir, down below, Phan Theit River, Phan Theit town, just south, air strip Phan Theit, LZ Betty, LZ Bozo."

Remphelmann could see the fishing village of Phan Thiet. As

if on cue, the pilot did a sweeping circle of the area. He saw Phan Theit, bisected by the Phan Theit River. It seemed a town of ten thousand people with the same Italianate type houses he had seen farther north. Neat whitewashed stone two story houses hugged the riverside. In the estuary of the river hundreds of fishing boats bobbed softly. Further off shore the South China Sea seemed rougher, but the river mouth gave an easy and calm harbor to the mariners who had angled this small inlet for thousands of years.

The helicopter again swooped in a long lazy spiral, this time as if it was a sea gull home from the sea, corkscrewing itself down a breeze and towards the military base. The military facility was just south of Phan Theit, deposited onto some primeval sand dune. Remphelmann could see a horrible abbreviated landing strip, surrounded by old French army buildings. Encircling that was a ring of US army tents and wooden hootches. Beyond that ring was the same engineered scar of red earth, sandbag bunkers, razor sharp concertina wire and free fire zone that had greeted Remphelmann's eye on the neck of the Cam Ranh peninsula. The huey fluttered down to a flawless landing in a heliport that was made of packed clay earth and surrounded by a knee high wall of olive drab sandbags. The loadmaster immediately hopped out from behind his machine gun and began to joyfully sling the cargo of the aircraft on to the ground. Remphelmann had the presence of mind to unlatch himself from his lap belt, grab his duffle and duck below and away from the whirling overhead blades of the helicopter. No sooner did he spot his gear over the sandbag perimeter of the helipad than a jeep came roaring up.

The jeep screeched to a halt in the red dust storm of the huey's blades. Out of the M-151 unlimbered one of the strangest physiognomies that Remphelmann had ever seen. He could see that the mirage approaching him was a platoon sergeant. That was clear from the sergeant's lapel insignia. But the man's physique was something to behold. He looked like a brick. The sergeant had the squarest head imaginable. It was shaped like solid concrete block. From this cube like head dangled a neck that looked like a short concrete post. Below that was a compact rectangular body that also looked liked a brick. Somehow, branching off this apparition were cylindrical arms and legs that looked like stone pillars. There was not an ounce of fat on this thing that approached, who hardly came up to Remphelmann's shoulder.

The sergeant came directly up to the officer and fired off a precision salute. "Lieutenant Winkleman, I presume! I'm Platoon Sergeant Shortarm, the non-commissioned officer in charge of the ordnance repair platoon. I understand you're my new officer type platoon leader!" The sergeant's east Texas accent was so thick that Remphelmann could hardly decipher the words.

"The name is Remphelmann, sergeant. Remphelmann is the name."

"Oh, I got it, sir; the name is Remphelmann, not Winkleman. The phone connection between here and Surf City Cam Ranh is worster than a hoot and a holler. They said you were a coming on the afternoon chopper. I got a mind like a steel trap, sir. Everything gets snapped in, but ain't nothing gets snapped out." The sergeant loosed a guffaw at his own joke. "Remphelmann, Lieutenant Remphelmann, Second Lieutenant Ronald R. Remphelmann. It had done be in the trap, sir. Thank you, sir."

"Well, thank you, Platoon Sergeant Shortarm." The Iowa boy was hugely gratified that the sergeant had not taken a condescending tone as everybody else had.

So, sir, grabs up your luggage and toss it here in the jeep. It's late in the day, I don't know whether to take you to chow, or to the amazing Major Dufuss, or off to the officers hooch. That's what we call the BOQ or bachelor officers quarters. However, old Major Dufuss probably already done decamped to the officers bar for the day."

"No, thank you, Sergeant Shortarm, I'm hungry, I'm tired, and I'm also sick of officers. Take me off the platoon, so I can orient myself to my duties."

"Holy Houston, dang Dallas and frig Fort Worth, sir! You're

the first officer down here at LZ Bozo that ever said such a thing! So we're off to your platoon, sir. Damn and damn!"

Remphelmann gently added, "Well, sergeant, duty first.".

"Bodacious Beaumont buffalo chips, sir! Off we go to your command. And, oh, by the way, young sir, begging the lieutenant's pardon, sir." The stocky man sniffled a laugh.

Remphelmann was taken aback by the sergeant's use of the old and honored phrase.

"You don't have to beg me, sarge. I was a private only six months ago."

"Shave tail officers, shave ass corporals and slick butt privates, I done been round the pump handle myself." Shortarm let loose with another round of earthy laughter, as he drove the jeep away from the helipad. "Oh by the way, did I say..."

"Say what?" a suddenly relaxed young officer replied.

"Did I say, 'Welcome to Que Ell One?'"

Chapter Eight

Platoon Sergeant Shortarm, the noncommissioned officer of amazingly compact body and tight muscle, contained a joyous soul within the firm brick-like firmament of his body. With boisterous, even boy-like good humor, he deftly drove the jeep from the LZ Bozo helipad and up a bumpy track that met with an army engineered mud rut that paralleled the so-called runway.

"Lieutenant Remphelmann, sir, you got to understand that I been in this here man's army for going on fourteen years now. The thing that goes with the territory of being a platoon sergeant is that I gets to re-educate every shave tail second lieutenant just out of officer school that gets the glorious title of platoon leader. Jest about the time I gets them educated, they get transferred, and all my cosmic wisdom that I here done imparted to the aforesaid young louie done gets flushed down the cosmic toilet and I get another young officer type and I gets to start all over from scratch. It goes with the job. As they say, a second lieutenant is useless, but he may grow up to be colonel or even a general. Louie's are useless, but you gotta start officers out somewhere. Being a platoon leader is the best launch point. Maybe you'll end up being the Admiral of The Ocean Sea, and remember me."

"I think I understand," said Remphelmann.

"Thank the kind young officer for his kind attention to the kind aforesaid matter," Shortarm prefaced before he continued. "What's I gotta do, every time you understand, I got's to start from the get go and educate each young louie as I gets 'em. So begging the lieutenant's pardon, I begins where I begin. There ain't any use in starting from the beginning 'cause there ain't no beginning. I just call's 'em as I sees them. There ain't no end, so's I cain't start at the end and work back. So's I start right here at the air strip." The sergeant stopped the jeep on a bumpy rise that overlooked the pathetic excuse for a landing field. "What I need now to do is to orient the officer to this here local terrain. This here rise is the best overview of the LZ. Does the officer know how to use a compass and read a map?"

"Yes, thank you, Sergeant Shortarm. I've always been good at that sort of thing."

"Thank the Lord," Shortarm grinned. "You'd be surprised how many officers can't read a map or direct themselves to the nearest latrine. So's I continue. If you look right down the runway, you will perceive that the heading is actually zero degrees, or due north as the civilians term it. Now down that away you will notice a large clump of whitewashed stone buildings smack at the terminus of the runway. That there is the original French headquarters of this here god-forsaken outpost. I might add a historical note. When the Frenchies tried to reoccupy Indochina after Double U Double U Two, they set up this fort and airfield. The idea was to control the Phan Thiet corridor that runs inland from here to Saigon. They's wasn't too successful. Just about the time these here froggies got their asses whipped up north at Dien Bien Phu, this place got overrun by the Viet Minh and all these cute little French troops what was stationed here got slaughtered to a man. Slaughtered! It was beneath their dignity to surrender. A regular Alamo. Of course, the Frenchies don't see it as a massacre, they calls it 'esprit de corps.' Go figure. By the way, lieutenant, I was stationed in Germany a few years back and my missus and me went over to France to see the sights. The food was real good but real unfamiliar. Did you know that you can't get french toast or french fries in France?"

"No, I didn't," demurred Remphelmann.

"Well, to continue. The lieutenant will see that there's a real short runway up that away that is made of concrete. That's a froggy leftover. It's only about a half mile long. Jest long enough to touch down a C-47 cargo plane. C-47 is military speak for a DC-3. Due to the prevailing winds off of this here South Chinaman Sea, the only way to approach this here landing field is to scream in low over the fishing town of Phan Thiet at tree top level coming out of the north agoin' southbound, flop down over them there whitewashed buildings and smack the concrete. Then you gotta roll out the aircraft. Since we got C-130 Hercules cargo planes the rollout is longer than the C-47's. So the Air Force engineers came in and extended the runway out over them lumpy sand dunes and paved it with PSP, you know, perforated steel planking. Landing here is fun. You scream over the rooftops of Phan Thiet, you slap your tires on that concrete and then take a roller coaster ride over the dunes till the airplane decides to stop. It's fun. But I digresses. If the young officer will sweep his eye from due north to due south, the esteemed officer will see a range of sand dunes, military tents and wooden hootches. Just over the dunes is that there South Chinaman Sea. That whole area is LZ Betty. The 1st battalion of the 999th Air Mobile Infantry is bivouacked over there. That's about 800 grunts. They gets the place of honor sandwiched between the airstrip and the sea. It's safer there at night. That's 'cause they do the heavy lifting around here, 'cause they gotta chopper out and do battle with our esteemed friends, the local force Viet Cong and the main force Viet Cong, mostly to the west of us, around Big Titty Mountain."

Remphelmann tried not to blush. "Big What Mountain?"

"I pre-anticipates my orientation lecture, sir. With the glorious officer's glorious pardon, I shall continue. If the lieutenant will face due south, that is 180 degrees of compass, he will see sand dunes stretched out to the horizon. All that out there is free fire zone, anything out there that sneaks up day or night, we whack them with all we got, machine guns, mortars and artillery. Does the lieutenant see, in the distance, two kinds of bunkers out there? Square type American bunkers made out of dark green sandbags, and funny little triangular shaped bunkers made out of concrete?"

Despite his thick spectacles Remphelmann could see clearly into the distance. "Yes, I see them well."

"Them sandbag bunkers are American and manned 24 hours at day. Them funny little triangle outposts are a legacy from the Frenchies. They gots good line of sight view and excellent fields of fire. But us Americans don't like 'em too much. The froggies got over-run here back in '54 and got killed to a man. Every GI thinks them concrete bunkers are haunted, haunted you know, by Champagne's and Provencal's and Brittany's. Slaughtered by the Viet Minh, a regular Alamo, you know. The froggies don't call it murder, you know, they call it 'esprit de corps'. The French they are a funny race. Did I tell you, you can't get french toast in France?"

"Yes, you did."

"So's I continue to inform the new platoon leader about the ground situation. If'n the platoon leader would be kind enough to face at the 270th degree of the compass, or due west as the civilians call it, the louie will get the grand view of LZ Bozo, the cemetery, the Phan Thiet river, Nui Ta Dom Mountain, Big Titty Mountain as we calls it, and continuing onto the north, as the civilians call it, or roughly 350 degrees heading, one will observe the western suburbs of the grand town of Phan Thiet. Now it would do well for the fine young officer to take cognizance. I sweeps my eye from the south. There is a continuation of the sand dunes and the free fire zone. Directly to the west, inside the barbed wire, the German tape as we calls it, is LZ Bozo, where all us rear echelon mothers, in the rear with the gear, in the fanny with the tranny, live and move and have our being. The observant trooper will see, directly to the west, down the sand dunes at a distance of one mile, or one and a half kilometers, one and a half clicks, as we say in the military, there's a most interesting topographical feature."

Remphelmann looked. A mile away was an absolutely amazing layout of six-foot high hillocks laid across the land. These hilly bumps covered at least a thousand acres. "What is that?"

"That, lieutenant sir, is the largest graveyard in all of Vietnam. You ever been to New Orleans?"

The young man had actually been to New Orleans. He had, at the advanced age of fifteen, gone from his home in Keokuk on a field trip with his high school marching band, to participate in a football showdown on some long forgotten gridiron. "Oh, I remember New Orleans well," he piped.

"Then you understand that in Louisiana, you can't bury anybody six feet under, cause the water table is so high. So's they bury you at ground level, to keep the whoreson high water from covering your whoreson dead bones. Same thing here in Phan Thiet. What's they do is lay the coffin on the ground and then they piles up dirt or sand to cover the box. Except in New Orleans, they stuff you in a stone cubicle above the water. But the principle is the same. Only problem, here at LZ Bozo, is that all them humps of sand over the dear departed give cover to Sir Charles, Prince Charles of Hanoi, who can then sneak up and shoot at you day or night. It's a regular frigging sniper's paradise down there looking up at Bozo."

Sergeant Shortarm bumped the vehicle down the dirt track that paralleled the runway. Off to the west, about a city block away, was what was now to Remphelmann a familiar feature. There was a long bulldozer scar in the earth another city block wide. Smack in the middle of that was a thick tangle of barbed wire. Actually it was what was termed in military slang, German razor tape. This tape was actually a coil of sheet steel, exactly like the metal used in making razor blades. The ribbon like material was honed to knife like sharpness and interspersed by jagged saw tooth serrations. It was invented during WW-2 by the Germans and was hell to infiltrate. Just behind the razor tape, at hundred yard intervals were dark green square sandbagged bunkers, each with firing ports, just as Sergeant Shortarm had pointed out along the southern perimeter. Beyond, far beyond, lurked the Phan Thiet cemetery and beyond that, Nui Ta Dom Mountain. Inside the wire was stretched a thin line of military stores in ubiquitous olive drab painted boxes. Canned food, folded tents, wax paper wrapped toilet paper and the infinite paraphernalia of military life and war. They passed an impromptu ammunition dump piled high with containers of artillery shells, machine gun ammunition and mortar rounds.

Shortarm, the jeep and Remphelmann came to the end of the runway. Just off to the east lay the gallicly ordered streets of the old French outpost. The sergeant turned west down into something of a gully. Laid out higgledy-piggledy was as collection of tents, wooden hootches and ramshackle warehouse buildings. He turned onto a dilapidated excuse of a parade square that was nothing but a mud flat consisting of the Phan Thiet sands and the ever-present red clay of Vietnam. He stopped and whirled his post-like arm around.

"Well, this it, lieutenant. First, over there is the forward support area command hootch, but Major Dufuss's jeep ain't there. He usually stumbles off to the officers club on the infantry side of the airstrip by this time. Can't let a war interfere with his drinking, ifn's you know what I mean. Next-door is the officers hootch, which is where you'll call home. That'll be you, the ordnance platoon leader, and First Lieutenant Duvalier, the transportation corps platoon leader, and First Lieutenant Shinebaum, the military police honcho. Scuttlebutt is we're gonna get a quartermaster corps captain, who's gonna double up as supply big-wig and executive officer to Major Dufuss, but I ain't laid eyes on him yet. There, over there on the far side of the parade square, you'll see four hootches all in a row. One each for quartermaster, ordnance, military police and transportation platoon HQ's. Back behind them is the barracks and bomb proofs for each platoon, and back of them is warehouses, motor pools and repair sheds. I'll dis-inform you to all that in the coming days."

"But now," Sergeant Shortarm looked at the green oxidized timex on his wrist. "My old mickey mouse says the big hand is on the twelve and the little hand is on the six, which means it's 1800 hours and time for the evening muster and time for chow. Oh, by the way, the enlisted mess is right over there in that old froggy stone building."

Remphelmann tried a compliment. "Platoon Sergeant Shortarm, I'd like to thank you for such a thorough introduction to the ground."

Shortarm shrugged off the comment. "Sir, I done originated and orientated and opinionated dozens of louies in my time in this here man's army over the last dozen years. The trick is if'n you remembers it tomorrow." At that the sergeant turned off the ignition key of the jeep, leaped out and strode off toward the ordnance hooch. Remphelmann bounced out also and followed the stocky man. As they approached the platoon office, Shortarm suddenly stopped.

"Sir, begging the lieutenant's pardon, sir. Wait here about ten meters off so's I can get my men unlimbered and in a decent formation." Remphelmann stopped. The lieutenant was suddenly self-conscious. He was about to meet the platoon that he would lead to military victory and certain glory.

The sergeant strode purposefully forward and stopped an arm's length from the screen door of the ordnance hooch. "Come outa there, you god damned whore mother slovenly excuses for swinging richards and soldiers! Come out, I say, I know y'all hiding under your hats in there! Get your smelly anuses out here and in line. We gotta new platoon leader here and he's gonna address y'all and hold a formal inspection. Get your butts out here and in formation, and pronto!"

Remphelmann waited with expectation, nay, with exultation.

He was about to meet his first combat command. In time honored military organization, a platoon generally consists of forty to sixty men. He was chagrinned to see only seven men spill out the door and form a sullen line in front of the hootch. Not only were they not the pristine figures that he had imagined in his adolescent mind, but also they were filthy men. Their fatigue uniforms were soaked with the humid sweat of the tropics, incrusted with the ever-present sand and red dust of Vietnam, and also were besmeared with the grease and oily fluids that seem to adhere to mechanics worldwide. Remphelmann was not only disappointed, he was crestfallen.

After the disheveled men formed into a dispirited line, Sergeant Shortarm made an about-face and approached the lieutenant. "Sir, military courtesy requires that I calls the platoon to attention. You will, as leader, give a short address to the men thanking them for their duty to god, country, flag, mother and apple pie. Then you will make a very brief inspection of each man on the square inspection format. Turn the platoon back to me and I will dismiss the platoon. I'll dismiss them to chow, in this case. What part of the ritual does the young louie not understand?"

"I understand perfectly, Platoon Sergeant Shortarm, except for the obvious fact that there is no platoon there. A platoon is 40 to 60 men and I only see seven men."

Shortarm sighed. "Sir, this here is a forward support area. What we got here is called, in military speak, is the cadre. That means, I got the whizzes from each mechanical specialty here, a tank mechanic, a truck mechanic, a radio repair mechanic, a shit can mechanic and a couple of go-fers. Ifn's we need additional personnel to accomplish the mission, I get on the horn, the telephone, or the radio or the telex, and I requisitions extra men to fulfill the job as needed. Meaning I call up Cam Ranh Bay Surf City and I begs more bodies for the breech. Then the 1369th Rear Echelon Maintenance Force, the 13th unlucky 69th cough suckers, they scrape the bottom of the barrel and sends down the worst excuses for mechanics they can spare. They sends 'em down by huey. In glorious summation, I repeat, the seven men here before the exalted officer is the cadre. They is the platoon!"

Remphelmann tried to research his thin army education for the best way to proceed. He failed. "So what am I to do next," he whispered.

"The lieutenant will follow parade ground procedure. I will call the platoon, so-called, to attention. You will speak to the men briefly, and equally briefly troop the line. Then you will turn the formation back to me, and I will dismiss them. Does the august young officer understand the directions which I here-in outline?"

Remphelmann understood nothing, but was game enough to try. "I understand."

"Very good, sir. But please, please, for pretty damn please, when you addresses the men, don't say the magic word."

"What magic word?"

"Don't say, please don't say, 'Que Ell One.'"

Chapter Nine

With the surety born of fourteen years in the army, Shortarm confidently swung about and strode fearlessly toward the thin olive-green line of amazing heroic soldiers. With a trepidation born of bluster, Remphelmann followed and attempted his first command.

The sergeant stopped a discrete ten feet away from the inglorious gaggle of human forms. "Platoon, ah-tense-shun!" The motley crew sprang like a steel trap to a rigorous attention. "What you will observe is your new platoon leader, Second Lieutenant Ronald R. Remphelmann, ordnance corps. He is now the commanding officer of this here platoon. Excepting, as always, when he isn't around. If the louie gives you an order, you will obey with the most military celerity. If you don't obey, you surely will face court-martial for not obeying a lawful order from an officer and a gentleman. If'n the lieutenant ain't around, and I gives an order, and you don't obey, I'll haul your raggedy ass behind the hootch and beat the living crap out of you, one and all. Understood?"

"I heard that one before, sarge," came a muffled reply from one of the seven.

"Shut your measly mouth, private!"

The sergeant about faced smartly, only to discover that Remphelmann was too far away. With his hand, he motioned the lieutenant to stand in front of him. Remphelmann got the hint and with alacrity positioned himself before Shortarm. "Sir, Lieutenant Remphelmann, sir, I hereby present your command to you. Military courtesy, in its hallowed tradition of the army, asks that the officer commanding make a short, really short speech, and then troop the line. Normally I would tell the platoon to open ranks, so's you could inspect, but seeing as how they's only one rank I will forgo that part of the ceremony." Shortarm about faced again to present himself to the soldiers. There was a deathly pause. Shortarm a-hemmed and then a-hemmed again. He whispered over his shoulder to the lieutenant, "Sir, it's time to make your introductory speech."

Remphelmann took the prompt. "Thank you, Platoon Sergeant Shortarm, for your kind introductory remarks. I want to thank all the soldiers here for the opportunity of leading each of you in this grand glorious struggle against the horrid communist menace. As John Fitzgerald Kennedy said in his inaugural speech,

'We shall go anywhere, oppose any foe, and help any friend...'"

A jaundiced voice came out of the rank. "Heard that one before."

Shortarm promptly intervened. "Einstein, shut your darned mouth, or I'll wail the crap outa you." There was a deathly silence.

Remphelmann, however, took the hint, and abbreviated his hopefully stock speech. "So, I would like to thank you all, for the pleasure and honor of leading you fine examples of military rectitude. As I inspect each of you I wish to learn something about each of you, so that I can associate your name, face and military skill so I may lead you better. Therefore, would each of you would kindly tell me your rank, name, and military occupation specialty, your MOS, and kindly, your home town."

Remphelmann froze. Over his shoulder Sergeant Shortarm said, "Troop the line, sir."

Military courtesy decrees that the officer commanding first address the senior enlisted man, to the right, but Remphelmann injudiciously went to the left and faced the junior private.

"Sir," said Shortarm in a small voice as he followed behind the young lieutenant, "Sir, you're on the wrong end. You otter start with the sergeants."

Remphelmann was unable to admit his egregious courtesy error. "Thank you, sergeant," he hastily improvised, 'but I like to start with the privates, they are the basis of the army."

Shortarm groaned.

Remphelmann squared off on the most junior private. Yes, private?"

"Private TeJean Thibodaux Boudreaux, sir. Wrench mechanic. Atchafalaya, Louisiana. Where yawl from?"

"Don't get familiar with the officer, Boudreaux, familiarity breeds contempt," barked Shortarm. Then the sergeant thought it appropriate to whisper confidentiality in the officers ear. "Thick as a brick and twice as dumb."

Remphelmann square faced the next man. "Hello?"

"Private First Class Pedro Dancing Deer Gonzales-McGillicuddy, sir, Truth or Consequences, New Mexico. Wheel mechanic, sir."

The lieutenant confronted the next man and then soldiers afterward.

"Private First Class Elvis Einstein, sir. Radio repair, sir. I'm the electronic whiz kid. Minnetonka, Minnesota.

Shortarm whispered. "Local smart ass, sir, thinks he knows everything, except how to keep his trap shut."

"Private First Class Joseph Schweik, sir. Armorer, sir, rifle and machine gun repair. Stump Jump, Ohio."

"He got the prize for worst-dressed trooper, sir. He can put on fresh starched fatigues, and in five minutes, he looks like a rat's nest," Shortarm proffered.

"Specialist Brunnell Scheissenbrenner, sir. Canandaigua, New York. I'm an artillery specialist, you know sir, tank guns, artillery, that sort of thing, plus anything else mechanical, but my main thing is to be the chief honcho headquarters shit burner. They call me Brownie, obvious isn't it?"

Remphelmann hesitated slightly. He leaned toward Shortarm. "What's this MOS of shit burner?"

Shortarm sighed, "That's a subject for tomorrow."

Remphelmann adjusted his demeanor before facing off on the two sergeants. Not only were they much older than he, they had the most forbidding and disdainful looks upon their faces.

"Sergeant Gerald Gruntz, sir. Tank repair foreman, and where I'm from isn't any of your business. Besides, I transferred from the infantry to the ordnance so I wouldn't end up in a hellhole like this, and I want to re-post back to Cam Ranh Bay."

"Stop your grousing to the lieutenant, Sergeant Gruntz," Shortarm unloaded on the man. "It's unseemly for a non-commissioned officer to gripe like that. Later on I'll pound your ass through an exhaust pipe."

Remphelmann was impressed, to say the least. He approached the last man in line.

"Staff Sergeant Adolph Goering Heimstaadt, wheeled vehicle foreman, meine kleine under lieutenant, danke you very much. Darmstadt, Deutschland, I mean Darmstadt, Germany. And before you ask, I vas not a nazi in the last kreig, I vas a vegetarian. Sieg heil!"

"Don't mind him, sir, he got hit on the head by a piece of shrapnel last month, and been talking funny ever since."

Again Remphelmann stood still, not knowing what to do.

Shortarm was again to the rescue. "Sir, put yourself front and center on the platoon. Then I'll come up and salute. Then you salute back. Then you say, 'Sergeant, you may dismiss the men'. Then I'll salute, then you'll salute and then I'll dismiss the formation."

Remphelmann made a beeline front and center. Shortarm made a beeline for Remphelmann. He saluted, Remphelmann saluted. Remphelmann said, "Sergeant, you may dismiss the men." Shortarm saluted. Remphelmann saluted.

Shortarm wheeled about and belted out, "Formation, dismissed! Chow time for you dog faced mongrels."

The line of men dissolved instantly and began to meander towards the old French mess hall.

Shortarm suddenly relaxed and turned back to the young officer. "Sir, I wishes to inquire after the officer's physical condition, if'n I ain't being too forward. You seem to be plumb tuckered. You have anything to eat lately? You had any sleep?"

Remphelmann began to reminisce out loud. "Well, the last real sleep I had was back in California. Then there was this endless plane flight where I kind of cat-napped in the seat, and then there was Long Bien overnight where I couldn't really sleep, and then a C-130 to Cam Ranh Bay, and then a huey flight to here. As for food, I think I had breakfast in Saigon at daybreak."

"Well, then sir, I'll makes you an offer you can't refuse. If'n I traipses you over to the officers mess over on the east side of the airstrip, you'll jest get more over-load and tucker. Them high falluting officers over that away will just bug you no end. How's about you come on down to the enlisted mess, chow down and I'll then take you over to the bachelors officer quarters in that hootch over there and, you can get some shut eye?"

"You have made me the offer I can't refuse".

"Then, let's mosey over to chow."

They moseyed. As they entered the chow hall, Remphelmann had foresight enough to remember another military absurdity. Whenever a commissioned officer enters an enlisted mess hall, some poor grunt has to recognize the officers presence and yell, 'Attention'. Then the unfortunate souls contained therein have to immediately leap up from their soldiers fare and stand to attention. The remedy for this is for the officer to bellow out, 'at ease, as you were' just as he enters the portal. Such procedurals are what have made the military so beloved over the ages. So, in his prescience, as Remphelmann entered, he yelled out in his well-practiced command voice, "At ease, as you were, carry on, at ease, as you were, carry on." The poor soldiers carried on.

Remphelmann and Shortarm stood in line with the other soldiers. Each retrieved a brown melamine tray, greasy knives, forks and spoons from a grubby colander and ambled down the stainless steel chow line. The menu de jour was fried ham steak, Texas rice, huge amounts of boiled potatoes, brown gravy, and to Remphelmann's infinite delight, a steel pan of the morning meal leftover, shit on a shingle, minus the shingle. He glopped all this on his tray and followed Shortarm to the sergeant's table. He sat with the sergeants and silently hovered the starchy food into his gullet.

As they sat and consumed, there was not a word to be said. The food hit Remphelmann's stomach like a great soporific and his head began to swim from lack of sleep. In this groggy state he looked around the mess hall. There was a mechanical ingestion of food and none of the bonhomie he had experienced in stateside mess halls. It occurred to him a series of phrases that he had read in his now forgotten youth, 'the hollow men, the dead men, partaking the feast of the damned.' Had he not been so tired he would have attempted to reference the quote. Was it T.S. Elliot, or the Bible, or Shakespeare or Schiller, or all of them? The silence was deafening. Shortarm finished his tray and Remphelmann followed. They deposited their trays at a station where a forlorn kitchen police private scraped the leftovers into a 55-gallon drum.

The two exited out of the mess hall onto the parade ground. Remphelmann again noted the earth beneath him. The parade surface was an odd mixture of oxidized clay and sand, and dusty pockets of red powdered dirt and remnant rain puddles. He thought briefly of a French impressionist painting. The sun was setting over Nui Ta Dom Mountain. This prompted Shortarm to conversation.

"The lieutenant will observe several things. First, Big Titty Mountain, out there on the horizon. That's the nut of the whole military operation, and why we is here. More on that tomorrow. Second, if'n you ain't familiar with the tropics, there ain't hardly any twilight in this neck of the woods. Either the sun is plumb up or five minutes later it's plumb down. Third, as we march, you'll see we are approaching the officers hootch, the BOQ, the bachelor officers quarters. This time of day, there probably ain't no one there. There are two types of officers in my experience, sir. There are the time-servers, the careerist bureaucratic slime balls, who want to cushy themselves, and there's the decents, who are out doing the slog duty. You'll find out for yourself who is who."

The two came to the officers hootch. It was of the standard type surrounded by sand bags hip high, 24 feet by 40, screen upper sides, sheet tin roof. They entered one end. Inside was a comical excuse for a day room. It was crowded with a rickety wooden bench, a sofa, a chair or two, a side stand with an electric hot plate, and to Remphelmann's consternation, a television set. It had never occurred to him that television was available in Vietnam. In one corner of the day room there was a metal locker. Shortarm went over, opened it, and withdrew two white army sheets and a pillowcase. Silently they went down a central narrow hallway. The remainder of the hootch was divided into prison cell like cubicles, with the added benefit of a door to each. The sergeant examined the flimsy doors. One of them was not locked. "This one is your Waldorf," he said flatly. He pushed the door ajar. He entered and Remphelmann, bag in tow, followed into the narrow confine. There was a small nightstand, a metal locker and a typical army steel pipe bunk. A grimy humidity soaked mattress was rolled up against the headboard, with a musty pillow on top. Shortarm deftly unrolled the mattress and turned to the young man.

"Well, sir, the tour stops here. You ought to crash. I'll be back at daylight to fetch you. That is of course, providing that Charlie don't decide to come over the wire on a midnight ride, or we don't get mortared again. Three times last week. If'n that happens I might be back to fetch you off to our combat position. But more of that tomorrow."

Remphelmann dropped his duffel, took the bedclothes from the sergeant and swiftly laid them out on the mattress. "Thank you, platoon sergeant."

"Ain't no need to thank me, sir, I'm jest doin' my job."

Remphelmann threw his baseball cap on the nightstand, sat and began to unlace his boots. Silently Shortarm went out the door and closed it. Immediately, he stuck his head back in the door for a final remark, "Oh, by the way, If'n any of your fellow officers wander in and start giving advice, it would be to your advantage to ignore any or all of them. Let me brainwash your young mind, starting at first light. Good night, sir." The door whispered shut.

Remphelmann suddenly realized he was alone. He had privacy for the first time in days. He shucked his boots, shuffled out of his fatigues, and briefly considered unpacking his bag. He re-thought and turned back one of the sheets. He lay down, carefully removed his thick spectacles and tucked them under his pillow. There was no twilight zone of drowsiness. He was instantly asleep, and did not have time to think of Que Ell One.

Chapter Ten

Remphelmann drifted out of sleep. He looked at the luminous dots on his nickel brushed beveled watch, a gift from his grandmother back on the ancestral farm. It was 0430 hours, 'oh dark thirty', he remembered the reveille joke. He heard stirring of other men beyond his luxuriously closed door. He contemplated getting up, but it was still dark. He decided to think for a moment and gather his wits. He fished his plate glass peepers from beneath the pillow and perched them on his nose. With this action he realized that he was bathed head to foot in sweat and his bed sheets were in a similar state. 'And it isn't even daylight yet,' he mused.

As he lay there, he recapitulated in his mind. 'Where was I sleeping, where am I now?' Four days ago he was on leave in Keokuk, sleeping in his boyhood bed. Three days ago, a BOQ bunk at an air base in California. Two days ago, catnapping on a jet plane next to a loathsome fat captain. One day ago, sweat drenched in the cattle barn at Long Bien, and this morning, sweat drenched again. 'And where, where am I? Vietnam, an insignificant fishing village called Phan Thiet, LZ Betty, LZ Bozo.'

There was a knock on his cubicle door. He promptly assumed

it was Sergeant Shortarm, there to fetch him. "Come on in, sergeant." The cheap doorknob jiggled but didn't turn.

"The god forsaken door is locked," a muffled voice replied.

Remphelmann arose, his boxer shorts clinging damply, and fumbled with the knob mechanism. The door finally opened. A dim light shone in the hallway, outlining the man at the portal. But instead of the platoon sergeant there was Captain Manteca! The gross, obscene corpulent whale like body of Captain Manteca! Manteca took one look at Remphelmann, swayed back in horror and screamed hysterically. "Oh, god! Not you! Not you, you little twerp! Oh god, we're all going to die! You, you! Since I met you on the flight, I knew you'd be my nemesis. You snot-nose, you're my doom! What a horrible twist of fate! You're an evil omen!" With that cheery greeting, Manteca grabbed the knob and slammed the door shut.

It was a good thing that Remphelmann had already collected his wits. He too shared mutual anticipations of doom concerning Manteca. Pretending to be unperturbed, he fumbled his hand and discovered that there was a light switch next to the door. He flipped it and a feeble bulb incandesced overhead, reflecting on the underside of the tin roof. Now with enough light to see, he immediately took his duffle, unpacked the contents onto the sweaty bed, arranged them and stowed most in the metal locker. He choose out a freshly starched set of fatigues, donned them, laced on his boots, doffed his cap and discovered that there was a small mirror glued to the inside of the locker door. He grabbed his shaving bag, unzipped it and found a currycomb to stroke his crew cut. He realized he had to do latrine business: urinate, defecate, shave, and maybe even shower. But he did not know where to go. Shave kit in hand, he went to the door.

At that moment, there was another knock on the door. Fearing the return of Manteca, he hesitated to reopen. "Yes?"

"It's Sergeant Shortarm, sir. Is you decent?"

Remphelmann opened the door with obvious relief. Before him was the squat square cinder block presence of Shortarm.

Shortarm guffawed in his usual boisterous good humor. "Good morning, sir. Begging the lieutenant's pardon, sir, but hell's a popping this morning, not from old Victor Charles but from administration happenings. You ready?"

"Yes, sergeant, but I have to do personal latrine office, if you know what I mean."

"Surely, lieutenant, follow me." Shortarm briskly turned and went down the officer hootch gangway, through the day room and out the screen door. Remphelmann followed and was relieved to see that there was no one else in the hootch, not even the loathsome bloat of Manteca. The sun had popped with alacrity over the horizon and the whole LZ was bathed in light. The sergeant stopped short just outside the hootch and began to wave his hand about.

"Firstly, sir, we got no flush toilets here. If'n you needs to piss, just haul it out and piss on the sand. There ain't no laws round here about public indecency. This here is Vietnam, not Vincennes. Remember the old Marine Corps jingle?

This is my rifle,
This is my gun,
One is for shooting,
The other's for fun.

So's if it's pee time, just unlimber your gun and whiz away. When you gotta shit, see that privy over there, that shit burner outhouse? That's for old number two. You ever shit in a privy?"

"My grand folks are all Iowa farmers, sir, I mean sergeant. I think I can navigate a privy."

"God must love the common folk, 'cause he made so many of them," Shortarm quoted Abraham Lincoln. Remphelmann actually knew the quote. Shortarm waved again. "Then over there is a little half hootch. In there is a shaving trough and a shower stall. The water is turned off this time of day, but there's enough water in the holding tank to gets a cold water shave. Then, when's the fine young officer done gets done with his morning ablutions, he will," Shortarm reversed the direction of his waving hand to wiggle it over the parade ground. "He will kindly present himself to his command HQ, the ordnance hootch over yonder, and we'll take it from there. I'm up to my ass in repair parts problems this morning, so I'll be on the horn, on the telephone, yelling and screaming and searching for an alternator for that Patton tank I got side-lined for parts. Plus, sir, there's a new brigadier coming into LZ Betty today, and he wants the FSA people from Bozo to sit in on his briefing. Damn considerate of Charlie not to make another night attack last night, simplifies the day's proceedings." With that Shortarm disappeared across the parade ground.

Remphelmann, modest young man that he was, could not bring himself to urinate on the ground. He proceeded to the privy and entered. However, rather than being greeted by the barnyard perfume that he expected, he was met by the overwhelming aroma of burnt diesel fuel. He looked down the outhouse hole and saw a half of a 55-gallon steel drum ensconced beneath the throne. Nature being what it is, he enthroned himself on the cheap white toilet seat and did his business. Thankfully several rolls of army crepe toilet paper were nearby. Finished, he exited the burnt diesel environs, and headed to the half hootch. As promised, there was a non-operative shower stall and a shaving trough with the merest trickle of stagnant muddy water oozing from the cold-water tap. He shaved. He exited the half hootch and looked to the west. The Phan Theit cemetery spread its funerary mass over the near distance. Much farther beyond, Nui Ta Dom Mountain loomed on the horizon. He could not, at first blush, call it Big Titty Mountain. Then he remembered an embarrassing moment from a high school geography lesson, where the teacher explained in the most solemn terms about the Grand Teton Mountains of Wyoming, just south of Yellowstone National Park. The straight faced instructor related that they were named such by a French-Canadian mountain man and trapper, who for reasons known only to a lonely explorer, coined the thrusting range the Grand Tetons, or Big Breast Mountains. The geographer hurried on with the lecture, but Remphelmann remembered the adolescence tittering of his classmates. He tittered again as he turned his back on Big Titty and went back in the officers hootch.

Again thankfully, the BOQ was empty. He tossed his shaving kit on his narrow bed and re-exited. In the distance, across the parade ground was the ordnance hootch and his first command. He straightened and re-straightened himself and marched with due solemnity across the mud.

PART THE SECOND

Que Ell One Introduces Itself
To Our Young Hero

Chapter Eleven

Remphelmann entered the ordnance hootch. As he walked in he saw Sergeant Shortarm at the back desk literally screaming into the telephone. At the front desk sat Private Elvis Einstein, who was doing a hunt and peck with a manual typewriter. The typewriter was stuffed with the usual stack of army forms and carbon paper. Einstein was a young man of medium height, sandy brown curly hair and neat moustache. His eyes were a deep intelligent brown, and the way they twinkled gave some hint of his bubbling mind.

"Well, good morning, sir," he said without the least military formality. There was no snapping to attention or salutes or stock phrases of army courtesy. Einstein racked the typewriter and re-adjusted the forms in the platen. "You know why the army always has to type every piece of communication in triplicate?"

Remphelmann knew a joke was coming but played dumb. "No, private, I don't."

"One copy goes up the chain of command, one copy goes down the chain of command and the third gets used as ass wipe." Einstein looked over his shoulder to the sergeant who was bellowing himself blue-faced into the telephone receiver.

Shortarm was exploding. "Lookee here, Jones, don't give me that crap! I need that alternator, and I need it on the next chopper. Don't shit me. I called Cam Ranh, they don't have one, but say you do. I tried to call you earlier and there was no connection. So I called Qui Nonh. They don't have one, but say you do. Damn it, don't give me the bad connection excuse." Shortarm yelled even louder. "Alternator, Tank. M48A3. Federal Stock Number 322-607-4517-893! God help you if'n I ever gets down to Long Bien, Jones, and see you, I'll beat your skull and brains into clam chowder and season it with garlic." Shortarm paused in his tirade and looked up to see Remphelmann.

"Oh, good morning, Lieutenant Remphelmann. I'm busy as hell trying to get a part. Tell you what. I'll have Einstein here show you the backyard, while I locate this here tank part. Einstein, show him the layout." Instantly he was back on the telephone. "Damn it all to hell, Jones, this ain't any part for one of your Saigon hooker motorbikes. This tank is down, we got action coming up, and my infantry needs this tank. You can't understand, cause you're sitting safe and secure on your whoopee cushion at Long Bien, but there's a frigging war out here, men are getting whacked and I need that tank running!"

Einstein ambled up from his typewriter and motioned to the officer. "If my dear sweet grandmotherly sergeant asks me to show you the backyard, sir, I'll condescend to show you the backyard. Off we go." The two went out the screen door of the hootch. They paused at the parade ground. "Sir, cast your hungry eye over the four hootches that face the parade. One, two, three, four. Quartermaster, ordnance, military police, transportation. Behind each is a barracks hootch for us enlisted types. Behind them is a sanitary half-hootch for shaving and showering. Behind that is the shit burner privies. Behind that, beyond the sissy bunkers, or quick reaction bomb shelters, is what we call the backyards. So let's tip-toe through the tulips, or follow the primrose path to perdition."

Einstein went down a pathway between the hootches.

Sure enough, in regular order behind the platoon HQ's, were the enlisted men's barracks, the hootches for clean up, and the outhouses with their now unmistakable smell of burnt diesel. There were also small structures about the size of a garden shed. They were made of railroad ties, interlocked log cabin style, with a covering of sandbags. These were the safety bunkers or bomb proofs.

A wide mud-rut street interrupted the living quarters from the so-called backyards. "You'll notice the quartermaster backyard is all temporary warehouses. The QM's supply most everything, from food to housing to clothing. If you can eat it, sleep in it, wear it, or wipe your fanny with it, they supply it. Next is us, the flaming piss-pots, or ordnance. We repair everything that moves. Trucks, jeeps, tanks, APC armored personnel carriers, artillery, you name it. That's a ramshackle warehouse for parts, and behind that, is a leaky pole shed, so as to keep the rain and snow and sunburn off the mechanics. But what we really need is two more pole sheds and tons of gravel to pave the yard. It isn't bad now, but wait until the monsoon season, you'll see. Note the patients of the day, two each five ton trucks, one for a gear stripped transmission, the other got a B-40 rocket in the ass and torched the rear drive axle. One each M-113 APC, armored personnel carrier, one track crapped from a road mine, and the piece de résistance, that devil of a Patton tank, M48. The alternator went up in a cloud of electrical smoke. That baby is our headache. It's down for parts, we haven't got the parts, and every anus orifice in an air-conditioned office in Saigon is telling Shortarm 'tough shit'. Well it is tough shit. That tank is a back up for the poor god forsaken grunts, and we need it up and running now."

Remphelmann interrupted Einstein. "Private, I thought you said you were a radio repairman."

"Yes, sir that's a fact. Over there in our warehouse I have a little room that I cobbled out of scrap lumber, to house my workbench and test equipment. A regular clean room. But I'm slow today, mainly because I go out to the customers and do a lot of preventative maintenance. So, today I'm tripling up as platoon clerk, general help and junior bottle washer".

"What about the military police backyard?"

"That is hard to explain to some folks, sir. Most people think of MP's as criminal cops, you know arresting barracks thieves, and cracking drunks on the head with batons. But here, it's best to think of them as traffic cops, or better yet as highway patrol. Look here; see Big Titty Mountain over there, ten miles to the west, 15 clicks? The road to Long Bien and Saigon winds around old Big Titty and then shoots off southwest to the Emerald City. So from the Saigon suburbs to Phan Theit, forty miles. Then the highway hits the coast here at Phan Thiet City and runs up the coast to Qui Nonh and Cam Ranh. This MP detachment gets to patrol the highway, fifteen miles to the west, just beyond Big Titty and fifteen miles up the coast road toward Qui Nonh. So, to make the short story short, they road patrol and traffic police and provide convoy protection. That's why you see all those jeeps with big radios and machine guns. Same with those two and half ton trucks, improvised gun trucks, with the steel plate sides and ma deuces glued on them. Ma deuce is the M-2, the bigger machine gun that spits 50 caliber."

"Yes, I do see," said Remphelmann.

"Which brings us to the last backyard. The transportation corps. See all those deuce and half's, and five ton trucks and ten ton tractors with the flat bed trailers? Their usual duty is to back-haul empty to the huge supply base at Long Bien, load up, and heavy lift supplies either to here and Betty and Bozo or continue up the coast to Qui Nonh."

"You've given me quite a timely insight, Private Einstein."

"Well, as my Uncle Albert Einstein used to say, time and space is relative. I might add, sir that lots of ignoramuses think that being a truck driver or a traffic cop in war zone is some sort of rear echelon safe day job. But sir, you don't want to be out there on that highway. Charlie, VC, Victor, Mr. Moto, local force Viet Cong, main force Viet Cong, North Vietnamese

Army, NVA, however you address him, he knows every ambush point on the road. Inscrutable, these orientals. Remember that the MP's and the truckers are road-bound. If the locals decide to whack our decadent capitalistic asses on the road, there is no place to hide. You either grip your steering wheel and pray or you bail your truck and belly flop in the nearest muddy ditch and pray. Speaking of prayer, have you met the chaplain yet?

"No."

"God in heaven, wait until you meet him. But my digression aside, sir. What I wish to impress on your splendid open mind, is don't think a Vietnam truck driver has got it easy. He gets the worst of two worlds. In one world he is endlessly shot at, and in a parallel universe he has not the where-with-all to fight back with other than a side arm or a carbine. At least the grunts have the tools and mobility for the job. But as my Uncle Newton Einstein was fond of saying, 'great masses of flying lead and steel warp the gravitational continuum.'"

"I'll contemplate that," said Remphelmann.

"Well, sir, I was asked to give you an overview of the cosmos of our backyard. It's galactic. I have imparted to you all that I know, but I quadratically calculate that the two of us are just as clueless as when we began. Let's go back the ordnance hootch, to the great eternal flame of the flaming piss-pot. If we are lucky, Sergeant Shortarm has expired of an apoplectic fit, with the telephone in his cold dead hand, or else he has recovered enough to make the balance the day miserable for me." The two returned to the platoon HQ. Shortarm was still alive.

The sergeant was ecstatic. He burst out in song to Einstein or to whomever. "Hot diggety Houston damn! I got the alternator on the way! I threatened Jones that I'd hang him by his cojones on a yardarm and he blinked. That alternator is on its way, noon chopper from Long Bien! I'm a regular whore humping diplomat!" Shortarm suddenly realized that the lieutenant was present. "Oh, begging the officers pardon, sir. Have you had breakfast yet?"

"No."

Shortarm looked at his green oxide watch. "Well, neither have I. And I ain't got time to buzz you over to the officers mess. Our chow hall is closing in five minutes. Let's 'di di mao', and pronto!" With that Shortarm catapulted from behind his desk and was out the door and on a double time. He sprinted across the parade to the old French mess hall. Remphelmann did not wait on ceremony but closely followed the trotting non-com across the muggy field.

═══ Chapter Twelve ═══

Across the parade, at the door of the old French mess hall, dressed in greasy fatigues, adorned with a be-smudged white apron, the corporal cook stood guard. In time honored army fashion, he had a cigarette dangling from the corner of his mouth.

It is difficult if not impossible to describe an army cook. The roots of military cuisine go so deep as to test the skills of the most astute military historian. Before Nebuchadnezzar conquered Mesopotamia, there was the army cook. When the Greeks stood ready to die to the man at Thermopylae, a cook stood in the ranks to hand out couscous and falafel. When Caesar's disciplined legions faced the horrendous human waves of barbarian French and Germans, an army cook stood ready with hard salami, roman bread, olive oil and a rather nice amphora of vin ordinare. When General Grant's army assaulted the Wilderness, an army cook stood ready with hardtack, salt pork, goober peas and an illicit keg of Kentucky whiskey. As the Marines stood toe to toe with a Pacific foe, engaging in bloody conflict, buttressing them was a cook ladling out reconstituted mashed potatoes, tinned ham shreds, beans, navy coffee and cans of horrid year old beer. Can any poet sing the praises of the army cook? Could Homer sing the cook's praises? Could Shakespeare attempt the impossible? Would Milton, in the midst of the Parliamentary wars, even start? Even Whitman, standing in the door where last the lilacs bloomed, nursing maimed soldiers in a fetid civil war hospital, could not begin to sing the simplest hymn to the army cook. How many soldiers, wounded unto death, shot through the eye, or leg blown off, called to their God, or even their mothers, when they could summon the army cook? What soldier, mortally stricken, having the choice of calling on priest or pastor or rabbi for some hopeful password to the world to come, the paradise of the good, the land of eternal joy, would not first call up the army cook and say, 'Oh, Cookie, before I shuffle this mortal coil, one last request! Greasy potatoes and shit on a shingle?' How noble the army cook, how steadfast, how forgiving of the faults and sins of others! Virgil would blush at his lack of literary powers.

The cook saw Shortarm advancing. He spit the cigarette from his lips and retreated behind the teak door and attempted to bolt it. Shortarm, undaunted, slammed his concrete mass against the ill-closed door and burst it open.

"Cookie, you slimy piece of shit," he cried triumphantly as he burst into the hall. "I got your ass now!"

"Hey, sarge, the mess hall is closing, go away." To add to the confusion, Remphelmann was right behind, of course announcing in his best command voice, "As you were, carry on! As you were, carry on!" Unfortunately, the mess hall was empty and his words of succor met the empty air.

"Closing my ass," the sergeant beamed. "It's three minutes 'til, and you'll chow down both me and my new platoon leader here, Lieutenant Remphelmann."

The corporal cook finally realized the presence of Remphelmann. He fired off a snappy salute. "It's not often we get an officer to come in here to our humble mansion de cuisine, sir, especially two meals in a row." The cook turned to Shortarm. "I'll let you in on a secret, sarge. I stole some eggs, not frozen egg batter, but some real live stateside eggs, flown in fresh, from the officers ration." The cook realized he had used the word 'stole' in an officer's presence. He hastily backtracked. "I mean I didn't actually steal them, sir, I kind of liberated them as excess inventory. The eggs are date stamped, sir, I couldn't let them go to waste. Waste not, want not."

Remphelmann admired the greasy corporal's bluster. "I'm sure the corporal is doing the army a service."

The cook continued. "So the country club menu of the morning is eggs, real eggs, anyway you like them." The cook paused to look down the remnants of food on the steam table. "Plus fried spam, plus hash browns, freshly made from last night's boiled potatoes, plus, of course, shit on..." he paused and eyed the lieutenant, "Uh, begging the officers virgin ears, sir, creamed chipped beef on toast."

"You mean 'shit on a shingle,'" Remphelmann corrected.

"Sir, yes sir. The officer will excuse that I haven't the necessary ingredients, the hollandaise sauce and such to prepare Eggs Benedict. If you haven't had my specialty of poached eggs on army toast with micro sliced spam slathered with home-prepared hollandaise, you haven't really experienced my culinary delight. War time exigencies, sir."

"What is this crap?" Shortarm interjected. "Cookie, if the lieutenant wasn't here, I'd up-end that ugly mug of yours in a bucket of shinola."

"You are ever the diplomat, sarge. So how about real live eggs? Sunny side up, over medium?"

In short order, the two hungry men had plastic trays full of stateside eggs, thin-crisped spam, hash browns, buttered toast and SOS. They maneuvered through the empty mess and seated themselves at the NCO table. Both ate heartily for a while in silence. At that juncture Shortarm pulled a small notepad from his blouse pocket and audibly sighed at his scribbled notes.

"Holy Dallas dog doo-doo, sir, I don't know where to start." He flipped the pages of the notepad. He produced the stub of a pencil and crossed out some items. "First, first to me anyway, this that Patton tank that's dead lined for parts in the backyard. Did Einstein show you the backyard?"

"Yes, sergeant."

"One down. That tank is non-operational due to a burnt out alternator. I've got a replacement coming in on the noon chopper from Long Bien. My main concern is to get the armored deck of the engine cover off so I can remove and replace the generator. That's up to Sergeant Gruntz, and me and some help. We gotta have that weapon ready by sundown, 'cause there's a push on for tomorrow morning. Que Ell One, you know?"

"No, I don't know,' said Remphelmann with a note of exasperation. "What is it with this Que Ell One? Everybody keeps telling me, Que Ell One, Que Ell One, but nobody explains."

"Well, I can't explain either, sir. It would take too long."

Remphelmann sat back, unsatisfied and exasperated.

Shortarm consulted his notes. "Two, your jeep. We's only authorized two jeeps here, meaning the ordnance platoon here at Bozo. One for me as platoon sergeant, and one for the platoon leader, that's you. But Sergeant Peckerwood done got your jeep. He had to go out to the artillery firebase, the FB, out there under the shadow of Big Titty. They's only got six 105's, and one of them 105's done blown a recuperator and is blowing so much oil that it don't even cushion recoil, much less return to battery. So's he took your jeep and went out to scope out the leak. Did you understand anything I jest said?"

Remphelmann did understand. He regurgitated. "An artillery firebase, an FB, is a position arranged so that the artillery can provide effective cannon fire within the range of the artillery so situated. In this case, there are six 105mm gun-howitzers, or tubes as the nomenclature goes, Model M-102's with an effective range of 11,000 meters or seven miles. The problem with one of the tubes is that the recuperator, which is rather like an oversized shock absorber mounted in line with the barrel, is, or was, leaking hydraulic fluid. If this shock absorber is non-functional, two things happen. First is that the recoil of a fired shell slams back the barrel in the carriage way, damaging the cannon mount, and secondly that the tube does not return forward to its proper firing position, or battery, thus rendering the howitzer inaccurate."

Shortarm had attempted to stab some SOS on his fork as Remphelmann spoke. The chipped beef hovered near the sergeant's mouth. "Holy Texarkana tortoise turds, sir. Not only did the army teach you that in officers school, but you actually understood it!"

Remphelmann was secretly pleased with himself.

"So where was I?" Shortarm scanned his notes, but then abruptly looked up. "Holy Sherman shit cakes, sir, I'm a hoping you don't take my Texas way of speaking too literal. I was raised, back there in East Rabbit Hutch, as Pentecostal Holiness, and I believe in the Word. My home preacher says I'm a goin' to go straight to hell for speaking blasphemously the way I do. But fourteen years in this here man's army done done me. Purgatory, perdition, patootee. I call 'em as I sees 'em. By the way, a speaking on religious matters, has you the so-called honor of meeting the LZ chaplain?

"No, but Private Einstein warned me."

"Holy Beaumont bull pucky, sir! He's one for the books. But where was I?" Shortarm again looked at his notes. "Well, sir, that done does the real life of all this, at least as platoon matters goes. But there be officer type stuff I leave to your highly competent hands. Here I go again, one, two, and three. One, they done shit-canned Brigadier General Slurpfannie. The new commander of Que Ell One is some character named Brigadier General Kegresse. He got a briefing at 1000 hours over on the infantry side of the airstrip. But Major Dufuss, oh god, done told all the FSA officers, the LZ Bozo officers, to meet him for one of his patented briefings at 0930 hours at the FSA command hootch. That means you, Lieutenant Remphelmann, ordnance, Lieutenant Duvalier, transportation, Lieutenant Shinebaum, military police, and some new character, a Captain Manteca, quartermaster, who's I ain't eye-balled yet. All gets to get an earful from Dufuss. God help the army. God help the republic. Y'all done with breakfast?"

"Yes."

Abruptly Shortarm left the mess table and strode out the teak door. Abruptly Remphelmann followed. The two quick marched across the parade, which was baking in an insufferable heat. The sergeant pulled up short at the FSA HQ hootch door. "Sir, here at that this here portal, I relinquishes. I done give you all the platoon news and all the real on the ground army facts. Here in after, you gotta do all the officer stuff. Shortarm raised his hand in benediction. "May the Lord bless you and keeps you, and may the Lord let his lights shine upon you." With that Shortarm scurried back to the ordnance hootch.

That left Remphelmann alone. He screwed his courage to the sticking point, straightened his starched yet soggy fatigues, and walked to the door of the FSA headquarters.

Chapter Thirteen

Remphelmann swallowed his sense of apprehension as he entered the FSA HQ. The layout of the hootch was similar to 1369th HQ in Cam Ranh, rows of desks with an aisle way between. Beyond that was a door to an inner sanctum. However there was none of the busy paper work shuffling that characterized the Cam Ranh facility. There was no one at any of the desks. Or so Remphelmann thought. As his eyes adjusted from the harsh glare of outdoors, he saw three men seated about a desk in the back. They looked up at the new arrival. Captain Manteca was seated behind the desk. As he eyed his young nemesis, he immediately planted his elbows on the tabletop and buried his face in his hands and gave out a pathetic moan. Seated in front of the stricken captain were two first lieutenants. One was a thin intense looking black man and the other a wiry Italianate looking fellow with the deepest sunburn tan one could imagine.

"Come on down, join the party," one of the lieutenants said.

Remphelmann maneuvered his way to the back. He had a fleeting idea that he should face up to Manteca's desk and offer a salute. His disgust at the captain's unmilitary demeanor dissuaded him from the thought. Manteca, for his part, did not seem to care. The young officer approached the three. "Good morning, lieutenant," he said to each of the juniors. The two nodded assent. "Good morning, Captain Manteca, so we meet again." Manteca unlaced his fingers from his face and moaned. There was an uncomfortable silence.

Remphelmann broke it by saying in his most chipper way. "I say, guys..."he hesitated slightly at his use of the word 'guys', but as he was now alone with company grade officers of approximately the same rank, he felt it apropos and continued. "Guys, I've got a little problem when meeting with other folks, that is associating names and faces and such. One of my tricks is to get rank, name, hometown and job outline immediately, and then I can organize all that in my mind. So, I'm Second Lieutenant Ronald Reagan Remphelmann, ordnance, mechanical maintenance, Keokuk, Iowa. Most folks call me Ronnie."

"I haven't a problem with that," said the black officer. He stood, and to Remphelmann's eye kept standing and standing. The man was at least six foot four but could not have weighed one hundred and twenty pounds. To characterize the man as a string bean or a pipe cleaner would have understated the case. He was in his early twenties. He stepped over to Remphelmann and extended an equally thin hand for Remphelmann to shake. The thin man had a cafe a lait complexion, close cropped hair and profoundly searching black eyes that drank in Remphelmann. "First Lieutenant Pierre Toussaint Gustave Duvalier, transportation, Chicago. I'm the local convoy commander. Everybody in rank range just calls me P.T." The two shook hands and the tall man went down and down into his chair.

The other lieutenant stood. Besides the incredible sun baked skin of this man, Remphelmann mentally photographed this officer's other features. He was older than one would expect for a lieutenant, about thirty. With his Mediterranean good looks, his aquiline nose, and steady green eyes, Remphelmann had him pegged as Sicilian-American, until he opened his mouth. "First Lieutenant Moise Aaron Shinebaum, military police. Sometime local sheriff but mostly convoy coverage and road patrol. You can call me Moise or Shlomo if you want, but most folks call me Porky."

Remphelmann was taken slightly aback that a Hebrew would have a nickname like Porky. Shinebaum, however, had a trick up his sleeve. The MP, who been speaking with a rather normal American accent suddenly affected a comical imitation of a New York City Yiddisher. "Remphelmann? Remphelmann? That's funny, you don't look Jewish."

The Keokukian started back, speechless. Then he sputtered, "Ah, I'm not Jewish, I'm Pennsylvania Dutch, Lutheran." He failed to catch Shinebaum's humor.

Shinebaum grinned and continued in the same fake accent. "Remphelmann, Stemphelmann, Lutheran, Smutheran. Ten thousand meshuggeneh goys I gotta put up with in Vietnam and now I gets you!" Just as suddenly the sunburned one dropped back in a normal American accent as he shook hands and plopped back in his chair. "Welcome, welcome."

There was another pause. The others seemed to take it in stride as the tropical heat on the tin roof raised the hootch to a broiling point. Remphelmann could not pause. "I understood that there was going to be a briefing here with the staff, I guess all of you, and the FSA commander, Major Dufuss. Then we are all to go over to the other side of the airfield, to the infantry HQ, where we are to meet the new overall commander, Brigadier General Kegresse."

"So far, so good," Duvalier said.

"So far, so bad," Shinebaum added. "You see Dufuss, Major Dufuss, in addition to his amazing ineptitude and lack of brains, likes to juice. Juice. So when he unpasses out in the morning, his first duty is not to God and country but to high tail it to the so-called officers club and quaff two or three or four bloody mary's, double shot the vodka please, so he can re-gather the little brain power he possesses."

"You've heard the phase, 'the cure is the hair of the tail of the dog that bit me?'" Duvalier added. "He's got to skin the dog. What we are doing is waiting for the illustrious major to get his infinitely small act together and hopefully find this hootch."

There was another uncomfortable pause. Suddenly Remphelmann blurted out, "What are we doing here?"

Spontaneously Captain Manteca exploded out of his torpor. "What are we doing here, what are we doing here? Why you scrawny adolescent twerp, you pimply little twelve year old; you hell forsaken kindergarten kiddy of doom! You answered that question already on the plane. We are here to fulfill the Texas School Book Repository fate. JFK's speech. Fight any foe, help any friend! Staunch the flood of godless atheistic communizing! End the Marxist peril! Stop the dominoes of South Asia from falling! Kill commies for Christ! Stab Stalinism abroad before it stabs us in the States! 'What are we doing here', you burble like an uncomprehending babe? We're here to die like cannon fodder, and die a horrible death!" Having exhausted himself of vehement remarks, Manteca re-introduced his fat face into his pudgy fingers and silently wept.

Remphelmann turned to the two lieutenants. "No, that is not what I meant. By the question, 'What are we doing here', I meant, what is the reason for being here in Phan Theit? Is there a strategic or tactical reason as to why this LZ is where it is?"

"Oy gevalt," Shinebaum said softly. "Ronnie, can you read a map?"

"Yes," said Remphelmann, "I can read a map."

Shinebaum turned to Duvalier. "P.T., the new kid on the block can read a map. That's better than some officers here about," Porky jerked his thumb at the blubbering Manteca. "Do you want to do the honors, or shall I?"

"I shall be honored," said P.T. "Ronald, Ronnie, see those two maps thumb tacked to the wall over there? Let's go look at them." Long tall Duvalier stretched out of his chair to the ceiling. He went to the maps. Ronnie followed. "Ah-hem," said Duvalier. "Ah-hem, I always say as I start a lecture or a briefing. Ah-hem.

You perceive two maps on the wall. One is a large-scale map of Vietnam. Vietnam in its entirety, the country both north and south, stretching from the Chinese border on the north including Hanoi and Haiphong, its port city, to Saigon, its environs and its port of Vung Tao and continuing south through the Mekong Delta to Phu Quoc Island on the far south coast, bordered by Laos, and Cambodia. Thailand is not too far distant. Also, you will see a smaller map showing that area of South Vietnam that outlines the area between Saigon, the road to Phan Theit, LZ Betty and a continuance of the aforesaid road northward to Cam Ranh Bay."

"Let's go for it," said Ronnie.

"First of all, you will notice that traversing the whole of Vietnam from north to south presents some geographical quandaries. Inland of the coastline for much of the country the Central Highland Mountains interfere with any rail, road, truck or automobile traffic. Up around Hanoi and Haiphong there is a broad and fertile plain. Way down south there is a broad and fertile plain around Saigon that tapers off into the Mekong Delta. When the French colonized this country in the 1880's, the first thing they did, to tie the country together, was to build a railroad that went from Haiphong-Hanoi down to Saigon, following the coast. Later, with the advent of the automobile, they built a national highway in parallel with the railroad. This national highway was and is a very rough trace. As part of the ongoing colonial war between the French and the locals progressed, lets say 1954, the Viet Minh bombed the living crap out of the railroad, every bridge, every causeway, every rail junction. The railway has never been rebuilt. That, in turn, throws the entirety of Vietnam's north to south communications onto this decrepit road in an attempt to keep not only military traffic but also the economic artery that ties all of Vietnam and especially South Vietnam together. Forget the military situation for a second and think about the poor Vietnamese. For example, if a business in Hue, up north, needs let's say, an electric motor, and that simple little item can only be found in Saigon, then it needs to come up the only national highway. Up north, in a vice versa way, there are tin mines. But if the tin miners need to ship tin out of the country to stay in business, now a days they have to ship the tin out of Saigon, or the port of Vung Tao nearby. Again vice versa. Folks up in Qui Nhon need rice, right? But the major rice growing districts are in the Mekong. So how do the folks up north get their rice? Over the national road.

"I'm beginning to get the picture, this national road is a chokepoint both militarily and economically. It's like if in the United States, someone was to cut off all rail and highway traffic between the east and west coasts, the economy would collapse."

P.T. Duvalier looked over at Lieutenant Shinebaum. "Hey, Porky, where did the army come up with this one? He can actually think!"

Shinebaum looked first at Remphelmann and then over to the comatose Captain Manteca, who was staring blankly at his desktop. "Yes, the newbie thinks and the newbie listens. I wish some one else would listen." Manteca was beyond listening. "So, carry on, P.T."

"Ah-hem," Duvalier cleared his throat. "I have a bad habit of saying 'ah-hem' when I lecture."

"It doesn't bother me," said Remphelmann. "You are saying the first intelligent things I've heard from an officer since I got in-country. I'm thankful. I am all ears."

"Well, then, ah-hem. I will now direct your closer attention to this larger scale topographical map of the Phan Theit corridor. You will observe that the national highway makes a sudden turn off the coastline here at Phan Theit and makes a beeline straight southwest to Saigon. I say beeline but a clear shot it is not."

Shinebaum interrupted. "Ronnie, look at the map. The Central Highlands come to an abrupt stop here. The national highway skirts the foothills of the highlands. The road winds around Nui Ta Dom Mountain, aka Big Titty Mountain, aka Whiskey Mountain, and goes up and down and around. Between here and Saigon there are literally a hundred and one points for ambush. The enemy can hide back in the hills, and then swoop down whenever it strikes their fancy and cut the road, and then head back into the jungle. You know how in all those Hollywood westerns where the posse says, 'we'll cut them off at the pass'? Well, the local force Viet Cong, the main force Viet Cong, and the North Vietnamese Army, the NVA, whomever, get to cut our foreskins at a dozen places just in the forty miles between here and Saigon suburbs." The MP lapsed into his fake Yiddish accent. "Oy, some meshuggeneh from Bialystok must had laid out dieses road."

"Thanks, Porky," Duvalier continued. "Where was I? The local topo map. Ah-hem. So you will see that the choke point, as you, Ronnie have so aptly called it, is this stretch of the National Road Number One. Now in Vietnamese, it is referred to as Quoc Lo Mot. Quoc Lo Mot translates to us as QL-l."

"Stop right there, P.T.!" Remphelmann exulted. "You said the magic word! Que Ell One! Since I got here in Vietnam, people have been telling me about Que Ell One this, and Que Ell One that, and now you are telling me it's a two lane highway!"

Shinebaum amplified. "Call it what you want. Quoc Lo Mot, QL-1, Highway One, Que Ell One, Queue Ell Uno. It's the scariest piece of pot-holed asphalt you'll ever traverse. For years now, there has been nothing but a seesaw battle for this god-forsaken slice of highway. The VC swoop down out of the hill country and cut the road. The U.S. Army or the South Vietnamese Army come in and clear the road. For a day or so, road commerce continues. Then the Charlie troops come back down and close the road. Then our infantry goes back up on Whiskey Mountain, or Big Titty, and re-opens the road. Then Charles sneaks back down and closes. He closes, we open. We open, he closes. Do you have any comprehension of how many thousands of soldiers, Viet Cong, South Vietnamese, or Americans have died for this crummy stretch of pathway? And to what end, to what conclusion?"

"No," offered Remphelmann, "I don't."

There was, in the near distance, the sound of a jeep growling up to the hootch. Manteca uncovered his eyes. "Do I die now or later? Here comes Major Dufuss. At least he has his driver driving, or else he'd smash into the side of the building."

Major Dufuss's driver came into the little building. He was a spare young man who had a sarcastic smirk permanently planted on his mug. He went to Captain Manteca and saluted in an insolent manner and announced. "The major, Major Dufuss, has asked me to announce to his staff that he will conduct a staff briefing in his office. If the illustrious officers will go to his inner office, the officer commanding, Major Dufuss, will be with the aforesaid staff shortly." The driver exited stage right with an obnoxious flourish.

The four staffers filed into Major Dufuss's office to wait, but not with bated breath.

Chapter Fourteen

The four officers had decamped to the major's office. There was a desk, an odd chair or three and a bench. They sat and waited. And waited.

After a decent, diplomatic and fashionably late arrival, Major Dufuss arrived. He appeared at the hootch door and began a regal dead march towards his office. Caesar in his glory entering the Forum would not have attempted such a maneuver. Into the office the officer paced. The four company grades stood to attention. Imperiously, the major passed between them. Dufuss walked straight to the front of his desk. However he kept on walking. He ran into the desk and sprawled ass over teakettle over the tabletop. The officers remained silent. After a bit of orientation the major realized where he was. With immense solemnity he recovered his regality and planted his feet on the floor. He saluted the desk and said to it, "Yes, the desk. A desk is here, here is the desk."

With utmost gravity he straightened his crisply starched fatigues, and using a series of square parade ground turns maneuvered to the rear of the obstacle. He drew himself up to his full height and extended his arms outward, fingers extended, and tripoded them on the tabletop. Whether it was for theatric display or as an inebriatic support was unclear. He nodded to the assembled officers with a Jovian distain and then sat down. Unfortunately he had failed to bring his swivel chair up behind himself. He sat, and promptly disappeared with a resounding crash behind the furniture. There was a discreet silence as the four waited for him to reappear. He eventually arose, deus ex machina, and regained his tripod like stance. He opened his mouth with greatest decorum and said. "Yes, the desk. This desk is a desk. The desk has a symbiotic relationship, which was shipped with the chair. The chair is behind me." He felt with exceeding gravity for the chair to his rear with one of his hands and located it. He swiveled it up, and with a slight nod to his admirers, lowered himself in it.

During this grand procession to the throne, Remphelmann had an opportunity to take the measure of the man. Major Dufuss was a man of about forty years of age. His physiology reminded Remphelmann of nothing better than a wilted asparagus stalk of a head and neck stuck in a green potato like body. The major's hair was a tarnished copper brown that seemed to compliment his vodka face and beady narrow green eyes.

"Gentlemen," he began. There was a slight pause. "Gentlemen," he began. There was a slight pause. "Gentlemen," he began.

Manteca thought it politic to bump the major off the stuck groove. "Yes, sir, Major Dufuss, sir. I believe that there is a briefing over at the infantry headquarters at 1100 hours. There is to be a meeting with the new Que Ell One commander, Brigadier General Kegresse. You told me yesterday afternoon to have all the rear echelon officers here, so that you could address the issue."

"Ah, yes, Captain Manteca, thank you for reminding me. My brilliant mind is overloaded with weighty matters of tactics and strategy. Did you say address the issue? That is indeed an odd turn of phrase. You see, 'issue' I understand. As a quartermaster I can issue tissues, but an address is something on the front of an envelope."

"Yes sir," said Manteca.

"Ah yes, it comes to me now. General Kegresse! Our sacred duty as rear echelon mothers is to give motherly support to the infantry in the field. We are the mothers, we are the supporters, and we are the athletic supporters. A supporter is etymologically akin to support, thus supporter."

"Yes sir," said Manteca.

"So, I have called this meeting to co-ordinate our support efforts, so that we can athletically support General Kegresse and his cannon balls, I mean his cannon fodder."

"Yes sir," said Manteca.

"So it is with the utmost gravity that I address you, my staff, as to the upcoming briefing with Brigadier Cannon Balls. This is why I called this meeting, to pre-brief your briefs, or your boxer shorts, before the main briefing, so that we present a unified face of jockey strap to the general's balls. We are here in the rear with the gear to buttress the butts of our heroic infantry with our straps, jockey or otherwise. 'Otherwise' is, in the Indo-European scheme of languages, cognate to the Japanese word, 'other-wise', meaning 'other-wise'. Inscrutable, these orientals."

"Yes sir," said Manteca. "You were going to address the issue?"

"Don't get snippy with me, captain. I am addressing the issue. That's why I called this meeting. To address the three envelopes of my three unit officers."

Manteca gingerly broached the subject. "Sir, there are four of us officers here, not three."

Major Dufuss slammed back in his chair. There was genuine concern that he might redeposit himself back on the floor. Crisis averted, Dufuss again pulled his swivel back to the desk. He looked at the assembled officers. He held up three fingers, then four, then three again. "Captain Manteca, there is something amiss here. I am supposed to have three junior officers here, but I descry four."

The captain began to show a tad of annoyance. He snipped.

"That sounds like a personal problem, sir, begging the major's pardon, sir."

Dufuss was unperturbed. He waved his fingers again, by three's and then fours. "First piggly-wiggly, my new executive officer and quartermaster, Captain Manteca."

"Present and accounted for, sir," said Manteca.

"Second piggly-wiggly. Lieutenant Duvalier, the transportation platoon leader."

"Here, sir," P.T. said.

"Third piggly-wiggly. Lieutenant Shinebaum, MP and road security."

"Yes, sir."

The fingers wavered again by three's and four's. To Dufuss's own amazement, he was left over by one digit. The major focused and refocused his eyes on his fingers and on the officers present and eventually settled in on the presence of Remphelmann.

"And who, and who, and who are you?" exclaimed Dufuss as he exited his bloody mary fog. Not having any presence of mind to say anything else, he repeated, "And who, and who, and who are you?"

Remphelmann immediately thought of a Disney cartoon, "Alice in Wonderland," or Lewis Carroll, and the imperious questioning of the queen at the mad hatter's tea party.

"And who, and who are you? You are not on the addressee envelope. Captain Manteca, what is this rough beast that slouches toward Bethlehem to be born?"

Manteca was silent. Remphelmann, however took the opportunity announce his meager presence. "Lieutenant Remphelmann, ordnance, 1369th. REMF, Cam Ranh Bay. I'm the new platoon leader of the repair detachment." He paused and then said, "Sir."

Dufuss exploded. "And why did you not, in time honored army tradition, first present yourself to my wonderful presence, that you are reporting for duty, and thus humble yourself before me?"

Ronnie dutifully answered, "Sir, Major Dufuss, sir. I was explicitly told by the commander of the 1369th Rear Echelon Maintenance Force, Lieutenant Colonel Slick, that I am to take orders strictly from him, and that your presence here is merely in an advisory capacity. Thus in the direct chain of command, Colonel Slick is my commander and not you."

"Slick? Colonel Slick! Why that little pussy hunter! He missed his calling. He could have been a gold tooth pimp outside Fort Bragg, before he qualified as an officer. Did he try to entrap you into his womanizing schemes?"

"Begging the illustrious major's illuminating pardon. I was told only to take direct orders from Slick and not from you. Colonel Slick's personal shortcomings, perhaps like yours or mine, is not to the military issue at hand."

Dufuss homed his gimlet eye in on Remphelmann. "And just how old are you, young sir?"

"Nineteen, sir," the young officer replied. He did not think it worth the bother to add 'and a half.'

"And just what are these appendages hanging off your nose?"

Remphelmann, ever obedient and ever deferential, nonetheless began to let some irritation show. "I assume the major is referring to my spectacles and my mustache, sir. I'm rather nearsighted. And my mustache is thin, sir. God, sir, issued both my eyes and upper lip. I take what I'm issued."

The word 'issue' seemed to take the major on a different line of thought. "Issue, military issue, tissue, toilet tissue, facial tissue, is what we issue. That's why I'm a quartermaster. The faster we issue the tissue and address the envelopes, the sooner we shall return to the United States, of heart felt longing." Dufuss paused for a second and looked at Manteca. "Did you know that in the English language, during its transition from Anglo-Saxon to modern English, that there were many conflations from the Celtic, Old Norse and Norman French? To wit: dress, address, tress, guess, bless, Kegresse and mess are all derived from the Latin."

Manteca sighed. "Sir, the briefing with Brigadier Kegresse."

"Ah yes, General Kegresse. The rumor about the upper ranks is that he is not any better than General Slurpfannie, of blessed memory. Slurpy was shit-canned for gross ineptitude and incompetence. Kegresse bodes no better. It's sad, so to speak, that in my fourteen years in the army, I have had to witness such deterioration in the quality of the officer corps. The military needs more men like me, men of competence, intellect and devotion to duty."

The fat captain tried again. "Major, the briefing?"

"Ah, yes the briefing." Dufuss some how gathered a modicum of coherence and spoke again. "For some reason I cannot fathom, the infantry over on the other side of the airstrip, at LZ Betty, seems to hold the forward support area troops, the rear echelon mothers over here at Bozo in low regard. Thus at the briefing with General Kegresse, we shall keep a low profile. Ask no questions, offer no ideas, stay in the background, ruffle no feathers, feather no truffles, scuffle no muffles."

"Is that all?" Manteca blurted incredulously.

Major Dufuss opened a side drawer on his desk. He produced a glass water tumbler, a quart of vodka, and an olive drab tin can, that had 'Juice, Tomato, Reconstituted, 64 ounce' stenciled on its perimeter. He sloppily poured a fistful of vodka in the glass, and then with the greatest care added two tablespoons of tomato coloring to the glass. He redeposited the vodka and the juice in the drawer and centered the glass in front of himself. He somehow recognized that the four officers were still standing at attention before him. "Oh," he said in an off-hand fashion. "The briefing has briefed. You are dismissed."

With that the officers saluted and exited. Remphelmann was last out the door and closed it gingerly behind him. The fabulous four escaped into the outer sanctum. Captain Manteca kept marching. He commented over his shoulder as he continued out the door, "I gotta go puke."

The other three fluttered to a stop and settled about the empty desks. There was a pause. Remphelmann noted a profound sense of resignation in Duvalier and Shinebaum. He could not hold his peace. "Hey guys, what is going on here?"

"What do you mean?" said P.T.

"What I mean is, I know I'm new and I'm green, and I don't know the ropes. But there is something wrong here. I meet the privates, both regular and draftee, and they seem OK. I talk with the non-coms, the sergeants, and they are decent, hard working regular guys. But then there are the officers. The lieutenants seem good enough, but from captain on up, well, I don't know what to say. We've got a saying back in Iowa, 'there's nothing worse than rolling out of bed and falling into the cesspool.'"

"I get your drift," said Duvalier, "But I've given enough orientation for one day. Shinebaum, Porky, you want to do the honors on this subject?"

"No," Shinebaum said flatly.

"Porky, it's your turn."

Shinebaum resigned himself. "Ronnie, no maps on this one. Think of the globe. Think of the world as a whole. Despite the fact that we're here in a real live knock down drag out war here in Vietnam and Indochina as a theater, that's only a part of the world picture. The big thinkers of the world, the pentagon types, the NATO types, the European types see the world like this. What is the main threat to Europe and the West? The Soviet Union. The tactical situation there? Northern Poland and the north German plain. Five million Ruskies and Warsaw Pact allies and a hundred thousand tanks are ready at a second's notice ready to drive the steamroller across Europe and take Paris and the Bay of Biscay for lunch. Vietnam is a sideshow. How do the pentagoners divvy up the available officer manpower? The best, and there are the best, are stationed state-side to form the strategic reserve, the next best are stationed in Germany to counter-attack at first notice, or serve as hor d'oeurves for the commie meat grinder. The leftovers are sent to Vietnam. Visualize it this way. Imagine a gigantic electro-magnet sweeping over the whole of the army. But instead of picking up stray pieces of scrap metal, it picks up all the losers, all the nin-com-poops, the incompetents, the shit-headed brass, the seriously left-footed officers. This magnet swoops them up, swings over the Pacific and dumps them en masse on the army in Vietnam. You think I am shitting you."

"No," commented Remphelmann, "You shit me not. But what about us, are we the dregs also?"

Shinebaum commented. "My experience is that the company grades, especially the lieutenants, don't have the careerist mentality, the lifer attitude. Most of them just want to do their duty to the best of their ability and disappear back into civilian life and be plain old decent citizens. But even amongst us, there is the crud. You think I am shitting you."

"No," commented Remphelmann, "You shit me not."

═══ Chapter Fifteen ═══

Captain Manteca returned from his hurl excursion. He sat in uttermost dejection at his desk and then looked at his watch. "It's pushing 1100 hours, we ought to get across the air strip." Without further ado, he walked out again, got in his vehicle and drove away.

Remphelmann offered, "I'm supposed to have a jeep myself, but evidently its out in the field with a certain Sergeant Peckerwood."

"Yes, he's out at Firebase Firefly babysitting that 105 howitzer with the blown recuperator," said Shinebaum. "Tell you what, why don't you and P.T. catch a ride with me over to the grunt side of reality. It's nearly time for our daily dose of humiliation." The three piled in Shinebaum's jeep, which was fitted with a large tactical radio and an M-60 machine gun affixed to a post that jutted out of the rear box. P.T. rode shotgun and Remphelmann maneuvered himself into the rear between the radio and the gun post.

Shinebaum drove up out of the gully and seaward along a narrow cobblestone street that was situated between the old French garrison and the airfield. Just then a Hercules cargo plane came screaming over the rooftops of the old buildings. It was not more than thirty feet over Remphelmann's head. As it passed over with a deafening roar of propellers, lowered landing gear and full flapped air braked wings, it ka-boomed onto the old French runway, lurched and then went crazy-quilt off the end of the paved surface onto the extremely uneven PSP. Remphelmann was scared shit-less. Duvalier and Shinebaum didn't even react. Ronnie admired his elders and betters and resolved to himself act with such aplomb.

Shinebaum turned his jeep south bound on a miserable road that paralleled itself to the runway. Eastwards were a hodge-podge of tents, wooden hootches, bomb proofs, sand dunes and beyond them, a fleeting glimpse of the South China Sea. Presently they arrived at an area that had been bulldozed flat. On it were situated several wooden buildings that were larger than normal hootches. Shinebaum pulled into a graveled hard stand and parked. The three got out and stretched their legs.

"Somebody orient me," pleaded Remphelmann.

Shinebaum sighed and pointed to Duvalier. Duvalier took the hint. "Four super size hootches, see? One is the battalion mess hall. It's big enough to feed the whole 1st battalion of the 999th Infantry. About 800 men in three shifts. Off to the side in that building is what passes for the officers mess and officers club. They don't actually cook in there; they bring the choice cuts of dog food over into there and set it into steam tables. In the far end of that hootch is what passes for the officers club. All it is, is a partitioned space, with some sofas and tables and a two by twelve excuse for a bar with stools. Dufuss lives there, the asshole. Only reason we normal officers eat there is so we don't disturb the enlisted men at their chow in their mess hall. Next is the general assembly hall. Triples up as recreation hall, movie theater, briefing place, television hook up, and god forbid, on Sundays as the chapel. By the way, have you met the LZ chaplain, Chaplain Captain Champagne, yet?"

"No."

"Be thankful to God you haven't."

At this point, Shinebaum thought fit to intervene. At first he began with his normal American voice. "Ah yes, the chaplain, the sky pilot, the even handed smooth voice of religious love and toleration." Then the MP flipped into his obviously concocted Yiddish comic voice. "Oy, and gevalt! Such a one! Such words as escapes his lips! This Heeb don't understand. The Torah, the book of the Jews, the Bible book of the goys, the words of Jesus and Mohammed, may they both be blessed and rested in pieces, haven't not been got so mangled!" Shinebaum reverted back to normal speech. "Ronnie, be careful of the chaplain."

"And the fourth big hootch?" Remphelmann queried.

"That's battalion headquarters, and the nerve center for operations for this area in general and Que Ell One in particular. Stay away from there, we rear echelon mothers are not welcome."

The three amigos wandered into the assembly hall. There were folding chairs laid out against the walls and more opened up in neat geometrical patterns facing a stage made of plywood and odd bits of lumber. On the stage was a lectern that probably tripled up as address platform, pulpit and bingo caller station. It was made of gloriously varnished cheap plywood. The three men silently sat as close to the exit as possible. Various worthies filed in and began to fill the seats nearer the stage.

Duvalier began to give a running commentary. "Ronnie, remember your officer school training. An infantry battalion, 800 hundred men, consists of four companies of two hundred men each. A light colonel commands that, with a major as his backup. There are four companies led by captains. First the headquarters company that's got the clerks and hangers-on plus the heavy weapons. That's the company that's got the heavy machine guns, the big mortars and an artillery forward observer that calls in the shots from the bigger artillery. Then there are the three maneuver companies. That's straight leg infantry, whose job is to pound the ground and get up to rifle distance with the enemy. Locally here, they all have joke names. The heavy weapons company call themselves the pathetic petard hoisters, recalling Shakespeare's phrase. The maneuver companies, alpha, bravo, charlie, nickname themselves A, the amazing shrapnel stoppers, B, the bestiary bullet catchers, and C company, the road mine charlie's. It's an army joke you wouldn't understand."

More officers and a few senior enlisted men began to enter into the hall. The company captains, their executive officers and lieutenants, master sergeants and platoon sergeants began to fill up the front rows of the seats. Remphelmann was drawn to the gaunt, almost cadaverous look of the men filing in. He was soon to learn the look of men who had seen too much. They all had, in varying degrees, what is called in military parlance, 'the thousand yard stare'. Blank looking faces, not focused on the close things at hand, but looking out a mile away, as if they were looking for enemy over the horizon or through the trees. Gaunt men, wiry men, their appetites for life gone, their humanity lost, looking, searching, dreading the report of a rifle in the distance. The sight of such humanity gone to ground was overbearing. Remphelmann suddenly realized that these officers were not some tin or plastic soldiers, they were men who daily took responsibility for two hundred men on the line, answerable for their orders to attack, mindful of their men's safety, devastated when a soldier was blown to bits and went back home in a body bag.

In the midst of this funereal procession a rather chipper lieutenant came up to Duvalier. This man was a latino of medium height and smooth black hair. "Hey P.T., the ultimate home boy! How are things down on the cotton patch?"

Duvalier answered, "Just fine, my New York friend, how are things up in Spanish Harlem?"

"Same old stuff you know, too many women, too little time. Who's the new kid on the block?"

Remphelmann started to get up but Duvalier motioned him down. "The shave tail is Remphelmann, ordnance, new in country, learning phase."

"Well we are not going to learn anything today. Scuttlebutt is that Brigadier Kegresse is no better than Brigadier Slurpfannie. I'll bet you that he gives the same stock, 'I'm fresh from the States, and my briefing was to 'har-de-har-de-har' to clear Que Ell One'. He won't know Que Ell One from his ass opening. You know, put your head in rectal defilade and suck wind. Wait and see. Another infantry general who's never seen combat is going to lead us to final victory. Bet you he'll give the same stereotypical crud! 'It's been brought to my attention, that Que Ell One is clogged up and I am going to unclog it. Heroic problems require heroic action'. I heard the same crap from General Slurpfannie, and you see where that got him."

Lieutenant Shinebaum softly said, "Shove it, Cervantes, you're still bucking for that Silver Star, or Medal of Honor. You'll use Kegresse for your own ends."

"Say hey, Porky, we all got to polish up our careers wherever we can. When I'm a senator from the empire state of New York, I'll let you lick my boots." With that Cervantes ambled away.

Shinebaum explained to Remphelmann. "Cervantes is the executive officer for bravo company, the bestiary bullet catchers. Technically he is quite competent. His real problem is that he is a glory hunter. Bad news. Glory hunters lack discretion. One of these days he will get his men in a jam, just to prove how macho he is. I've seen the type before."

To Remphelmann's bewilderment, Major Dufuss and Captain Manteca slid unobtrusively into the hall and seated themselves in a most inconspicuous manner next to the three lieutenants. Promptly the commander of the battalion, Colonel BeLay filed in and took his place in the front row of the folding seats.

There was a loud call from the back of the assembly hootch. "Attention, attention, the general is approaching!" Everybody stood.

The brigadier swept in followed closely with his aide-de-camp. The brigadier was to Remphelmann's eye exactly like Colonel Slick, perfectly starched fatigues resisting the humid Vietnamese air. The smart hair-do, military short but with barber drawn lines, seemed familiar. The flunky behind him held a three-ring notebook full of essential and secret information. As the general swept through the hall with an air of self-imperative fit for a king, he nodded officiously left and right to the officers and sergeants present. He mounted the makeshift wooden stage and adjusted himself at the cheap plywood lectern.

"Good morning to all concerned. You may be seated. I am Brigadier General Keith Kegresse. After a brief but through briefing in Saigon I have discovered that I have the glorious opportunity to lead a coalition of troops along the vital corridor between here in Phan Thiet back towards to Saigon. You here in Phan Thiet are the backwards soldiers."

A universal groan went up amongst the assembled men.

Kegresse took this as an opportunity to launch further into his address. "As you may not know, my career background is sterling. I am a careerist flunky who has managed to avoid difficult duty all my life. Thus you, my assembled underlings, will appreciate my remarks."

A universal groan went up amongst the assembled men.

"Thank you for your appreciation. I need to add that I am trained, completely trained, by the grace of God and the United States Army, to fight on the northern plains of Europe. Massed armor and tanks, massed battalions of artillery. Massed against the horrid socialist menace. Thus in my brilliant estimation, the situation in this backwater is hardly worth mentioning. I have only to give a few orders, to my massed tanks and overwhelming artillery, to clear out this corridor between here and Saigon."

Somebody piped up. "Sir, you have only three tanks and six 105mm howitzers in the whole corridor."

"Did I hear that? Defeatist talk!" Kegresse turned to his aide-de-camp, Captain Lickspittle. "First, Lickspittle, take that man's name for disciplinary action, and then inform me of the number of tanks and artillery pieces that I have at my disposal."

Captain Lickspittle looked up to find that the anonymous

reporter had sat down. He looked at his notebook, and said. "Sir, you have three tanks and six howitzers."

Kegresse fumed. "Defeatist talk, I'll have none of it. Now according to the map plan I received at the general officers mess in Saigon, where, by the way the seven selection breakfast buffet was execrable, I received orders to clear out this roadway, bounded on the north by the Central Highland Mountains and the delta plain of the Mekong on the south. This drivel of a road was called National Road One at the map briefing, or as I have been informed, Barbeque Elbow One.

Lickspittle hastened to correct. "Sir, Quoc Lo Mot, or Que Ell One, sir, the main highway to Saigon..."

"Damn you, Lickspittle, don't give me any gomer talk. Why don't these damned slope heads speak English? It's an affront to western civilization. Now where was I? The north German plain. I was never in a war, but that is beside the point. My training is to attack and attack Patton-like against the evil enemy menace. Therefore I'll attack. This is like the Hertgen Forest, the Bastonge Bulge, and the causeway to Sainte Mere Eglise. The fact that I am in Vietnam has no bearing on the situation. It's simply a map exercise. Therefore, I, and I alone shall clear Barbeque Elbow One, I and I alone shall wipe this mere roadbed of a paltry fifty miles, wipe it clean I say, of the dreadful Russian and nazi combined menace!"

Lickspittle attempted to correct. "Sir, the current enemy is the main force Viet Cong, especially the 804th battalion. They are couched in the hills about Nui Ta Dom Mountain. Their objective is to cut Que Ell One from here in Phan Theit to Saigon."

"Don't confuse me with facts. I've already made up my mind. We are going to smash through the enemy defenses and make Barbeque Elbow One safe for god, mother and the flag. I have pre-ordained that."

Colonel BeLay, the long beleaguered commander of the 1st Battalion, 999th Infantry, stood. "Sir, this battalion has been defending this stretch of road for two years, sir. Fine words butter no parsnips. Clearing the road is no great feat. It is the difficulty of driving the enemy way beyond Whiskey Mountain and far back into the Central Highlands. After the enemy has been backed off the road corridor, only then shall we have a decent secure road."

"Look here, colonel, I'll have no negative talk at my briefing! I have, while ensconced at the general officers mess in Saigon, been given a total briefing as to the situation. On a map, mind you! There is no problem, butters or parsnips. I have an unalterable will to clear this road through the Hertgen Forest, over the causeway to Sainte Mere Eglise, and open the way to victory."

Lickspittle intervened again in a small voice. "General, sir, the Hertgen is in Germany and the Sainte Mere is in France. We are in Vietnam."

"Don't confuse my crystal mind with minor details, my incompetent aide-de-camp!" Kegresse exploded. "The map situation is the same. Onward to victory!"

Colonel BeLay was still standing. "Sir, niceties of map exercises are nice. But the situation on the ground..."

Kegresse cut him short. "Colonel, I have decided! I am the decider, and I have decided. Silence. As to the rest of you," the brigadier waved his hand to the assembled multitude, "As I get back into my personal helicopter, and go back to my meager air conditioned four bedroom house on the general's circle back at Long Bien and have to suffer though a paltry three course luncheon at the general officers mess, I shall bemoan the fact that you peons have not lived up to my expectations. However, I have every faith that some day you shall all rise to my exalted vision, and lay your gut-less little lives on the line for the benefit of my career and honor. Enough has been said. I take my leave now." With that General Kegresse swept regally down from his podium and the makeshift stage and exited out of the hall.

Chapter Sixteen

The brigadier had left. The infantrymen, who had been expecting the worst example of leadership, found it. No one stood on ceremony as they left. P.T., Porky and Ronnie rose and ambled out to the jeep. They sat in it for a moment. Lieutenant Cervantes came up and taunted Duvalier. "See, see," Cervantes gloated, "Another totally out of touch brass hat. Did you hear him? The general officers mess is not to his liking. He doesn't know Que Ell One from the autobahn to Frankfurt."

"Buzz off, Cervantes, and keeping looking on the ground, you might find your hero snatchers metal in the dirt." Cervantes smirked off.

Major Dufuss and Captain Manteca exited the hall. Dufuss made a beeline for the so-called officers club. Dragging with dejection, Manteca touched base with the three lieutenants. "At first, the major thought he ought to call a meeting with the FSA staff. Then on second thought he decided to postpone it indefinitely. Then on third thought, he though he had better inspect the tomato juice quality at the officers club. Lieutenant Duvalier, did you know that your people are scheduled a back haul to Long Bien? Ammunition stocks are at a low, food stocks at 40%."

P.T. acknowledged. "Yes sir, movement orders are already cut."

The captain turned to Shinebaum. "The intelligence estimate is only a company of VC are gunning for the road tomorrow."

Shinebaum amplified. "Yes sir, I already talked to the battalion S-2 staff. The skinny from the South Vietnamese is that the enemy, the Viet Cong local force, will try to cut about Ap Loi Du just short of Firebase Firefly. Ambush alley. We've got to cut loose two trucks full of howitzer ammo, and repair parts for that 105 that is side-lined for parts, plus the Patton tank if it's roadworthy."

Manteca groaned to himself, before he turned to Remphelmann. He groaned again and said. "As for you, my fine feathered friend, I rue the day I first laid eyes on you. My nemesis, my bad luck charm."

Remphelmann had begun to season rapidly. Before he knew it, he snapped back to Manteca. "Sir, you may not like the cut of my sail, but we have a job to do."

Manteca tried not to show his astonishment at the young officers newfound assertiveness. "Well, then, your two front burners are some kind of howitzer part, a re-pooper-actor..."

That's a recuperator, sir; it's basically the shock absorber on the cannon. Sergeant Peckerwood is, as we speak, out at Firebase Firefly, assessing the situation. When we get a firm idea, Peckerwood and the artillery mechanic will go out there and repair it."

If Manteca was impressed, he did not show it. "And there is our only tank, our Patton, our M48, which is dead-lined, side-lined for an electrical part..."

"The part in question is the alternator. Platoon Sergeant Shortarm has located the part at Long Bien. It's due on the noon chopper and the estimated time of repair is sundown."

Manteca sighed. "It's a good thing I haven't anything left to hurl. My next priority is to rejoin Major Dufuss. He has promised me more bon mots of his military wisdom, as well as actual on the ground facts, if only I can sift the facts from the farts out of him. He is sorely perturbed about the quality of the tomato juice." With that, Manteca turned and hung ten for the officers club. As he dragged himself away, he was heard to mutter, "We're all going to die."

Shinebaum started up his vehicle and the three officers slid away back to the FSA. They retraced the dusty yet muddy track back down the side of the runway and across the cramped cobblestone that hugged the north end of the runway. Another aircraft, a DeHavilland Caribou, came screaming over the roof tops of the old French garrison and did a squat onto the crumbling concrete and then went willy-nilly down the roller-coaster PSP, flaps full down, propellers reversing, brakes squealing and shuddering to an uncertain halt down the sand dunes. Neither Shinebaum nor Duvalier noticed, and Remphelmann pretended not to notice either, despite the fact that the landing seemed to be more a controlled crash rather a commuter flight sliding into a stateside airport. Shinebaum's jeep slid down the gully to the now familiar environs of LZ Bozo, its parade ground and its collection of hootches. Porky parked the car in front of his own MP platoon and without comment went inside his HQ. Duvalier unlimbered his long thin frame from the shotgun seat and turned to Remphelmann. "Well, Ronnie, the end of the line for another day of officious officialdom. Another new brigadier, another asshole to deal with, but the same continuing problems. We've got to get west sixty clicks to Long Bien and back tomorrow. Same logistical problems, 16 tons and what do we get, another day older and deeper in debt. My platoon problem is to info my men. I don't need to tell them what to do. They know what to do. All I have just to do is update them. New corridor general, new brilliant idea that he's going to clear Que Ell One. My people will just piss and moan and groan. They have heard all this before." Without further ado, P.T. disappeared into his platoon hootch.

Remphelmann untwined himself from his position around the machine gun. He tried to straighten his formerly crisp starched fatigues only to find the scorching Vietnamese humidity and heat had withered his clothes into a soggy mass of clinging cotton and polyester nothingness. Nonetheless he arranged his officer-like dignity and strode through the ineffectual screen door of his command. He was strangely seized by an odd thought to assert his command authority.

"At ease, as you were, carry on," Remphelmann announced grandly to the occupants of his grand headquarters. Unfortunately the only two occupants of the hootch were Private Einstein, who was continuing his hunt and peck on the ubiquitous three form, two-carbon sandwich of some meaningless military communication. The other presence was Sergeant Shortarm, who was behind the other desk bellowing as usual into the telephone.

"Oh, how are you," said Einstein without the least bit of formality. "You've been to the briefing with the new honcho Brigadier Kegresse. I bet he said something really stupid, like "I'm here to clean up the mess, the objective is making Que Ell One safe for Superman, Batman and the Green Hornet. Dah, dah, dah, same old cheerleader pep talk. Same old same old. Right?"

Remphelmann was about to respond, when he was suddenly brought up short. Einstein knew more than he did. Ronnie paused diplomatically.

"So," Einstein continued. "It's like my Uncle Heissenburg Einstein liked to say, 'At the quantum level, there's a whole lot of shaking going on, at the level of the microcosm, quantum uncertainty'. Of course, my Uncle Albert always got in a snit fit about that and always insisted that 'as above, so below' and countered that if at the large cosmic level great majestic harmony prevails, so there must be the same at the microcosmic. They always used to argue to point at the after dinner whisky and soda. Same here in Vietnam, cosmic certainty at the top, quantum indetermination at the bottom."

Remphelmann had no idea what Einstein had just said. Thankfully, Sergeant Shortarm slammed down his telephone with a great smack of satisfaction and beamed his jovial face up at the lieutenant. "Hot holy Harlingen damn, sir. Amazing Amarillo armadillo assholes, sir! What a turn of events. That damned alternator for the tank is due to touch down at the LZ Bozo helipad in fifteen minutes, plus I expects Sergeant Peckerwood back from Firebase Firefly at any second with a diagnosis on that there howitzer recuperator." Shortarm beamed again. Remphelmann stumbled in his mind.

At that very moment, a jeep, plastered, coated, caked red with Vietnamese dust and mud, from windshield to tires, came tearing across the parade ground. "Well, here he is", said Shortarm, peering out the screen walled windows of the hootch. Let's mosey out and see what he's gotta say." Shortarm bounded out from behind his desk and out the door, with Remphelmann in close pursuit.

The red slopped jeep squealed its muddy brakes to a halt. To say it was caked would have been an understatement. The vehicle and its driver were one seamless whole of clay slip. It was as if the whole assemblage had been through a vast dripping car wash of vermilion goop. There was the slightest of pauses. A golem like wraith that appeared to be a human being disentangled itself from the jeep and stood up. It, whatever it was, peeled a pair of goggles from its face. Remphelmann was pleased to discover a human form beneath the mutative statue. It grinned. It had white teeth. What was amazing to Remphelmann was the body of this living thing. He imagined that if he took a thousand coat hanger wires and several sets of pliers and tried to twist them into a simian form he could approximate the form that uncaked himself before him. A lean medium height man was just visible underneath the crud. The golem shook the mud from its hands. The mouth opened. "Shortarm, excellent news. Blown recuperator, my ass. Leaky seal, loss of fluid, and that's it. New seal, fresh fifteen gallons of shock oil, and we're back in business. I'll take the gun mechanic out there tomorrow and we got that little puppy of a cannon back up!" The form noticed Remphelmann. It saluted. Remphelmann saluted back.

Sergeant Shortarm sidled up to Sergeant Peckerwood and whispered in his ear. "Here ye go, Billy," Shortarm informed, "This here is the new platoon leader, fresh from the States, fresh from Cam Ranh Surf City."

Peckerwood shot an amazing clot of mud out of his red-caked mouth. "Those assholes up in Cam Ranh really, really screwed up again. Not another Captain McSweeney!"

"No it's ass backwards from that, they done sent us an officer with a half a brain and half a sense of duty."

"God no," Peckerwood spat again.

"God yes, so you make up nicety nice to the young lieutenant. We might have a man on our hands."

"Man, my rosy red ass, how old is that thing?"

"Old enough to have a coherent brain between his ears. That's a damn sight better than we've had lately."

Peckerwood strode the short distance between himself and Remphelmann, who had held himself at a respectful distance. "Sir, sergeant E-5 three stripe, Sergeant Peckerwood reporting, sir." With that the terra–cotta figure snapped off another salute to the officer.

"Very well, sergeant. I am Second Lieutenant Ronald Remphelmann. I have been assigned here to lead the ordnance platoon." Remphelmann paused slightly and launched into his stock speech. "I wish to learn something about you, so that I can associate your name, face and military skill, so that I can lead you better. Therefore would you kindly tell me your rank, name, MOS, and kindly, your home town."

Peckerwood knew the routine. "Sir, Sergeant Billy-Bob Bob-Billy Peckerwood. Artillery mechanic foreman. West Rabbit Hutch, Tennessee."

Remphelmann was again faced with a bit of American geography. It seemed that Shortarm had been hatched in a hutch, or a rabbit warren, or something. His personal compass deflected. "East Rabbit Hutch, or west, or north?"

"I knew you'd ask that, sir, because Sergeant Shortarm here is from East Rabbit Hutch, Texas, whereas I hail from West Rabbit Hutch, Tennessee. So you see that East Rabbit Hutch is to the west in east Texas, whereas I was born in West Rabbit Hutch which is to the east in the southeastern section of Tennessee."

"Ah, I see," Remphelmann faked. He did not see at all.

"Maybe I ought clarify." Shortarm interjected. "You see even though Peckerwood here and I ain't related, we is related. You see, we is seventeenth cousins fourth removed. We both stem from the same two groups of Scotch Irish emigrants what came to West by god Virginia, afore the revolutionary war. Them two families involved were the Rabbits and the Hutches. Now when that there revolutionary war was over, that opened up the Ohio and Tennessee valleys to settlers. Some of the Rabbits and some of the Hutches went west. Some of them went to Kentucky, some of them went to Tennessee and some of them moseyed out to Texas. So some of the Rabbits married the Hutches, and some of the Hutches married the Peckerwoods, and some of the Shortarm's married the Hutches who was married to the Clintons. But I digresses. Thus the north Rabbits went west to east Texas, while the west Hutches went south to east Tennessee. All this is clear. So Peckerwood and I ain't related, but we is related."

Remphelmann's head was in a bit of a swim. "And how do you know this?"

"Ah, shucks," demurred Shortarm. "I don't know a damn thing about it. But my great-aunt Lulu Belle follows all this stuff. She researched all these things and sent me a family tree. Even she couldn't figger it out so's she contacted them Mormon folks in Salt Lake City, who is real big on that there genealogy stuff. They sent her a manila envelope full of papers. You know, them Mormons are weird, they believe in all this stuff about genealogy and baptism of the dead, and polygamy and such. They's weird. If a Mormon guy got the hots for a chick, first he marries her and pops a couple babies out of her and then divorces her and moves on to the next hottie. All the while claiming they is still married in heaven. And so on. But us Pentecostals, we jest get married once and make cute little critters on the side, what with our wives third cousin womenfolk, third removed. And all the time I gets to acclaiming I ain't repented my carnality enough. It's work."

"Don't give me that Pentecostal crap, Shorty, I'm a Birmingham Baptist, through and through."

At this juncture Remphelmann thought it politic to bring the conversation back to business matters. "So, Sergeant Peckerwood, what about this 105mm howitzer out at Firebase Firefly and the recuperator?"

"I'm glad you asked." Peckerwood seemed to be relieved from a tad of family infighting. "You see the artillery called up us up and thought the recuperator was blown clear out of tolerance and alignment. But I went out there, and all it is, you see, was that the rear recuperator O-ring failed, and let the shock absorber oil leak out. I disassembled the puppy and micro metered the bore and the piston. Those parts are all fine. All that tube needs is to replace the o-ring seal and replenish the oil and it's back in business. I got the o-ring and the oil right here in LZ Bozo. Tomorrow morning's trip and that gun is back up and firing."

Conveniently a helicopter made a swooping circular pass over LZ Bozo. "Hot holy Dallas doggies!" exclaimed Sergeant Shortarm. "That there's the noon chopper from Long Bien. That damn alternator better be on that flight or there's hell to pay. Peckerwood, you oughter go hose yourself down, get some clean fatigues and hightail it over to the maintenance shed and get the engine cover uncorked on that Patton. Round up anybody you need, even if they're busy on something else. Einstein's typing in the hootch, and Scheissenbrenner's doing his thing, and Gonzales-McGillicuddy is dissembling the ass differential out of that five-ton. And of course, you know the lieutenant here got firsts dibs on this here mud pail of a jeep. You have to relinquish it to him."

"Well, rank hath its privileges," Peckerwood retorted. "I'll have that tank engine cover off in a jiffy as soon as I shower and change." Peckerwood shot off.

"You know how to drive a stick shift, sir?"

"Yes, thank you."

"Then this here jeep is yours. I suggest we hop in and drag main down to the Bozo helipad and see if that whorebaby alternator is done delivered."

The two slopped themselves into mud caked jeep and went off to the helipad. As they arrived the helicopter's rotors had just swung to a stop. There was a metal canister the size of a steamer truck being unceremoniously toppled out of the helicopter's cargo bay. The loadmaster had jammed his body against the huey frame and literally kicked it out with his feet. The box fell with a thud over the chopper skids onto the PSP.

"Hey, god damn you, you damn propeller head! Be careful with my goods," Shortarm screamed as he bounded from the jeep.

The air crewman flipped Shortarm his middle finger. "Screw you and horse you rode in on."

"It's a good thing you're in somebody else's unit, you useless twirly-birder! Otherwise I'd straighten out your attitude with my knuckles!"

"Kiss my rosy red, sarge. I'm a short-timer. I got ten days left in country. You don't like my attitude, put it in rectal defilade."

Shortarm turned to Remphelmann, who had unglued himself from the clay soaked seat of his new jeep and was now at the sergeant's side. "Gol' darn draftees, sir, no respect. No respect for ranks, no respect for government property. Here, see here, there's carry handles on this alternator case. You grab one side and I'll grab the to-other, and let's hoist it in back of your jeep." The two manhandled the heavy case into the back of the muddy vehicle. They reseated themselves and started to drive away.

The insolent loadmaster yelled after Shortarm. "Hey sargie-wargie, bite mine!"

Shortarm ignored the parting insult. Remphelmann was having a difficult time operating the clutch and brake of the car due to the clay slop in the foot wells. "This jeep is a real mud bucket," he quipped.

The sergeant guffawed. "I tells you what, lieutenant, you done christened this here M-151. As the day wears on I'll have Gonzales-McGillicuddy take your jeep over to the air force crash station, have him hose it down with a fire hose and then paint a name on the hood of this thing. Gonzales is one of them low rider types and got a steady hand for painting in that old English character style. He can mark it up 'Mud Bucket' if you like!"

Remphelmann laughed, "Whatever you say, sergeant."

They wound their way back to the ordnance area. Peckerwood, newly pristine, already had the men using a wrecker truck hoist, lifting the heavy armored engine cover off of the tank's rear deck.

The rest of the day went to Remphelmann's infinite delight. He helped the men change out the alternator on the tank, which promptly started up with a satisfying roar. Then he crawled underneath a five-ton truck with Gonzales and helped him disassemble the rear axle loose from the truck. There was indeed a massive melted hole in the differential where a Viet Cong rocket had trashed the gears.

If there were rumblings of mutiny in the crew, that an officer was actually helping the men, getting greasy and dirty and back sprawling in the mud, it was remarkably mute. In fact, the men were amazed that an officer would help them. They whispered amongst themselves at such unseemly behavior. The sun began to set. Shortarm approached the lieutenant.

"Sir, my mickey mouse is pushing at 1800 hours. I gotta break my men for evening chow. Now normally you officer types is supposed to gather for evening briefing at the FSA HQ but skinny is Major Dufuss is on a tomato juice inspection. I suggests to the lieutenant that he moseys over to the BOQ, clean up, shower up, starch up and interfaces with the officers over there about officer things and officer chow. I talked with Cookie and he don't want you again at the enlisted mess. You officers are a disruption in the daily routine, begging the lieutenant's pardon. I gotta put off Gonzales washing your jeep until tomorrow."

Remphelmann suddenly realized that he was not only exhausted, but that he, as well as the men, was caked cap-a-pie with sticky red mud. He took the hint. He went back to his dirt-encrusted chariot, and growled it over to the BOQ. The other officers jeeps were there: Duvalier's, Shinebaum's and Manteca's. He entered his home.

Chapter Seventeen

Remphelmann came home, home to his front door. But on the other side, he knew not what. Mud caked, he walked in. He was greeted by the sound of a television set. On the audio was the familiar voice of Captain Kirk, of *Star Trek* fame. "Beam me up, Scotty. Beam me up. There's no intelligent life down here."

Remphelmann looked about. He had not really gathered in the small annex of the hootch that had presented itself to him earlier. It was a small room, with an army issue couch, two rough wooden benches and a low coffee table. On a plywood sideboard was a two burner electric hotplate. To one side was a smallish refrigerator of Korean manufacture. There was a black and white television set. There was a water cooler with a five-gallon jug and no cooling. Stuck in a corner of the sofa was Captain Manteca who was transfixed on the television screen. He was mumbling to himself. "Beam me up, beam me up."

Remphelmann tried to make small talk. "I didn't know we had television here in Vietnam."

"Armed Forces Radio and Television Network. The Vietnamese can't afford TV but we can. This station is out of Saigon. Reruns and propaganda news. Reruns of *Gunsmoke*, and *Star Trek* and

Bob Hope, plus *The Flying Nun* and *My Mother The Car*. Noon to 2200 hours daily, but at least no commercials." Manteca finally peeled his eyes from the small screen. "God, lieutenant, you're filthy. Mud and grease. The mud I can understand but the grease? Have you been helping your men?"

"Yes."

"That's a bad sign, twerp. You are supposed to stand aside and give godlike orders, but not get down in the dirt and do real work. It's conduct unbecoming an officer."

Remphelmann stifled his tongue.

Manteca continued. "You know where the shower hootch is? You got clean fatigues?"

"Yes," replied the young man.

"No enlisted mess hall tonight, no going across the airstrip to the officers table. I requisitioned T-bone steak, pre-baked potatoes and iceberg lettuce for us. I'm going to barbeque here on the back porch."

Remphelmann found his way to his cubicle and snatched up a clean set of tee shirt and underwear. He located his flip-flops and skivvied down, throwing his dirt caked outer clothing in a heap in a corner. He made his way to the half hootch and got butt naked under a showerhead. There was a bar of lye soap and a dingy towel nearby. He turned on the hot and cold taps, but all that exited the showerhead was a muddy red stream of ice-cold water. He showered anyway. After toweling down, he donned the fresh pair of shorts, the tee shirt and clean fatigue trousers and flip-flopped back to the officers BOQ. He went to his cubicle and thought about re-donning his boots. He realized that he was already sopping wet from the tropical climate and thought better of the idea.

He went back into the day room to find Manteca still transfixed on the boob tube. Also there was Duvalier, who was seated on one of the benches. He was tonging out ice cubes from a plastic bucket into glass tumblers and had a can of lemon-lime soda already open. He produced a quart of gin and poured a healthy shot into a glass for Manteca along with a modicum of fizz, who instantly guzzled it like mother's milk. Duvalier gave a smile of amusement and refilled the captain's glass. Then he poured a discrete shot and carbonation for himself, which he tasted sparingly. "Hey, Ronnie, after work highball?"

Remphelmann responded, "I rarely drink."

Duvalier said. "Well, this is a rare occasion, but suit yourself."

Ronnie reconsidered. "That soda looks good and cold. I'll take that, plus maybe a jigger of gin."

Duvalier laughed more to himself than Remphelmann. "Don't say jigger to a jig-a-boo. It sounds racist."

P.T. did the honors and handed the drink to Remphelmann, who was immediately aware of its coldness on such a hot day. "Thanks," he thanked.

"There's more where that came from." Duvalier was already mixing up a third drink for Manteca, who had done the disappearing act with the previous libations. Manteca was still narrowed in on the television screen. *Star Trek* had just come to an end.

The fat one was still mumbling, "Beam me up, Scotty, there's no intelligent life down here," when an abbreviated five minute newscast came on.

A rather emotionless sergeant announcer announced: "Back in the United States, there is continued rioting in the negro areas of Newark as disaffected slum dwellers torch their own neighborhoods. In Chicago, longhaired hippies and sundry anti-war protesters continue to have violent street clashes against Mayor Daley's heroic police who are attempting to renew law and order on Cook County streets. On the sports front the New York Yankees are attempting to snap a seven game losing streak by playing the Brooklyn Dodgers, that is the Los Angles Dodgers, at Chavez Ravine. Here in country, our heroic marines are facing down the North Vietnamese at the DMZ. Our glorious air force is bombing the bridges at the Phu Phu River with great success.

Here in the fourth corps area, the body count is excellent as the 77th Infantry continues to whack the be-joneses out of the local force VC at the Beaver's Beak. Now it's on to an exciting re-run of *Gunsmoke* starring James Arness and Dennis Weaver."

The screen flickered slightly and *Gunsmoke* appeared. In the classic opening shot, Marshal Matt Dillon faced off on Main Street with an obvious villain. There was a quick draw of six shooters and the bad guy crumpled into the dust.

Manteca automatically reached for another drink from Duvalier. "I don't want *Gunsmoke*, I want Kirk to keep calling, "Beam me up, beam me up." The *Gunsmoke* episode began to unfold in its stereotyped manner. Marshal Dillon was sitting in the office. Chester came limping in and hysterically announced, "Marshal Dillon, Marshal Dillon, there's a god awful fight down at the Long Branch Saloon between some cowboys, and Miss Kitty says you ought to come quick."

Lieutenant Shinebaum came in. "Guys, it seems there is a change of plans. I just came from the S-2 intelligence desk. It looks like the minor road cut tomorrow by the local VC is just a ploy. The 804th main force Viet Cong is planning a cross-the-wire attack here at Bozo tomorrow night. South Vietnamese intelligence puts all this at extreme probability. The road convoy to Long Bien is on hold. Not in the morning, maybe two days out."

Remphelmann took this opportunity to show his ignorance. "South Vietnamese intelligence? Are they trustworthy?"

Shinebaum flushed slightly with anger and then remembered he was instructing a newbie. "Ronnie, you have got to remember that this war is not between the United States and the Vietnamese. We are jammed between the rock and the hard place of an internal civil war. The South Viets are doing their damndest to resolve the war with the North Viets to their benefit. They speak the local language, they know the local terrain, and they know their intelligence sources. It's their own damn country, for God's sake.

If the ARVN's, the Army of South Vietnam intelligence service says something is afoot, it's afoot."

Duvalier stood. "Thanks, Porky, I better go tell my platoon sergeant to stand down from the road march and prepare for a Charlie midnight. Hey Manteca, I hear you scored steaks, baked potatoes, sour cream and salad."

The fat boy peeled his eye from the television and replied. "I've got the charcoal lit and simmering down. I'll put the meat on the grill in thirty minutes."

"I'll be back in twenty," Duvalier said. "Let me go update my platoon." He went out the door.

"Same for me," said Shinebaum. "Back soon." Porky started for the door.

"Should I go tell my platoon sergeant?" Remphelmann asked.

"No," considered Shinebaum. "Best not. Your platoon wasn't in on the movement order. It's best not to rile your men with too much information. Your Sergeant Shortarm is already in on the grapevine and will do what's needed. Let sleeping dogs lie." Shinebaum left.

That left Manteca and Remphelmann alone. The captain was obviously deep in the cup. He continued to watch *Gunsmoke*. Marshal Dillon had restored order at the Long Branch. Doc Adams had a cowboy laid out on a faro table and was preparing to extract a bullet from the ham of a Hollywood ham actor. Manteca suddenly turned to Remphelmann with a silly gin grin. His whole demeanor toward Remphelmann had flipped. "And so, my good buddy," he blubbered, "And how did you end up here at the ripe old age of nineteen?

Remphelmann, unused to alcohol, had let the mere shot of spirits go to his head. He also slid into bonhomie. "Do you mean the Army or Vietnam or both?"

The lardo maneuvered himself up from his ensconce and made his way to the bottle of gin, the plastic bucket of melting ice and the can of soda. He refreshed his ammunition and reseated himself with an oily oomph on his seat. Miss Kitty was helping Doc Adam to deftly extract the fake bullet from the actor's Hollywood ass. Manteca drank more deeply. "'Drinking little, drunkens one, but drinking largely, largely sobers one again'. Well, the Army, or Vietnam, or both."

Remphelmann could not resist. He also refreshed his tumbler. "Well first, sir, I'm not nineteen, I'm nineteen plus. I'll be twenty years old in a couple of months. But to start, I started in college on a scholarship."

"Oh, you were on scholarship? What were you, a football player? No, you're too skinny. A track runner?"

"I was an oboe player."

"What kind of game is oboe? Is that Canadian or something?"

"No, I'm a musician. An oboe is a musical reed instrument, rather like an over size clarinet. But I lost my scholarship."

"And just how did that happen?"

"I got fisted in the mouth by my aunt and busted my lip. I couldn't play due to the scar tissue, so I lost my scholarship. So I waited for the draft and..."

"Just a minute, you got busted in the chops by your aunt, and split your lip."

"Yes."

"And just what series of circumstances led up to your aunt busting your chops?"

Remphelmann demurred at first but then continued. "Well, a diplomatic silence should be in order to avoid a rather tangled turn of events. However, my uncle was drunk and my aunt was drunk. The two really were about to come to blows. I stepped between to serve as mediator, but as events transpired, my aunt swung at my uncle, slugged and missed, and hit me instead. My lip is gone."

"The world is full of unexpected tragedies," Manteca commiserated.

"So I lost my scholarship and my college deferment, and so I got drafted."

"Oh what a tangled web fate weaves, when first it practices to deceive."

Remphelmann somehow knew Manteca had mangled a quote from some English dramatist, but the horrid effects of gin on his unready brain caused a lapse of referents. He continued his sad tale of descent into the clutches of a military life. "So, I got drafted and went to basic training. And I took this series of mental aptitude tests, including the Officer Qualification Test. Some specialist took me aside and told me I scored high enough on the OQT to be eligible for officer candidate school. Well, I thought, I had never thought about being an officer, but if the army offered, well, you know? I mean my chance of being an oboe player with a busted lip? So, well, the idea of being an army officer seemed like a change of career."

Manteca felt the need to interrupt. "Don't you have to be twenty-one years of age, or be a college graduate, or go to Reverse Officer Training School, ROTC or something like that?"

"No, the army regulations state, you only have to pass the OQT and be eighteen and a half."

"Damn," swore the chub, "Where is this man's army going?"

"So," continued Remphelmann. I went before something called an officer candidate review board. There were three captains who asked me all questions about current events, and moral rectitude, and devotion to duty. They said because of my OQT scores and the fact that I could express my self and that sort of thing, so I qualified. They never asked me about my failed career as an oboe player and how my lip got mangled, an embarrassing event I'd like to forget. So they signed some document and sent me to OCS, to officer candidate school."

"Why didn't you go to Fort Benning and become an infantry type, or Fort Sill and train for the artillery?"

"Well, as you can see, I'm mighty nearsighted and the regulations say, the medical regs state, to get in the combat arms you go to have twenty-twenty vision so you can shoot rifles and artillery and tank guns and such. So that meant for me no infantry, no artillery, and no armor. So this board says to me 'we have got to recommend you to the combat support troops. How about the transportation corps?' Well I never drove a truck in my life. 'Well how about the quartermasters?' 'What's that I say'? 'Supply', the review officer says. I can't even match my socks, much less go to the grocery store. So that was out. 'How about ordnance?' What's that, I say? 'Ordnance is the repair of guns, ammunition, tanks and armored personnel carriers, you know, mechanical things'. 'Machines', I spoke up. 'I once helped a fellow musician unstick a trombone slide.' 'Tell us more', the review captain said. 'Well, I once unstuck a lock by squirting oil in the keyway. So I repeated the same operation by helping this trombonist disassemble his slide and squirt some oil into the workings'. The review officer beamed, 'so you are a regular mechanical genius! We'll recommend you for the ordnance corps, Aberdeen Proving Ground'. 'I said whatever you say, sir.' The next day I got mimeographed orders for APG. I went there, took the course, kept my nose clean, and here I am."

Manteca maneuvered his way off the sofa to Duvalier's fixings. He reconstituted his juice. The can of lemon-lime soda had gone empty. Manteca klutzed his way to the small refrigerator and found a tin can of cola. There was a sign of the time lying on the plywood counter. It was a triangular pointy thing that was used to open beverage cans in the ante-diluvian age before pop-tops. He used it with dexterity and filled his gin tumbler with cola. He relapsed himself on the sofa and peered at Marshal Dillon.

Remphelmann, abuzz with a whole shot and a half of gin, began to blabber. "So I told you how I got here, what about you?"

Manteca was not at a loss for words. "Well, you see, I'm an ROTC officer. I was totally useless in college, and totally useless at campus life and totally useless during my two-year term as an active duty reserve officer. And then something happened after

I returned to civilian life. I found I was totally useless even as a civilian. So I went back into the army, where my incompetence is not noticeable."

"Yes?" Ronnie prompted.

"In addition, you see I have this hang-up. It's called cross-dressing. Not that I'm queer or anything, but I like to wear women's underwear."

"I see", said Remphelmann, not seeing at all.

"So I walked out of a transvestite bar outside Fort Ord, drunk off my ass, and the local cop comes up and busts me for public intoxication. They hauled me off to jail; strip searched me and found my lime green panties and bra. I was in a fix. Thankfully my wife showed up and weaseled me out. But all this gets reported to the Fort Ord Provost Marshal. So, to make a long story short, I volunteered to go to Vietnam to avoid a rather embarrassing situation." Manteca drew deeply on his tumbler, and then asked. "Do you like to wear women's underwear?"

Involuntarily Remphelmann began to look for an exit. The only thing that saved him from a hasty retreat was the simultaneous entrance of Shinebaum and Duvalier.

Chapter Eighteen

The only thing that saved Lieutenant Remphelmann from running from the presence of Captain Manteca was actually two things. First, it was Vietnam and he had no place to run to. Secondly, it was the angelic arrival of the Heeb and the Schwartze. Both came bearing gifts. Lieutenant Duvalier had another plastic bucket of ice and an amazing bottle of Calcutta scotch whiskey. How scotch could be made in India was a mystery to Remphelmann. Shinebaum had an entire carton of C rations, twenty-four breakfast meals including ham and scrambled eggs, pork sausage and breakfast beans, and bacon bits with oatmeal. He also had two cases, 24 cans, of the world famous Vietnamese beer '33', or 'Ba Muoi Ba'.

The captain was semi-comatose on the sofa watching *Gunsmoke*. He stirred to consciousness as the two arrivals stowed away their bringings. "You know, I've been watching *Gunsmoke* for years and there has never been an episode where Marshal Dillon ever screwed Miss Kitty. Do you think the marshal got a secret sex hang-up?"

Shinebaum and Duvalier rolled their eyes at each other, before Porky prompted the damp slug. "Captain Manteca, I checked out the charcoal on the barbeque grill out back, I think they are near ready to flop on those steaks."

Manteca woozed up from his alcoholic cocoon and wandered out the hootch's screen door. Remphelmann, suddenly soothed by the presence of the other two lieutenants, decided to follow the lard butt. On the perimeter side of the BOQ was a rather neat patio about twelve feet square. It was paved with scrap PSP obviously stolen from the air force engineers. This was surrounded by a low wall made of green sandbags two rows high. There was a barbeque grill that had been crafted by a handy mechanic. It was a steel ammunition case, lid removed, welded to pipe legs. Therein handmade Vietnamese charcoal had burnt down to a fine gray glow. Ranged against the hootch wall were patio chairs and a bench made of scrap lumber. A makeshift picnic table completed the ensemble. The only thing that seemed odd was a small bomb shelter at the far edge. It was a squat beehive of interlocked railroad ties overlaid with sandbags.

Manteca waxed enthusiastic about the view. "What a beautiful sight. Look at the sterling view down the free fire zone, to the razor wire and the bunkers, and beyond that the famous Phan Thiet Cemetery, and in the glorious distance the Nui Ta Dom, Whiskey Mountain, Big Titty Mountain! Any Bel-Air real estate agent worth her salt could sell this hootch to a millionaire on the view alone." He found a metal hook, raised the grill, which was made of a piece of scrounged expanded sheet metal and smoothed the charcoal down to an even bed. "Ah, the barbeque is ready. Let us call our fellow cohorts out and grill up a storm."

The officers were soon assembled. Manteca, despite his inebriation, proved a deft cook. He laid foil wrapped baked potatoes to one side of the grill, arranged the lettuce salad and army bread on the picnic table along with military margarine. Duvalier and Shinebaum were mostly silent. Remphelmann, who an hour before had protested at alcohol, observed the other three enjoying boilermakers of warm Vietnamese beer and ice cubed glasses of neat Calcutta scotch. He joined them. The sun sank with suddenness over the western horizon. Manteca had scored a stainless steel baking pan and after baptizing the steaks in a fine bath of vinegar, salt, pepper, army ketchup and a dash of tabasco sauce, laid them on the grill. The four sat with some contentment. A single light from inside the hootch cast a bare glow on the patio.

Suddenly, all hell broke loose. Remphelmann had discerned earlier that there was a mortar platoon attached to the LZ Betty infantry. It was a heavy mortar unit that shot 4.2 inch shells, four-duece in the army slang. A tremendous whoop of many shells went arcing up about a half kilometer south of the hootch. In the far distance, far beyond the razor wire and the bunkers and the free fire zone and the Phan Thiet cemetery, at the extent of the horizon, 105mm howitzer tubes erupted. Their faint muzzle flashes spoke in the extreme distance. There was a pause of about twenty seconds. Whiskey Mountain exploded in the far dark, in roiling waves of red fire. There was wave after wave of outgoing mortar rounds from the LZ. There was another similar blast of far distance artillery muzzles. Again the Big Titty was ablaze with fire. Remphelmann wanted to know what was happening but Manteca silently retrieved the steaks from the grill and all present quietly ate their repast. The waves of mortar and artillery continued for another fifteen minutes. Just as suddenly as the fireworks had begun, they ended. By then the steaks had been consumed and the officers had ended their meal. Remphelmann could contain his wonderment no longer. "What was that all about?"

Shinebaum explained. "It's called 'H and I'. Harassment and interdiction fire. We, at least the South Vietnamese, know that the Viet Cong are massing on Nui Ta Dom for a push. So they know that we know that we know, so we H and I them. They do the same back to us. Maybe tonight, maybe tomorrow. It's all part of the game."

Manteca gathered the leftover cooking utensils and plates and mounded them on the picnic table. "Who KP's? Who kitchen police's all this?" Ronnie asked.

Manteca explained. "We've a got an old Vietnamese woman, a hootch granny. A Ba. Tomorrow morning she'll show up from Phan Theit, clear the dishes off to the mess hall, tidy up, sweep the hootch, change linen and then wash and starch our uniforms."

The three ranking officers left and went to their sleeping quarters. That left Remphelmann alone. He pondered whether to sit in the dark or retire. He decided that sufficient to the day was the evil thereof and crept back to his cubicle and his bunk. The lone light bulb went out and Remphelmann sank into another exhausted sleep.

The next morning, at oh dark thirty, the officers hootch stirred to life. A wind up alarm clock went off someplace. Bodies began to move in the dark. Remphelmann, now used to sleeping in his own sweat, arose and did his latrine, shave and thankfully, due to the unexpected presence of muddy waters flowing in the half hootch, showered. Towel clad, muddy red wet, he went back to his cubicle and donned the last of his clean fatigues. By this time his hootch mates had disappeared. However there was note hanging on the screen door. It was from Shinebaum. It directed Remphelmann to the electric hot plate. Inside a saucepan of simmering water were numerous cans of C rations. Remphelmann fished them out, opened them with a handy can opener and had a hearty feast of canned scrambled eggs, canned saltines and spaghetti with meat sauce. He got his boots re-laced and went out into the rising sun. His jeep was sitting there. Although his platoon HQ was only a hundred yards away he fired up the car and drove over to the ordnance building with a dubious air of officiality. He parked and walked confidently into the hootch.

"Holy El Paso pest puckies," exclaimed Sergeant Shortarm. "What an amazing morning. We done got the tank up and running, we done got a handle on that there howitzer recuperator, we done got the five ton truck ready to reinstall the back axle and we done got no harassment and interdiction from Charlie last night. Complete and total success."

"I'm glad to hear that," offered Remphelmann.

"However," offered Shortarm in return. "Skinny is, you got a meeting with the major at the FSA headquarters in fifteen minutes, plus, and I hate to say this, we gotta lift the axle assembly on that five ton truck in about a half hour. We're short two arms and two legs to lift it. Could the lieutenant come back from that highly important meeting and help us? I mean we're short on men, and damn sir, holy Sugarland shit chutes, you did help us enlisted types yesterday and did actually get dirty. After your staff meeting, could you actually help?"

"Certainly," Remphelmann said.

"Holy Austin assholes, sir. Then you scoot off to your meeting, and we'll await your help." Remphelmann got back in the jeep and trundled over to the forward support headquarters. The other officers jeeps were already parked there. Ronnie went in. The four officers waited for the arrival of Major Dufuss.

"Besides the fact that we are all going to die," Manteca prognosticated, "I'll bet Dufuss enters stage center, four bloody mary's to the wind, and with the same broken record announcements." The captain prophesied correctly.

Major Dufuss's jeep arrived. There was a pause. His condescending driver smirked in, relayed the same instructions to the officers, which was to retire to the major's office and wait. The four retired and waited and waited. Ultimately Dufuss appeared at the HQ door and made a beeline for his desk. He marched like a drunk on a straight-line cop test and again smacked into his desk. This time, rather than roiling cup over coffee pot, he stopped and regained his balance. He swung out with his arm and snatched up a handy chair. Using that as a step stool, he mounted up and stood at attention on his desk.

"Gentlemen," he started, but seemed to realize he was facing the back wall. "Gentlemen," he started again.

Skip E. Lee

Manteca prompted, "Sir, Major Dufuss, sir, begging the major's tomato juice pardon, sir, we are behind you, sir."

Major Dufuss stood still for an interminable moment. Then he abruptly about faced, heel to toe. Manteca wondered if he would have to catch the major in his pirouette, but the major showed a true vodka balance and landed smartly in the right direction. He raised his arms in benediction to his assembled staff, looking rather like Moses on the mount, speaking down to the twelve tribes. "Yeah, verily and I say unto thee, I have just returned from the Mount Sinai of the infantry headquarters. The road movement to Long Bien has been delayed until tomorrow. The battalion S-2 hath announced that a small scale attack is going to be made on LZ Bozo tonight but that in the morning Que Ell One shall be clear unto the promised land."

"Is that all, sir?" Manteca queried.

"Captain Manteca, one will note that my instructions are not only final, finalized, fine and alliterative, but literal. Literal is, in the Indo-European scheme of languages, also cognate to the Algonquin and Cherokee tongues, namely Lilliput and Lu-Lu."

"Most certainly," Manteca groveled.

"Then, that is all, you are all dismissed." Dufuss still had his arms stretched out in imitation of a savior on a cross.

The four officers beat a hasty retreat out the door. Remphelmann, last in line, gingerly closed the office door ritualistically behind him. The officers did not stop in the fore-room but made a strategic withdrawal out the door to their jeeps. Not a word needed to be said. They hopped in their respective vehicles and went back to their duties.

══ Chapter Nineteen ══

"Do I have any messages or instructions from Cam Ranh, or Surf City?" Remphelmann said to Sergeant Shortarm as he met him inside the ordnance building.

"When it comes to guidance from Surf City to LZ Bozo, we might as will be on the dark side of the moon. Tell you what, sir, my educating you is getting near the end. I've told you all of what I know, and I'll bet a horny toad's ass you's now just as ignorant as me."

"Quite the contrary, sergeant, you've been most helpful so far."

"Thankee, lieutenant. But on to business. First the tank is up and running and the tank commander Sergeant Nocks came over and took 'er for a spin. The new alternator is making good juice, but the diesel fuel injection is running sluggish. So Sergeant Gruntz and Boudreaux are sorting that out now. Plus he's got an intermittent short on the radio. Einstein's got that pulled and is researching that. At some point this morning we want to reattach that ass axle on the five ton. Gonzales-McGillicuddy as we speak is tuning up the engine. That there truck is an old gas-guzzler left over from Korea, no fuel injection and it's backfiring like

Boston baked beans. Sergeant Peckerwood and Scheissenbrenner are rebuilding a spare equilibator mechanism for one of the howitzers out at Firebase Firefly. That leaves the armorer Schweik. You know where Einstein's clean room is?"

"Yes."

"Schweik's work bench is next that. He's got a back load of M-16 rifles and an M-60 machine gun he's trying to get repaired. Did your meeting with Major Dufuss get anywhere?"

"No. Outside of the fact the convoy to Long Bien on Que Ell One is cancelled until tomorrow morning."

"Figgers. The infantry types like to keep Dufuss in the dark. Dufuss would mess up a wet dream if he had any real facts. The real facts, as the poop goes, poops like this. Shinebaum and his people got cut orders for road security all the way to Long Bien. Lieutenant Duvalier and his truck platoon get to dead head empty back there and pick up supplies. That there Patton tank what where we is tuning up is going on the march as far as Firefly. Sergeant Peckerwood and Scheissenbrenner are tagging along with the recuperator seal for that 105mm gun to install it. Plus the South Vietnamese are organizing a convoy for their own purposes that will do a simultaneous road march. Also there seems to be a whole gaggle of Vietnamese, civilians, cars, motorbikes, trucks and what not that been waiting to get up Que Ell One. Poor buggers in Phan Thiet, civilians that is, their whole local economy is in collapse. Can't ship any civvie goods in, can't ship any civvie goods out. Everybody in Phan Thiet has done be plumb broke."

"How do you know all this and the officers don't?"

"Lookee here, lieutenant. There done be three streams of information here in this man's army. The first is the enlisted man's rumor mill, which is just that, rumors, bullshit, piss water, lies, conjectures, wild speculation and outright crap. Secondly, there is the officer information channel, which is so full of legalistic whys, wherefores, suppurations, supposed secrets, provisos, tactical tit wringing, strategic moonbeams and possum poop as to be damn near worthless. Then there is the sergeants grapevine. Sergeants run this here man's army. We gotta have actionable information, 'cause us god forsaken non-commissioned types gotta do all the heavy lifting. We gotta keep the privates in line and gotta keep the officers in line. We gotta make sure the army really functions. So's we got our own channels of information. If'n you want to know what's really goin' on, ask the old sarge."

"Thank you, sergeant, I'll remember that."

"So, sir. I gotta get back on the horn and try to rustle up parts. I suggest to the esteemed young officer, that he go out in the yard and politely snoop. I mean, find each man, find what he's doing, what his job and problems is. Don't stand on no ceremony. Let 'em get on with their duty, and kind of sort out in your own mind how's you can help and maybe lead." At that point the telephone rang. Shortarm answered and immediately began to scream obscenities into the receiver. Remphelmann straightened up his soggy fatigues and went on a politically snoopy inspection tour.

The first person he met was Sergeant Heimstaadt, the truck repair foreman. Heimstaadt and Gonzales-McGillicuddy were figuring out how to the hoist the rear axle into the back end of a five-ton truck with only mud underneath and no jacking tools. Remphelmann presented himself to the senior enlisted man.

"Hello, Sergeant Heimstaadt."

"Und guten morgan to you. You see that my mechanic, Herr Gonzales-McGillicuddy und I been trying to make the axle fit to the frame of this truck. We have the axle aligned but, we lacks the under hoist to maneuver it into the correct."

The New Mexican was lying in the dirt, a large bolt in hand, attempting to align the axle. The two mechanics had jury-rigged some heavy wooden boards as a kind of fulcrum and lever to lift the thousand pound axle into its approximate position.

"Hey, lieutenant. Flop down and push up on the other side."

Remphelmann plopped his back in the mud, and using

his legs, he pushed the heavy axle up. Gonzales-McGillicuddy swore softly in Apache, Spanish and English and the axle located itself and the bolt twisted in. "Hey, lieutenant, thanks, easy gravy." McGillicuddy slithered through the mud and placed a corresponding bolt on the other side. "Duck soup," he announced to both sergeant and officer.

"Der lieutenant will appraise that der axle is hereby in alignment, for which many gotter danken. You are a help. As der American redskin say, 'Mucho las mucho gracias'."

"I said nothing of the sort," said Gonzales, "I said thanks. Now I gotta find the spring hangers and u-bolts and the brake line connections." He crawled up from underneath the truck and straightened his mud-caked body. "Also, I gotta re-tune that old gas engine. The timing is so off it hardly runs. It just coughs, backfires and quits. Oh by the way, lieutenant, Sarge Shortarm said I ought to take your jeep over to the air force fire station and hose it down. He said I should paint up a nickname on the hood if you want. I'm real good at the old English style lettering stuff. I'm with a low rider car club in Truth or Consequences, you know bajito y suavito, low and slow. I tag everybody's car with a placa."

"What a funny name for a town, "Remphelmann mused.

"Yes, and in Truth or Consequences, we Mexican-Apache-Irish types got a joke. That is 'in this town we got very little truth but a whole lot of consequences'. You want me to spiff up your coach now or later?" Remphelmann handed Gonzales-McGillicuddy a spare jeep key. "And just what's the nickname you want inscribed on your jeep, sir?"

Remphelmann said, "I mentioned it as a joke, but Sergeant Shortarm picked up on it. I'm going to christen it the "Mud Bucket."

"Say that again, sir?"

"Mud Bucket, Mud Bucket".

"Got you, sir." The New Mexican was away in a flash. The officer wandered into the ramshackle parts warehouse. He found

Private Einstein twirling the knobs on an oscilloscope as he probed the inside of the tank's radio.

"Hey there lieutenant. How's your hammer hanging?"

"Just fine, Private Einstein. What are you up to?"

"This is the radio out of that Patton tank that's out in the yard. It came in on a repair tag claiming 'intermittent short'. It seems there is a cold solder connection between the voltage regulator and the super-heterodyne circuit. I'm trying to pinpoint it now. Do you know anything about radios and electronics?

"After I get past the on-off switch and tuning dial, I'm lost."

"Then I won't bother you with the details. But it's a transformer connection. As my old Uncle Conrad Lorenz Einstein used to warn me, beware of the Lorenz transformations."

Remphelmann took that as some sort of electronic arcana and moved off to find Private Schweik at his gunsmith's bench. Schweik tried to stand at attention but Remphelmann waved him down. "As you were, private, I don't want to interrupt you, but tell me what your doing." During the brief moment Schweik had bobbed up and down, Remphelmann saw how disheveled the armorer was. He was reminded of the Sergeant Shortarm's earlier characterization of the man's slovenly appearance. There was a famous newspaper cartoon character of World War Two vintage about a hopelessly inept soldier of doleful demeanor and atrocious personal appearance named 'The Sad Sack'. Remphelmann instinctively wanted to moniker Schweik with the same label.

"Sir, what I have here is about a dozen M-16 rifles out of whack, and two 45 caliber colt pistols with bad feed. The main patient today in the emergency room is this M-60 machine gun that I'm working on now. This puppy got dropped in a muddy rice paddy. The gunner was real busy sending postcards to Charlie at the time and kept on firing. The mud acted like liquid sandpaper and screwed the action up royal. I've had to replace the whole gas piston assembly and now I'm head spacing the bolt back into tolerance with the breech, you know?"

Remphelmann knew. He left and went to a rough shed behind the parts warehouse. There on a table made of scavenged boards supported by 55-gallon drums was the howitzer equilibrator Sergeant Shortarm had referred to. Remphelmann knew from his training what an equilibrator was. It was something on the order of a set of giant balancing springs that held the gun tube in balance over the howitzer main frame. Sergeant Peckerwood and Specialist Scheissenbrenner were adjusting the massive coil springs that were housed in the assembly of parts.

"Good morning, Sergeant Peckerwood, good morning Specialist Scheissenbrenner."

"Oh god sir, don't be so damn cheerful," moaned Peckerwood. "I've got the mother of all hangovers."

Remphelmann researched his military etiquette. For a non-commissioned officer to show up in a hangover state was bad, but to admit it was even worse. But Remphelmann also knew that he could not remonstrate with the sergeant in front of others, for fear of humiliating the man in front of his subordinates. Remphelmann kept a diplomatic silence while Peckerwood continued.

"I '33'd myself," the sergeant continued. "'Bomnee bombed' myself near to perdition. You know what I mean by bomnee bombing myself?"

"No."

"Well, sir, first of all you have to understand the beer situation. First of all, the best beer comes from the States, and the next best beer comes from the Philippines and when we can't get either of those we move on to the world famous Vietnamese '33' brand of beer. Ba Muoi Ba in the local lingo. Now don't get me wrong. The Viet is as good a brew master as anybody in the world. But you see, this is the tropics, and what they do is add the smallest smidgen of formaldehyde to the beer. It being the tropics and the heat and lack of refrigeration. They don't want their beer to go sour in the heat so they dose it with a tiny whiff of formaldehyde."

"Formaldehyde!" exclaimed the lieutenant, "That's embalming fluid!"

Peckerwood rubbed his temple to increase the blood flow to his aching head. "Sir, its only embalming fluid in a big dose. Actually in a small amount it gives a bit of kick to the brew. But if you have the 'fatal glass', as W.C. Fields would say, 'Katy, bar the door!'"

Remphelmann thought it politic to go to the job at hand. "Well, what about the equilibrator?"

"It's fine, sir. Nothing is broken. It's simply out of adjustment. We've re-toleranced the frame and Scheissenbrenner and I are now re-torqueing the spring tension back into specifications."

The young officer turned to Specialist Scheissenbrenner.

"And how are you this morning, specialist?"

"Just fine, sir. Just fine. But you've missed my morning duty. Perhaps the most important job here at the LZ, the shit burning routine."

Remphelmann suddenly felt as if he was out of the information loop. Was there a need-to-know that he was not plugged into? He queried. "Just what is it about this often mentioned shit burning that I have not been appraised of?"

"Oh sir," Scheissenbrenner rejoined with a small twinkle in his eye. "It's damn near a Vietnam theater top-secret operation. Originated at the top levels of the Pentagon. I couldn't really tell you in words but if you were to show up thirty minutes after the mess hall closes on any given morning and meet me, I could let you in on the secret."

Remphelmann turned back to Peckerwood. "So what else is on the agenda?"

"The main thing, sir, is getting out to Firebase Firefly. Getting that tube with the punk recuperator seal is priority one. Plus that Patton tank must be ship-shape for the trip. The armor sergeant has some kind of covering mission out there in that rice paddy. Seems Charlie is on the push. A day or so of wake up probes, and then a knock down drag out fight for control of Big Titty Mountain and ownership of Que Ell One."

"Thanks for the information, sergeant. You non-coms have a better handle on the situation than anybody else."

"We sergeants own this man's army, sir. Privates and officers just rent space."

Remphelmann snooped on. He found Sergeant Gruntz and Private Boudreaux working on the tank. They had just used a crane mounted on the back of a truck to lower the massive engine hatch over the engine bay and were busy bolting it down. The engine hatch was a seeming cross between armor plate and the world's largest sewer grate. The gratings or louvers allowed the heat of the engine to escape. Integral to that were smaller hatchways that allowed a mechanic to reach in and adjust the inner workings of the engine. Remphelmann deftly swung up on the engine deck. "Good morning, Sergeant Gruntz, how are things going?"

"Like shit as always, sir. Pure crap. The alternator works just fine, Einstein's got the radio out to find why it shits out on and off. Now Boudreaux and I have to diagnose why the injectors aren't running smooth. Hopefully it's just crud in the lines or one of the fuel filters is waxed up, but with my luck the guts of the injector body is screwed and we'll have to replace it."

"Do you have a new injector assembly on hand?"

"Yes, damn it, but takes all day to weasel the old one out and plug the new one in and get it tweaked. Damn it, sir, I transferred out of the infantry into the ordnance, so I don't have to pull this kind of duty. LZ Bozo is a shit hole and I'm tired of being in shit holes and getting shot at. I had Private Einstein type up a new request for transfer, in triplicate. If you were to sign it and send it up, maybe I could get sent back to Surf City and civilization."

"I'll look into it, Sergeant Gruntz," Remphelmann soothed. Then he turned to Private Boudreaux. The young private was installing a gigantic bolt with a very large ratchet wrench. His eyes were beaded and his brow furrowed, as if the mere installation of a bolt was requiring the sum total of his mental abilities. Remphelmann had the sudden insight that here was a man who could not walk and chew gum at the same time. He was soon proved right. "So, Private Boudreaux, how are you?"

The Louisianan instantly stopped his taxing intellectual labor and the physical dexterity of screwing home the bolt. "Dang them, sir, this bolt is a-taxing my brain. It ain't a wanting to go home smooth." Boudreaux then beamed. "Yes, sir, did I ever tell you sir, how is that me and my Cousin Pierre ever got out of the bayou and back into Atchafalaya for a wake?"

Remphelmann was at a loss. "No, Boudreaux, you haven't."

The cajun's face instantly relaxed its mentally contorted brow and Bordeaux's lips began to speak. "Oh, goody, sir. See it goes like this. Me Cousin Pierre and I decide to go to town. See, we get in Cousin Pierre's pick 'em up truck and scampers into Atchafalaya. So we gets to town and both of us has a big cold Nehi cola drink at the gas 'em up station, and then, and then," Boudreaux paused slightly as if he had lost what little train of thought he possessed. He regained it, slightly out of the station, and continued. "So we went over to Grandpa Fontenot's house. Gran Mama Odell isn't not to home. Ain't not sooner we sits down than Gran Papa tells Pierre to take these here two envelopes over to the Breaux Bridge Pharmacy and done have a prescription fulfilled. Well, we are dutiful grandsons so we got in the pick 'em up and went over to Breaux Bridge. The pharmacist, Mr. Brossard, done open the first letter and it done asked for a horse killer dose of cyanide to kill Gran Mama Odell. Well, the pharmacist, trying to keep a professional posture, done said to Pierre, 'I'm sorry, but under the circumstances I can't sell you any cyanide'. But Cousin Pierre done produced the second envelope inside of which being a photo of Gran Mama Odell, perhaps the ugliest and meanest looking woman the pharmacist never met. That there pharmacist blushed and replied, 'Sha, Pierre, I didn't know Gran Papa Fontenot had a prescription!' To make the story short, shortly thereafter we had a great funeral and a grander wake, ah-gar-own-tee."

Remphelmann had no ready answer. He could only reply, "Perhaps you should finishing bolting down the engine cover." Boudreaux knitted his intellectual brow and returned to screwing down the bolt.

Remphelmann, having trooped after the last of his platoon stalwarts decided to make a diplomatic retreat to the ordnance HQ. No sooner than he made the entrance to the hootch than Gonzales-McGillicuddy roared up in the lieutenant's newly washed jeep. Emblazoned across the vehicle's hood, in old English lettering, rather like a prison tattoo, already dry in the scorching sun, was the name 'Mudd Buck It'. Remphelmann admired Gonzales-McGillicuddy's obvious grasp of English spelling.

"That's a fine job of car wash and sign painting skill."

"Thanks lieutenant, but the main chore of the day is getting that old five ton truck to get its ass axle finished up and to get the engine running smoothly. It back fires like a taco folding beaner eating burritos. And that's the most important mission of my day."

Sergeant Shortarm stormed out the hootch. He took a small glance at the washed jeep and barked to Gonzales-McGillicuddy. "That's there looks just fine, private, now hightail out and get that five ton engine running." Sergeant Shortarm recognized the officers presence. "Holy Midland menstrual monthlies, sir! The horn is burning up with intelligence skinny. Charlie did be doing a diversionary here on Bozo tonight, and a road interdiction tomorrow."

"How do you know all this?"

"Sir, contrary to popular opinion they ain't no secrets in no frigging war zone. The enemy knows what we're up to and we, by a damn sight, knows what they are up to. So a mortar attack tonight, maybe a quick shot at the ammo dump and tomorrow the fun and games of Que Ell One. Does me a favor, sir, I gotta get back on the horn. Holy Houston horseshoes, hells-a-popping. Go light a fire under Sergeant Heimstaadt and the frigging Apache Mexican. Make sure they get the five-ton engine up and tuned.

If'n need be, throw in a cuss word or too." With that Shortarm went back in the building and hollered the most sailor like talk into the phone.

The ever-dutiful officer wandered back into the maintenance yard, to find Gonzales butt skyward hanging over the fender of the truck while Heimstaadt sat in the drivers seat, cranking the engine and goosing the throttle.

Chapter Twenty

Heimstaadt sat in the driver's seat of an old large truck, the five-ton cargo truck that had just had the axle replacement. He was alternately cranking the engine and flipping the foot throttle back and forth. Underneath the hood Private Gonzales-McGillicuddy was twiddling an infinitesimal calculus of carburetor settings and advancement of the electrical distributor, that spider like web of doohickeys that send impulses to the spark plugs. Neither Newton with his fluxions, nor Leibnitz with his calculus and differentials, nay even that great mechanic Riemann, whatever their theoretical postulates in the academic and intellectual worlds, could attempt what a Mexican and a kraut could actualize in the real.

The real was, the damned old truck wouldn't start and run. The best minds of a generation had been driven to madness, stark, raving, on the Korean era beast. It started, it ran, and it died. It died, hiccupped to life, and sputtered to an ignominious conclusion. Every mechanic at the landing zone, real or wannabe, had tried his expert knowledge, or his shade tree experience, or his voodoo on the machine. All had traced the most meticulous troubleshooting diagnosis in checking fuel, cylinder compression, spark, errant leaks, electric wiring, gasket integrity, filters and whatever secret knowledge that they might possess on the recalcitrant machine. All had tried, Shortarm, Peckerwood, Gruntz, Scheissenbrenner, Boudreaux, and various hangers on. Nothing would bring the Frankensteinian corpse to life.

Sergeant Heimstaadt and Gonzales-McGillicuddy were trying again. Remphelmann stood at a discrete distance. His knowledge of engine repair had got no farther than cleaning spark plugs on his grandfather's tractor back in Iowa and he thought it politic to stand on the shoulders of giants such as a heinie and an Apache.

Heimstaadt cranked and throttled. Gonzales fiddled and burned. He twisted the distributor back and forth in its socket. Heimstaadt button pushed and flatfooted the pedal.

Suddenly the beast not only started but also roared. It roared like a tiger. It roared so much that a copious cloud of blue and white smoke blew itself from the exhaust. It reverberated and ran! Gonzales pulled himself from under the hood and gazed in astonishment at Sergeant Heimstaadt. Heimstaadt also had a look of amazement that would have graced the Second Coming. The sergeant ran the engine for 30 seconds or so at a race.

From around the ordnance yard there were glances of approval from all present. Even Einstein and Schweik came out of the warehouse to admire. Sergeant Shortarm appeared out of the ordnance headquarters hootch, hands to heaven, to glorify the resurrection. Heimstaadt continued to race the engine. Satisfied that it was running and running cleanly, he eased off the throttle. The engine spun smoothly down. Finally he let the truck return to idle. McGillicuddy stood on the fender of the truck. Heimstaadt beamed from behind the driver's seat.

There was a breathless admiration from the assembled onlookers. Breathless like nuns in their orisons having all prayers answered. It was a transcendent moment. A spiritual epiphany. A theophany from God to individual grease monkey souls.

Then it happened. The truck backfired. It didn't just backfire, it fired back. It didn't just let a polite po-tooty from the anus, it didn't just fart commodiously, it backfired to the point that a resonating explosion exited the tail pipe. The fire from the exhaust shot in a twenty-foot blowtorch across the yard. The sound was deafening, nay, earth shaking, no, it was an ear splitting experience.

Remphelmann was not in the least perturbed. After all a backfire from a gasoline driven engine was not new to him. Farm trucks, tractors, even automobiles backfired. What amazed him as he gathered the vision through his thick glasses was the reaction of all the men within eyesight.

Sergeant Gruntz and Private Boudreaux were on the tank's rear deck. In a superhuman leap Gruntz was headfirst down the open turret hatch of the machine. Boudreaux did an amazing back flip off the iron deck and smacked back down into the mud. Schweik and Einstein, who were just outside the warehouse door, did something similar. Schweik, as if on a trampoline, went flying back through the warehouse door. Einstein did something else. He twirled his arms about his head and did a strange maneuver rather like folding his arms pretzel-like about his head. His legs did the same folding up maneuver. As he instantaneously went to ground, he rolled into crumpled position. Scheissenbrenner and Sergeant Peckerwood dived beneath their worktable and disappeared. On the errant truck, Sergeant Heimstaadt evaporated underneath the dash. Gonzales-McGillicuddy did a backing turn, rolled into a compact ball and fell like a roly-poly insect into a muddy puddle to the side of the truck fender. Sergeant Shortarm, arms raised like an Old Testament prophet seeing the rejuvenation of the dead, went into a convoluted mass of collapsing arms and legs and disappeared behind some sandbags. Only Lieutenant Remphelmann of the ordnance was left standing.

Then as suddenly as the situation had unraveled, the situation raveled up again, as if a short nap had re-knitted a night of care. Sergeant Gruntz and Private Boudreaux were back on the tank engine cover. Sergeant Shortarm was afoot and walking back to the ordnance hootch. Specialist Scheissenbrenner and Sergeant Peckerwood were back to adjusting the howitzer part.

Heimstaadt was back at the driver's position of the truck and restarted it. It ran smoothly. It purred like the proverbial kitten. Gonzales was back under the hood of the five-ton doing some kind of final adjustment. Private Schweik, his clothing no worse for sartorial wear, appeared at the warehouse door, looked briefly and disappeared back to his workbench. That left Private Einstein who had pretzeled himself so sufficiently into a mud hole that he took a bit of time to extricate himself. Lieutenant Remphelmann approached the radio repairman. Einstein was actually using his forefinger to dig mud out of his mouth, gums and tongue.

"What is this all about?"

"What's what all about?"

"Everybody went fanny over tranny into the dirt."

"Oh, that." Einstein coughed red mud from his throat. "Herky-jerky."

"Huh?" said the officer with incredulity.

"The herky-jerky, you know, like the title of that song, that soul brother dance tune you hear on the radio. 'Hey, Baby, Let's Do The Herky-Jerky'."

Remphelmann did not understand. "I do not understand."

"The herky-jerky, the duck and cover, the dick in the dirt, the bend over and kiss your ass goodbye, the flop and pray, the belt buckle in the bush, the titties on the tarmac, the bellybutton in the bayou, the gut in the gutter, the kiddush in the crud. You know."

Remphelmann did not know. "I don't know what you're talking about."

Einstein finished hacking mud up from his windpipe. "Oh right, sir, I see now. I forgot you're a new kid on the block. Whenever, in a war zone, you hear a loud unexpected noise, it's one of two things. It's either outgoing or incoming. By outgoing I mean we, the good guys, are shooting something at the bad guys. Like for instance, an artillery piece goes off, or a mortar, or a machine gun, outgoing, outbound. So you reflexively duck to make sure outgoing fire doesn't hit you. Outgoing. Friendly fire.

But what if the reverse is true? According to my Uncle Richard Feynman Einstein, time is not only reversible; it's a sum over histories. But I wander from the subject. If the enemy, the bad guy is shooting at you, you do what comes naturally, that is to get out of the line of fire. Make a low profile. Make yourself as small a target as possible. So when you hear a loud unexpected noise, you don't know whether it's good, bad or ugly. Your instinctive reaction is to go to ground instantly. Only then do you reassess whether the situation is copasetic or not. Safety first. When in doubt, drop out. Duck first, investigate later.

"I think I follow your drift, Private Einstein. But to me it seems rather a caricature of over-reaction."

"Well, sir," Einstein spat a final wad of muddy mucus from between his teeth. "You might think it an over-reaction, but wait till Charlie gets you in his sights. I bet you'll herky-jerky just like any other man with a sense of self-preservation."

"I think not," Remphelmann replied with a false bravado.

"Funny thing sir, the herky-jerky. I've heard many men describe the phenomenon, and everybody all over Vietnam has got a slang term for the reflexive behavior, but I will as, Boudreaux says, I guarantee, ah-gar-on-tee, that you'll be dancing the herky-jerky like a champion soon enough." Einstein blew a final snot of mud from his nose and disappeared back to his work station.

The rest of the workday seemed to settle into something of a routine. Remphelmann kept going back to the ordnance hootch to ask if there were any orders from Cam Ranh. There were none. He waited until the men had returned from noon chow and suddenly felt hungry. He still did not know what the officers mess protocol really was, and was loath to find out. The thought of boiled C-rations came to mind, but he dismissed it. Finally he got in the 'Mudd Buck It' and drove over to the enlisted mess. The mess door was unlocked. Remphelmann went in. The place was empty of men. Cookie, busy barking clean up orders at the kitchen police, saw him. The cook put a finger to his lips. Soon, silently there was a melamine tray of left over cheeseburgers and potato griddle fries.

Remphelmann went back to the ordnance area and politely snooped for the rest of the day. The sun set. He did the 'Mudd Buck It' back to the officers BOQ.

Shinebaum was sitting in a slump. He was obviously on the first drink of the evening. It was some concoction of canned cola and Philippine rum, dashed on ice. He invited Remphelmann to make himself one to 'be sociable'. Remphelmann complied.

"What's with the convoy tomorrow, Porky?"

"Everything is up in the air, the usual hurry up and wait."

The two sat for some time in silence. Shinebaum poured him self another libation. He suddenly brightened. "So, Ronnie, I like names. How in Yahweh's sweet name did you every get a moniker like Ronald Reagan Remphelmann?"

"Well, you know how mothers are."

"Indeed I do."

"My mother was in a movie theater in Keokuk with my aunt. Nine months along when her water broke. They went straight to the hospital and I popped right out, all smiles and smooth bottom. When my mom got the first contraction, she, well you know, she's something of a soap opera fan, she was bawling over some tear-jerk scene in the movie and didn't know whether it was the movie or me. So the nurse says, 'what's the name for the birth certificate', and my name slipped right out of her mouth. When my dad heard this he was pissed cause they, mom and dad, had agreed on Woodrow Wilson Remphelmann. But the deed was done."

"I don't get it," Porky replied.

"Oh, the movie was 'The Hasty Heart', starring Patricia Neal and Ronald Reagan."

Shinebaum laughed as he got more drinks arranged. "So tell me more, how did you end up in Vietnam?" Remphelmann repeated the short inglorious biography he had related to Manteca the evening before. "An oboe player with a busted lip, too blind to be combat arms, named after a 'B' movie actor, and now an army officer!" Porky laughed more to himself than Remphelmann.

"So the tables are turned. How, if you're Jewish, did you get a nickname like 'Porky'. Are you really Jewish?"

"Don't ask about my nick-name. That's a story for another day. But I am Jewish. I'm about as heeb as you can get, full blooded Puerto Rican kike. You doubt me, no problem, I can drop trousers now, you can do the short arms inspection and see how the old circumcision is going."

"I'll pass on that," Remphelmann replied.

Shinebaum was sliding down the cup. "Being a heeb among all you gentiles, gives me the heebie-jeebies. Being the only kike amongst you Christ-crazies makes me claustrophobic." Porky's remark was in good humor and Remphelmann took it in good humor.

"O.K. so how did you end up in Vietnam"? Ronnie enquired.

The Philippine rum had cheered Shinebaum up and made him more voluble. "So I got to hear your short biography. I heard yours, you hear mine."

"Sure."

"My dad is a German Jew. In 1939 he was one of last of undesirables to get out of Hilterland before the war really started. He got a visa to the United States and got on an ocean liner, and got the hell out of Dodge. But when the boat gets to New York, the authorities refused landing rights. Typical anti-Jew crap. So the boat goes instead to Havana, Cuba, where the refugees were allowed to land. There my Dad gets a job with some import-export company. Being a semi-religious type he goes to the local synagogue. But the local temple is old time Moreno Sephardic Spanish Jews, and my dad is a kraut Ashkenazi. However, being young and horny and on the make, he meets my mom, who was and is, about as strict a Sephardic as you can get. Again, lust and love triumphs over picayunish religious differences and they get married. All the time my dad is trying to finagle his way into the United States. No luck. In 1943, though he gets a chance to go to San Juan, Puerto Rico. So mom, dad and my two older sisters hop scotch to Puerto Rico. Later than sooner I get born. Finally after the war, dad and the family get a visa and it's off to Milwaukee."

"Pabst Blue Ribbon, the beer that made Milwaukee famous."

"You got it. So I grow up a German Ashkenazi slash Spanish Cuban Sephardic slash Puerto Rican from Wisconsin. I was confused about my heritage."

"Figures," added Remphelmann.

" So I go to college for two years, but I'm bored. So its 1964. I get a wild hair up my ass to go to Israel and live on a kibbutz. It was a kind of proto-hippie kind of thing for a nice young Jewish boy to do."

Remphelmann commiserated. "Say no more."

Shinebaum kept talking. "So I'm a kibbutznik. So I'm bored tending broccoli. So I join the Israeli army under an assumed name as a private and get the bottom end job, straight leg infantry. So the 1967 war, the Six Day War starts. So I end up on the Golan Heights banging away at the Syrians, who are quite good soldiers by the way. Bullets whizzing and mortars banging down and artillery making mincemeat of the terrain and a few of my buddies. So the war is over, my enlistment is over and I go back to the University of Wisconsin and do pre-law. But the war made me crazy you see. So I do ROTC and get a commission. I wanted to go JAG, Judge Advocate General and be a military lawyer, but I only got a pre-law, so they assigned me to the military police.

"I'm losing track of the biography."

"No, it's simple. You see I'm on the Golan Heights. A firefight. A bullet went right past my head, singing right next to my ear. At first I was scared shitless. But then a sudden thought came into my head. It was a quote from George Washington, who at Braddock's Defeat, came under heavy musket fire from the French and Indians. The bullets were doing that, singing as it were. Washington got a horse shot out from under him and got another bullet through the frock of his coat, and another bullet singing past his ear. But afterward he wrote a letter to his brother, and confided, 'There was something charming in the sound'. That's something like me. I am not a war lover, I am not a hero, but when the bullets fly, there's something charming in the sound. I felt then, and I feel now, a certain exhilaration in being alive, being close to certain death and yet alive. The every day tedium of life pales in comparison when you come to the nexus, to the geometrical center of human experience. Somehow being in battle trumps all human experience. That thought brings me back, perhaps like a moth to a flame. But most of life is really boring and war is the ultimate edge. There is nothing like being on the cusp of death, to make you feel alive. Maybe I'm a war lover. I hope not. This is too introspective for me. What about food?"

Manteca entered the hootch. He had stainless steel pans of hot food that he had cadged from some nameless mess. Lieutenant Duvalier was right behind.

"Say hey, Manteca." Porky had brightened up. "What's under the lid? Thank God, we've got a quartermaster who's on the ball. Stealing, uh, liberating, food, booze, c-rations, cigarettes and god knows what."

"I don't steal, begging the lieutenant's ass. I re-allocate resources."

"What's on the menu tonight?"

"What, on the army's infamous 21 day rotating menu, is the worst of the worst?"

"Easy," said Duvalier, "Day 17, liver and onions, liver fried green and white onions burned brown."

"You said the magic word," Manteca said with a hint of sadism.

A collective groan went up.

"No," the quartermaster continued, it is day 17 of 21, liver and onions for the troops, but I've got beef ravioli, real French

Vietnamese garlic bread and all the trimmings. Asparagus tips with mock béarnaise, green beans with bacon bits, Caesar salad with ham chunks, and cold cans of real state-side Jax Beer!" A sigh of relief went up. "Let's haul our sorry parade out onto the patio and chow down."

The group did just that. As they ate Remphelmann felt constrained to bring up business. "What's the story about your convoy tomorrow?" he asked P.T.

"The same information and lack of information. Our own S-2 is clueless from our own sources, but the ARVN intel is that there will be some kind of attack tonight on our wire here at Bozo and Betty. Their sources think it just might be a little H and I, harassment and interdiction, just to keep us awake tonight. But you never can tell. The real bug-a-boo is what Charlie is planning for the convoy. There's indication that something is up around 'Ambush Alley.'" Duvalier pointed off the patio towards Whiskey Mountain on the horizon. "Over there, Que Ell One does a series of dog-leg turns through some ravines and it's choice terrain for a meat grinder. We don't know whether the Viet Cong will have local force VC, black pajama types, just to give us the 'slam, bam, thank you, ma'am', and di di mao or whether the main force VC battalion wants to have a slug fest. Tomorrow will tell."

"Dee Dee Ma-ow?" Remphelmann queried.

"Di di mao. It's Vietnamese. Literally it means 'let us go,' but depending on the context and tone of voice it can mean anything from getting your kid ready for school di di mao, to a fishing captain telling his crew to sail out of port di di mao, to the worst kind of situation di di mao. Which can translate as 'let's get the hell out of Dodge' or 'run like hell' or as the French have the saying, 'suave qui peut', 'save who can', 'every man for himself'. Context, you know."

Remphelmann looked a little closer to home. "But you said an attack on the wire tonight. Staged from where, against what? For example, that sand-bagged bunker fifty meters over there.

159

Who mans that at night? Where would Charlie want to hit the perimeter?"

"Damn it, Ronnie, you ask to many obvious questions. In any normal circumstance, the FSA commander, Major Dufuss would brief you on these subjects, but Dufuss is as worthless as teats on a boar hog. Speaking of hogs, Porky, can you fill new kid in, while I fetch up some more ravioli?"

The Philippine rum had found a friend in Shinebaum, who was ready to pick up the conversation. "Ronnie, you've asked several questions. First, Charlie's disposition. The whole of the LZ is surrounded by sand dunes to the south and west. Free fire zones for two kilometers. To the north is the city of Phan Thiet. The VC aren't stupid. If they mounted an attack from town, we would have to fire back and waste Phan Thiet. That would not only piss off the South Vietnamese, the Viet Cong have an interest in protecting the civilians too. After all this is a civil war. If the VC attacks from town, we waste the town, and the civvies will blame the VC for the casualties. No win situation. That leaves the northwest perimeter and the beautiful world famous Phan Thiet cemetery, one and a half clicks out. Long-range machine gun fire, spotty AK-47 rounds, long distance bazookas, RPG's, and easy mortar range. So they muster up in the no-man's land of the cemetery and go from there."

Remphelmann gazed out at the cemetery in the fading light. A hundred thousand people, five hundred years of humanity slept snuggly beneath the hummocks.

"So," continued the heeb. "Their main objective, from their only jump off place is LZ Bozo. The ammo dumps, the petroleum storage, the quartermaster supply yard. Us!" Shinebaum mixed himself another rum and cola and continued. "I'm getting tired of talking but here goes. See that sandbagged bunker out there, about fifty yards out? Next to it is one of those old French concrete bunkers. Now when the security threat is low they allow us rear echelon mother types, the REMF's, to man those bunkers at night. That gives the poor god-forsaken grunts a chance to get back across the airfield and get some well-deserved sleep and rest. But tonight, the threat level is high, so the infantry is going to occupy it. They don't trust us amateur soldiers when Charlie is on the make."

Dinner was soon over. The sun was down. There was no artillery attack on Nui Ta Dom Mountain. The officers drifted off to their cubicles. The lights went out. Remphelmann lay down on his soggy mattress and looked at the luminous dots on his wristwatch. It was 10 o'clock, 2200 hours. It had been an eventful and informative day. As he tucked his thick glasses under his pillow, he had a fleeting thought. It was about Private Einstein describing the herky-jerky. Ronnie laughed to himself. The herky-jerky. What a ridiculous phrase. What an over-reaction from his men. As he slipped into unconsciousness, he chuckled again, 'herky-jerky'.

═══ Chapter Twenty-One ═══

Remphelmann slept soundly. He knew not whether it was the sleep of the blessed or of the damned. Out of his slumber there was an unusual sound. He turned in his rack and ignored it. However, there were shouts, if not screams. Not the scream of a hysterical, but the calls of grown men, seasoned men, answering some problem.

"Incoming, damn it. Incoming!" Ronnie looked at his watch. It was 2:30 in the morning. Beyond the luminous dial there was pitch black. "Power off, flashlight time." He heard the now familiar voice of Duvalier. Under his cubicle door he saw the flicker of an electric torch. Then there was a most horrendous crash some twenty feet away, followed immediately by an indescribable sound, at least to Remphelmann. It was a sort of punching sound, like the sound of a sledgehammer hitting kasha-thunk against a car fender. A ka-ching, ka-cring sort of patter followed that noise on the tin roof of the hootch.

"Bunker time," came the voice of Shinebaum. "Crawl baby, crawl!"

Remphelmann leaped out of bed. Not knowing what to do, he thought it appropriate to put on his fatigue pants. He opened the door. There was barely enough ambient flash light for him to see Duvalier and Shinebaum low crawling down the hallway on elbows and knees. They were heading for the hootch door. He tripped over Shinebaum in the narrow hallway but kept his balance and straightened.

"Get down, damn you," Shinebaum yelled at Ronnie.

Instead Remphelmann continued to stand upright. He glanced about in something of a confusion. There was another mighty blasting sound at some distance from the hootch that lit the night air. The whole of the night sky went orange-red. Remphelmann looked up at the underside of the tin roof. Splotches of crimson light were shining through puncture holes in the sheet metal. Then there were jagged holes of additional light winging through the roof with the same metal punching sound. "What's that?" he naively asked.

"That's frigging mortar shrapnel going though the roof, you frigging idiot. Get down!" Remphelmann did not get down. Instead he looked with some amazement at the roof being punctured again. This time a stitch of holes went horizontally in a straight line through the roof like a sewing machine. It seem as if every fifth hole was accompanied by a streak of tail emitting light. 'What's that?' he said again.

One of the two low crawling figures screamed, "That is frigging machine gun fire and tracers, you living idiot. Get down and crawl!"

Despite the novelty of the situation, Remphelmann could not contain a burst of philosophy. "Why are these people shooting at me? They don't even know my name!"

"Get your rosy red new kid ass on the deck and crawl for the bunker, asshole!"

It finally occurred to Remphelmann. He was being shot at. Of a sudden, all mental computation left his brain, and he crumpled en mass. His arms flew up and twirled themselves around his head and neck. His knees bucked in a contracting spring movement and he found himself in a tangled mass on the concrete hallway of the hootch. He unwound and began to crawl toward the bunker with the other two lieutenants. It suddenly occurred to him that he had done the herky-jerky, the cojones on the concrete, the peter on the pavement.

"Where the hell is Manteca," one voice asked.

"Still in the rack," the other answered. "Manteca, Manteca, are you still alive?"

A childlike moan came from behind Manteca's closed door. "We're all going to die."

"Dead or not, get your fat ass off your bunk and bunkerize yourself."

From somewhere a parachute flare had lofted itself into the night and suddenly the whole LZ was bathed in a white thermite glow of ghostly dancing light. Remphelmann saw himself, Duvalier and Shinebaum scraping knees toward the hootch door. Suddenly Manteca's bloated form, stark ass naked, burst through his door and began a run for the exit. Stark ass naked except for a steel helmet on his head. In the wavering light of the parachute flare he attempted a mad dash for the hootch exit. Despite his bulk he overleaped the three men on the floor like a football player dodging bodies, hall walls and any other obstacle in between. He sprinted for the exit. He yelled his pet phase again, this time at the top of his lungs, "We're all going to die!" However, rather than expiring to his greater reward, he leap-frogged the three prone men and dashed with force for the door. Alas, his aim proved less than his valor. He ran straight into the door frame, smacked helmet first with a horrendous crash into the wooden door post, and fell back, totally cold cocked onto the worm-like line of low crawlers.

There was a muffled gurgle of "Help!" Remphelmann realized that the corpulent mass of Manteca's dripping flesh had smothered the lanky and underweight frame of Duvalier onto the concrete. Duvalier's face was literally being smothered by the captain's huge soft underbelly. Duvalier gasped his last. Remphelmann, with a mighty heave, rolled the quivering whale-like carcass of Manteca off the black man, who gulped for air.

"Holy Jesus," remarked Shinebaum, who had evidently forgotten his religious preference. "How do we get this thing to the bunker?"

Remphelmann was again at the ready. "Let's just hook him under the arm-pits and drag." Drag they did, oblivious to the abrasion it might cause to Manteca's pristine derriere. Out the door they went across the PSP of the patio. They dumped the captain unceremoniously in the bomb shelter. Only when another burst of machine gun fire squirted over their heads did they realize they had been standing up. Both did the herky jerky again into the dirt.

"Holy Mother of God," exclaimed Shinebaum again. "Where's super-schwartz?"

To the immense relief of the two, P.T. came scraping around the corner of the hootch in a crab-like sort of way. He had his flashlight clenched in his mouth. They all made it to the bunker entrance as a horrendous roar came out of the perimeter bunker. An American machinegun had opened up and was raking the open ground between the wire and the cemetery. In the near distance was the thunking sound of friendly mortar fire outbound that landed in the free fire zone.

The four huddled in the bunker. Manteca regained consciousness and was mumbling to himself from underneath his steel pot. "Honestly officer, I'm not a cross-dresser, I was only trying the high-heels on for size." This meant nothing to Porky and P.T. What it meant to Ronnie, he really didn't care.

The whoosh of mortars, the chatter of machine gun fire, and the landing of artillery rounds into the free fire zone seemed to creep outward towards the cemetery. Then as suddenly as it all began, the noise stopped. Somewhere on the far side of the airstrip a siren wailed up and died away.

"All clear," said Shinebaum.

"What's next?" asked Remphelmann.

"First, we must get the butterball man back to his bunk. Then we have to check on our men. Do you have a flashlight?" asked Duvalier.

"I've got one in my locker. Fresh batteries."

Manteca was still blubbering in the corner of the bomb proof. "Of course I wear a size sixteen, you think I want to look like a tight dress bimbo?"

Shinebaum shook the captain. "Captain Manteca, snap to. Can you walk?"

Manteca raised his weary head. The steel helmet was still jammed down over his nose. "Of course I can walk." He stood up and fell over. He stood again. "See, I can do it all by myself!" He fell again and re-righted himself. "Am I dead yet?"

"No, you useless piece of shit." snapped Duvalier. "Let's woozy you back to your bunk." The three lieutenants maneuvered the jellyfish back to his cubicle and threw him on his bed.

"Look, Ronnie," Duvalier continued, "Grab your boots and your flashlight. Go to the ordnance hootch and work your way back through the enlisted hootches to the bunkers. Make sure your men are all right. I'll do the same, as will Shinebaum. Hey Porky, what about the quartermaster men? Manteca is out for the count."

"Never fear, Shlomo is here," retorted Shinebaum. "I'll cover both his platoon and mine."

"Great," concluded Duvalier. "Let's meet back here in five minutes and compare notes. I'll call S-2 and see what the skinny has to say, plus, ha-ha, I'll see whether Fearless Leader Dufuss is in the same world as we are."

Remphelmann went into his room in the dark and found his flashlight. It worked. He hurried on his boots and flew out of the BOQ towards his area. The platoon hootch was empty. The enlisted barracks were vacant. He found the bomb shelter and yelled, "Is everybody alright?"

Sergeant Shortarm appeared out of the doorway. "Holy Dallas dingle-berries, lieutenant, are we having fun yet?"

"Is everybody all right?"

"Sure as San Antonio shit, sir."

Remphelmann ducked inside the bunker and shone the flashlight around. All of his men were there. They, to his surprise, were squatting there in semi-boredom. He tried to re-call names, but his mind drew a blank. All he could conjure up was Private Einstein's first name. "Elvis, are you alright?"

Private Einstein burst into song, recalling somebody's hit record. "It's alright, Papa, any way you snooze."

Remphelmann racked his brain. "Sergeant Gruntz?"

Gruntz snapped back. "Damn it, sir. I transferred out of the infantry to the ordnance so I didn't have to put up with this shit. Do you have my transfer request?"

"Sergeant Heimstaadt?"

"I vasn't a nazi in der last kreig, I vas a vegetarian!"

Thus satisfied that his men were all right, Remphelmann high-tailed it back to the officers BOQ. Soon Duvalier and Shinebaum joined him. They compared notes.

"My men are O.K.," said Remphelmann.

"My men are alright, Jack." Porky chimed. "So are the quartermasters. The quartermasters got some shrapnel in the area but no casualties or equipment damage."

"My people are fine, also," Duvalier added. "Plus I called S-2, it was only an H and I run by Charles. Harassment with a small 'h'. Plus I tried to ring up old tomato juice Dufuss. No reply." Duvalier paused. "Then that leaves Manteca. Ronnie, do the honors."

With great trepidation, Remphelmann approached Manteca's door. The door was still open. He found the lard bucket squirming on his mattress. "Captain Manteca, sir, begging the captain's fat fanny, is the captain alright?"

Manteca still had his helmet shoved down around his eyes. "Oh, leave me alone, you little twerp, you little nemesis of my baneful existence. We are all going to die."

Remphelmann closed Manteca's door and scrambled back to the other lieutenants. "Captain Manteca is indisposed."

Shinebaum looked at his watch. "It's 0330 hours. We've got a movement order for 0430 hours. Enough sleep for tonight. We've got a full days work coming up." The three sat for a minute in quiet contemplation.

There was a silence in the heavens, which did not reach the space of a half an hour. It only lasted a half a minute. Then an explosion of unknown origin rent the veil of the temple. It was only a truck backfiring. Nonetheless, Remphelmann twirled himself into a pretzel and fell onto the concrete floor like Paul on the road to Damascus. Shinebaum and Duvalier were too jaundiced to move. But they did not laugh nor did they show any sign of derision to the young officer.

Remphelmann lay knitted on the ground. His first thought was 'Que Ell One'. There was another first thought. He had learned to do the herky jerky.

Chapter Twenty-Two

Remphelmann pulled himself off the concrete floor with an air of sheepishness. Neither Shinebaum nor Duvalier noticed. Shinebaum was right. There would be no time for more sleep. Remphelmann showered and shaved by flashlight. The hootch granny, whom Ronnie had yet to meet, had washed, ironed and starched a set of jungle fatigues and hung the clothes in his locker. The young man carefully dressed and went back to the ordnance hootch. The electrical power had been restored and the little HQ was ablaze with light and alive with activity.

Sergeant Shortarm, as usual, was screaming obscenities into the phone trying to rustle up repair parts. Einstein had found yet another set of forms to type. "Hey, lieutenant, I've got Sergeant Gruntz's request for transfer all typed up. Do you want to throw it away now or later?"

Remphelmann ignored Einstein only because Sergeant Shortarm got off the phone. "Holy Childress horseshit, sir. A busy morning and a busy day coming up. Did you like Charlie's alarm clock?" The squat sergeant snickered to himself.

Einstein chimed in. "Skinny is, sarge, the new louie has

169

learned to dance. He was doing the herky jerky to a new tune, only about an hour ago in a Hollywood bungalow."

Shortarm fell over himself laughing. "I love how you young kids come up with new phases for the same old thing! It might be Hollywood herky me jerky me off to you but it's still dick in the dirt to me." Shortarm paused. "Lieutenant, I keep telling you how my education to you has done been done. God bless when I have a thought, it's dangerous! But seeing as how Sergeant Peckerwood, his man and maybe Schweik are going to go with convoy as far as Firebase Firefly, I thought you oughter tag along and see what's they do in the field."

"That's an excellent idea."

"Glad you liked it, sir. My advice cement is that you goes along. Politely snoop as to their jobs and problems. Have Sergeant Peckerwood introduce you to the firebase commander Captain Lanyard. But be real careful and dip-a-low-mastic. Them cannon cocker types don't like the rear echelon mother friggers messing around their territory. Kind of explain real nice-like that you realize their difficulties. And that you are there to provide logistical support and repair support and customer support but jest don't say you are there for athletic support!" Shortarm laughed at his own joke. "Our job is to give the front line grunts as much help as possible and then get out of the way of their shitty duties. Plus another thing, skinny is that Captain Lanyard done developed a case of the heeby jeebs and the stare. Handle him with inspection gloves."

"Thanks for the advice."

"So," Shortarm continued, "The convoy is forming up. You can hear all them trucks starting and huffing and puffing to life. Maybe you oughter tour the other platoon HQ's. Introduce yourself to Sergeant Piggott, who is Lieutenant Shinebaum's highway cop. He'll be commanding the MP jeep. Then find Lieutenant Duvalier's best man, Sergeant Ciezarowski, who will be convoy road captain. Win friends and influence people. It's good for your immortal soul as well as your practical ass." Just then the telephone rang and Shortarm answered. "Don't give me any crap about that deuce and half gearbox. I said I want it, and I want it now!"

Remphelmann did as ordered or rather as suggested. He went over to the transportation hut and walked in. Several people attempted to stand, but Remphelmann called, "As you were." He looked about. "Is Lieutenant Duvalier here?"

"No sir," answered a stocky blond sergeant with a broad flat face and granite like cheekbones. "He's out in the yard, doing the convoy form-up. I'm Sergeant Ciezarowski, can I help?"

"I'm going to be going along with Sergeant Peckerwood and his mechanic as far as Firebase Firefly, so I thought I would inform Lieutenant Duvalier."

"Good thing you dropped in here, sir. I have to make a road convoy log of every truck that goes along to get along, plus all personnel involved. That way if you get blown up, we can identify the body." Ciezarowski grabbed a clipboard. "Let's see, Peckerwood and his man have that ordnance deuce and half, convoy order number seventeen. That number will be chalked on the truck. I'll add your name to number seventeen. Let's see, that's Lieutenant Rempleskin."

Remphelmann corrected the man. "That's Remphelmann."

"Yes sir," the man corrected himself. He looked at the nametag sewn above the officers fatigue pocket and wrote down the name.

Remphelmann went over to the MP hootch. There was the same shuffle of feet and Remphelmann's now stock order, "As you were. Is Lieutenant Shinebaum about?"

A rather swinish faced sergeant promptly answered. "Sir, no sir, he's over across the airfield getting the last minute intelligence poop. I'm Platoon Sergeant Piggott, Mr. Shinebaum's general factotum and water carrier. Can I help?"

Remphelmann remembered Shortarm's phrase as he continued. "No, I'm just here to let you know I'll be accompanying

Sergeant Peckerwood and friends to Firebase Firefly. I'm going along to win friends and influence people."

Piggott snorted. "Sir, begging the officers butt, sir. If you want to win friends, you can do all that here at dear old LZ Bozo, but if you want to influence people, wait until we get out on the road. There's a half dozen places between here and Firefly where the Viet Cong want to influence you. After all it's Que Ell One. If you want to influence people, influence Charlie. I might give you the opportunity."

Remphelmann did not really know what Sergeant Piggott meant, but he pretended he did. He left and went back to the ordnance HQ. Shortarm was on the phone as usual but hung up abruptly when the officer entered. "Holy La Mesa linguini's, sir, day light is breaking and it's time for you to get on the road. Where's your flak jacket, steel pot, and M-16?"

Remphelmann offered that he had none of those accouterments. Shortarm disappeared for a second and returned with a steel helmet, a flak jacket and a rifle with a bandolier of six twenty-round magazines. "Holy Odessa assholes, sir, I done forgot to outfit you yesterday. The pot, the flak jacket, they kind of self explanatory, but as to the rifle. Private Schweik done refurbished it. It ain't really zeroed in. If'n you get to use it, aim for two hundred meters and spray and pray. When you get back Schweik will take you off to our shooting range and you can get it dialed in to your specifications. We'll make you a sure fire Dead Eye Dick." Remphelmann clambered into to the flak jacket, adjusted the headband on the helmet and plunked it on. Then he draped the bandolier of magazines over one shoulder and the M-16 over the other. Somehow in his celluloid imagination he felt like he was a soldier.

Remphelmann went out into the back yard. The sun had broken abruptly over the horizon and the heat began to build. The trucks, smoking a combination of diesel and gasoline exhaust, were maneuvering into a convoy line. Remphelmann counted back along the numbers chalked on the fenders of the trucks and found number seventeen. Peckerwood and Scheissenbrenner were in the cab. The requisite repair materials were stowed in the back.

He maneuvered himself into the cab of the truck. The convoy smoked itself out of the Bozo compound and headed towards the exit of the camp. MP's with clipboards counted out each truck. The convoy of thirty trucks came to a halt on a muddy flat, just south of Phan Thiet and parallel to the main highway, Que Ell One. The Patton tank lumbered into view and inserted itself at the end of the line. Two jeeps roared up. One held Shinebaum, and the other, Duvalier. Both jeeps carried a driver, the officer in the front passenger seat and a machine gunner posted at the back of the vehicle along with a large radio. Remphelmann dismounted himself from his truck and walked up to Shinebaum's jeep.

"It's your lucky day," Porky announced. "Sergeant Piggott said you wanted the grand tourist view. You want to ride with your damn repair parts, or with me in the lead, or in the number one gun truck?"

"Uh," stammered Remphelmann.

"Consider yourself volunteered. Sergeant Ciezarowski is manning the forward 50 caliber on the gun truck, and he's short a grenadier. Can you shoot a 40mm grenade launcher?"

"Uh," repeated Remphelmann.

"Great," said Shinebaum with glee. "Go up to chalk number two and see Ciezarowski. That's the deuce and a half truck with the home built armored plating. The one that's painted up 'Flaming Panther Piss'. Painted up in old English lettering by your man Gonzales-McGillicuddy. Go, you lucky devil."

Remphelmann hitched up his trousers, flak jacket, M-16 and magazine bandolier. He found the gun truck as advertised. It was chalk two, a two and half-ton truck that had an oddball assortment of steel plates applied helter skelter to the cab and back of the truck. Here and there green sandbags had been stuffed in odd places. A 50 caliber machine gun with mounting ring had been jury-rigged facing forward over the cab top. That allowed a gunner to sweep a full circle around the front, sides and back of the gun truck. The machine gun dripped copious belts of ammunition. At the back a smaller M-60 machine gun was mounted on a swivel post. Sure enough, painted on the side was a pink panther cartooned in garish colors, leg cocked and emitting a stream of yellow urine that morphed into a hose of flame. Remphelmann hardly had time to admire the artwork when the looming voice of Sergeant Ciezarowski came booming down from the top of the contraption.

"Good morning again, sir. Good morning. I hear you volunteered to be my grenadier for the Firebase Firefly leg, you lucky son of a gun!"

"How do I get up there?" puzzled Remphelmann.

"Get on the drivers running board. You'll see steel straps welded up the side. Just use them as ladder rungs, stairways to heaven, and you are here."

Remphelmann clumsily mounted as instructed, and finding himself at the top of the steel plate, with woeful un-aplomb descended into the belly of the beast. The inside walls of the steel box was lined with sandbags. The sandbags were backed up with spare truck wheels complete with tires, with only a narrow passageway between the front and rear gunners position. To Remphelmann's mortification he found sad sack Schweik at the rear machine gun position.

"Top of the mother blessing morning to you sir," Schweik sang. "This detail beats the shit out of repairing rifles. Plus as McGillicuddy had to go to the dentist in Cam Ranh and I'm on convoy duty, that doesn't leave anybody left at LZ Bozo to do shit burner duty. How will the republic survive?"

Sergeant Ciezarowski escorted the young officer to the middle of the gun nest and thrust a stubby shotgun-looking weapon into Ronnie's hands. "As you are my ace grenadier, I suppose you know your weapon of choice." Remphelmann, deftly as he thought, received the weapon and looked it over. It was a standard grenade launcher. Sergeant Ciezarowski let loose with a wad of tobacco juice that sailed cleanly over the steel plate.

Remphelmann, beyond amazement, marveled at a tobacco chewing Polish-American that dipped plug. He had seen the disgusting habit among his grandfather's aging farm friends, but thought it extinct in modern society. He was wrong.

"Well, I got to shoot four rounds with it in officer candidate school."

Ciezarowski let loose with a wad of brown saliva that sang happily over the armor. "It's simple enough. What you have here is a single shot shot gun. First, toggle the breech. Open this lever with your thumb, break the barrel open, take a round from the bandolier here, stick the round in and click the barrel snap up. Then you flip up the sight, that's ladder like widget on the top. Click the sight bar to say 200 meters and pull the trigger. It'll bloop a 40mm grenade exactly where you point it and bring a happy little can of whoop ass on those that gratefully receive."

"Bloop?"

Sergeant Ciezarowski again deftly spit a lethal wad over the plate. "It's called a blooper, because it hasn't a sound like a shotgun. It has a low velocity powder charge to propel the grenade. It makes a puffing sound or blooping sound, well, like 'bloop.' And off it goes. If I have to start shooting with my ma deuce, figure out the range, one hundred meters, two hundred, three hundred, and bloop as many rounds as you can at my point of impact."

"Yes, sergeant," demurred Remphelmann. "Load, range and fire as many rounds as possible."

"What we want to do if we get attacked," Ciezarowski paused only long enough to spit accommodatingly over the armor, "Is to bring the maximum amount of smoke on Charlie's ass. Begging the lieutenant's short arm, sir, suppressive fire is a wonderful way to win friends and influence people."

There was the low blip of a police siren from Shinebaum's MP jeep. The convoy went into gear and proceeded a bit farther up Que Ell One.

Chapter Twenty-Three

The convoy was bunched up on the mud flat next to a poorly paved two-lane highway, the only road to Saigon, Highway QL-1. The trucks were bumper to bumper. Soon Lieutenant Shinebaum's jeep took a U-turn from the head of the convoy and made an inspection of the 30 trucks. Shinebaum's driver did a slow crawl along as Porky carefully checked off each truck against his clip-boarded list of vehicles. On the rear platform of the jeep, the M-60 pedestal gunner adjusted a nylon web strap around his waist to keep himself from being pitched from the rocking 4 by 4. Satisfied that all the vehicles were in order, the MP jeep sped back to the point position. Again a short wail came from the jeep's siren. Shinebaum's driver guided the lead machine off the mud flat and onto Que Ell One.

The trucks began to follow. But rather than bunching up butt cheek to belt buckle, each machine waited until there was a hundred yards, a hundred meters, between each truck. Remphelmann's ride, the 'Flaming Panther Piss', waited until Shinebaum was on the road. Then his gun truck followed. After that Duvalier's jeep came on line and after him, the remaining transportation corps supply trucks, deuce and a half's, five tons, and ten ton semi's hauling empty flat bed trailers. At the tail end of the American convoy there was the Patton tank, another jury-rigged gun truck and a follow up MP jeep. It took a half an hour to string the convoy out onto the pot-holed asphalt.

As Remphelmann's truck clambered onto the tarmac, he saw another convoy stringing back into the western edge of Phan Thiet. There was an ARVN MP jeep and improvised gun trucks fore and aft of a forlorn gaggle of some fifty Vietnamese civilian transports, trucks, mostly lorry types, with an odd semi-truck sandwiched in-between. There were decrepit Renault sedans with goods piled in precarious high hats on top. There were equally beat up Citroen taxicabs hauling tiny homemade trailers full of soggy cardboard boxes.

'I guess all those civilian trucks are full of nuoc mam, and salted fish and dried seaweed and pickled sardines. The economic lifeblood of the poor fishing village of Phan Thiet', Remphelmann mused to himself. 'These poor folk are sitting on a fortune of fish sauce and unable to sell it.' The sudden vision of an evil VC came to his mind. A Viet Cong in black pajamas lurking in the bush with a Chinese made rocket propelled grenade. The VC fired, the rocket screamed into the side of one of the Vietnamese lorries, and in a hellish explosion two thousand glass liter bottles of nuoc mam vaporized, sending a brown black mist of chunky fish sauce up in a mushroom cloud of doomed financial dreams. The thought was so loathsome, he banished it from his mind. He rearranged several of the sand bags in the center well of the gun truck to provide a seat, then sat and observed.

The convoy got underway. Shinebaum was in the lead, followed at a distance of a hundred yards by the Flaming Panther and hundred meters behind that, Duvalier. It took nearly an hour for the two convoys to leave the suburbs of Phan Thiet and sort themselves like a string of pearls onto Que Ell One. The US convoy maintained a slow steady pace of twenty miles an hour, each machine a hundred yards apart. In the distance behind

Remphelmann he saw the Vietnamese convoy had bunched together almost bumper to bumper.

Remphelmann was puzzled. He made his way up to Sergeant Ciezarowski, who was keeping keen eyes across the open rice fields. "Hey, sarge, why are we spaced so far apart?"

The pollack spat another commodious wad of juice over the metal transom. "Look here, lieutenant, its just like they taught you in officer candidate school. What is the range of a Russki 12.7 caliber large machine gun?"

"1000 to 2000 meters."

"And the effective range of a B-40 Chinese rocket propelled grenade?

"400 to 800 meters."

"And the useful distance of an AK-47 rifle?"

"300 to 500. Three to five football fields."

"So," pontificated Sergeant Ciezarowski, "If we have a kilometer of road and our little brown brothers open up and we are all bunched together bumper to bumper, asshole to belly button, begging the esteemed officer's pardon for a earthy expression, within a space of a 400 meter kill zone then the gomers could wipe out the whole convoy. If we string out on the road that only gives them four or five trucks to target instead on the whole she-bang."

"Low profile," marveled Remphelmann.

"Low body bag count." retorted Ciezarowski. "Another thing. If we get incoming, the lead truck drivers, the unsung heroes of this unsung war, are supposed to race forward out of the kill zone. The truck drivers in the rear are instructed to stop or even back up, and the gun trucks, that's us, are to drive straight into the targeted zone and then as the tactical manual says, 'find, fix, and destroy' the enemy gun emplacements. That's why I have my ma deuce, and young sad sack Schweik has his M-60, and why you have a hundred rounds of 40mm grenades."

Remphelmann thanked Ciezarowski for the short lesson on tactics and returned to his sandbag perch. The open rice paddies on either side of Que Ell One became more sparse and farther from the road. Que Ell One began to climb to a higher elevation and narrowed onto an upland where the jungle began to crowd the shoulders of the road. Remphelmann became alarmed. The closeness of the vegetation seemed to hide snipers. The outcropping rocks surely had Viet Cong observers behind each layer of red crumbling shale. The trees and brush grew thicker.

As they ambled along at a slow pace, Sergeant Ciezarowski pried himself away from his position at the 50 caliber, crawled up the sandbags and urinated merrily over the edge of the steel bulwark. Then he danced back to Remphelmann. "You see how we are getting out of the rice paddy flats into the woods? It's called the Le Hong Phong Forest. See how Big Titty Mountain is getting bigger? Prime VC territory. Ambush Alley. Kill zone time." The sergeant started to roll back to his machine gun, balancing against the rocking motion of the gun truck.

Suddenly a green Very pistol smoke flare came sailing back along the length of the road, evidently fired from Lieutenant Shinebaum's jeep. Simultaneously the radio operator in the gun truck cab stuck his head out the window and yelled to Ciezarowski, "Devil's dogleg!"

"Devil's dogleg?" Ronnie queried.

The gunner stopped his motion toward the gun ring. The steel plated side on the gun truck was covered with a thick film of red dust. Ciezarowski used it as an impromptu black board. He drew an elongated 'Z' with his finger, with the middle leg far longer than the top and bottom. "We've got a hard right turn, here at the bottom of the 'Z' and the long middle leg which is a click long, a kilometer long, which goes through a kind of defile with hills on either side. If Sir Charles wants to say hello, he'll have a machine gun at one of the points of the 'Z' so as to rake the whole length of the road and infantry one side or the other to spray the column with AK or rocket fire. It won't happen today though, it's the wrong phase of the moon." Ciezarowski returned to his gun.

They entered the right hand bend and sure enough there was a kilometer of road, tightly defined by encroaching hills and dense jungle. They traveled though the straight space and out the hard left turn that defined the top of the 'Z'. Ciezarowski and Schweik had their heads on swivels, scanning the brush. Out of the 'Z', Remphelmann thought himself safe when all of a sudden behind them a huge noise broke loose. He could hear the large ripping sound of machine gun and rifle fire, along with the strange whooshing sound of B-40 rockets.

Instantly Shinebaum and his jeep made did an abrupt 180-degree turn and headed back into the 'Z'. Behind Remphelmann, one the truck drivers in the bad stretch of the dogleg had popped a red smoke grenade. Duvalier's jeep bumped up the margin of the road and took Shinebaum's place at the head of the column. The driver of the 'Flaming Panther' did an impossible u-turn on the narrow road and roared after Shinebaum. The group re-entered the long stretch of the dogleg and Shinebaum's jeep roared to a stop near the red smoke grenade, which was spewing a vermilion cloud on the road shoulder. None of the six trucks in the 'Z' had stopped. The gun truck pulled up a hundred meters short of the MP's. Ciezarowski intuitively began to plaster the western side of the defile with machine gun fire. As Ciezarowski's tracers bounced into the trees, sad sack Schweik opened up onto the same target area. Ciezarowski looked back to Remphelmann between measured bursts from his 50 caliber. "Bloop, damn it, bloop! Three hundred meters!" Remphelmann went into a dreamlike, robotic mode instantly. He felt as if he was swimming slowly in crystal clear jell-o. He snapped the toggle and opened the breech of the grenade launcher, slipped in a round from the bandolier, sighted three hundred and fired and fired and fired.

The enemy machine gun fire, which up until then was spraying the trucks, as the truckers were gunning their engines to get out of the kill zone, had moved their streams of fire rather inaccurately to the 'Flaming Panther'. Remphelmann heard, as if he were in the bottom of a well, machine gun and AK rounds pinging on the steel plate or buzzing past his ears. A blur went over his head and then another. He thought about bazooka rounds, RPG's, and thought he heard them explode somewhere on the far side of the truck. He thought, he thought again, and then he stopped thought. He was puzzled that he felt outside of himself, looking down on himself as if he were an eye in the sky, flicking the lever on the grenade launcher, snapping open the breech to eject a spent casing, loading another round from the bandolier next to him and firing and firing and firing. The pounding of Ciezarowski's 50 caliber was reverberating endlessly in one ear, then the staccato bursts of Schweik's M-60 was beating counter time in the other. It did not seem surreal, it was surreal. Remphelmann ejected, reloaded, aimed and fired and fired and fired.

Out of this cacophony Remphelmann heard the voice of Sergeant Ciezarowski from a million miles away. "Cease fire!"

The silence was deafening.

The voice of Ciezarowski came again, this time only a hundred miles away. "Damn." The sergeant paused long enough to hack an amazing brown wad from his lips over the rim of the armor with its newfound bullet divots. "That wasn't anything today. I can't even classify that as a proper ambush. I guess Charles didn't have it in his heart today. Maybe he didn't eat enough kim chee and wheaties for breakfast."

Remphelmann looked down the length of the truck to his armorer, Schweik, who was clearing back the bolt of his machine gun. Schweik pushed his helmet back and was smiling from ear to ear. "Dang me, lieutenant," Schweik remarked. "I'm grinning like a possum eating defecation, because I didn't get hit. And you know something else?"

"Yes?" Remphelmann responded.

"This sure beats the crap out a burning shit at LZ Bozo!"

Shinebaum appeared in his jeep and stood up. Behind him his pedestal gunner was clearing the belt feed of his M-60, whose barrel was sizzling from the heat of use. Porky yelled up to the ma deuce gunner. "Sergeant Cee, everything's clear. About face, get back up to the chalk two, nobody hurt, no disabled vehicles, thanks for the help, easy money." Shinebaum started to sit and motion to his driver to go back to the head of the column, when he was brought up short by the eyes of Remphelmann. "Hey there, Lieutenant Remphelmann of the ordnance!"

Ronnie's ears were ringing endlessly, but he caught Shinebaum's address. "Yes?"

Shinebaum sat and tapped his driver on the shoulder. Then as his vehicle began to move back to the front of the convoy, he laughed over his shoulder. "Welcome to Que Ell One!"

PART THE THIRD

Our Young Hero Gets Acclimated
To Que Ell One

Chapter Twenty-Four

The convoy restarted its orderly procession through the Le Hong Phong Forest, in a manner similar to Dorothy and Toto on their way to see the Wizard. There were no lions and tigers and bears, however. Remphelmann was beyond recollection of the previous moment's events, but he had an eerie and truly spooky feeling. When the firing was going on, he had the remarkable feeling of being suspended above himself, as if he was on a gossamer umbilical cord, looking down at his own mortality. However both Ciezarowski and Schweik had put their heads back on their terrestrial swivels and were scanning the environs for more immediate earthly troubles. Remphelmann did the same. But he could not shake that singular vision of looking down at himself through an infinite ocular pipe, the distinct visual cue of looking at his own humanity as if through the wrong end of a telescope, small, distant, yet crystal clear.

At some point after the convoy had completely cleared the devil's dogleg, they came clear of the forest and the rocky defile. In the near distance Whiskey Mountain loomed up in a conical shape, easily reminding any soldier of a starlet's best features. The Le Hong Phong swept away to the north and up the side of the foothills rather like an undulating green carpet, a corrugation of tangled trees and underbrush. The road began to follow a narrow levee road that shot straight through rice paddies. Farmers knee deep in the water were setting out rice seedlings. The planters ignored the Americans, but as the ARVN and civilian convoys passed through, there were waves of the hand and smiles of the face.

They drove up a slight rise to some rocky ground. The outcrop continued to the north up to the piedmont of the Central Highlands and to the south some distance. On the southernmost end of the rocky way Remphelmann saw a battery of six 105mm howitzers. The compound was a seeming triangular affair of green sand bagged structures scarred into the red earth. A perimeter of concertina razor tape surrounded the encampment, which in turn seemed like an island in a sea of rice paddies and dikes. The sun was arcing toward noon and the sunlight sparkled through the impoundments of shallow water and green plants.

They reached a spot where a graveled track sprouted off Que Ell One and wended to the firebase. The convoy came to a temporary halt. Two five-ton trucks loaded with artillery ammunition peeled out of the convoy and felt their way toward the firebase. Another truck, a deuce and half full of food and provisions, rabbit-tailed after. Finally the Patton tank lumbered in.

The ordnance truck with Sergeant Peckerwood at the helm and Scheissenbrenner doing the shotgun sidled up to the 'Flaming Panther Piss'. Sergeant Ciezarowski lobbed another heroic load of brunette spittle from his cheek. "Lieutenant Remphelmann, sir, the bus stops here, at least for you. I want to thank you for your enthusiastic yet poorly aimed blooper shots. Now get off of my truck."

"Thanks for the experience, sergeant, I learned a lot." Remphelmann did an ungainly dismount over the side of the armor plate.

"Hey, Schweik," the sergeant yelled. "Get your slovenly ass out from behind that gun and di di mao!"

"Ah, sarge, do I have to? I was having fun! This convoy duty might be work to you, but as for me, it beats the shit out of the shit burner detail anytime."

"Get off my truck."

"Anything you say, sergeant."

"By the way, Schweik, you look like crap. Your uniform wouldn't grace a gunnysack. When was the last time you put on clean fatigues?"

"Gosh, Sergeant Cee. I broke starch just this morning."

"I swear to the Black Virgin of Krakow, Schweik, you could put on a set of dress parade blues and five minutes later look like you crawled out of a pig sty."

"Ah, you're just jealous of my youth and good looks."

"Get off my truck, sad sack!"

As Schweik clambered over the steel, he blew Ciezarowski a kiss. "I love you too, sergeant."

Bite my hemorrhoids, private."

Remphelmann and the armorer clambered into Peckerwood's limousine. They hurried off to follow the other supply trucks and the tank into the firebase.

The seeming triangularly of the firebase from Remphelmann's original point of view was something of a mis-description. Actually the firebase had been laid out by the engineers and artillery to take the best advantage of the ground. It was in more of a lozenge shape. The six artillery tubes were set out in two parallel groups of three. In the center of the oblong was a low bunker of sandbags that served as the fire control center. On the four corners of the perimeter were machine gun bunkers. Scattered hither and thither in the intervening spaces were squat army tents that had sandbag revetments humped man high around them. The layout was not a parade ground exercise, but made a splendid use of the terrain. The convoy trucks squeezed through a narrow opening in the wire next to one of the gun bunkers. As if on signal, men appeared from underground. The two five ton trucks with the ammunition sidled up to ammo bunkers and the magically appearing men swarmed after them like ants. They quickly began to unload the trucks and hurry the wooden boxes of ammunition into insect like lairs. Peckerwood maneuvered his truck to one of the guns.

"See here," Peckerwood spurted. "Lieutenant, this is the gun tube with the leaky recuperator seal. We've got about an hour and a half of work. That is with me and Scheissenbrenner doing the honors. What with ragbag Schweik that means two and half hours, and what with a new kid lieutenant, that means four!" Peckerwood laughed as the four un-piled from the cab. The three enlisted men scampered to the bed of the truck and began to unload the repair parts and the mechanical tools. Remphelmann took the hint and stood discretely to one side.

The mechanics tore into to the howitzer's innards. The artillery gun layer, a smooth faced sergeant, appeared and paced up and down, like a young father doing observance over his young wife's birthing process. The gun layer alternated between speaking softly to Peckerwood the obstetrician, to pacing again to the side, to going up to the gun and stroking its breech, and whispering sweet nothings to the optical mount, to caressing the gun's aiming machinery, to a distracted pacing, to yet another quiet conversation with the tube. It was a touching display of husbandry, fatherly concern and true love.

At some point during this birthing or rebirthing, an artillery captain appeared and stood at some distance to peer at the goings on. The captain stood stock still as if he were a post or a lump of coal. Remphelmann was immediately aware that the captain was the same Captain Lanyard that Sergeant Shortarm had mentioned. Ronnie's first thought was to approach the senior officer of the firebase, but he remembered the cautionary comment from his platoon sergeant. Instead he went to Peckerwood, who was busy yelling at Scheissenbrenner and Schweik. "Sergeant Peckerwood, is that captain over there the firebase commander? Sergeant

Shortarm told me to treat him with kid gloves. What should I do?"

Peckerwood looked about. Scheissenbrenner, Schweik and the gun layer had stopped stock still at Remphelmann's question. The sergeant had a cloud of sadness descend on his face and at first said nothing. Then he motioned Remphelmann to one side out of the earshot of the other men. "Sir, of course you got to introduce yourself. That's officer protocol. That's part of why you're here. Your job is to coordinate with the other officers. Your job as a rear echelon support officer is to make life bearable for the front line combat types. But sir, talking to Captain Lanyard is like walking on eggs. You see, Captain Lanyard has got, I can't say it! It isn't the heebie-jeebies, he has neither the heeb nor the jeeb. God help us, sir, he's been in-country eleven and half months and he's due to be rotated home. But, sir, sir, damn it sir, he's developed the world's worse case of the 'thousand yard stare'"

Remphelmann rocked back on his heels.

The thousand yard stare. The kiss of death. The most horrible of all horrible psychological fates that any soldier can experience. It is not like having your arm blown off, or your legs shredded into stir fry meat. That is human. A minced leg might be repaired or sawed off in a hospital. It is not watching your comrades vaporized into a red cloud of bursting hemoglobin. That is a different story. It is not lofting dead men into a meat wagon. That is the every day work of gravediggers and ambulance attendants. It is the death of one's innermost self, the thousand yard stare. Numbness, the overcooked glaze and gaze of one who has endured too much of man's self-inflicted cruelty. The dazed, mindless, wooden reaction of a magically moving corpse. A different reality opens up, closes down, and skirts to the edges of perception. Slack lips, a sleepwalking demeanor, a drilling focus of the eyes that is unfocused, looking a million light years into the distance, detached, beyond the death wish, wall eyed and evacuated of humanity. The idea of death is transcended because death has passed beyond a man's consciousness. There is no tint of terror. Any hint of terror resides in the dim past of human feeling. A dead man is walking and talking and looking not at you but a cosmos a thousand thousand thousand yards beyond any human sacrifice that one could offer to any blood altar religion. The look zeroes in. The most horrible of horribles is the gaze of the man with the thousand yard stare. He looks you straight in the eye. In a living man the stare looks un-quenching into your retina and soul. That is the frightening power of a living man with a powerful eye. The man with the thousand yard stare, he stares, stares at your eyes, but the point of his eye drills through your optic nerve, through your brain, out the back of your skull, into the infinitude of space. Horrible, horrible, most horrible.

Remphelmann approached Captain Lanyard and saluted. "Sir, Lieutenant Remphelmann. I am in charge of the ordnance platoon at LZ Betty. Can I be of any assistance to you?"

"No, thank you, lieutenant. It is well, and all manner of things are well. Your men are repairing that gun tube quite satisfactorily. Plus, it appears that the ammunition is being unloaded and stored with great alacrity and care."

Remphelmann could not help feeling squeamish at the captain's gaze. Lanyard was looking the young man straight in the eye with an unwavering look. But to Remphelmann's view, the look, the set of the face, at first reminded him of a wooden sculpture. Then Remphelmann flashed on a memory from his youth. There had been a car accident in Keokuk. A man had somehow run into a telephone pole. The car had wrapped itself around the pole. The driver was still seated in the wreck, one hand on the wheel and the other on the gearshift. The driver was dead but his eyes were still wide open. The corpse continued looking at the horizon. The captain's eyes were the same eyes, alert at the wheel, ready to shift gears, but dead to the immediate presence of reality. Only the far away look portrayed any hint of a human presence. Remphelmann squirmed.

Finally Ronnie mustered the presence of mind to say, "Well

sir, if I or any of my men can be of assistance..." His voice trailed off.

"No, thank you, lieutenant. I'm happy, my men are happy. We have a planned fire mission for tonight. There is going to be action on Nui Ta Dom tonight and every tube counts. Are your men squared away? You will not be able to backtrack to Phan Thiet until tomorrow morning. Do your men have shelter for the night? Do they have food, hot food?"

"I'll have to speak with Sergeant Peckerwood, I really don't know."

"I'll have my battery top sergeant co-ordinate with your sergeant. My company cook is arranging hot food. Perhaps we have sleeping berths for your men. Hot food is good for the morale of soldiers. Hot food is good. But more important is a safe place to sleep. All soldiers need a safe place to sleep. Sleep. Sleep for soldiers is a good thing, a consummation devoutly to be wished. Sleep." Captain Lanyard continued to gaze at Remphelmann as if time had ceased to exist.

Remphelmann twisted in his boots. "Sir, if everything is fine, I'll take my leave."

"Yes," said the artilleryman. "Every thing is fine. And all manner of things are fine," but his gaze drilled through Remphelmann's head. Ronnie saluted and moved out of the captain's emotionless presence.

Remphelmann went back to his men. The repair of the howitzer was going quite well. The battery sergeant appeared and invited all to chow. The cook had found a dozen large cans of whole cooked chicken in the delivery from the provisioning truck and had whipped up an impromptu meal of shredded chicken and noodles, along with army bread that had been flow in by helicopter at daylight from the LZ Betty kitchen. There was a solemn assembly in the tent that served as the chow hall. Everyone ate their fill. Remphelmann sat at a picnic table with Captain Lanyard, but not a word was said. After lunch the ordnance men went back to the ailing howitzer and completed their repairs. The sun was setting with great alacrity over the horizon.

Sergeant Peckerwood approached Ronnie. "Sir, the repair is completed but obviously we can't test it now. There's a fire mission later in the night. I'll camp out next to the gun and send my men off to sleep. The battery sergeant found them all a dry bunk, but I have no idea how to bed you down."

"I'll just stretch out in the cab of our deuce and a half."

"Suit yourself, sir." Peckerwood then went over to the left wheel of the gun carriage, squatted in the dirt and fell instantly asleep.

Remphelmann went to the cab of the ordnance truck and unlimbered as much as the space would allow. The sun snapped down. Remphelmann was totally exhausted, mentally and physically. Only as he attempted to stretch out did he realize that he was still outfitted with his steel helmet, flak jacket, army flashlight in a thigh pocket, his M-16 and the bandolier of magazines. He decided to not take them off. He re-arranged his gear, took his thick eyeglasses and tucked them into a cranny of his helmet and attempted to sleep. Sleep he did, but then he would jerk awake. Visual images raced though his mind. The small time ambush at the devil's dogleg. The sound of the grenade launcher. The dissociated feeling of being in the air looking down at his body. He drifted back to sleep, then jerked to consciousness again. The face of the thousand yard stare, Captain Lanyard's face, haunted Remphelmann's mind. He fell fitfully into another state of semi-sleep.

Red flames irrupted from inside his closed eyes. He looked at his watch. It was midnight. The guns, all six guns of the battery had blasted off in unison. Remphelmann tried to stand upright in the confines of the cab only to smack his helmet on the headliner. The guns roared again and again. Only then did Remphelmann remember his duty. Where was Sergeant Peckerwood? He fished his eyeglasses from his helmet, his flashlight from his hip pocket, flicked it on and made his way to Peckerwood and the repaired gun.

"Douse that frigging flashlight!" somebody yelled. Remphelmann snapped it off and somehow made his way to the howitzer. It went off with a tremendous roar. In the muzzle flash he saw Sergeant Peckerwood fondling the recuperator that had just been repaired. With the next flash he saw the outline of the gun layer sighting through the optical sight. Voices in the darkness were yelling arcane commands to the gun layer and the rest of the crew. Somebody spoke, "Charge three. Point detonation." Hands twirled in the darkness. A round went into the breech. "Fire." The howitzer let loose with a deafening blast.

Remphelmann found Peckerwood in the darkness. "Is everything going alright?" The artillery piece blasted again. Ronnie was deafened.

Peckerwood answered. "I don't know. What I mean is the recuperator has stopped leaking. The recoil is working fine. But how are the guns are doing the whack on Charlie? That I don't know." There were more muffled commands in the darkness and all six guns erupted again. Remphelmann actually fell butt behind most in the mud. He picked himself up. He had the sensation of being temporarily deaf. He was in fact deaf. The two ordnance men stood to one side as the rounds blasted in rocket arcs out of the muzzles and onto Whiskey Mountain. As each shell left the breech there was a pause of some thirty seconds, and then in the distance, on the flanks of the mountain, fire erupted. This went on for twenty minutes. All of a sudden, all was quiet.

"What's that mean, I mean, why have they stopped firing?"

"Beats the hell out of me, lieutenant. The battery gets the order to fire from the forward observer. The battery fires at the co-ordinates. They fire until the FO says stop. That's all I know. But we've got a couple of hours until daylight." With that Peckerwood folded up against the wheel of the howitzer and dropped into a nap.

Ronnie went back to the cab of the ordnance truck and tried

to go into oblivion. That he did, but in the intervening moments he was yanked awake. He kept having the same detached feeling he had before. Flashes of the ambush on Que Ell One, and his brief interview with Captain Lanyard. It was the feeling of being a million miles from home, of being on the moon and yet looking backwards at himself. He could not articulate the experience to himself, so he did not try. He fell into a trance. A trance that mimicked sleep but was not sleep. A simulacrum of rest. The fitful rest did not last. An hour before daylight, Schweik was knocking at the door of Remphelmann's hidey-hole.

"Hey, lieutenant, you like pancakes and spam? The battery cook is a frigging genius. He can whip real food out of nothing."

Ronnie followed the mechanic to the chow tent. No one stood on military etiquette. There were indeed pancakes, syrup and thin sliced fried spam to be consumed. Remphelmann went back to the picnic table where Captain Lanyard was eating his meal. The lieutenant sat and ate his meal in silence. Finished, he thought he would do an indirect verbal approach on the captain again. "Sir, if there is any thing I or my men can do to assist..."

Lanyard looked up from his flapjacks. "No, lieutenant, all is well and all manner of things shall be well."

Remphelmann verbally stumbled forward. "That was some heck of a fire mission last night."

Lanyard's oaken expression went through Ronnie's eyes. "Last night, yes, the fire mission. Preplanned fires and a few co-ordinate corrections. That was last night; last night was a long time ago. All is well and all manner of things shall be well."

Remphelmann mumbled some kind of excuse and left the captain's non-presence. He went looking for Sergeant Peckerwood. Peckerwood and Scheissenbrenner were minutely inspecting each howitzer for the least of malfunctions. "What's happening, sergeant?"

"Sir, Brownie and I are doing preventative maintenance. We're looking over each tube with a microscope. We ask each man in the gun crew to report even the slightest thing out of order. Of course the artillery types know their stuff and keep the gun squeaky clean but anything we can do to help, well, we help." Remphelmann followed the two on their hospital rounds. They took a surgical interest in their observations. Thus satisfied, Peckerwood turned to his platoon leader. "Sir, the subject of the back haul to LZ Betty comes up. We are going to form up a mini convoy and head home. That's just the four of us trucks. The two five ton ammo haulers, the quartermaster provisioning deuce and a half, plus our ordnance taxi."

Remphelmann hid his alarm. "A back haul? No convoy protection?"

"Ah, no." Peckerwood explained. "You've got to understand, again and again. Charlie isn't stupid. He knows, as you college boy types know, about energy conservation. He generally doesn't like to waste time, men or ammunition on small potatoes. So we'll just buzz off home. Of course, that isn't written in stone. He might do the unexpected. But the Arvin engineers swept the road at daybreak and declared it clear of ambushes or road mines. So we have got an eighty-twenty chance of smooth sailing."

The little convoy did form up. The ordnance truck did the point lead. As there were no machine guns available, Scheissenbrenner did shotgun, with his M-16 lagged out the passenger side window. Peckerwood told Schweik to grab a position at the tail gate of the truck with his rifle, and 'suggested' to Remphelmann that he might plant him self with his M-16 over the top of the cab. The other trucks did likewise, driver behind the wheel, assistant driver at the shotgun position, with the odd man stationed in the back, M-16's at the ready. At the razor wire gate, Peckerwood stopped and unlimbered from behind the wheel. He yelled up to Lieutenant Remphelmann, "Dang and hang, sir! I forgot to ask if you wanted to finish up conversation with Captain Lanyard! Should I stop so you can re-matriculate?"

"No," Remphelmann lied. "We had a long conversation at breakfast."

"Hot diggety damn, then sir, the circus wagons are now going down the road."

The little convoy wound out of the firebase. It re-connected with Que Ell One at the foot of Big Titty Mountain and turned back east toward the South China Sea. Remphelmann scanned with difficultly the path that he had traversed the day before. He was into the devil's dogleg before he could re-gather his wits about the previous day. Only an otherwise unnoticed clump of trees served to re-orient him at the place he had so ineffectually shot off the grenade launcher the day before. Even quicker than that, the little line of trucks was back to the suburbs of Phan Thiet and speedily crawled off the two-lane pavement onto the LZ Betty approach. They wound through the security gate and were soon at the LZ Bozo parking area. Remphelmann had been checking his watch. What had taken four hours the morning before was retraced in less than forty-five minutes. Nui Ta Dom Mountain in the distance was no longer an oddity on the horizon, it now to Remphelmann held a permanent and real place in his sense of landscape. The little line of trucks disbanded. Ronnie went back to the ordnance hootch. Sergeant Shortarm was there to greet him.

"Holy Huntsville horse hocks, sir, did you have fun out in the field?"

"Yes."

"Did you get a good gander at that there garden spot of Firebase Firefly?"

"Yes."

"Y'all have a good talk with Captain Lanyard?"

"Yes."

"Poor old Captain Lanyard, poor feller done plumb lost his marbles, yet still keeps his act together. Mebbe I'm next." Shortarm laughed the laugh of the knowing.

"I hope not."

"Howdy doody, lieutenant, you look plumb tuckered. Mebbe

you all ought a scoot off to your BOQ and shower and shave and mebbe take a nap."

Remphelmann took the hint. He dragged off to his hootch, showered, shaved and lay down in his bunk. However, he did not nap. He fell into a comatose, almost catatonic state. Nonetheless, he kept jerking awake, with three things slapping into his brain. First was the horrid vision of Captain Lanyard's face. Second was an endless repeat of that dissociated state when he was being shot at and his mind had floated far above his body. Third was an almost map-like replay of every meter of Que Ell One.

══ Chapter Twenty-Five ══

There is something near and dear to every soldier's heart. It is not what some ruminative thinks, or the musings of Ivy League bound psychologists or even the nap repair of an armchair general. It is the need of any soldier or sailor to have a quiet crap. Before Attila the Hun sent his men into battle, he arranged latrines for his men. Caesar, prior to his battle with Vercingetorix in some horrid place in frog-infested Gaul, had his engineers design up to the date toilets. A great number of failed battles in the American Civil War were not due to strategic lapses, but were occasioned by a untimely and non-perspicacious inattention to the houses of office. More soldiers died from dysentery than battle wounds. Any United States historian worth his toilet salt will recall the nasty results of First and Second Bull Run. Manassas aside, the lack of decent sanitation has pre-occupied the finest and dullest minds of military history.

Can anyone, prior to the glorious battle of Trafalgar, fault Admiral Nelson for his inspection of the heads? Did Napoleon, cogitating on his brilliant divide and conquer at the Lodi Bridge neglect to provide pissoirs and poop chutes for his hard pressed and undernourished poilus? Did Blucher on his way to help Wellington at Waterloo fail to arrange dog watering and bowel relieving stations for his Prussian hoards? The subject is vast, almost all consuming. There is nary a footnote in Gibbon's *Decline and Fall of the Roman Empire* on this important subject. Yet the topic is known and beloved by all military men. It is the stuff of legends.

This subject did not escape the best and brightest minds of the Pentagon. The engineering manuals of the United States military give ample testimony to this subject. However, the local topography of Vietnam adds a particular fillip to this subject with a small geographical dilemma. That is the water table. Dig a hole in many places in Vietnam and the hole immediately fills with ground water. This is a godsend to rice farmers but an immense difficulty to any military man attempting to excavate a latrine. The subject brought the Pentagon to a halt. Superannuated engineers were brought from retirement to deal with the problem. Military historians went back to Marius to seek the solution. Frantic telexes were sent to the British for their ex-colonial advice. Oriental scholars from Yale pored over crumbling manuscripts from the Ming Dynasty. Everyone hypothesized, quasi-realized, semi-failed and re-constituted the dilemma in their capacious brains. However it was a lowly janitor in the Pentagon that solved the problem. He was an elderly man of brown skin who had been raised in the swamps of South Carolina. He inadvertently swept in on a think tank of the most brilliant, who were drawing flow charts and moon shot solutions. Over his broom, he chanced to mention that the solution was to crap on a pile of soggy wood, douse it with runny pine tar and set it alight. The offending bacteria would be thus incinerated. The resulting soil and ash could then be confidently recycled into fertilizer for poke salad and tobacco. Star spangled fireworks erupted all over the District of Columbia. Cannons were shot off from the bulwarks of Fort Meade. Physicians and surgeons from Reed Army Hospital raced to the chapel to kneel in thanks. The brown broom pusher was conviently forgotten, but the relevant epiphany was not. Burn the shit!

Think tanks from the Rand Corporation, high intelligence boffins from Harvard, brilliant physicists from Berkeley rushed to solve the practical problems. The solution was breath taking in its simplicity. Burn the shit! Their brilliant advice was incineratingly simple. Design an outhouse. On the back of the outhouse just below the toilet seat arrange a back door or trap door that would accommodate the lower half of a sawed off 55 gallon drum. After twenty or thirty men had crapped or peed into the remnant metal container, haul it out, stack it in a loose row with other such drums, douse the containers with a mixture of gasoline and diesel fuel and set the whole thing alight. A regular Hindu funeral pyre of mankind's detritus would go up in a glorious antiseptic roar. Sanitary and clean except for the resultant smoke and fumes. Would Vulcan and Pasteur bow down to the incense thus created? Yes.

Legions of army engineers, blueprinted plans in hand, descended on the long-suffering land of Vietnam. From the generals to the colonels to the majors to the captains, this new discovery was promulgated. Slide shows of the relevant technology were given to breathless staff meetings. Field expedient methods were devised to build the privies and slice up steel drums. Petroleum specialists were engaged to calculate the exact number of gallons of flammables needed to accomplish the mission. Congress allocated millions for the project. Everyone involved breathed a collective upwind sigh of relief. Senators were re-elected for their leadership on the issue. Then the best and brightest retreated to the safe suburbs of Arlington and celebrated at barbeques in their middle class backyards.

This left only the implementation of the project. Would a colonel of engineers deign to address the practicalities of the problem? No. Could the great sanitation experts of the medical corps take time from their practical duties of slicing and dicing to attend to the earthly implementation of the new plan? No.

The problem devolved. The generals passed it to the colonels. The colonels passed it to the majors and thence down the chain of command to the captains, lieutenants, senior sergeants, junior sergeants, corporals, specialists and privates first class. At the bottom of the heap the buck stopped. The sad sacks, the specialists on the out with their sergeants, the poor privates doing company punishment for real or imagined offences were the final precipitants of this vital duty and the military trickle down.

Thus spoke the military from on high. Thus spoke Zarathustra. Thus spoke the sergeants. Those thus spoken to, at least in the environs of Landing Zone Bozo, were Scheissenbrenner and Schweik. Specialist Scheissenbrenner, artillery repairman, Private Schweik, sometime small arms gunsmith. They were the lowest of the low on the totem pole of Mars local favor. Thus to them went the glory of implementing the grand strategy of shit burning.

It was their best of times; it was their worst of times.

It was the age of sanitary wisdom, yet the age of a defecator's foolishness.

It was an epoch of true belief, yet containing a stench of incredulity.

A moment of gasoline flashing light, a season of diesel fuel smoking darkness.

A spring of hope extinguished in a monsoon of despair.

There was a shit burner with a large jaw with neat clothes,

Pulling the steel can thrones of Scone from the back of the outhouse with a steel hook.

There was a shit burner with a slack jaw with disheveled fatigues,

Dribbling petrol and diesel on the stacked metal rounds.

Everything before them, a zippo was produced by one of the two sovereigns,

And a scrap of newsprint went alight.

Clearer than crystal, the plain face of flame went fair faced

Into the pyre and the defecations of a hundred men

Went like loaves and fishes into the humid tropic air.

Lieutenant Ronald Reagan Remphelmann of the ordnance stood to one side as the two high priests of clean living watched their bonfire erupt. "My god," he watched in amazement, "That smells like shit!"

"Aw," said Specialist Scheissenbrenner, "You get used to it, just like everything in a war zone. I got used to it during my first tour here."

"First tour? You mean you are here on the second go around? Why for god's sake?"

Scheissenbrenner motioned to both Schweik and Remphelmann to get out of the down wind waft of the flames. Then he continued his explanation. "I didn't think I'd come back, you know. But when I went back to the States I didn't like the peacetime army. So I let my enlistment run out and went back to Canandaigua. But that was even worse. I didn't fit in anyplace. At home, at work or anyplace. I didn't even feel at home at home. I wasn't wanted there. I didn't understand people any more. My own father said to me 'Son, I don't know what happened to you in Vietnam, but you aren't the son I raised. You are like a spaceman that stepped out of a UFO, since you were in Vietnam, I mean. I don't know what happened to you over there. But you are different. Son, you are not fit for human consumption. We don't want you around, because you are acting so weird.' My own father said that that. My own father cut me loose! So I thought and thought and I went back to the army recruiter and told him I wanted to re-enlist. The recruiter sergeant said 'sure enough, you want to go to Germany or you want some nifty job at Fort Polk, Louisiana, or...' and I said 'No sirree Bob, I want to go back to Vietnam'. The recruiter sergeant didn't blink an eye and said 'specialist, you are gone.' And I was gone, gone in the blink of an eye, and here I am, where I feel totally at home."

Remphelmann turned to Schweik, who was not to be outdone. "Sir, I can't answer like Scheissenbrenner. I'm a draftee. When I go home, back to Stump Jump, Ohio, I'll stay home come hell or high water. But look around. I'm burning shit for a living. But that reminds me of a day or so ago. Remember when we were on the highway? And we got shot at by Charles? Well sir. I will tell you, if I have a choice of being here and burning shit, or out on the highway taking my chances, I'd rather be out on Que Ell One."

Ronnie had had enough of the top-secret pentagon manure immolation. He excused himself from the two high priests of defecation and tried to find fresh air. Alas, the diesel smoke and its perfume clung to his clothing. He went back to the officers hootch to change. He knew that of his three changes of clothing all were in soggy, sweaty and grime besmeared condition, but decided to do a change out to something that was less odiferous.

At the hootch he noticed three zinc washtubs arranged just outside the door. One was filled with fatigues in soapy water and two held more clothing in various stages of rinse. An impromptu clothesline was stretched next to the door. He went in the screen door. There was the instant aroma of a clothes iron and sizzling spray starch. Then he saw her. A woman! The ugliest old crone that could be imagined. A wizened slack framed old Vietnamese lady dressed in black silk pajamas. The woman smiled at Ronnie. She was missing half of her teeth, and those that still adhered to her gums were stained purple black from a lifetime of chewing betel nut. She was at an ironing board, electric iron in hand; spray starching and pressing olive drab cloth. "Oh, Trung Uy Rem-full-man, finally we meet!"

Ronnie realized he had just met the hootch granny. She was the one who had been doing his laundry. He put her together from previous conversations. She had been let in the gate of the landing zone by military police, both ARVN and American. Her job, like other hootch grannies and hootch maids, was to relieve the soldiers of basic things like changing bed sheets and washing fatigues. Hootch girls were hired by the local mayors, vetted by Vietnamese intelligence, and sent into the American environs at the magnificent sum of seventeen cents an hour to clean up, wash up, sweep up, do kitchen police and sundry other housekeeping chores. They were not whores or pimps or drug providers or spies, at least to the undiscerning eye.

Seventeen cents an hour was a princely sum in those days, and the whole idea was to provide employment to otherwise impoverished women in a war zone. They swept, they washed and starched clothes, they cleaned dishes and took their meager earnings back to town to provide largesse to their war-torn kinfolk. It was a wartime expediency. Mere American privates in their barracks got the benefit. Cleaned starched fatigues and fresh bed sheets were a godsend to exhausted men who worked and even fought twenty-four hours a day, seven days at week.

So Remphelmann tried his best diplomatic approach on the bony old woman. "Thank you so much for your help. I need a clean set of fatigues."

"Oh, Lieutenant Remphelmann, Trung Uy Rem-full-man, already you got fresh starch in your cell."

Ronnie went in his cubicle and found a pristine set of clothes hanging in his locker. He changed out and re-appeared to the ba, the grandmother. "I feel so clean," he remarked.

The hootch granny laughed. "I like that. So, I clean and sweep and iron, wash the patio dishes, but what you like from town? I supply, you like."

"I really don't need anything."

"Oh Trung Wee, oh, GI! You too modest. All GI got money, all GI need something! You like girls?"

"Yes, I like women."

Good. I bring you hot eighteen-year-old hootch maid from Phan Thiet. She likes boom-boom GI officer very much!"

"No!" said a startled Remphelmann.

The old witch giggled. "Oh, then! You like young boys? I bring you hot young boy with fanny cranny. You boom-boom in the bottom! Yes, you like?"

Remphelmann was horrified. "No!"

The ba fetched a piece of betel nut out of her pajama waistband

and chomped on it. "Oh, then you like ganja, hemp, mary juana, opium? Yes, you like?

"No, no, and no!"

Trung Uy, you funny numbah ten GI! You not like fun? Maybe you think I dinky dao old woman? You right! I dinky dao old hootch granny! Dien cai dau, same-same as crazy!" She laughed uproariously.

Remphelmann took this pause to exit the hootch and go back to his work.

The granny had just ironed a set of clothes for Captain Manteca. She scurried them into the lardo's room and hung them in his locker. She noticed that the captain had left a pile of military communications on his bed. Her command of English did not rise to the level of reading, but she felt there must be something of importance there. A shaft of sunlight crossed the bed. She rearranged the stack of papers in the sunny beam. She fished in the top of her pajamas and produced a small minox type miniature camera. One by one, she snapped the pages, singing at each page, "Dien cai dau, dien cai dau." She finished her photographic mission and went back to the day room. She ironed more of Manteca's fatigues. Then she sang again "Quoc Lo Mot, and Que Ell One."

Chapter Twenty-Six

There was a persistent yet polite knock at the door of the BOQ. Remphelmann roused himself at the sound. Intuitively he knew he was alone in the hootch. Duvalier and Shinebaum were still on the road. Manteca had a habit of not being anyplace where anything was happening. Remphelmann crawled out of his bunk and answered the door. Standing in the morning gloom were, of all people, Privates Boudreaux and Schweik.

Schweik piped up. "Sir, it being Sunday morning and all, and seeing how the chaplain is going to hold Sunday morning service over across the airfield and all, and seeing how you have a jeep, and seeing how TeJean and I are the religious type, we thought maybe you could ferry us over to the early morning service."

How could Remphelmann refuse? He excused himself long enough to dress and bade the two privates to clamber into his jeep. "Isn't there a bus service or whatever to get you religious folk to service?"

"In theory, sir," offered TeJean. "But in reality we alls gets to sleep in an extra hour on Sunday, and tain't none of the truck drivers or sergeants wants to stir, ah-gar-on-tee."

As the three began their jeep ride and crested over a rise to see the South China Sea. Boudreaux began to speak again. "That's what 'em you call it one big salt pass and it done refresh a fishing story in my mind. Seems my cousin Pierre and I went salt-water fishing in Pierre's boat. We came to cross with Alphonse. His boat be done loaded with fish. Pierre do ask what his secret was. Alphonse said, 'Jess go out through that pass in the water over dere 'tween the islands until the water gets fresh. Stop dere and drop yer line. Abundances.' All excitements, Cousin Pierre fired up the motor and headed through that pass. When we got a little ways out Pierre tol' me to fill up a bucket and taste the water. I, TeJean Thibodaux, comply and say 'It's salty.' So this going on for hours, Pierre agoing out the pass further and further and stopping and me tasting the same bucket for fresh. This here goes on till we dang near sundown. In the middle of nowhere and no fish. So Pierre say to me 'taste the water bucket one last time.' But I reply, 'But Pierre, there's no more salt water in the bucket.'"

Remphelmann turned his young mind to logic. Was Boudreaux's statement a mere non sequitur or a misplaced syllogism or pure nonsense? He was saved by Schweik's voice.

"You know why I like to go to chaplain's meetings, sir? Because when I re-up I want a military career as a chaplain's assistant. Eighteen more years in the Army and I can retire and be straight with God at the same time."

Remphelmann queried. "Schweik, you don't strike me as a lifer. Eighteen more years?"

"Oh," quipped Schweik. "I'm like the chaplain you're going to meet. I lie a lot."

The three pulled up next to the meeting hall next to the infantry battalion headquarters. The long low building quintupled as enlisted men's day room, movie theatre, TV space, briefing platform and now on a Sunday as religious sanctuary. The three chumps entered. Gathered near the front rows of the briefing platform was a small assemblage of the faithful. Twelve in number. All were the leftovers from the infantry battalion, those who had not been called out to the field to fight the dragon on Big

Titty Mountain. Much to Remphelmann's consternation, in the back most rows seated on opposite sides of the meeting hall were Sergeants Shortarm and Heimstaadt. Shortarm on the left had his head down. He plucked a pocket copy of the New Testament from his blouse and opened it. On the right Heimstaadt sat with an absolutely huge copy of the Bible, big as a briefcase and a hand span thick. The binding was of worn and dog-eared leather. Dithering, Remphelmann approached Heimstaadt. He noticed that the bible was written in the ornate old German fraktur script, replete with swoops and curls and rhomboidal umlauts. Remphelmann wanted to ask why the privates had begged a ride when obviously there were two sergeants there. He was cut short.

Heimstaadt looked up from his book. "Mein Gott in Himmel, lieutenant! Don't you approach! Forbidden! It's Sontag. Gott in Himmel day. And don't even thinking I be a bible forcer. I'm no bible nut case. I'm a vegetarian!"

Remphelmann took the hint and snuggled into a middle row of the hall, halfway between the two back cornering non-coms and the poor soldiers at the front. He did not wait for long for the service to begin.

The chaplain swept into the meeting hall. He was a tall muscular man with a smooth face and longish blond hair. Draped over his fatigue blouse was an ornate prayer shawl. From the look of it could have easily been Catholic, Jewish or Lutheran. The chaplain did a rolling walk up the aisle. "Glory, glory, glory to God in the highest. I am Chaplain Captain Champagne, your sky pilot for this leg of your journey to the Promised Land. Glory and glory again." He mounted the platform as if an annointed one on the mountain, ready to impart wisdom sayings to the underling smallholders below him. He bowed again to the left and to the right. "Glory and glory. I repeat I am Chaplain Captain Champagne, currently assigned to this landing zone as your spiritual leader. Glory is to God and the United States Army!

I have muddy boots as I trek among my flock, as the messiah also muddied his sandals."

Remphelmann happened to notice that the chaplain had spit shined boots without the least clod of dirt upon them.

The chaplain continued. "I give you ministry in action. Adventure and challenge. I serve those who serve. I give and you receive. Your faith will be enriched, as I enrich you, challenge you and strengthen you as you carry out your duties. I am your spiritual leader in the spiritual community known as the Army."

"Blow it out your ass," Remphelmann heard Sergeant Shortarm exclaim from behind his left ear.

"Glory to God in the highest," the chaplain ejaculated. "Another testimony to the puissance of the Lord. And glory again, that we have not in the flock today any Christ-killing Jew boys nor any papist back-sliders!"

"Blasphemer! Anti-Christ!" Remphelmann heard Sergeant Heimstaadt exclaim from behind his right ear.

"I hear the celestial voices," continued the chaplain, "Calling me on to exposit on the word of the Lord. Let us kill commies for Christ, the little yellow hoards of Buddhist reprobates, and smite the philistines for their unbelief."

"Cite chapter and verse from the evangelists for that," shouted Shortarm from behind.

"Glory! Another proof of scripture is forthcoming!" replied the chaplain. "But tarry a moment. I'm so busy in the life of the faith community! I serve, with dirt stained sandals to expand my ministry, immovable in my desire to bring the true gospel to the Greeks, gentiles and sundry heathen."

"Including der Dutch Germans? Who you call heathen, Satan filled liar!" This word of faith came from behind Remphelmann's right shoulder.

The chaplain continued unperturbed. "I was asked to provide chapter and verse. I will do so. The reading today is from Romans Thirteen, verses one and two:

'Let every person be subject to the governing
authorities. For there is no authority
except from God, and those that exist
have been instituted by God.
Therefore he who resists the authority resists what
God has appointed.'

That quoted, my sermon today is on unquestioning obedience
to your military superiors."

"Taking God's Word out of context and twisting it around?"
Sergeant Shortarm offered at the top of his lungs. "You snake in
the grass!"

"Glory," Captain Champagne went on. "What does the
scripture mean? What it means is what I say it means, because
I am higher in authority than you. Glory! Our two sequential
leaders back in Washington, Lyndon Baines and Richard
Milhous, both the godliest of men, operate at the highest level.
Which means they get their authority not from the electorate but
by divine right, the divine right of kings. Therefore each of you,
my bleating little flock, had better follow orders or else."

"You sweared to defend der Constitution of the United States
and yet tell us this? Swinehund!" Heimstaadt rang loudly.

"Glory. God will smash the unrighteous under his thumb
like a man squashing a loathsome spider, fellow soldiers. The
army's orders are God's orders. Don't ask questions. Mindlessly
obey your Lord!"

Shortarm was on his feet, waving his fist. "You want take
God's word out of context and use it to y'all own advantage? Take
this, First Peter, chapter two, verse sixteen!

'Live as free men, yet without using your freedom as a pretext
for evil,
But live as servants for God.'"

Shortarm flopped exasperated and then leaped again. "You
womanizing, whore hunting scum bag excuse for minister of
faith!"

"Thank you, case in point. That same citation continues, 'Honor the Emperor...Be submissive to your masters.'"

It was Heimstaadt's turn again. "The evil that men do live on after them!"

"That, my dear sergeant, is from Shakespeare's 'Julius Caesar' and not Holy Writ. Glory! Now as it is Sunday, the officers mess is opening an hour late. I like to be first in the chow line, so I will abbreviate my sermon. But first I see we have a new member of the flock, a lieutenant there in the middle row. Lieutenant, would you kindly accompany me after the service. Let us break bread together and praise the bounties of God. Glory!"

Remphelmann knew he was stuck and nodded a silent assent.

"So to close. Army chaplains are expected to observe the distinctive doctrines of their own faith while also honoring the right of others to observe their own faith. Rabbis, ministers and priests are in our holy ranks. That said, I hope god fries all the kikes, and skewers all the pope benighted wops on a stake."

Both Shortarm and Heimstaadt were on their feet again chanting, "Evil, evil."

Champagne spread his arms in benediction. "May the Lord bless you and keep you. May the Lord bless your brainless adherence to authority and grant you a thousand dead godless atheistic gooks in the weeks to come. Amen, amen and amen. Glory!"

The little gathering broke up. Shortarm and Heimstaadt stormed out. Boudreaux and Schweik wandered back past Remphelmann.

"Say, men, if you hustle maybe you can hitch a ride with the sergeants. You can see I have to go to breakfast with the captain."

"Sure enough, sir," said Schweik. "Isn't that preacher something? He sure doesn't pull any punches."

Boudreaux looked blankly at the lieutenant. "Sir, that sermon done reminded me of a story. Y'all see, my cousin Pierre and I was out craw-dad hunting..."

"Perhaps some other time, private. I have to go with the chaplain."

With the chaplain he went. He traversed the distance with him to the officers mess. Indeed they were the first in line. He was surprised at the sumptuous repast laid artfully out on a buffet table rather than the usual steam line. There were white china plates and real cloth napkins. Instead of freeze thawed scrambled eggs, there were real poached eggs swimming in hot butter. Instead of spam chunks there were real slices of smoked ham. Instead of the ubiquitous army bread slabs, there were piping hot rolls fresh from the oven. The two made a selection from this smorgasbord and went to a back table. Real combat officers began to filter in. They looked haggard. Some had the distant eyes Remphelmann had seen in Captain Lanyard. They picked lightly at the available food and made a point of avoiding the chaplain. Manteca bounded in, all eyes for the sumptuous repast. He shoveled obscene amounts of food onto three plates. Balancing them carefully, he noticed Remphelmann and Champagne and made a beeline for the opposite corner of the hall. He planted his commodious butt into a chair and turned his back on the two. He began to shovel food like a pig at a trough.

Another infantry officer came in, selected his food and went to join his compadres. He noticed Chaplain Captain Champagne. "Hey, chaplain, hey holy joe, how was your poon-tang foray in town last night?"

"Glory!" exalted the chaplain. "I brought the ever-living gospel, not to three, but to four young slant eye sluts last night."

"Fry in hell," the infantryman snarled as he sat as far away as possible.

Remphelmann had gotten used to being at a loss for words. He remained silent and paused before dishing into the poached eggs. It crossed his mind to give holy thanks for the food, but decided to wait for the chaplain.

The chaplain proved to be rather fastidious at his table manners. He arranged his food neatly, carefully spread the cloth napkin out on his lap and laid out his silverware with care. Then he plowed with gusto into the food. He did not condescend to say thanks to the Big Man.

This prompted the lieutenant to words. "You don't say grace?"

"Grace? Grace? Blow grace out of your ass."

"Pardon me, sir. But from what I've seen and heard, you seem to have a rather dissolute lifestyle. How can you reconcile it with your religion?"

"Who says I have any religion?"

"But you are a ordained minister and a commissioned chaplain."

"Hell's bells. Religion is a load of crap. The first thing that happens when you go to seminary is that you do an intensive, exhaustive study of scripture. You find out soon enough that it is all nonsense, all bullshit. It's a written mishmash of myths and pseudo-history and con artist tales. All that fairy tale crap is then wrapped up in quasi-mystical language. It became quickly apparent to me that it, religion, is all arrant nonsense."

"So" Ronnie offered, "don't you at least believe in God?"

"Who's got time for that dog doo doo? There's no evidence of a god. Who cares anyway?"

"Then why do you go through this charade of belief? How do you reconcile your unbelief with your outward vocation?"

"Shit. Did you ever see a used car salesman that believed in what he was doing? Shit no. He has simply discovered an easy way to con suckers out of their money. Car salesmen need a job, I need a job. It beats working for a living."

"I think I'm beginning to see where you stand."

"It's like being a child psychologist, my job. Your audience is just like children. What you need to do is feed them bedtime fairy tales, like the Brothers Grimm. Stories like God loving you even if you parents don't. Or the glorious supposed after life, and heaven being peachy keen, and that this crummy life is just a way station on the way to a paradisiacal bliss. Plus a few boogey man stories hiding under the bed. Feed the suckers what they want to hear. Our job as chaplain, or priest or whatever, is to baffle and bamboozle the babies of life. Our job is to feed the ignoramuses what we term as 'noble lies'. Otherwise folks get depressed over the reality of Darwinian existence." Champagne paused briefly. "Do you want me to give you extreme unction?"

"But," protested Remphelmann, you're not a Catholic. How can you give extreme unction?"

"Hah," laughed the captain. I'm a military chaplain. I've memorized the whole bag of tricks. You want it Catholic, I give it to you Vatican style. Are you a Protestant? You get it Methodist, Baptist, whatever. You're Jewish, and I give it to you Heeb. By the way, speaking kike, I'm really good at the eighth day circumcision. Are you circumcised? I'll circumcise you right here and now. This steak knife has a bit of ham juice on it, but what the hay!"

Remphelmann dropped his fork, "Uh, thank you. I think I'll pass." The young man had lost his appetite. He retrieved his fork. "So you're just a religious and philosophical charlatan?"

"Thank you. But actually I do have a religious philosophy."

"And that is?"

"Perhaps you know about the famous Russian monk, Rasputin. You know, the one that held such sway on the last Russian Czar, Nicholas and his Czarina?"

"Yes."

"He belonged to an obscure off shoot of the Russian Orthodox Church. This off shoot was in turn an even more obscure off shoot of the Philokalia off shoot of a Greek Orthodox off shoot of a Byzantine Christian Orthodox off shoot."

"I've lost track of these off shoots."

"It matters not. This hidden sect of a sect of a sect was preoccupied with sex. The basic idea was that you couldn't really be saved until you had been thrown down into the depths of all manner of depravity. Depravity! Vice! Sexual, moral, legal!

Then and only then could you call upon the saving pardon of the Savior to rescue you from the total abyss of sin. Thus I, as my spiritual exercise, am forced, forced I tell you, to engage in the most degrading forms of sexual debasements so that my redeemer can offer me the most glorious return to spiritual grace! Only with the worst work of the devil prompting me to satiation of my most earthly lustful desires, can I be enabled to the point where the Holy Ghost can descend, and through his glorious mediation, raise me up and cleanse me."

"That is quite interesting," Remphelmann offered. He cast in his mind for suitable exit from the captain's presence.

"Hey, all this holy talk is making me horny. What say you and I jump in my jeep and buzz off to Phan Thiet City? The best place in town is 'Long Tall Sally's'. I assure you, it's the best little whorehouse in Vietnam."

Remphelmann stammered his declination. "Well, uh, thank you, sir. But, uh, I have work to do over at LZ Bozo. Lots of repair and maintenance problems, you know. Duty, you know."

"Duty, my ass, lieutenant. The only thing is this world is the duty of self gratification."

Remphelmann blurted his farewell and hurried back to his jeep, the 'Mudd Buck It'. He scooted back across the airfield to the putative safety of his LZ.

Chapter Twenty-Seven

All human beings, besides being subject to terrain, weather and taxes, are subject to death. Burial practices vary across the world from cremation to entombment to burying in the ground. The Phan Thiet region of Vietnam is and will be no different than that of other regions. The usual practice in Vietnam is ground burial, but in the Binh Thuan province there is an additional problem. That is the water table is unduly high. Common decency being what it is, to preserve the Shakespearean whoreson dead body from the whoredaughter damp, dictates that the mortal coil be laid to rest at ground level. The well to do, having the financial means, traditionally build a small tomb like structure, or erect an above ground honeycomb affair, a condominium so to speak, into which to slide a coffin. The humble folk however, lacking the money, economize by laying the coffin directly on the ground and heap six feet of dirt over the corpse. Those familiar with the burial areas of New Orleans or Amsterdam or similar soggy cities, would both, living and dead, feel comfy with such arrangements.

Another fact is that in Vietnam, as in many other cultures, the time honored practice of ancestor worship is widely observed.

Family members are buried cheek to jowl unto the tenth or twelfth generation. As a kind of holiday, the extended family will go to the cemetery on certain holy or commemorative days, and have a grand picnic. They will party and have meaningful conversations with great-great-great grandma. The men will sample rice wine or beer, the children will play hide and seek around the various mounds and structures, and the women folk will serve up a grand repast and re-new family relations. After leaving ritual meals at the foot of the resting places for their recently and remotely passed family members, there will be a joyful procession back to town.

The Phan Thiet Cemetery has all these wonderful features to the maximum. It is at least four hundred years old. It is located on a series of eroded red clay benches, full of slight ravines. As far as the eye can see there are thousands of hummocks of man high dirt, interspersed with the stone or concrete tombs of the more prosperous class. Wreaths of flowers, prayer flags, pinwheels and bunting abound. The gravesite is primarily Buddhist with the usual iconography, but since the introduction of Catholicism by the Portuguese in 1600's, there are many crosses to admire. Additionally there is a local religion, Cao Dai, a wonderful mixture of Buddhism, Christianity, Daoism and Confucianism. There are no separate religious sections to the place. Buddhists, Christians and Cao Dai mingle happily together in death as well as in life. The Vietnamese people are gracious and tolerant folk, whether encorpsed or enlivened.

The only downside to this happy place was its proximity to the old French garrison and airfield. The landing zone was a mere kilometer or so uphill from this Elysian paradise. It was not lost on the locals that the cemetery was a wonderful start line for any military operations against the enemy du jour.

The 804th Viet Cong Battalion main force consisted of 800 regular paid troops with professional officers. They wore regulation uniforms when it suited their purposes and carried AK-47 rifles, kalashnikovs, light machine guns and B-40 Chinese manufactured RPG's, rocket propelled grenades. As such they were a highly mobile light infantry. The only thing they lacked was artillery. They made up for this by becoming grand masters at the use of the 82mm soviet mortar. However the mortar was a rather bulky affair, requiring one man to carry the heavy base plate, another to lug the aiming bipod, a third to hoist the mortar tube, and several others to mule along the large rounds of ammunition. Logistics being a major problem with any army, the Viet Cong cast far and wide for ways to pre-position mortars prior to any attack.

Cao Nat Lanh and his buddy, Ngo Dinh Bao, were working an ornate coffin through the streets of Phan Thiet City. They had it balanced on their heads as they dodged pedestrians, motorbikes, pedicabs and the occasional old Renault. They were clad in the everyday garb of Vietnamese workingmen, the famous black silk pajamas. They were heading down to the wharf where fishing boats bobbed on the incoming tide. The passersby stepped nimbly aside and obviously admired the workmanship of the wooden casket, which was beautifully lacquered in gloss black with red polished teak inlay panels and gold gilt ornaments.

Cao and Ngo passed by a local cop, who was patrolling the quay bound street. The policeman was an amiable fellow, who had an ancient French Lebel Modelle 92 revolver strapped to his waist.

"Hello there, who's inside?" the cop asked.

"Oh, nobody yet," quipped Cao, "But soon, but soon."

"Who will be the occupant of such a fine little house?"

"You know the old lady Anh, who lives over Nguyen's machine shop?"

"Oh yes," offered the policeman. "She has been feeling poorly of late."

"No, not her," Cao corrected. "It's her brother. He lives up in Ap Bong Tra, he's a goner. He even sold off his rice cache to buy this piece of polished wood."

"And he died?" inquired the policeman.

"Well, not yet, not yet, but he sees the pure land coming and wants to go out in style. We're going to store it in the back of Nguyen's machine shop until needed."

"We all have to go, sooner or later. So this old man of Ap Bong Tra, he's Catholic?"

"No, Buddhist."

"Pity, the cop sympathized, "I hope he doesn't spend to much time in purgatory before he sees the true savior."

"I don't know," Cao continued. "He's Pure Land Buddhist, working his beads with every ounce of his failing strength, chanting 'namo amitaba, namo amitaba' endlessly. His main concern to just to get planted in the cemetery next to his family."

The policeman touched his cap in salute. "May God, Jesus, Buddha and his family look kindly on his voyage."

The two ambled down the road onto the quay and maneuvered the coffin into Nguyen's shop. Inside the establishment was an ancient French metal working lathe, a Chinese bridgeport mill and the perfume of lubricating oil and cutting fluid. Metal swarf littered the tile floor. They set the coffin down on a set of sawhorses. "What's happening?" Cao asked.

Nguyen was a prematurely wizened man in his fifties. He sported a thin goatee of gray hair. He stood back from the drill press he was operating and flipped off the electrical switch. "You know Tri Ang? He's got that red fishing trawler. The drive to his diesel injector snapped. It's an old Perkins diesel, Hong Kong style, and well, no parts. Because of the war there's no parts for anything so I'm in a hurry to fabricate a new injector coupling. I had a time coming up with the raw material."

Cao sympathized. "No parts, no raw material. Where did you get the steel?"

"Oh, you know that American, Private Scrounge? He was in here yesterday looking for a half kilo of hemp, marijuana they call it, and I said I need a piece of steel 25 millimeters in diameter by 60 millimeters long. He said 'sure' and an hour later he was back with a really nice piece of axle shaft from a blown up truck, perfect. I'm latheing it down now to make the part. Tri is in a hurry. If his boat engine doesn't work, no fishing, no money, no food. I'll have it done by sundown and he'll be ready to fish by the next tide."

"Good, good," Cao nodded.

"So how is our friend in the casket?" Nguyen asked. Nguyen and Cao went to the door of the shop and cased the street. Satisfied that there were no prying eyes, they went back inside. Cao and Ngo lifted the lid. Inside was a soviet style 82mm mortar round and a large piece of gas pipe about four feet long and three inches across the mouth. Nguyen marveled at the pipe. "That's a beauty. High quality steel and near the right inside diameter. Where did you get it?"

Cao laughed, "Our friend Private Scrounge. I ran into him at Long Tall Sally's. I told him I needed a piece of pipe thus and so in size to repair an irrigation pump. Then I arranged with Madame Sally to have one of her girls give him a free ride with more to come if he could locate the goods. Next day he was back. He got another boom-boom on the house and I got the tube."

Nguyen fished a micrometer out of a tool chest and carefully measured the inside of the pipe. "Ah, yes, excellent. I'll just have to bore and hone only a little. And I'm glad you brought me a sample round. The copper driving band on the mortar shell is the most important tolerance."

"Then," continued Cao, "Weld an end cap with a firing pin on the bottom and it's ready to go."

"I have to ask. Why improvise? I'm an old weapons technician from the Viet Minh days."

"And a hero of Dien Bien Phu."

"I was no hero, I was just doing my job. Now I'm doing my job again. But as the French say, 'La guerre c'est non fin.' But I ask again. Why improvise? You need a base plate. You need an aiming bipod. Surely we have good Chinese mortar sets?"

"That is exactly the point. We have good chi-com mortars but this is going to be a set and forget and run like hell weapon. We don't want to waste a good tube, base plate, bipod and aiming telescope. We'll put your machined tube and a sack of instant set concrete in the coffin, and add ten rounds of ammunition. Then we'll carry the dear departed to the cemetery and lay him to rest. When night comes, we go back to the graveyard and disinter the old man. Then we'll set the throwaway tube in a good triangulated position with the butt in a hole of the wet concrete and drop the ten rounds on LZ Bozo. Then we'll di di mao. By the time the GI's get the distance and azimuth we'll be long gone."

Nguyen stroked his wispy beard. "C'est la guerre."

Chapter Twenty-Eight

Something was wrong. Something had gone horribly wrong. Remphelmann had on this Monday morning after the chaplain's service gone about his daily business. He interfaced with his men. He waited for a phone call from his superiors in Surf City, a communication that never came. The road convoy that he had accompanied two days before returned. Lieutenants Duvalier and Shinebaum led the line of trucks back into the LZ Bozo confines. Men were busy unloading the trucks. Porky and P.T. kept huddling together, and then breaking apart. One went to the nearest telephone and the other to a jeep-mounted radio.

Sergeant Shortarm was wringing his hands.

"What's up?" Remphelmann queried his sergeant.

"Holy Marfa miscarriages, sir. I don't know, but the general feeling done be done awful. Something real shitty done happened out on Big Titty Mountain."

Remphelmann looked out across the western distance. Beyond the Phan Thiet cemetery lay Whiskey Hill. From the distance whole flights of huey helicopters were winging in. Some of the choppers whopped up the rise and landed at the infantry helipad on the far side of the airstrip. Two helicopters with red crosses squatted down near the first aid station. Another inserted itself on a narrow lane between the ammunition dump and LZ Bozo. It was the closest point to the Graves Registration facility. Shortarm went at a dead run over to the military police building and was soon back.

"Holy Harlingen horse crap, sir. The mission on Big Titty done gone wrong, and I mean big time. Seems there was a ground movement that the grunts were evoluting, and wham, a huge Charlie counter–attack. And the shit done did fly."

Remphelmann gathered his wits enough to go over to Lieutenant Shinebaum. Porky had a tactical map laid out on the hood of his jeep and was screaming into his radio. Sholmo paused soon enough. Ronnie naively asked, "What's going on?"

Shinebaum exploded in a rage. "It's Kegresse. It's that damned idiot Kegresse! The infantry battalion commander had a tactical plan to go up the Hoa Thanh ridge and got countermanded by that blithering fool. Kegresse was up in his huey, playing god of the maps and had all of bravo company change direction and attack up the Song Can gully. My god, it wasn't just a miscalculation, it was a frigging ambush pocket. Charles opened up with crossfire and wiped the whole company's ass! Frigging Kegresse! Fool idiot! He maneuvered two hundred men right into a dead duck kill zone!"

Remphelmann peered at the topographical map. "The Hoa Thanh ridge? The Song Can gully?"

Shinebaum threw down the microphone of his field radio. He buried his face in his palms and rubbed his dirt-encrusted face. Then, obviously to distract himself from the current situation, he pointed with a dusty finger at the map. "Look, damn it, Remphelmann. If an infantry force is going uphill towards a mountaintop, you take the high ground as you go. In this case, we either go up the Hoa Thanh ridge or the parallel high ground, the Phu Loi spur. The enemy knows this. They had positions blocking the ridge spines. So what does this god-forsaken asshole do? He countermands the high ground approach, and has the men slither up the intervening valley! That leaves Charlie clear to shoot down in a cross fire from the heights! Frigging god damn blatant stupidity. Shit, shit, shit!"

Out of the blue, Major Dufuss's driver, the smarmy smirky one, ran up to Duvalier and Remphelmann. The smirk had left his face. "Thank god, I found two of you, gentlemen, sirs. General Kegresse is due to land here at the LZ in about thirty minutes. He's going to hold a holy hell dressing down conference at the meeting hall. Major Dufuss says all the Bozo officers need to meet him ASAP, as soon as possible, at the FSA hootch. Damn, sirs, I never saw the major so out of joint! Do the gentlemen know where Lieutenant Duvalier and Captain Manteca are?"

Shinebaum answered. "I just saw them over at the quartermaster warehouse, helping to unload a truck." The major's driver was away like lightning. Shinebaum folded his map into his armpit and he and Remphelmann ran through the dirt towards the forward support headquarters. Manteca and Duvalier, who were double-timing from the quartermaster yard, met them. They piled en masse through the door.

"Come into my office, into my office," they heard Major Dufuss whine. They crowded through the door to find the major pacing to and fro behind his desk. Dufuss paused long enough to klutz into his desk for his vodka and tomato juice. He flopped a drink together and chugged it. "This is dreadful."

"What's going on?" Manteca asked.

"Damned if I know, all I know is that something went badly, badly wrong on today's Nui Ta Dom Mountain clearing operation. At least a dozen men killed. Now Kegresse is looking for scapegoats for something he did or didn't do. He's called an immediate staff meeting for all the LZ officers. That asshole is going to pin blame, and I'm sure I'm one of the targets. Oh god, my career." Dufuss chugged the rest of his bloody mary and prepared another.

Dufuss's driver charged into the office. "Sir, the staff conference is going off in ten minutes, sir. We just have time to get across the airfield." Dufuss and his driver piled into the major's jeep and roared away.

Manteca's coach was close to hand. The four junior officers ran for it. "Ronnie, you drive," Shinebaum ordered as he sat in the passenger's seat. "Manteca, Duvalier, clamber in the back and I'll explain." The fat man and the black man piled in. "Go, Remphelmann go." Remphelmann slammed the jeep into gear and followed the billowing dust of Dufuss. As they drove across the airstrip to the infantry side, Shinebaum pulled his map out from his armpit and presented it to the rear space passengers. Remphelmann could hear Shinebaum explaining about the Song Can gully and the Hoa Thanh ridge. Remphelmann kept glancing back though the rear view mirror. Manteca's face was blank with incomprehension, but Duvalier's visage scowled and turned dark with constrained rage.

They wheeled to the parking area. The meeting hall was being jammed with officers and senior NCOs. There was a sense, not of panic, but a manly seething silent emotion that swept the room. Remphelmann could not imagine what was going on behind the grim visages of the officers who were assembling. He was now aware of the thousand yard stare. He was now aware of the blank hope-forgotten look of dust becaked men who had been too long in the field. Some of the sergeants and officers had dried blood smeared on their uniforms and hands. The five rear echelon types hid on a back row. Dufuss cowered. Shinebaum and Duvalier sat edgily on their seats.

There was a shout of "Attention." Lieutenant Colonel BeLay walked in grimly shouting, "As you were, be seated." The colonel went to the front row and collapsed into a chair. Remphelmann was aghast at the colonel's Styx-like demeanor.

There was another shout of "Attention." Every one leaped to their feet. This time it was Brigadier General Kegresse, followed by his aide-de-camp, Captain Lickspittle. Kegresse swept regally up the aisle. There was no call of 'As you were.' Kegresse made a slow march up the middle aisle and mounted the stage and the podium with his doormat in close attendance. Only after he had situated his kingly presence behind the plywood altar did he condescend to softly remark, "Gentlemen, be seated." He screwed the most condescending scathing look he could muster on his face and glanced that over his captive audience. Then he spoke again.

"The only reason I stooped to call you scurrilous losers to a meeting was to berate all of you for your absolutely atrocious performance today on Newsy Tom-tom Mountain."

"That's Nui Ta Dom Mountain, sir," Captain Lickspittle hurried a small voice into the general's ear.

"Damn it, Lickspittle, don't correct me."

"Sir, yes sir."

Kegresse clamped his hands on the podium. "The tactical movements on Whiskey Mountain were not to my liking. You little ants on the ground could not possibly see what I saw from my eagle eye perch in my personal helicopter. Your advance from the forward edge of the battle area, until you made contact with the enemy was amateurish. Your approach up that ridge, the Howie Toothy spine..."

"Sir, begging pardon, sir. The Hoa Thanh ridge..."

Kegresse snapped, "Damn it, Lickspittle, don't correct me!"

"Sir, yes sir."

"I gave excellent orders from my overhead position, high enough from ground fire to assure my personal safety, to redirect your attack in a mode that would protect you from hostile fire. Thus the order, my direct order, was given to re-direct your assault up the Fu Manchu valley."

Lickspittle intervened again, "That's the Song Can wash, sir."

"Damn it, Lickspittle, don't correct me."

"Sir, yes sir."

"Where was I? Ah yes. The blame for today's failure! I am free of any culpability for the unfortunate results. My brilliant orders were clear. The failure to take the objective and the resulting minor causalities, the blame for all that, I lay directly on the incompetence of Lieutenant Colonel BeLay."

A collective sledgehammer hit all the men in the room. Soldiers were knocked back in their chairs at this verbal attack. The whole room gasped in a single breath.

Being in the military and under martial discipline is a difficult life. Few things are sacrosanct when it comes to personal feelings. A certain amount of brutal fact-finding and blunt talk is part of the occupation. But one thing is never done. Never. That is to berate, belittle or humiliate a subordinate soldier in public. To dress-down a military man in front of his equals or lower ranks is a thing never to be undertaken. There is no quicker route to individual or group morale destruction than to humiliate a man in front of his peers. Kegresse had done just that.

Colonel BeLay started in his chair and then went immobile. That did not stop others from leaping to their feet. One infantry officer shouted, "Damn you sir, Colonel BeLay is an honorable man! How dare you?" Another, blue-faced, spoke in heated terms. "Minor casualties? Minor? Twelve men killed in action and twenty-three wounded. Minor? And you countermanded the ground commander's attack plan?" A third shook his fist. "Eagle eye view? You re-directed a perfectly designed attack off the ridge into a kill zone gully! And you're not to blame?"

"Silence, men! Silence I say!"

Even in the back of the hall there was commotion. In the far pocket sat Major Dufuss and Captain Manteca who were quaking in their boots for fear of their beloved careers. Remphelmann was as usual speechless. That did not stop P.T. from exploding out of his seat. Shinebaum attempted to restrain him, to no effect. Duvalier burst out in anger. "Shame, shame, shame on you! You impugn the name of Colonel BeLay? BeLay is on his third tour here in Vietnam. He has the Bronze Star, the Silver Star, two Purple Hearts and the Distinguished Service Cross from Korea. Seventeen years of heroic service and you humiliate him unjustly before his men?"

Kegresse saw an excellent opportunity to change the subject. "You, you in the back. You, you my little negroid friend. Are you an officer?"

'First Lieutenant Pierre Duvalier, sir. Are you an officer?"

"Enough snippy talk from you, colored boy! You should know your place."

Duvalier started to reply but Shinebaum literally wrested the man down in his seat and slapped his hand over P.T.'s mouth.

"Lickspittle, take that coon's name and rank down for disciplinary action."

"Sir, yes sir."

Kegresse straightened his uniform. "So. All this simply reinforces my preconception. Here in Phan Thiet I have an incredibly useless and worthless group of so-called soldiers. My helicopter awaits. As I return to my air-conditioned quarters in Saigon and drag my weary soul off to the general officers mess, I will rue the day that you slovens were placed under my command. Today was to be the San Lo breakout, the Stalingrad pocket counter-attack, and instead I got a private's fart. As I sit to dinner, what's today's menu? Bruised broccoli with béarnaise, beef bourguignon with sour cream and noodles, washed down with California merlot? Oh I shall mourn. I shall mourn you incompetents. Gentlemen, that is all." With that Kegresse swept out of the hall, Lickspittle in tow, and boarded his helicopter.

The infantry officers began to crowd around the hero BeLay. BeLay sat immobile in a catatonic frenzy. Major Dufuss turned to Manteca. "Thank god, he didn't call us out, that would have been the end of our careers." Manteca nodded assent and offered, "Perhaps the major and I should find some tomato juice." The two wandered away, it never entering their minds that two such rear echelon losers would have ever appeared on Kegresse's radar screen.

Shinebaum had restrained Duvalier's neck with an impromptu hammerlock, which he released in increments as P.T.'s rage ebbed.

Remphelmann could only remark, "Twelve dead, twenty–three wounded. And all the general had to say was incompetents and béarnaise sauce? And all this because of Que Ell One?"

Chapter Twenty-Nine

Why are funerals so sad? If in the grand scheme of things death marks the grand march into a greater life in heaven or paradise or the world to come or the pure land, why do people grieve? Surely a life in the immortal pristine, transiting from the nasty realm of human material existence, would mark an occasion of joy rather than dirge. Is there a more earthly reminder? Could it be that widows go penniless and orphans starve or that a family unit would disintegrate or some lawyer or politician or banker would lose a client? The Irish, a perverse race, perhaps have a better idea. Hold a wake. All the living march off to the pub and celebrate the release of the suddenly dead to an indeterminate fate, but blare horn, voice or harp at the predicament of the living.

Thus in Phan Thiet such a funeral march took place.

It seems that the old man of Ap Bong Tra had been transported to the old lady Anh's apartment over Nguyen's machine shop. The doctors were seemingly helpless to stop the old man from regaining the pure land. He, to all officialdom, dropped dead. The coffin, that ornate casket which had been conveniently stored in the back of the machine shop was brought from its short stay, hauled upstairs and poor old man, now dead as a doornail, was ostensibly inserted within, lacking formaldehyde and perfume. It was expedient that he be buried in the Phan Thiet cemetery with all possible sanitary haste.

The erstwhile officials of this timely removal were in fact officers. Cao Nat Lanh, a company commander of the 804th Viet Cong Battalion, main force, was dressed in the simple black dress of a peasant. His partner in deception was the redoubtable Lieutenant Ngo Dinh Bao, he of the strong and silent mode, also dressed in mufti. They assumed a straight face and a calm stance was they maneuvered the coffin down from old lady Anh's apartment. After a brief pause in Nguyen's machine shop, where inexplicably the improvised mortar tube, a bag of concrete and ten rounds of mortar ammunition were added to the lacquered container, they were met by a covey of coffin handlers who helped load the overweight box onto a hand drawn hearse. The procession of mourners set out. There was the usual herd of sad family and friends, casting muted wails and imprecations upon any transient evil spirits that would attempt to follow the old man to his resting place with his ancestors. Prominent among them was Remphelmann's hootch granny, flowing crocodile tears. Even the local cop, Lebel revolver at his hip, could not help but tip his cap to the old man making his final tour.

They wended their way westwards out of the city into the broad expanse of the cemetery. After a bit of casting about in the maze of graveyard pathways they found the family mound of the Anh Clan. Gravediggers had just completed excavating a niche in the side of the hillock just large enough for the old man's varnished travel trailer. To Captain Cao's own surprise and delight the grave shovelers had moved to an adjoining mound and were digging furiously in the heat. They were excavating a similar niche on the hummock of a Catholic clan. Presently another funeral procession came along with another assemblage of hearse haulers, mourners and a Catholic priest, replete with flowing brightly embroidered robe and swinging censer wafting glorious incense smoke. Captain Cao hid a smile. The putative priest was his fellow soldier Major Thich Xuan Doung, executive officer of the 804th Viet Cong. After lingering a decent interval at the internment of old man of Ap Bong Tra, Cao sidled over to the Roman officiator.

"Peace, blessings, and prosperity, my good man." Cao said to the fake priest.

"And the same to you and yours."

"So?" queried the captain.

Major Thich stopped swinging his billowing censer and glanced about to make sure no prying ears of the innocent or the South Vietnamese secret police were within earshot. "There's been an upgrade in plans. Your coffin has the mortar tube, the fast dry cement, and ten rounds of 82mm mortar ammunition?"

"Yes."

"In this casket we have 30 more mortar shells. As much as we could stuff in the box without arousing attention. Enough said. Plus the command is thinking about a direct attack on the Ami's wire. Enough said. See you here at midnight." The major went back to his funeral, and Captain Cao to his. The gravediggers humped a bare minimum of dirt on the coffins. A ritual last meal was judicially placed on porcelain plates; a cupful of rice, a tad of dried fish and some sprinkles of nuoc mam. These were placed next to the interned coffins. A few words were said at both funerals to finish up the necessities of passage to the great beyond and both funeral parties went back to Phan Thiet City. The sun was close to the horizon.

It was nearing midnight. Remphelmann was asleep in his rack. Ronnie had quickly learned the sleep of the damned. A sleep of comatose blankness followed by a fidgety stirring of semi-consciousness, followed again by a thankful timelessness of incomprehension. Remphelmann startled awake. He looked at his glowing dot wristwatch. It was exactly midnight. A mortar round screamed overhead and landed on the far side the airstrip. And then another and another. Without thinking he was up from his bunk. A tee shirt, fatigue pants and boots flew onto his body. There was another salvo of mortar shells and post haste Remphelmann found himself herky jerked on the floor. The LZ generator blinked out. He grabbed his flashlight and flicked it on. He unwound himself and raced into the hallway of the officers hootch.

"Douse that frigging light," Remphelmann heard Duvalier bark.

"What am I supposed to do?"

"You're an officer, damn it. Check on your men." It was Shinebaum's voice.

Remphelmann scurried through the little building into the open. The landing of the mortar shells and their bursting light gave him enough orientation to leapfrog across the parade to the ordnance hootch. The hootch was empty. He worked his way back through the thin series of buildings, the enlisted barracks and stumbled into the bomb shelter. He flicked on his flashlight.

"Holy Kerrville crap, sir, douse that light!" It was the comforting grandmotherly voice of Sergeant Shortarm. Ronnie snapped off the light.

"Who is here?"

"Everybody, sir. Me, Peckerwood, Gruntz, Heimstaadt, all the NCOs. Einstein, Boudreaux, Scheissenbrenner, Schweik, Apache Gonzalez-McGillicuddy. That's nine. All present and alive. Plus you. That makes nine plus one." Despite himself Remphelmann blipped on the flashlight and in an instant counted nine men. That left one short till he realized he was the tenth.

"Slap that beam off, damn it, sir." It was the voice of Sergeant Gruntz. The flashlight went blank. In the darkness the voice of Gruntz continued. "Sir, I transferred out of the infantry to the rear echelon mothers, so I didn't have to put up with this crap. Did you get my request for transfer?"

Back in the cemetery the 804th Viet Cong mortar team had been busy. They had silently crept from the village of Ap Boi into the graveyard. They had stealthily moved through the winding pathways and hummocks of the cemetery and found their clay-covered coffins. After a few shovels full of dirt were removed, the coffins were at hand. The quick set cement was mixed with a carboy of water dosed with calcium chloride, the better to make the concrete rapidly set. A bucket-sized hole was excavated. The cement mix was slopped in. The impromptu mortar tube was plopped butt-first into the concrete. An artilleryman, hiding his head under a blanket, had laid a crude aiming sight made of a piece of wood against the steel tube. Using a compass, a plastic protractor, a plumb bob and a match he had aimed the mortar barrel towards the LZ a mile away. They had settled back for a quarter hour while the concrete set up. The time appeared. The ten rounds from old man of Ap Bong Tra's coffin were hung and dropped, hung and dropped and went in a flashing arc towards both LZ Betty and LZ Bozo. They were quite inaccurate but that was not the point of the exercise. Just as the last round of old man's casket was let loose, the additional thirty rounds of the other box were on their way to the jury-rigged firing platform.

There was a pause in the ordnance bunker. Remphelmann asked what to him was an obvious question. "Sergeant Shortarm, should we move our men up to the perimeter bunker?"

"Holy Nacogdoches nits, sir. No. The infantry got control of the firing line tonight and they don't want us gumming up the works."

"I don't understand this," offered Heimstaadt. "Ich has been no Charlie cannon fodder. Ich been a vegetarian."

Boudreaux chimed in. "That done dere remind me of a story. Seems me and my cousin Pierre re-cedes to go to Ponchatoula to see Auntie Clotile. We get in Pierre's pick-um-up truck and..."

"Oh shut up, with that pick up truck crap, TeJean," exasperated Private Einstein. "Did my Uncle Newton Einstein ever tell you in high school physics that the energy of the mass of a moving object is proportional to its weight times its speed? That means one of those mortar rounds landing out there will slice you in fifteen pieces."

One of the mortar rounds from the cemetery took an errant

path from its intended trajectory towards the infantry side of the airstrip and landed smack on top of the sandbagged bunker. A horrendous reverberation knocked every man's trousers back into their pockets. The men inside did the herky. Sergeant Peckerwood called out, "Is everyone O.K? 'I'm O.K., you're O.K.' Just like that book I never read. Tennessee, where are you?"

Gonzales-McGillicuddy staggered up, deafened by the explosion. "Tennessee, hell, where is Truth or Consequences?"

Sergeant Gruntz felt the necessity to repeat, "My request for transfer..."

Schweik had to add, "I just broke starch and now my uniform has dirt from collar to inseam."

Lieutenant Trang Ngoc Trong was advancing up the slope to the LZ with two squads of infantrymen. It was against his better judgment to do so. He had been trained at the Ecole Militaire just outside Paris. Paris, at this juncture, would have been a better venue than advancing uphill from a graveyard into the teeth of the American's barbed wire. However, orders were orders. His orders were to go forward to within two hundred meters of the Yankee wire and spray the front line with as much lead as possible. His two squads had a light machine gun each plus ten trusty souls with AK-47's to provide cover. Some of the men lugged B-40 rockets. They snaked up through the ravines to a comfortable distance, emplaced and then let loose with a holy hell of machine gun, RPG and rifle fire. They did not care much what they hit. There was little to aim at in the darkness. The objective of the exercise was to spray and pray. They prayed. They sprayed.

A whole shower of bullets ripped into the ordnance bunker. Zips of lead screamed past the bunker and many dug into the sandbags. The simple Viet soldiers had no concept of what they were going to say, but somehow a resounding voice came up from them. Perhaps they had seen a John Wayne movie. Perhaps they had been coached. In one voice they called across the intervening ground. "Marine, you die! Marine, you die!" Someone had failed to inform them that they were facing army men. Hundreds of bullets smacked into the bunker with the rear echelon ordnance men.

The last scream of "marine, you die" and the last spray of AK light rounds and some heavier machine gun bullets came rather inaccurately over the bunker. At this juncture Scheissenbrenner decided to freak out. "What's wrong with these sons a bitches? We're army, not gyrines. If the bastards want to kill me at least they should get my service right. What's their problem? Maybe they're been watching some old Hollywood stuff on the late show?"

Sergeant Peckerwood made the mistake of remarking, "What the heck, Brownie? Maybe you should set them straight. Tell them off." Scheissenbrenner proceeded to do just that. He leaped up and ran to the exit of the bomb proof and began to yell at the Viet Cong.

"You stupid assholes, we are army, not marines! If you want to kill us, fine, at least call us by our right branch." Tracers zinged around Scheissenbrenner's head.

Sergeant Shortarm had the presence of mind to cinch up his flak jacket, duck out the revetment and snag the specialist by the boot. He dragged the vocal one back into the bunker. "Holy Alpine anuses, Scheissie, free speech done got its time and place!" The stocky NCO threw Scheissenbrenner into a corner of the bunker.

Back in the cemetery, Lieutenant Ngo, who was watching the mortar rounds plop onto the LZ, deftly came over and smacked the impromptu mortar tube back into alignment. His soldiers were continuing to drop rounds into the muzzle of the machine. The mortar rounds began again to arc over on the far side of the airfield. The rounds of both coffins were soon exhausted. He yelled to an aide, "Recall the infantry" and led his mortar men out of the cemetery. The call went up the line to the riflemen. They disappeared. They di di mao'd. As suddenly as the attack had begun, the attack was ended. Silence prevailed.

Back at the LZ the American infantry fire stopped. There was a dead silence in the ordnance bunker. It was over.

Chapter Thirty

Lieutenant Remphelmann began to settle into the daily routine of his duties. Every day brought new problems both in his small world and the small worlds of LZ Bozo and LZ Betty. The poor god forsaken infantry were sent out to Que Ell One and its nether reaches around Whiskey Mountain to 'clear and secure', or 'search and destroy' to no avail other than have men choppered back to Phan Thiet exhausted and spiritless. On a daily basis they went out and on the same basis they came back, short a man or two wounded or body-bagged.

Remphelmann soon learned that being an officer in the real army had nothing to do with heroic leadership or fine words that buttered parsnips, but the small time minutiae of daily duty. Making sure the men were fed and housed was a concern shared by all, especially by the men themselves. Soldiers are a self-sufficient, self-centered and self-comforting breed.

The young Keokukian found the worst problem in his narrow job was locating repair parts for his mechanics and having them forwarded to a seeming backwater. He sat at the feet of the master in this regard, Sergeant Shortarm. From him he learned the fine art of sending endless telexes and the grander art of getting on the poor telephone connections and screaming bloody murder. He could never summon the courage to scream obscenities at the top of his lungs, but he developed his officerly phone demeanor to the point where he could locate parts and demand immediate shipment.

One of the oddities of this practice was that he could call the Cam Ranh Bay supply depot and get parts, but he could never get any guidance or help from his putative battalion headquarters, from Colonel Slick to Captain Dunghill on down. At least on that front he was the loneliest man in town, a forgotten functionary at a forgotten outpost. He had on one occasion been forced to call battalion headquarters. It seemed that the inimitable Private Schweik came down with a stomach complaint, due to bad water and sticky heat and had been sent back to the hospital in Cam Ranh for a wonderful dose of anti-biotic injections and a short leave at the battalion sick bay for a rest. Remphelmann called his battalion HQ to check up on his armorer. He called and announced himself as Lieutenant Remphelmann, platoon leader in Phan Theit. The voice of the clerk on the other end said, "Who?" Ronnie repeated himself. The clerk continued to maintain non-recognition. Remphelmann then demanded to talk to Colonel Slick. After a judicious pause a voice answered. It was Captain Dunghill. Gruffly he asked who was on the line. Remphelmann repeated himself. He repeated his name, rank, and leadership position and inquired as to the status of Private Schweik.

"Who the hell are you?" Dunghill commanded.

Remphelmann like a broken record repeated his name, rank, assignment and his concern for the heroic Private Schweik.

"Ah, yes I remember." Dunghill coughed. "Remphelmann. You are the little twerp we eighty-sixed off to Bozo. I can't even remember what you look like. Colonel Slick is not available. He went off to a putting green and golf tournament at Long Bien and is not near a phone. What whiney little complaint do you have?"

Remphelmann repeated his request for further instructions and his concern for his armorer.

"Damn it, lieutenant, I don't even know or really remember where LZ Bozo is, and I don't care. As for this butthead Schweik, he's just a serf, a mere blip on the radar screen. Who cares about privates? By the way, Colonel Slick is going to come down to Phan Thiet in a day or two. He isn't coming to see you or any of the losers down there. He has arranged a meeting with General Kegresse to discuss an important strategic matter. Expect him by huey in a day or so. That's all." The phone line went dead.

Remphelmann was back on the phone in a second. This time he called the supply clerk in Cam Ranh. It seemed that there was a truck, a five-ton truck that was used to haul ammunition to Firebase Firefly. The clutch had gone up in smoke and seized. There was no way to send ammunition from the ammo dump at LZ Bozo out to the guns. Captain Lanyard had called and in his hollow voice insisted that the truck be made operational. That was the imperative on Remphelmann's list. The supply clerk promised that the clutch assembly, which weighed two hundred pounds, would be on the morning chopper. Remphelmann closed the phone call and told Sergeant Heimstaadt to stand by and await the repair part at daylight.

The next day came. The morning helicopter from Cam Ranh came in. Remphelmann was waiting in the 'Mudd Buck It' for the promised part. As the whirling blades chopped down, Ronnie clambered under the blades to grab the clutch assembly from the machine. Instead, what did he find? Colonel Slick in all his glory!

Slick dismounted like a roman centurion. Finding Remphelmann at hand he barked, "Who are you? You've got ordnance insignia on, you must be somebody under my command."

Remphelmann saluted. "Lieutenant Remphelmann, sir. I'm your platoon leader here in Phan Thiet."

"Oh so you are here to chauffer me to my meeting with

General Kegresse. I remember you vaguely, from my interview with you at Cam Ranh HQ. You are the useless little shit I banished to oblivion. Well, never mind. Are you prepared to jeep me over to the officers mess, so I can discuss weighty matters with the general?"

"No sir, I married up with this chopper to get a clutch plate assembly. Surely the clutch is on the huey."

The loadmaster from the helicopter sauntered by. "Hell no, we bumped your cargo. We were at maximum weight when the colonel showed up unannounced. It was two hundred pounds of cargo or two hundred pounds of officer. Guess what got bumped."

"Ah yes, rank hath it privileges!" Slick gloated. "Is that my jeep over there?"

Remphelmann was furious but held his tongue. The colonel went to the 'Mudd Buck It'. He discovered the rear view mirror as he plopped into the passengers seat. He carefully removed his hat, produced a comb and began to groom his spotless hair arrangement.

Remphelmann climbed into the driver's seat. "Sir," he asked. "I came here to the helipad to get a clutch for an ammunition truck. But now the part, which is needed desperately by the artillery, was kicked off so that you could fly on this helicopter."

"Lieutenant, you have no idea what is important in the upper reaches of the military. What is more important in the grand scheme of war, a colonel meeting a general to speak discretely together, or a clutch plate for a truck?"

"Here at LZ Betty, here at Bozo, here at Firebase Firefly, here where infantrymen slog and die, the clutch is more important."

"Nonsense, bull-crap. The higher level communication is more important than a few grunt lives." Colonel Slick finished his primp in the mirror. "So off we go. I'm to meet General Kegresse in ten minutes. Away, young man."

Remphelmann drove the colonel across the airfield. He kept obsessing on the fact that a vital piece of war material had been dumped to allow Slick onboard. They arrived at the officers club just as General Kegresse's helicopter touched down. Evidently it was an unplanned visit. Officers streamed out of the battalion headquarters. The infantry commander, Lieutenant Colonel BeLay, came bursting out of the situation bunker and began to line up in receiving formation with his staff. However General Kegresse exited his aircraft with nary a glance at his men, and swept into the club with Colonel Slick toadying respectfully behind. BeLay darted to Remphelmann. "Lieutenant, what the hell is going on?"

Remphelmann related Slick's unannounced appearance, the non-arrival of the clutch assembly and Slick's demand to be driven to meet Kegresse for 'a high level meeting'.

"High level meeting, my ass!" BeLay exploded. "Damn it, I'm the boots on the ground commander at this LZ and the frigging general doesn't even recognize my presence!" BeLay had worked himself into such a state that his face had turned beet red. Veins were popping out all over his neck and face. Every man present turned their view to the closed door of the officers club.

Kegresse had seated himself at a corner table. It being morning, the place was empty. "Damn, no air conditioning."

"I agree, sir," Slick offered.

"How about a drink, Slick. Scotch and water, and ice, if this hellhole has any."

"I'll call for a bar-tender."

"No, no witnesses, no eave-droppers. Go find the drinks by yourself."

Slick went behind the impromptu bar, found a bottle of Johnny Walker, club soda, glasses and even some ice. He swept all onto a tray and went back to Kegresse.

"Sit, sit, my dear Horatio, and make us a libation. You know it was a stroke of luck that we met yesterday at the golf tournament. Did you know that the golf course at Long Bien, designed and built by our heroic military engineers, is the only one in Vietnam?"

"I agree, sir."

"No wonder Vietnam is a third world country. Look at the terrain! Trees, pasture, dirt, sand, water hazards are here, plenty of servile slopes stand ready to caddy, but no golf courses. They deserve to be bombed back to the Stone Age, except that they are still in the Stone Age." Kegresse laughed at his little joke.

"I agree, sir." Slick had seated himself and prepared the drinks.

"So, as I said it was a stroke of luck that you and I were in the same foursome. It was a pity that we could not discuss the matter at length. Prying ears, nosey do-gooders. God, they're a pain in the ass."

"I agree, sir."

"I'll quickly recapitulate. Ever since I got in country, I've been hearing about the fabulous sums of money to be made in the heroin trade. I have made discrete inquiries. The usual method is having a graves registration type in Saigon fill an airtight aluminum coffin with two hundred pounds of the stuff, arrange fake paperwork and have it shipped out to the States. That is a brilliant idea. However, in the short time I have been here two things have transpired. First, I have developed a contact that can get any amount of the finest golden triangle heroin, 95% pure stuff. A hundred kilos for a paltry sum of dollars. Or two hundred or three hundred. Whatever I want. However the graves registration method is already spoken for. Thus I have a ready source of supply but I still lack a method of transshipment. Then again, a stroke of luck. I got to my exalted rank through a series of strokes of luck. This stroke, I met you at the golf soirée and heard your idea." Kegresse fixed himself another johnny and fizz and sat back.

"I agree, sir." Slick mixed himself a drink. "Now comes my method of shipment. Every replacement engine for any vehicle that comes into Vietnam is shipped in an airtight metal canister. Armored personnel carrier, deuce and half, track, ten-ton truck, even tanks have their engines sent in a metal box. When the engine is swapped out at a repair facility, let's say my repair facility, the old engine, greasy, muddy, filthy is put back into the original crate and shipped back to the United States for rebuild. Off it goes, generally to Rock Island Arsenal, Illinois, where it is directed off to sub-contractors for rebuild or re-manufacture. So my scheme is to fill a junk engine with plastic bags of heroin, stuffed to the gills with the white powder, white money, and fake paperwork so that it goes to a rebuild of my choice in Chicago who will be little other than a dead-drop. Thus we can have hundreds of pounds of the good stuff shipped direct from Cam Ranh to Chicago. If customs were to inspect the box all they would see was a greasy, filthy, mud incrusted engine. My lackeys will gut the engine of crankshaft, pistons, all the internal workings, stuff it with smack, replace the oil pan and slather it with crud. No one will be the wiser."

"And how much, poundage wise?

"I've done the volumetric and weight calculations already. A five-ton truck engine weighs over 1,100 pounds. I could hide four hundred pounds, no problem."

"Brilliant, brilliant, Slick."

"I agree, sir."

"Well, my helicopter awaits. I must be off. With luck I can make the lunch at the general officers mess. Medallions of filet mignon, wrapped in bacon, sautéed mushrooms. Sourdough bread flown in fresh from San Francisco. I'll contact you later with the finer details. We shall both be rich. After all, how could I retire on a mere general's pension?" With that, Kegresse swept out to his waiting helicopter.

Lieutenant Colonel BeLay and his staff were still at receiving formation. Kegresse ignored them and went into his huey, which went up into the blue.

Colonel Slick followed out and went straight to Remphelmann. "I ordered the supply chopper to wait until my return. I must be off to Surf City."

Remphelmann was in a quiet riot. He ferried Slick back to

the Bozo helipad. At the approach of the 'Mudd Buck It' the helicopter began to spool up its engine and engage its rotors. Remphelmann sat motionless in his seat. Slick removed his hat, re-arranged his silver hair in the rear view mirror and stepped out. He looked back at the hapless young man. "Lieutenant Rempelstilt, when a superior officer takes his leave, you are to salute." Grudgingly, Remphelmann saluted. Slick went into the belly of the huey. The rotors bit the air and in a cloud of red dust the contraption rose up and flew off. The helicopter made a beeline up the coast, following an imaginary yellow brick road to an imaginary palace of Oz.

═══ Chapter Thirty-One ═══

America's intelligence community, ensconced in the pentagon, beautiful suburban Langley, Virginia, and Foggy Bottom, District of Columbia, plus lesser-known venues of operation, such as the Chelsea Hotel in New York City and Heidi's Hideaway in Los Angeles, is never wrong. At the least, they claim an infallibility that a pope would blanch to venture. In Vietnam they were never wrong. Not once.

Thus when a coded message came through that the Russians were going to smash across Central Asia in an astounding blitzkrieg and Dieppe the Americans into the Mekong, or better yet Dunkirk them against the La Manche of the South China Sea, warning flags flew. Ambassadors quivered in their silk slippers. Generals packed their bags. CIA agents made arrangements to ship their paramours to Hawaii. Alas, the rumor proved such.

On the other hand, the best and the brightest of Harvard, Yale and Podunk State had a scathing disregard of the South Vietnamese intelligence community. After all, how could a ragbag of unintelligent orientals know any thing about their own country? After all, how could someone who spoke Vietnamese as their native tongue gather intelligence about the Stone Age rice farmers that polluted the countryside? What did they know about Marxist-Leninist-Maoist-Stalinism? The fact that the finest of Vietnamese leadership had been trained at the Ecole Militaire, the Sorbonne, and the Lycee was a further proof. After all, the mere whiff of pollution of the frog language into an oriental mind was a certain route to brain death. Added to that, that the jungle bunnies had been so indoctrinated by french-fried socialist thought processes, gave easy proof that the restless natives had no idea what side was up. What did the Vietnamese know about Vietnam?

So Lieutenant Ronald Reagan Remphelmann of the ordnance wound his weary way back to the officers BOQ as the sun threatened to set. He unclammed himself from his sweat, grease and dirt encrusted clothes and flip-flopped for the cold water shower. He was met by Lieutenant Duvalier of the transportation.

"Hey. P.T., what's happening?"

"Thankfully not a thing. The skinny from ARVN intelligence is that another push on Nui Ta Dom and Que Ell One is off for a couple of days. We look forward to a night's rest. Which brings up the subject of evening chow. Rather than the enlisted mess, or the horror of the officers mess, or the joys of C rations, I called Captain Manteca. He promised oodles of noodles. Spaghetti with spam chunks. Round steak fried in cottonseed oil. Dehydrated broccoli browned in beef fat. Freeze dried ham steak reconstituted in hot crisco. A repast fit for kings. The only thing we are missing is booze."

Ronnie showered and changed into a fresh set of starch. As he wandered back to the BOQ he saw that Manteca had delivered as promised. Laid out on the picnic table was a spread worthy of an English baron. There was even cole slaw to boot.

Shinebaum was there also. He also bemoaned that fact that there was no call for alcohol. At that unfortunate lament, Chaplain Captain Champagne roared up in his jeep. He had a huge plastic tub filled to the brim with Rochester Cream Ale and ice. Everybody moaned at the unwelcome appearance of the Holy Joe, but that was tempered by the huge quantity of canned cold American beer.

"May the Lord bless you and keep you! The angle of the dangle is proportionate to the heat of the meat! Up in heaven an angel I hope to moor, who prays like an saint, and screws like a whore." With that Chaplain Captain Champagne lugged the huge tub of cold beer on to the picnic table along with Manteca's smorgasbord. With a flourish he produced that now long forgotten instrument of joy and torture, a triangular beverage can opener. In those long past days before the self-opening can, beer was lodged in steel topped containers. The archaic instrument was designed to lever into and pierce a pyramid shaped hole into such relics as steel beer cans. "Behold the keys to the kingdom. Behold the entering wedge for Satan. Back in the real world modern engineering has just invented something called a pop-top can. It consists of a little lever on an aluminum lid. You flip a little tab and the can pops open. Amazing. Yet here we know nothing of God's newest works. Thus I present you all with the tool of true salvation. The church key." Champagne began to open beer cans at a prodigious rate.

All present began to dig into the picnic. Big Titty Mountain, the Phan Thiet cemetery and Que Ell One began to fade into the twilight's last gleaming.

What did not glimmer nor fade was the chaplain captain's sermonic mood. "Pray tell, young Lieutenant Remphelmann. What was Jesus's first miracle?"

Ronnie thought a second. "The miracle at Cana."

"And," prompted Champagne, "what was that miracle?"

Remphelmann thought two seconds. "At the wedding feast, Jesus turned water into wine."

"Proof enough," exclaimed the chaplain. "Let us drink deeply to the savior's primary manifestation."

Lieutenant Duvalier guzzled two cans at a swoop but paused long enough to remark. "I'm AME, African Methodist Episcopal, and being Calvinist in principal, and Southern Baptist in practice, I grew up in that milieu. If you have just one beer, you are going to hell and fry forever. If you give into the demon rum even to the point of a bottle of three point two, it's over, you are no longer of the Geneva elect." P.T. grabbed another Rochester Ale.

"Precisely my point", gloated the chaplain. "The way to heaven is to detour through hell."

Captain Manteca was dishing up food while guzzling the brew. "All this can penetration reminds me of the Uniform Code of Military Justice, you know, the war articles. Did you know that as a simplification of law to suit wartime combat zone conditions, that all sexual offices are subsumed under the general act of sodomy?"

Champagne burst into a gleeful laugh. "Oh tell me more, tell me more."

Manteca continued. "Yes, under article ten, section seven, any genital contact of any sort, whether consensual or forced, is simplified into the sodomy clause."

"Oh, I'm in heaven," squealed the chaplain.

"And the operative phrase is, get this, 'Any penetration, however slight, is sufficient to complete the offence'. That includes heterosexual, homosexual, or bestiary."

"Glory to god in the highest, 'any penetration, however slight is sufficient to complete the offence.' The hand of god moves in mysterious ways!" The chaplain exulted.

Remphelmann groaned silently to Shinebaum, who groaned silently to Duvalier, who groaned. P.T. saw the perfect opportunity to change the subject. He produced a bottle of nuoc mam and began to sprinkle it on not only his food but onto the plates of the others.

"Oy and gevalt," Shinebaum faked horror, "Is that stuff kosher?" He was spearing a slice of reconstituted ham.

"You've ruined my food," Manteca recoiled in fright. "It's that horrible gook fish head crap sauce!"

Duvalier paused and then elucidated. "Nuoc mam, sir, is not

fish head crap. It is a savory sauce used around the world in all maritime nations, from Japan to Spain. The Romans called it 'garum' and it was as highly valued as wine. The cognoscenti of Pompeii considered the fish sauce of Portugal the cat's pajamas. Do you want to know how it is made?"

"Spare me the details," interjected Remphelmann. "I was going past the nuoc mam factory yesterday with Sergeant Peckerwood. Even he gagged."

"Captain Manteca, do you eat canned sardines or anchovies?"

"Yes, the Norwegian kind. Delicious. But what that got to do..."

P.T. continued. "Nuoc mam is roughly the same. You take the finest freshest anchovies right here in Phan Thiet, caught off the coastal banks, and bring them to market. There they are rinsed, drained and mixed with dried sea salt in a two to one ratio. Then they are packed into wooden vats, and mellowed for a half year. The fermented mash is then decanted into earthenware crocks and aired out."

"Puke!" Manteca was nauseated.

"The resulting mixture is then colandered though cheese cloth, bottled and shipped."

"Vomit!" rejoined Champagne. "Rotten fish juice. The work of the devil. Where is Rasputin when I need him?"

"No," Duvalier rejoined, "Fermented and savory."

"Then why doesn't it stink of dead fish?" Ronnie asked. He had actually tasted the sauce on his plateful of food.

"Good nuoc mam smells like the salty sea, not like fermented anchovies. It has the fresh taste of the open ocean. Up north in China and such, they dilute it with soy sauce. But here in Vietnam and places south the local folks prefer it neat."

"Oh," groaned Manteca, who nonetheless tasted the stuff. "That's why the Roman Empire fell."

Duvalier continued unperturbed. "The three premium brands in Vietnam are from Phu Quoc, Phan Thiet and Nha

Trang. However, the connoisseurs all judge Phan Thiet's as the best."

The party continued. The chaplain captain kept opening Rochester Cream with his church key. All drank and ate, and drank to amazing excess.

Shinebaum was beyond repair. "Ronnie, do you know why my own family calls me 'Porky'?"

"No," slobbered Remphelmann.

"Shut the shit up, you imprudent little brat. That's a family skeleton in the closet."

Champagne added his two cents worth. "Ronnie, you never asked me my domination. I belong to the same line as Saint James of Swaggart, the 'Church of the Holy Hooker'. Glory amen! Let me put my glory pole into her glory hole! All praise to the sacrament of the perpetual orgasm! Let my testicular juice unload into any female's fertile field!"

Manteca could not resist. "According to the UCMJ, 'any penetration, however slight, is sufficient to complete the offence'".

Remphelmann had double vision. "I've lost track of the conversation."

Duvalier was up to the confessional. "You know, I never trusted white trash."

"Trust, my Heeb ass," Shinebaum chimed in. I don't trust American Jews. American Jews are powerless pussies. Whenever there's a problem in Israel, the slime ball New York kikes raise one hand and plead 'I'm an American, what's Jerusalem got to do with me?' And when there's a problem in America, they throw up the other hand and whine 'what's the United States to do with me? I'm a Jew! Next year in Jerusalem!' Gutless wonders, American Juden!"

At some point, all the patio characters disappeared. Champagne drove away. Duvalier, Manteca and Shinebaum were gone in the darkness. That left Remphelmann alone in the gloom. He stumbled his fingers around the last of a warm beer can. He looked out into the blank darkness, beyond the sandbag revetments, beyond the razor wire, and beyond the cemetery to the small ribbon road lost in the black of night. There in the swimming nothingness was Que Ell One.

=== **Chapter Thirty-Two** ===

Graves Registration is a polite euphemism. It is really the nasty business of collecting corpses or pieces thereof from a scene of military carnage, identifying the bodies or portions thereof and finding some way to store them in a sanitary manner until a sane disposal method can be worked out. Thus a graves registration unit has a happy blend of meat wagon haulers, morgue attendants, forensic sleuths, cold storage technicians, shipping clerks, and only on rare occasions the task of actually registering a grave. The misnomer in modern times dates from a late great war, also known as World War One. The heroic cannon fodder of that trench war could not be shipped back to the United States for a proper patriotic burial. It was decided to follow the English method, that is, to cram the hero into a makeshift wooden coffin and arrange the Spartan in a convenient field. Six feet deep, six feet from tombstone to tombstone and a spacious ten feet between rows. A geometric landscaping was the order of the day. The gravediggers had the duty of registering the plots, thus the moniker. This method of burial, no doubt gleaned from Hamlet's gravedigger and sexton, man and boy for thirty years, if lucky, could yield Yorick's skull for a soliloquy. This way of burial ran true from

World War One through World War Two and Korea. Modernity intervened. With the rise of portable refrigerated morgues, new forms of pressure injected formaldehyde, the infamous rubber zip lock body bag and jet planes, the Athenian could be whisked back to the USA and buried at home in a spiffy aluminum coffin. Such are the wonders of modern military mortuary science.

Of this, Remphelmann had been informed, if not forewarned. What he did not know was the untimely appearance of Captain Manteca in the ordnance repair yard on a certain day. Remphelmann was minding his own business and the business of his men. He knew that there was a big push on, on Whiskey Mountain and Que Ell One. The helicopters had been loading grunts out since early light. The artillery, both from LZ Betty and Firebase Firefly had been whacking out rounds at a prodigious pace. Something big was unfolding on the Big Titty, but neither Remphelmann, nor his trusty Indian scout, Sergeant Shortarm, knew what was afoot.

Thus, untimely ripped from the womb, the fat abortion of Captain Manteca came screaming into the ordnance yard. "Die, we are all going to die!"

Remphelmann seemed to recall Manteca's pat phrase and rejoined. "Yes, at some point, but what is the point?"

"All shit has broke loose on Big Titty. General Kegresse has launched another one of his Gettysburg attacks in the wrong place. The bodies are everywhere. We need body bag backup."

"What has this to do with me?" Remphelmann protested. "Graves registration is a quartermaster responsibility."

"I sent the graves registration squad out to Ap Noi Lon. They're stuffing guts like crazy. But at the devil's dogleg Charlie planted a land mine. An armored personnel carrier, a M-113 went up, flipped turtle and there's a hell of a mess."

"That sounds like a personal problem, Captain Manteca."

"It was until Colonel BeLay called me on the horn. He said to dragoon the ordnance people if necessary. So you are necessary."

Remphelmann protested again. "I, we, know nothing about graves registration."

"No problem, over at the stiff cooler, the last man left there is Private First Class Frankenfood. Take at least three men; go to the graves registration hootch. Get Private Frankenfood to organize a shovel party. A huey will be there in ten minutes to ferry you out. Collect the bodies from the road blast and wing back what's left."

"What about you?" Ronnie snapped back.

"Me, me? I've got noon chow to organize! BeLay speaks, you snap to and obey."

Remphelmann gathered up Einstein, Schweik and Gonzales-McGillicuddy and hustled them over to the graves registration hootch. A helicopter was landing on the nearby helipad. Remphelmann went into the GR facility. Private Frankenfood was in the process of shifting a body-bagged corpse off a gurney and double stacking it into a refrigerator drawer containing another occupant. "Howdy and duty, and happy day, lieutenant. Can you help me stack the hamburger onto the lasagna? Get on the far side of the gurney and help me heave." Remphelmann positioned himself on the opposite side of the trolley and helped boost the body bag onto the down stairs resident. Private Frankenfood slammed the drawer shut as frost boiled out of the cooler.

"I've got three men, plus myself. Manteca says to help. What can we do?"

"I can hear the meat wagon chopper touching down, sir. You and your men need to grab two of those stretchers over there plus six body bags off that shelf and heft them into the huey. Plus see those shovels over there? Best take four."

Remphelmann called in his men and got the requisite equipment loaded onto the waiting helicopter. As soon as the men were positioned inside, Frankenfood darted out of the mortuary hootch with a loose armful of industrial rubber gloves. He hopped aboard. The door gunner of the huey twirled a finger at the helicopter pilot and the machine was airborne.

The devil's dogleg, so far away on the pavement of Que Ell One, was only five minutes airtime as the carrion bird flew. The helicopter did a quick recognizance circle around an armored personnel carrier that was blown to bits in a ditch just off ambush alley and made a tight landing on the roadway. With professional aplomb Frankenfood was out of the chopper and waving Remphelmann and his men to follow.

The personnel carrier was a total mangled mess of bent aluminum plate, caterpillar tracks and twisted machinery. Evidently a land mine had been planted under Que Ell One, and when it exploded the M-113 went up like a tin can over a firecracker and twirled off the road into an unrecognizable lump in the roadside gully.

"Thank god," Frankenfood exulted as he surveyed the carnage. "At least the explosion blew off the rear loading ramp. Easier ingress, as we say."

Remphelmann was appalled. The land mine had bent the floor of the personnel carrier into a vee shape. Inside were not the bodies of men; there was a potpourri of unrecognizable bloody body parts. Einstein looked and puked on his own boots. Gonzales–McGillicuddy turned and gagged at the sight.

"Isn't it odd," Frankenfood remarked to the young lieutenant, "That when a soldier is alive, he isn't worth shit, but the second he dies, he has to have the highest regard from society. When he's alive, screw him. Now that he's bacon bits he is top priority. We have to make a noble show to prove he did not die in vain."

Remphelmann stifled his urge to retch. "To hell with the speeches, private, what do we do?"

Frankenfood cast a practiced eye on the scene. "Well, sir, I can see eight boots. And I can see four steel helmets. And I can see four rifles. So get your men to lay out four unzipped body bags here on the ground. Then we don gloves and shovel. If you see two size ten boots, left and right, throw them on the rubber. Then we work our way in. Look for pants and shirts and belt buckles, and if you can find torsos or heads, try and figure what jigsaws up with what. If you can find dog tags, that's a help. When we have the big chunks divided up on the zip locks, then we simply scrape up the guts. That's a matter of proportion rather than identification. Figure that the average grunt weighs 160 pounds. If we can scrape enough offal out of the wreck to equal a hundred pounds per hero, we have enough to zipper up and haul away. We'll take the dog food back to LZ Bozo, freeze it, and ship it to Hawaii. They'll try to make sense of what's in the bag. Honolulu will then repackage what they can and aluminum box the remains. Back to mommy and daddy in Bakersfield and a hero's funeral."

Remphelmann and his men did as told. The four body bags were quickly filled and zipped up and on the chopper. The detail and their grisly cargo were quickly back at the graves registration helipad. The bodies were soon in the stiff cooler. Frankenfood pulled a case of Texas Star beer out of a hiding place and threw it on top of a morgue tray of triple stacked corpses. "Hey, lieutenant, you and your men were a real help. Come back in an hour or so and you got cold beer."

Schweik, McGillicuddy, and Einstein were dazed and wandered back to the ordnance area. Remphelmann paused outside. He stood and looked out over the perimeter, past the Phan Theit cemetery, towards Nui Ta Dom Mountain and Que Ell One. Then he vomited. He vomited again. He vomited until he dry heaved. Then he could vomit no more.

Chapter Thirty-Three

Something again had happened on Que Ell One. What it was, was not clear to the rear echelon mothers at LZ Bozo. True to form Lieutenant Remphelmann knew nothing. It was the morning after Ronnie's induction to graves registration. The sun was not even above the horizon. Sergeant Shortarm knew nothing, and only hung his head, which was a surprise. Remphelmann asked Lieutenant Pierre Toussaint Beauregard Duvalier, who maintained a noble silence. He asked Lieutenant Moise Aaron Shinebaum, who only groaned. Something had happened and it was not good.

"Crap." That was the word from Private Einstein. "Crap, sir, crap again. It seems that General Kegresse countermanded ground orders again yesterday, and the latest push on Big Titty went big time wrong again."

"Tell me more."

"As my uncle Leibnitz Einstein liked to say, the monadological interactions of mind and matter..."

"Spare me the physics crap, Einstein. What do you know?"

"Thirty-seven dead. And eighty wounded. That's out the grunt battalion's strength of eight hundred men."

Remphelmann swore. "Oh, my God."

"What we did up yesterday on the devil's dogleg, the body bag detail, was a mere fractal. The whole clearance of Que Ell One went up in a pure bloody far space vacuum energy mist. And who is to blame? The skinny from the privates is Kegresse. Of course the brigadier is looking for scapegoats. Again."

Major Dufuss had learned from the regulars across the airfield that a formal morning roll call was to be held, replete with starched uniform formations and flying flags. The reason was to honor the honest dead, the hapless thirty-seven decent souls that had sacrificed all for the military glory of a few yards of highway asphalt. Blown to bits on Que Ell One were good young men, altared up to the greater glory of war. There was even to be a twenty-one rifle salute.

Major Dufuss, oblivious to the real meaning, decided in his schnapps addled wisdom to imitate. The men of LZ Bozo were to be rousted out early from their bunks, told to dress their best and stand by.

Major Dufuss's brown-nosed driver sent word that all FSA officers were to assemble at the Bozo HQ for the most important of meetings. Manteca, Shinebaum, Duvalier and Remphelmann duly reported to the major's inner sanctum. The sun began to simmer over the South China Sea. Arranged in two neat rows they sat and waited, and waited.

The door splattered open and Major Dufuss stumbled in. "As you were," he grandly announced. He went straight to his desk and flipped completely over it, disappearing behind its gray immanence. He reappeared, found his chair and seated himself "Gentlemen, be seated." The officers present were already seated. "It has been bought to my attention that there were a few casualties yesterday on the highway."

"Sir, thirty-seven dead and eighty wounded."

"Is that larger than a dozen?"

"Yes sir, by a few."

"So it has been brought to my attention that a memorial

morning formation will be held across the airfield to commemorate those fallen few that gave their last measure of devotion to our noble cause and the security of my pension. That ceremony is to be held at 07:30 hours. Complete with a playing of taps and a twenty-one-gun salute. In mirror of that grand display, our rear echelon troops will execute the same ceremony. That is, to come to attention in parade ground formation and bid fondest farewell to those who served so valiantly to protect the officers club." The assembled junior officers had nothing to add. However, Major Dufuss did. He launched into a political diatribe. It is sacrosanct that military officers hold themselves aloof from politics and adhere to the narrow duty of war fighting. This was lost on Major Dufuss.

"What we have here is an ocular mal-occlusion of retinal and political renalism. It should be obvious that the Vietnamese have no concept that we are dimming the war, much less the battle of Que Ell One."

"Sir, yes sir." Manteca offered.

"Thank you, captain. As you and I are students of philology and language deviation, you will of course observe that the root word behind intellectualism is from the Sanskrit, entre-delictable-ism, thus dialectics. The whole font of the misconduct of the war is that we have all these inter-rectal pointy-headed ineffectual intellectuals back in Washington doing all the tactical thinking for us. If left to the men on the ground, clear soused-a-phoned men with practical priapism would do the planning. The root word says it all. Vodka equals victory. Washington jerks are junk. The east coast cone headed indirectuals who read all the smart ass print like the New York Times and Harper's Fairies, and Playboy have no idea about the facts on the ground here in Korea."

"That's Vietnam, sir, not Korea."

"Shut your insolent mouth, fat boy."

"Thank you sir. And the reason for you calling this meeting?"

"To co-ordinate a morning formation to honor the dead,

damn it! Parade formation in fifteen minutes." Dufuss attempted
to open his desk where the vodka and tomato juice were stored.
Alas, he had mislaid his key. He tugged forlornly against the
drawer handle. "Gentlemen, as you were, you may be seated.
I mean you may be excused." The four officers exited as Dufuss
fought the good fight against the locked liquor cache.

It was seven fifteen. 07:15 hours. The four young officers had
only ten minutes to inform their men, get them out of quarters or
early work and arranged on the parade ground. The men did so,
unwilling schoolboys dragging themselves not into the teacher's
presence, but the semblance of a line. Captain Manteca positioned
himself in front of the gaggle and waited for the appointed time
and the imminent arrival of Major Dufuss. Dufuss wandered
out of the command hootch and made a beeline for the unseen
officers club on the far side of the airfield. When he discovered the
airstrip in front of himself he about faced and went in measured
step towards the cemetery wire. The assembled FSA troops were
out of the corner of his beady eye.

In the distance the bugle call of assembly blared for the unseen
grunts. Captain Manteca, with a rare degree of puissance, stepped
to the center of the gaggle of men and officers. He thought a
moment. Was he call 'Battalion, attention?' He had no battalion
of eight hundred men in front of him. Was he to call 'Company,
attention?' He had not the 200 hundred to so address. Where
was Major Dufuss to relieve his distress? The redoubtable major
had about-faced at the barbed wire and was wandering towards
the officers club again. Finally the captain of butter bottom
proportions thought 'Group!' Thus prepared he yelled in his best
parade voice, "Group..." Remphelmann heard P.T. and Porky
bark, "Platoon..." so Ronnie barked or yelped in a high voice,
"Platoon..." In his best voice Manteca cried "Attention." Instead
of the crisp snap of well-shined heels clicking into attention there
was the dull gravelly sound of muddy boots dragging across the
dirt.

Manteca, sweating the fat man's sweat, was at a loss. In the distance he saw Major Dufuss wandering back toward the parade line, and was temporarily heartened by Dufuss's near arrival. However the major staggered in his peregrinations and went off toward the FSA headquarters. Not to be embarrassed, Manteca thought through the drill manual and the order 'Open, ranks,' came to his commodious mind. So he squeaked, "Open..." The three lieutenants relayed the command. "Open..." The only difficulty was that there were no ranks to open. "Ranks!" the captain concluded. The three lieutenants echoed. The confusion amongst the rank and file was predetermined. There were no files to open. Some of the men stepped three steps forward, some two steps, while others moved not at all.

Manteca was out of ideas. In the distance he saw Major Dufuss circumambulating the headquarters hootch. At the loss of another drill ground command, he croaked, "Inspect the Guard." Duvalier and Shinebaum immediate saluted, did an abrupt about face and moved to the lead of each uneven file. Remphelmann clumsily imitated them. Following Shinebaum from the corner of his eye he slowly stepped one by one in front of his men. First from Sergeant Shortarm, to the other non-coms and on down to the glorious privates. All that remained at the end of the line was Private Schweik. Schweik said. "Sir?"

Remphelmann snapped back "You are not to speak while under inspection, private."

"But," Schweik persisted. "Sir, lieutenant sir, begging the officers pardon, sir! If raise my hand, can I be excused? I don't want to be here in this man's army any more. If I raise my hand, can I go home?"

"Request denied." Remphelmann said with sadness.

Manteca was beside himself with drill and parade formality. Major Dufuss had made a circle of the FSA hootch and disappeared inside, obviously to unlock the cosmic secret of how to re-open his vodka tomato repository.

Then happened one of those atmospheric auditory oddities that only military men understand. Far away across the airfield the roll call of the grunts was heard. An officer called out in solemn tone the name of each sterling young man who had perished the day before. "Not present, but accounted for," was heard from an equally somber sergeant. Then there was a seven-gun salute fired by riflemen into the empty air. This was repeated two more times until a total of twenty-one rounds had resounded into the morning mist.

"Assembly, dismissed!" Manteca cried in relief. The whole gaggle of rear echeloners melted in a scurry in the red dust.

Lieutenant Remphelmann was left standing alone at the head of a non-existent formation. The twenty-one guns had become a memory in the distance. All he could think of was the body bags on Que Ell One.

Chapter Thirty-Four

The rainy season began to show. First there was a day of drenching rain, followed by a respite. Then it deluged for three solid days and nights, only to break again.

The total environs of LZ's Betty and Bozo turned to a quagmire of red sloppy mud. The whole of the Bozo work and parking compound became a mass of slithering goop. The ordnance men pulled an armored personnel carrier into the yard for transmission repair only to have its tracks sink into the ooze until the machine's belly plate sucked into the mud. Sergeant Shortarm, usually not prone to musing, mused to his lieutenant. "Sir, holy McAllen mudpuppies, sir, we're up to our bungholes in clay soup. If'n we could somehow get the army eagle to shit a hundred tons of gravel and make a real pole barn to keep the rain off, mebbe we could get some work done."

This set Remphelmann to thinking. There was a rock outcropping at the far end of the airfield. Maybe engineers could blast and pulverize rock and spread it on the yard. Sergeant Ciezarowski informed him that a huge store of telephone poles, roof trusses and sheet tin was moldering away at Long Bien. Maybe Lieutenant Duvalier could back haul the materials on one of his trips. Sergeant Peckerwood learned that a platoon of engineers was hard standing a chopper pad at Ni Hau Tran not far away. They had the equipment and the expertise. Maybe they could be detailed to do the job. There were a lot of 'maybes'.

Remphelmann was not dissuaded. He broached the subject to Duvalier, Shinebaum and Manteca at the evening patio. All were enthusiastic about the idea. However the captain was suddenly a wet rag. "You see, you can't just shit these things out. There has to be an engineering order from the engineer corps office in Cam Ranh." Remphelmann formulated a plan. He would go to Cam Ranh, enlist Colonel Slick's imprimatur, go to the engineer office and request an engineering order.

Remphelmann called his headquarters in Cam Ranh the next morning. True to form nobody knew who he was, or where Phan Thiet was. Ronnie had finally learned the fine art of jawboning and ultimately got Slick on the phone. Much to the lieutenant's surprise, the colonel not only remembered him but also was also enthusiastic about hard-standing the work area. "Get on the noon taxi, come back here to Surf City and I'll have a driver fetch you and take you to the engineers. This will be a real feather in my cap! It'll look like I'm doing something for the boondockers."

In short order, Remphelmann gathered his flak jacket, rifle, and a civilian ditty bag with a clean change of clothes. He thought he could change out of his mud-spattered fatigues at some point. Sergeant Shortarm limousined him down to the helipad just in time to pile into the noon huey and immediately Remphelmann was up and away.

Ronnie was now no novice helicopter passenger. He had been well seasoned by his numerous flights up and down Que Ell One, but he was not one to be jaundiced by aerial views. The chopper sped north along the coast and Remphelmann re-marveled at the lushness of the countryside. Soon the peninsula of Cam Ranh and its beautiful bay came into sight. The huey fluttered down into the army compound and alighted at a helipad. Remphelmann, ditty bag, steel pot, rifle and flak jacket, dismounted.

The same motor pool jeep driver that had met him before, Private Oliva, the Jersey City greaser, Private Oliva of the pimply face, the oleaginous duck-ass haircut, and the smart-ass attitude, greeted him. "Say hey, lieutenant." The private slacked off a perfunctory salute. "You still alive? Skinny is all youse cannon fodder down in Phan Thiet are getting whacked on a regular basis!"

Remphelmann was now at ease with disrespectful enlisted men. "All in a day's work, Oliva. It don't mean nothing. How's things here in real echelon paradise. Is the surf up?"

"I'm from Jersey City, lieutenant, us block kids don't surf anything but the Atlantic City boardwalk and women's boobs. I been told to take youse to see Colonel Slick, but he isn't around the battalion HQ. He's up at the field grade officers digs hiding from the heat in his air conditioned trailer." Remphelmann clambered into Oliva's jeep and they bumped away. Rather than turning to the industrial complex of warehouses, company streets and sundry headquarters, Oliva turned up a paved road that wound up a low range of hills. To Remphelmann's surprise there was a neat mobile home sub-division set on a wooded hillside overlooking a small lake. The mobile homes, set on winding lanes, had neatly manicured lawns. An abbreviated golf course of four links, a driving range and a putting green lay just downhill. He could hear the unmistakable popping of numerous shotguns from the woods next to the lake. He could hear the cicada like drone of air conditioning units installed in the trailers.

Olivia caught Remphelmann's surprise and explained. "Ain't this the frigging life of riley, lieutenant? Youse see that if youse a field grade officer and above, you don't have to sweat life out in a hootch. Majors, light colonels and up get quartered in two bedroom mobile homes shipped straight from the States. Hot and cold running water, electricity twenty-four hours a day, air conditioning, complete kitchens with utensils, civilian beds, the whole works. They even get food delivered hot from the officers club. Skinny is they get hookers delivered hot from off post. But what the hey, rank got its privileges. You got an air conditioned trailer down there in Phan Theit?"

"No," Remphelmann said ruefully.

Olivia pulled into the mobile home park and stopped at one of the pristine trailers. An officer came out of the door, collins highball glass in hand. Remphelmann recognized the red faced Captain Dunghill. Dunghill shouted out, "Don't drop the twerp here, for god's sake. Colonel Slick is down at the skeet range, take the drip over there." Olivia faked another sloppy salute and drove away. They wound through the mobile home park and skirted the little golf course. The greaser continued his impromptu tour lecture. "They say there is a full golf course in Long Bien. The dinks, god bless them, haven't ever heard of golf, so there's no indigenous golf courses in the whole country. Here, the bigwigs had the engineers cobble up a driving range for the brass. Rank hath its privileges. Plus this little lake, Tiger Lake, got a boat dock, sailboats, and skinny is they had it stocked with fresh water fish so the highest of the high can dangle an angle. But for me, I like the skeet range. Free shotguns, actually riot guns, free ammo from army stocks, how they get clay pigeons, god knows. Rank hath... but lo and behold, Colonel Slick!"

The jeep stopped at a professional looking skeet range, replete with white painted fences delineating semi-circular firing lanes, which were paved with gravel. To one side was a white enclosure spewing clay pigeons on a regular basis. Slick and another colonel were crying, "Pull" and shooting away with glee at the traversing clay discs. Remphelmann got out of the jeep, slung his rifle over his flak jacket, and approached his commanding officer.

"Sir, Colonel Slick, sir. Lieutenant Remphelmann of Phan Thiet, reporting as ordered."

Slick sneered at the young man. "Damn it, Remphelmann, why are you lugging that flak jacket and rifle? Does this look like a war zone? And look at your uniform! Covered with mud! Slovenly, slovenly!"

Remphelmann had no answer other than to say, "Sir, you

ordered me up here to address the issue of getting a gravel hardstand and a pole barn for my men down in Phan Thiet, at LZ Bozo."

"Ah yes, now I remember. My career curriculum vitae needs to show that I take care of the losers in the field." Slick interrupted himself to call to a sergeant hidden in the white shack. "Pull," the colonel ordered. A clay pigeon flew from a spring loaded throwing arm and sailed across the skeet range. Slick fired a blast from his shotgun and missed. He turned to Oliva. "Driver, shuffle this thing off to the corps engineers office, and dump him on Major Bridgeless."

"Are there any other instructions, sir?" Remphelmann asked.

Slick again called, "Pull." Another clay pigeon flew. Slick shot again and missed again. "No, lieutenant, go to the engineers and explain the need for gravel and tin roof in your god-forsaken forgotten little mud patch. By the way, my sources tell me you actually like it down there at LZ Betty, and going into the field. Do you need to see the shrink? Do you have a death wish?"

Remphelmann found himself suddenly angry. "Sir, instead of concerning yourself with skeet and golf and lakes stocked with fish, couldn't you concern yourself with winning the war?"

Slick sneered at Remphelmann. "Lieutenant, we are! I repeat, we are! We are winning the war!" He again called "Pull." Again a clay target flew from the trap shack and again he missed. Slick turned back to the junior officer. "That is all, lieutenant. Leave my presence."

Remphelmann went back to the grease ball's jeep and they drove off to the engineers office. Again they transpired though the industrial zone and went up another hill. At the top was an amazing sight. It was a building of grand ante-bellum proportions, painted gleaming white, surrounded by porches and columns, plus huge plate glass windows with commanding views of the whole Cam Ranh peninsula. It looked for the entire world like an upscale hilltop restaurant that would have graced a swank Georgia country club. "What in god's name is that?" Ronnie marveled.

"Youse jerking my chain, lieutenant? That's the officers club. I figured that would have been your first stop when you hit country. What you being an officer and all."

"It's obscene", fumed the officer. "What a waste of materials and money."

At the bottom of the drive that led to the restaurant was a row of concrete office buildings, far more substantial than the hootches and Quonsets that graced the industrial park. Oliva pulled up to the office complex where a sign proclaimed:

II Corps Permanent Engineering Office
U.S. Army MACV
"Building a Better Vietnam"

Oliva paused the jeep long enough for Remphelmann to get out. "Say hey, lieutenant, my cousin Vinnie from Newark is a cook up there in the officers club. I can sneak in the kitchen entrance and have a quick visit, if it's alright with you." Remphelmann acquiesced.

Remphelmann went in the glass door of the engineers office. Insufferable air conditioning iced the air. A surprised clerk saw the young man's flak jacket and rifle. He greeted him with "Sir, we don't normally allow firearms in here."

"I'm just in from the field, and I've no place to secure my weapon."

"Well, you're an officer, I guess it's O.K. What do you need?"

"I'm here to see Major Bridgeless."

"One moment, sir," the clerk went to the back of the office complex to a private office and returned. "The major will see you now."

Remphelmann went to the office door. Just outside a haggard lieutenant sat at a steel desk. He was an emaciated man not much older than Remphelmann. His pock marked face bore the brunt of many acne scars. He stood. "Remphelmann, I presume? My name is Amidenus, engineers. You're the one looking to gravel and monsoon roof that area down in Phan Thiet."

"Yes."

"I've done a bit of work myself down at LZ Betty. You got a tough row to hoe. But give the major your best sales pitch."

Remphelmann went into the major's office. Major Bridgeless was a tanless toad of a man who barely seemed to notice Remphelmann as Ronnie saluted and stated his need for hardstand and rain cover for his beleaguered men. Bridgeless stood and turned away and looked out a large plate glass window at the officers club on the hill. Then Bridgeless launched into something of a practiced diatribe.

"Stop there, lieutenant. I've heard these whiney, driveling requests before. The situation is this, and straight from pentagon directives. The war is all but won. The grand plan is to do here what we have done in Japan and Korea, improve permanent infrastructure for a long-term occupation. It is not in the budget to provide temporary facilities at god forsaken little mud holes like Phan Thiet. The powers that be and the budgets that be can't waste the taxpayers money on keeping slime ball little mechanics out of the mud in the field. I'm seriously over budget here at Cam Ranh. For example, I've ordered travertine marble flooring from Italy to tile the general officers dining room at the officers club, but it is delayed in transit." Bridgeless swept his hand out the plate glass window at the abomination of a building on the hilltop. "Priorities are priorities! Officers club construction is more important than mere war conduct construction."

Remphelmann lost his cool again. "Major, you say the war is over. I don't see that. All around us, men are dying, men are slogging, and working and fighting in the mud, men are doing duty, even bleeding, in the pouring rain. Why can't we concentrate on winning the war, before we concentrate on building officers clubs?"

Bridgeless went ballistic. "What? What! That's defeatist talk! What's happening in the field is mere mopping up operations! If you are not able to win the war in your mind, seated at the officers club bar, how can you affirm the final victory on the ground?"

"Begging the major's pardon, sir. Have you ever been out in the field? Men are fighting and working and dying. Men are getting stuffed into medivacs and body bags. Have you ever been in a combat zone?"

"I am in the combat zone!" Bridgeless sputtered. "All of Vietnam is the combat zone. Cam Ranh is the combat zone. The officers club is the combat zone!"

"I pity you," Remphelmann said quietly.

Bridgeless literally leaped over his desk, grabbed Remphelmann by the collars, and began to scream, "Defeatist! Commie sympathizer! Fifth columnist sub-human!" Bridgeless's neck veins were bulging purple.

"Sir," said Remphelmann quietly, "Can you release my collars so I can breathe?"

At this fortunate juncture Lieutenant Amidenus entered the office. "May I intercede, major?"

"Intercede my ass! Get this loser creep out of my office!" The major released his grip on Remphelmann. "Out, out, damned spot!" Remphelmann and Amidenus beat a hasty retreat. Remphelmann did not salute as he exited. Bridgeless turned to his window view of the officers club. "Oh," he lamented, "Where oh where is my marble, where is my travertine?"

Amidenus escorted Remphelmann back through the office and out the door into the afternoon sun. "Do you have transportation?" the acne faced asked.

I let my driver go up to the officers club kitchen. Seems his cousin is a cook up there. He ought to be back soon."

"Then," offered Lieutenant Amidenus, "Let me show you something. I have my jeep here. Let's take a little look-see at something." The two got in the engineer's vehicle and drove over an intervening hill. Below them in a sandy wash was a barbed wire enclosure the size of a football field. Inside, parked bumper to bumper, were hundreds of construction machines. Bulldozers, paving machines, concrete trucks, backhoes, rock drills. All lay rusting in the sun. "See all this," Amidenus offered. "These machines are nearly brand new. All of them have less than 500 hours on the clock. They were used to build the airfield and the facilities here at Cam Ranh. Brand new and deteriorating into junk."

Remphelmann was puzzled. "Why don't we turn all this over to the Vietnamese? They could use them for nation building. You know, for building houses and roads and schools and that sort of thing. I mean aren't we here to help the Vietnamese? All that 'hearts and mind' propaganda?"

"Look", Amidenus offered. "The whole idea of this war is to make money for the big companies back in the States. The manufacturers of this construction equipment make huge profits sending millions of dollar worth of equipment here to be used once and then written off. The point of the war is not to win hearts and minds as you so naively put it. Nor to stop the spread of communism, or stop the political dominoes from falling, or any such thing. The point of the war is a charade to make money for the fat cats."

"But people are dying. Vietnamese are dying. Americans are dying."

"Not a problem. The taxpayer foots the bill for the death and the dying and the veterans after-war expenses, and the merchants of death book the profit tax-free." Amidenus drove a chastened Remphelmann back to the engineer office. Oliva was there. "One other thing, Ronnie, I've been down to LZ Betty. I know you need that gravel and roof tin and pole barn. You'll get it."

"How? Major Bridgeless..."

"Screw the creep. I know how to forge engineering orders. Your men need help."

"Thank you."

"No need to thank me, my sympathies are with the men who are living and dying out in the field. Look at it this way. Instead of friends in high places, maybe the grunts and the rear echelon assholes might think 'they have a friend or two in low places.'"

There was no need for Remphelmann to salute a fellow lieutenant, but he did anyway as he transferred into Oliva's M-151. Amidenus went quietly back into the engineer office.

"Say hey, Mr. Remphelmann. Hot damn! My cousin Vinnie was on duty and the chow for tonight is grand! Boneless chicken breast, rice pilaf. Parsley potatoes! Damn you officers and your privileges. Vinnie let me scarf down the early cooking. Should I chauffer youse up to the officers club so you can get first dibs?"

"No," mused Remphelmann. "I want to go home."

"I want to go home too! Jersey City, here I come."

"No I don't mean that. I want to get back to Phan Thiet."

"You're a wild and crazy guy, lieutenant. The sundown chopper to Betty is leaving in fifteen minutes. Sure youse don't want to camp over here in Surf City and party?"

"I want to go home."

Oliva fired up the jeep and blasted down the road like a demon on the New Jersey turnpike on his way to Atlantic City. The sundown huey to Phan Thiet had already begun to chop air as the jeep roared up. Oliva leaped out, elbows out, palms flat, waving the door gunner down. "One hundred fifty pounds of meat for Miss Betty!" he screamed at the man. The gunner gave a thumb up. Remphelmann leaped in. The pilot bit air again and Remphelmann was in the blue in an instant.

Remphelmann sighed. He was going home. Home to Phan Thiet and Que Ell One.

Chapter Thirty-Five

Remphelmann had arrived back in Phan Thiet, crashed on his rack, slept the sleep of the hopeless, and arose the next day. Bleary, jet-lagged, culture-lagged, he went to the ordnance hootch. Private Einstein was typing away at the ubiquitous army forms and whistling to himself. This was a bad omen.

"Good morning, Vietnam. Good morning, LZ Bozo, and good morning, Lieutenant Remphelmann!"

Ronnie sensed a trap. "Out with it, Einstein."

"You want the physics, or the poetry, or the facts?"

"Crap on your mother's grave," Remphelmann found himself swearing.

"Thank you, sir. First the physics. It seems my uncle Niels Bohr Einstein got all bollixed up with the dual quantum problems of what comes first, the chicken or the egg, and it's necessary corollary, why did the chicken cross the road. So he crossed the road, only to find his doppel-ganger there to meet him. It's called time simultaneity."

"Einstein, you've been too frigging long in country."

"Thank you, sir. Second the poetry. Shakespeare's sonnet number thirty, from which I elide:

'When to the sessions of sweet silent thought,
I summon up remembrance of things past,
And moan again the fore-bemoaned moan,
And weep afresh from woe to woe new paid...'"

"Bite my ass, Einstein," Remphelmann burst out. "Get to the point."

"General Kegresse is coming today for a full scale inspection of the LZ. He had another big time loser day on Big Titty Mountain and Que Ell One, and he's loaded for bear, looking for scapegoats. 'Oh, what tangled web we weave...'"

Remphelmann swore for the third time, "Crap, shit, and damn!"

Sergeant Shortarm, ever the bull in china closet, came bounding through the door. "Holy Sherman shit-cakes, lieutenant, Brigadier Kegresse..."

"I heard already."

"And Major Dufuss done called a meeting for the rear echelon officers at his command hootch, in ten minutes."

Remphelmann set his jaw and went towards the FSA building. Duvalier, Shinebaum and Manteca fell in with him. A portent of doom gathered over their weary heads. They filed in the door only to find Major Dufuss's office door open. Dufuss was seated at his desk. He had his face buried in his hands. Tears were leaking through his fingers and he was moaning over and over to himself, "My career, my pension."

The four stalwarts trooped in and stood at attention. Dufuss was oblivious to their presence. Presently Captain Manteca coughed politely and said, "Major, we are here."

Dufuss looked out from his palms. His eyes were sob red and trickling freshets of moisture. "Gentlemen, you may be seated." They sat.

Dufuss wrung his hands in a pitiable manner. "Gentlemen, as we speak, Brigadier Kegresse is doing a formal parade inspection of the infantry battalion. He is not pleased. He stuck his incompetent nose again into yesterday's combat operations on Whiskey Mountain, which resulted in the predictable result. From what I hear, he is berating every officer in the battalion in the most un-officerly and demeaning manner in front of their men. This is a disaster of the first water. What is worse, is that..." Dufuss looked at his wrist watch, "is that he is due over here in ten minutes to repeat the dressing down with us, the poor innocent forward support troops! All of you are to have your men in parade formation instantly. I will be out shortly to head the unit. Gentleman, that is all. Go, go quickly, and may god have mercy on our immoral souls."

As the officers filed quietly out Dufuss was seen attempting to open his liquor drawer. It was jammed shut. He grabbed his wooden nameplate from the front of his desk, and using it as a crowbar, pried the offending metal open with a resounding bang. His trembling hands went to his medicinal goods. As the last of the officers exited, he was heard to lament, "My career, my career."

The officers rustled up their men to a semblance of a parade line, privates to the end and sergeants to the head of each file. Then they stationed themselves three steps ahead and centered on their respective units. Dufuss appeared, buoyed by his excursion into the liquor cabinet, and made front and center of the formation just as Brigadier Kegresse rolled up in a jeep.

Kegresse was standing up in the vehicle with a scowl on his face, obviously trying to imitate a General Patton grand arrival. He had evidently seen a recent Hollywood movie and thought imitation the sincerest form of flattery. The brigadier dismounted, deus ex machina, and swaggered up to Dufuss. Swagger he did, as he carried a swagger stick in his hands. He had an iron grip on the stick with his right hand and was thumping it ominously into the palm of his left. A swagger stick, though beloved of British and German officer types, was and is frowned upon by the U.S. Army. The display smacks of class division, of which America is thankfully absent. Kegresse went to Dufuss, who was literally quaking in his boots.

Dufuss attempted to salute. Instead he stabbed himself in the eye with the gesture. "Sir, Major Darrell Dufuss, sir! The forward support area troops are ready for inspection, sir!"

Kegresse flicked his swagger stick in a nonchalant manner. He saw the four junior officers three steps behind Dufuss and three steps ahead of their men, centered on their respective soldiers. Kegresse sneered at Dufuss. "Tell these useless excuses for officers to close file behind you. I want to talk to them." Dufuss stood frozen in high anxiety. He hadn't the least idea how to order such a maneuver. Thankfully the junior officers displayed individual initiative and swept shoulder to shoulder behind the craven major. Even at that, Kegresse ignored them, stepped to their rear and trooped the line of enlisted men. He walked the file of men, ordnance, transportation, quartermaster and military police, looking at each with the highest distain. At the end of the line, he about faced and walked back with the same contemptuous air. That is until he got back to Private Boudreaux. Boudreaux, in a fit of idiot's delight, spoke up.

"Howdy doody, General."

From the corner of his mouth Sergeant Shortarm barked, "Shut up, TeJean."

Kegresse stopped and stared Boudreaux down. He read the privates nametag. "Boudreaux, huh? Louisiana cajun."

"I swan, General, how'd yawl know?"

"I'm never wrong, private."

"I hain't never seen a general close up before, general. That reminds me of a story, sir. Seems my cousin Pierre and I decides to go the Louisiana state fair. We gets in Pierre's pick-em-up truck and..."

"For god's sake, shut up, Boudreaux! Shut your useless trap." Shortarm snarled again from the side of his clenched teeth.

Kegresse swaggered back to the line of junior officers. He scrutinized them. Major Dufuss still stood three steps in advance of them, and was petrified, staring into empty space. Kegresse planted himself squarely on the officers and sneered again.

"Useless, damned useless!" he announced to the four within earshot of the enlisted men.

In the enlisted row, Sergeant Peckerwood blew such a fuse at this breach of military decorum that he fainted and fell, and crumpled soggily into the mud.

"First, you, you tub of lard. How much do you weigh?"

"Two hundred ninety, sir."

"I order you to lose seventy five pounds immediately."

"Sir, yes sir."

"Second, you four eyed little stripling. How old are you?

"Nineteen, sir, actually my birthday is two days from now and I'll be twenty."

"I have no room in my army for boy lieutenants, but I'm stuck with children and sundry incompetents. How can you see out of those coke bottles?"

"I might be near-sighted, sir, but I rifle qualified twenty shots dead center at two hundred meters."

"Another smart-ass adolescent."

"Sir, yes sir."

"Third, and you?"

"First Lieutenant Moise Shinebaum, military police. Road convoy security."

"You cowardly heebs couldn't shoot you way out of a paper bag. You're a disgrace to the officer corps."

"If you say so, sir. I noticed you like to fly over Que Ell One, but when was the last time you put boots on the ground around there?"

"Impertinent talk from an untermensch. "Fourth, speaking of untermensch, what are you? No, don't answer. You are that uppity nigger I remember from my last briefing here."

Duvalier decided to jerk the general's chain. "Sir, First Lieutenant Pierre Toussaint Gustave Duvalier, transportation corps, at your service, sir. But I must ascertain to the esteemed general that I am from the state of Illinois. According to the present statutes of the aforesaid state, my last negro ancestry was my great-grandmother, who was an octoroon from Louisiana. Thus I am legally a white person."

Kegresse rocked back on his heels if only for a moment. "Louisiana! Illinois law! Then tell that cajun from Louisiana to front and center," the brigadier fulminated. Boudreaux was soon at foot and was delighted to be the center of attention. "Now see here, my little colored officer, my little Lieutenant Flip. This is a man from Louisiana, a man, not a buck. He is white and you are black. Period, end of sentence."

Boudreaux in all simple-minded sincerity piped up. "But general, sir, I hain't white, I'm black. You see my great-gran-mama was an octoroon from Illinois, and 'cording to the miss regurgitation laws of the sovereign state of Louisiana, any black blood in the family, no matter how far distant down the family tree, done here do qualify me as a colored fella. Practically, I'm 110% cajun, but legally I'm a negro, ah-guar-on-tee."

Kegresse was not prepared for such wisdom from babes. "Let me get this straight. This lieutenant here, looks black, acts black, talks black, is black, but is legally white. You, Boudreaux, look white, act white, are white, but you are legally black."

Boudreaux beamed. "Yes sir, general, sir. An' nicest thing about bein' colored is that I got natural rhythm."

Whatever failings Kegresse had in tactical understanding, he knew he was verbally boxed in, and retreated forthwith. "That is all, private!" The cajun disappeared. The brigadier stiffened. He cast a haughty glance at the four officers and again huffed loud enough so that the enlisted men could hear. "Yesterday's abysmal performance on Whiskey Mountain and Que Ell One was due, not to my explicit, clear, and brilliantly conceived orders, but due to the incompetent execution by the officers on the ground. That includes you worthless rear echelon mama's boys, you sniveling little pack of octoroons, fat babies, striplings and gutless kikes. Henceforth my orders will be obeyed!" With that Kegresse wheeled, stomped to his jeep, stood Patton-like in the passenger seat, swept his swagger stick like a field marshal's baton, and was driven away.

The entire formation hung in deathly silence, first for a minute, then two. Captain Manteca whispered to Major Dufuss, who was frozen in attention staring forward into space. "Major, sir, it's time to dismiss the parade." There was no answer from the redoubtable Dufuss. Manteca repeated the prompt. There was still no movement on the major's part. The fat captain gathered his bearings, about-faced and yelled, "Group, dismissed!" Shortarm and Einstein grabbed the crumpled form of Peckerwood from the dirt and hauled the unconscious form away. The other enlisted men evaporated in a heartbeat.

The four officers with great wariness approached the statue-like form of the major. Dufuss was catatonic, rigid, and blearing obliviously into the distance. Manteca fronted on the major and waved his hand before Dufuss's eyes. There was no response, not even an iris quiver. "Stone cold into the ozone," the chub remarked. He pushed on the major's chest and Dufuss rocked back like a toppling pillar. Duvalier, Remphelmann and Shinebaum caught him as he fell. He was rigid as a log. "What do we do?"

Shinebaum responded. "Let's heft him up and take him back to his office." This they proceeded to do. The four young officers hoisted Dufuss coffin-like onto their broad shoulders and dead-marched him into the FSA. Once in the office, they attempted to put the brave soul on his feet, but he toppled over. "What do we do?" Manteca repeated.

Duvalier had the best idea. "Let's prop him on the wall and run like hell." They propped Dufuss at a thirty-degree angle, nose first. When they let go, the magical body wedged itself against the surface like a piece of wood.

"Gentlemen," Manteca announced, "Extra-ordinary times call for extra-ordinary action. I have been sequestering a bottle of Martel brandy under my bunk for the most perilous of times. That time is now. I propose we run like hell and uncork that bottle."

"The motion is seconded." Shinebaum seconded

"The motion is passed," Duvalier concluded.

The four piled for the exit in a four stooges rush. Dufuss was left leaning against the wall, stiff as a carp. The officers did not double-time, they ran for the BOQ.

Chapter Thirty-Six

It was two days after Kegresse rained on the parade, in a figurative sense, that it began to rain on the parade ground, literally. Not raining, not pouring, but deluging Noachian monsoon cloudbursts. Gully washing, streaming, and rivering heavens of unending water zipped open in torrential founts on the humans below.

The day Kegresse's joyful bouquets of unbounded love were handed out, Duvalier and Shinebaum had led a convoy out of Phan Thiet to Saigon on Que Ell One, slightly buoyed by a healthy snort of Martel. It was not soldierly to snap a quick one before work, but again it was extraordinary times. What was wonderment to Remphelmann was the safe return of Porky and P.T. from the uninviting gullet of the road. What was more than wonderment was that both men came storming after Ronnie.

"For god's sake, Remphelmann! What the hell did you do?" Shinebaum swore.

Hell if I know, what did I do?"

"For god's sake, Remphelmann, we got to Long Bien and we had engineers yelling and screaming to load up, priority one! Telephone poles. Pre-mixed sacks of dry concrete. Roof trusses.

Sheet tin. The whole nine yards. You not only got your one uncircumcised monsoon barn, but two. Whose ass did you kiss up in Cam Ranh three days ago to make this happen?"

P.T. added, "A regular pain in the transportation ass, Ronnie. Three, count 'em, three flatbeds of construction material. A cornucopia of ready-made super hootches. Who's ass did you kiss up in Cam Ranh three days ago to make this happen?"

The superman of all sergeants, Sergeant Shortarm, leaped sandbags and tall buildings in a single bound and ran up to the three.

"Holy Port Arthur pimple-poppers, Lieutenant Remphelmann! Who's ass did you kiss up in Cam Ranh three days ago to make this happen?"

"What are you saying?"

"Sir, two hours after midnight the whole 444th Engineer Company came into the LZ, went up to that rock outcropping south of the airstrip and is getting prepared to blow the whole thing to smithereens. They's company sergeant was yelling at me where the hell to spot the rock, dump the gravel, build the maintenance sheds and the whole texican enchilada."

At that moment a tremendous explosion went off at the distant rock pile. The crew looked down the length of the airfield. Even as the dust and rock flew, bulldozers and front-end loaders were scooping rock into one end of a portable rock crusher while dump trucks were filling up on the other side with the macerated stone. Within minutes the dumps and an accompanying grader were in the drenching rain spreading the gravel out on the mud rut streets and work areas. More engineers appeared and with a truck mounted posthole digger drilled holes. Other sappers with a forklift yanked telephone poles off of the flatbeds and vertically positioned them into the holes. Yet another crew bucked hundred pound bags of ready-mix off another trailer into a motorized cement mixer, which slopped wet concrete to form the post bases and a concrete floor. Yet another crew craned roof trusses into place and power nailed sheet metal roofing onto them. Within an amazing grace of two hours, the whole of the support area yard was graveled, hard-standed, monsoon roofed and done. A hard-bitten engineer captain stormed into the area and demanded that a certain Lieutenant Remphelmann had to sign off on the engineering order. Ronnie trepidated himself into the engineer's presence and signed a formidable piece of paper. The sun burnt engineer swore. "Damn your soul, lieutenant. I don't know whose ass you kissed up in Cam Ranh, but now you got your devil damned gravel and rain cover. You're either a kiss-ass or one mean ass-kicking son-of-bitch. I never had a hotter engineering order than this one." With that the whole of the 444th Engineers drove into the noonday spitting rain and disappeared up Que Ell One.

All the men of LZ Bozo were ecstatic. They began to drive trucks, jeeps, and armored carriers up and down the formerly muddy premises, crunching the gravel into a smooth pavement. They whooped and hollered and honked horns. Sergeant Peckerwood, uneasily recovered from his fainting spell on the parade, danced a jig up to Ronnie. "Damn my Tennessee derriere, I don't know whose ass you kissed up in Cam Ranh three days ago, but thank you! Whose ass did you kiss, by the way? You must have friends in high places."

Remphelmann recalled the acne scarred Lieutenant Amidenus, who had promised to forge the engineering order. "No, Peckerwood, I don't have friends in high places, you have friends in low places."

Remphelmann suddenly felt sick. Ever since coming in country he had shrugged off heat exhaustion, doubtful food, diarrhea, sleep deprivation and honest moments of fear. But he had never felt sick before. Then he suddenly remembered. It was his birthday. He was twenty years old. No one else knew or cared. Perhaps his mother or father or grandmother remarked the day, but they were millions of miles and memories away from his reality. He waited until Sergeant Peckerwood had left and then he doubled up with cramps. Ronnie found out his platoon sergeant. "Sergeant Shortarm, I don't know what's up. I feel like crap. Maybe I've got the flu or something."

Shortarm was wonderfully supportive. "Holy Dennison dingle berries, sir. You ain't no malingering son of a bitch. If'n you all feels punk, feel punk. Maybe go home and grab your bunk."

Remphelmann did just that. He went to the officers hootch and lay down. The rain was deluging in torrents. He lay on the bed, listening to the water pelt the roof. Then he did something he hated, dreaded, and was loathe to do. He began to introspect. 'Why am I here? What am I doing here? What am I doing? What is this I've gotten myself into? What is meaning? What means life? What means death? What is puking over body bags? What is the reason I've humiliated myself to achieve this parlous state? What is Que Ell One? What is Vietnam? What is America? What is that weird feeling I get when I'm shot at? What, what, what?' He wanted to vomit, but realized there was nothing to vomit but his own soul. Remphelmann was a decent middling Protestant, but he obsessed on Saint John of the Cross, the Spanish mystic, and John's description of the 'dark night of the soul'. Empty, forsaken, having had a taste of spiritual agape, only to lose it, candle-less in the lack of light, lost to the foundations of his soul.

The rain continued to drench down. Remphelmann was seized by an immense claustrophobia. He staggered off his bunk and went into the BOQ's little dayroom. He saw the bottle of Martel resting on a side stand. It was still one-third full. He grabbed it. He wanted to guzzle, but the ghostly specter of being a barracks thief came to mind. There is nothing lower in life than a barracks thief. He consoled himself that Manteca had left the brandy for public consumption and grabbed it. The rain was hammering on the tin roof. Ronnie stumbled out the door to the 'Mudd Buck It'. Gonzales-McGillicuddy had fitted the canvas bow-hoop top the day before and it was reasonably dry. The lieutenant fired up the machine and drove along a muddy track to the far end of the airstrip.

He found a parking vista that gave a view of the whole LZ. Despite the horrendous downpour, flights of hueys were taking off from the infantry side of the field. The mortar platoon began to hang and fire four-deuce ammunition into the sky. In the distance he heard the echoes of the howitzers at Firebase Firefly. The rain cleared only for an instant and he saw roiling swirls of black smoke where the artillery was striking on the side of Whiskey Mountain. He uncorked the brandy and did not sip, he chugged.

The alcohol did no good. His mind raced with thoughts and images. 'Why were we fighting over this useless mountain and its insignificant road? Why, day after day, week after week, did the army shove the Viet Cong off Que Ell One, declare victory and leave, only to have the Cong sweep back out of the Le Hong Phong Forest, retake the road, declare victory, and leave? Why this endless seesaw of blood and intestines of young men, both American and Vietnamese, both corn farmers and rice farmers, over a filthy piece of asphalt? Why?'

The demons of war would not leave his head. He gulped the bottle again. 'Why? What horrid misanthropic streak of madness in the mind of man would make mankind do these things to one another? Why the waste of human life, why the waste of man's economic treasure? Why the waste of men and women's hearts? Why the waste, why the consummate stupidity of whole nations in driving the Alpha of destruction to such a pointless Omega?' Remphelmann drank again and realized he had emptied the bottle. He restarted the jeep and wended through the pouring sheets of rain. He found himself navigating his way by drunkenly paralleling the barbed wire entanglements of the western perimeter. A World War One British song or ditty began to surge though his drunken brain.

"Don't ask where the sergeant major went,
He took no leave to the ville of Ghent.
Don't ask where the sergeant major went,
I'm sure he's not too far.

He's not a spying from the churchyard spire,
He's not trench crawling in the muddy mire.
He's not home drinking with the county squire.
He's a hanging on the wire."

The vision of his graves registration duty flopped into Remphelmann's mind. It flopped into his mind like flopping a rancid steak before a junkyard dog. A vision of human lungs, human legs, human heads, human hearts hanging on the wire, like so much damp laundry, steaming their last humid human body heat into a fruitless air.

It took every ounce of Remphelmann's addled brain to find his hootch. He stumbled into it and aimed for his cubicle, which to his swimming brain now resembled a sarcophagus. He saw the bed, his homely bunk, but never made it. He collapsed corpselike on the concrete floor. He had a fleeting horror of nightmares, but even that passed and he slipped into unconsciousness.

Part the Fourth

Our Young Hero Gets A Vacation From Que Ell One To The Mountains

Chapter Thirty-Seven

Sergeant Shortarm was holding a telex in his hands as Remphelmann entered the ordnance hootch. A telex was something printed out on a yellow sheet of paper, rather like a telegraph bulletin. Things like this were delivered through a signal corps detachment teletype writer machine, guarded by competent clerks, encoded, passed by cryptography, decoded, and had the same moral force as a signed typed-in-triplicate order. Telephone orders paled in comparison. Shortarm puzzled his short brain. "Holy Hondo horse heinies, sir. Look at this."

The teletype read,

FSA BOZO ORD DET.STOP. IMMEDIATELY SEND TWO TRACK MECH TWO WHEEL MECH ONE ARTY MECH. STOP. NECESSARY TOOLS PARTS AND RESPONSIBLE OFFICER. FB DA LAT. NO DELAY HELI TRANSP CLEARED MOVEMENT NOW. STOP. REPEAT NO DELAY. STOP. HIGHEST PRIORITY.STOP. NO INTERVENING HQ. STOP. SIGNED GENERAL GEARLOOSE ORD COMMANDING

The telephone rang. Shortarm grabbed it. "Bozo Ord... Hell

289

if I know! Do the math. Six men, personal gear, flaks, pots, rifles, figure 250 a man, that's 1500 pounds. Hell if I know...! Tool chests are heavy. Figure one wheel at 300, one track at 400 and one arty at 300. That's less the bore scope, which is another 200. Figure 1200 pounds. Hell if I know! All I got is this piss yeller telex. No other info. We don't know where Da Lat is, who we gotta support, what their equipment is or what's broken... Hell if I know! We can't estimate repair parts weight till we know what we need, you frigging idiot. Can you lay on a re-supply chopper from Long Bien later, if they got the parts? Hell if I know! Tell me what you know." Shortarm listened intently and then spoke again, "Yeah, and your grandmother sucks little green wienies!" He slammed down the phone.

Remphelmann had gone to a series of maps thumb tacked on the hootch wall. He found Da Lat, which was a town in the Central Highlands about sixty air miles to the north. There was a small civilian airfield and an area marked Firebase Da Lat with a helipad.

Ronnie was now a seasoned professional and took charge. "Look, sarge, here's Da Lat. Rustle up Boudreaux and Gruntz for tank repair, Heimstaadt and Gonzales-McGillicuddy for trucks, and Scheissenbrenner for artillery. I'd rather have Peckerwood for gun repair but he's out at Firebase Firefly. I could send you as responsible NCO but then that leaves Bozo naked. I'll go. What was that phone call?"

"That was the helicopter company dispatch. They got a Chinook laid on to land here in thirty minutes. They're trying to cram 14,000 pounds into a 12,000 payload. But here's the skinny. There's a huge VC attack near Da Lat. Kegresse, that idiot, has been ordered to move a whole battalion of his 999[Th] Infantry out of Long Bien into the gap, to support the 2nd of the 604th which is already there. Plus the Arvin's got a whole brigade, 3000 men, working the hills west of the town. It's awful, I guess. Charlie's creaming everybody's ass straight through the grate. But we're knocking Charlie's pants in the pavement."

Remphelmann mused aloud. "No intervening HQ, thank god. That means I can leave Colonel Slick out of the loop. Thirty minutes to get men and goods down to the helipad. Put a rocket up the men's asses. It's time to get the hell out of Dodge."

Twenty-five minutes later Remphelmann, his stalwart men and their equipment were spotted at the helipad. Also there was a detachment of five medics with case after case of medical supplies. There were two quartermasters with a small trailer-mounted water purification unit. A truck from the ammunition dump backed up, its bed full of boxes of machine gun ammunition. A large cargo helicopter with a boxcar like body and two enormous rotors set fore and aft came in for a landing. It was the Chinook. The blades did not stop spinning. A rear ramp lowered. Remphelmann, his men, and their equipment charged in followed by the medics and their gear. The quartermasters dragged the water machine into the belly of the beast and began to lash it down. The Chinook loadmaster was screaming bloody murder. He had a clipboard and pencil and was scribbling figures like mad as he estimated weight and balance. He paused long enough to add his sums. Then he motioned to the ammunition truck and counted off boxes of machine gun rounds as ammo humpers loaded the rear of the machine. At a certain point he drew his forefinger across his throat. The loading stopped. The rear ramp went up. The Chinook lumbered heavily into a light monsoon rain.

Remphelmann was seated at the front cargo door, next to the door gunner. As the Chinook sweated itself into the air, directly below him was the cemetery and the little town of Phan Thiet. He incongruously thought of Keokuk. The cargo chopper made a heavy, ponderous climbing arc toward the north and the Central Highland Mountains. Remphelmann looked again as the rain spewed beneath his view. He could still see the dim trace of Que Ell One.

Da Lat is the most beautiful town in all of Vietnam. Located 5000 feet above sea level in a lush mountain setting, it is situated where three river valleys converge. Surrounding the city and its enfolding mountains are glorious teak forests full of three hundred year trees, tea and cinnamon plantations, and the odd wheat or barley farm. A great part of the city's charm is its climate. A mile high, the terrain offers a cool European climate, with fine misty rains, romantic pea soup fogs, and nighttime temperatures sometimes close to freezing.

The architecture is delightful. The invading French, eschewing local building styles, built the town up from a hill station and lumber camp in grand French provincial style. The city is built of carefully cut stone, the two story houses covered with red terra-cotta roofs. The various sections of the city hug the terrain in an organic manner, with the side streets zigging and zagging any which way on the hilly topography. The main thoroughfares boot lace down the slopes of the three valleys to a grand finale where the three rivers meet at the city park. Any snail slurper would feel immediately at home, and if they ignored the quoc ngu Vietnamese lettering on the shop signs, could easily mistake it for a snug little town in the Terre de la France, or the Pyrenees du Haut.

One of the oddities of the town's existence is that it owes its founding, of all things, to the Great European Bicycle Craze of the 1890's. The French had made numerous attempts to colonize Vietnam ever since 1847. They took Saigon in 1859 and then didn't know what to do with it. Tea, silk, and cinnamon exports could barely pay the imperial bills. The Gauls haphazardly and in often comic-opera style extended their operations until they completed the take-over of Cochin, Annam and Tonkin in 1874. Nonetheless, Europeans considered the country a backwater. That is until the bicycle craze.

The safety bicycle, the bicycle as we currently know it with equal sized wheels and chain pedal drive, was invented in the 1870's. Mr. Dunlop, of perfidious Albion, invented the air filled rubber tire, the Brothers Michelin patented a superior version in 1891 and suddenly the world wanted bicycles. A problem was the lack of rubber. The only source was the Amazon. Both British and French stole cuttings and seeds from the secretive Brazilians and planted the caoutchouc wherever they thought it would grow. Vietnam blossomed with a million acres of rubber trees and the boom was on. Newly minted rubber barons infested Saigon and built lavish villas and lascivious life-styles. To escape the steamy flats of the Mekong delta, they built a cog railway to Da Lat and started a mountain retreat in the cool mist of the hills. In those heady days, a Frenchman was not a Frenchman unless he owned a palace in Saigon, a beach house on the sea at Vung Tao and a villa in Da Lat. For some obscure reason, by 1954 all the French had left.

The Chinook bearing Lieutenant Remphelmann and its enthusiastic cargo of rear echelon mama's boys made a slow sweep over Da Lat. The monsoon rain, misty at this altitude, had broken. Ronnie had an eyeful of the town, and the battle in the distance.

Black puffs of artillery smoke were blowing though the jungle. A flight of four Thunderchief jet planes, nicknamed 'Thuds,' swooped out of the sky and laid neat rows of napalm into the trees. The cargo chopper went down the valley and came on the firebase and landing zone. There was a traffic jam of epic proportions at the small helipad. A short distance off, a battery of howitzers was blasting rounds at something six miles away. A flight of eight hueys was circling, landing one at a time to disgorge their men. Squads of infantrymen were disembarking, running to the side and re-grouping. Then it was the Chinook's turn. Remphelmann had wormed his way to the back of the cargo bay. As the chopper landed and lowered its ramp, he leaped out. A captain, obviously a helicopter pilot, ran up. Amid the pandemonium of movement on the ground and circling aircraft overhead, Ronnie and the LZ master quickly conferred. An instant later, Remphelmann was back in the Chinook yelling orders to everybody, whether he knew them or not. Every man jack heaved to. Within seconds all the men had gone aft, grabbed the machine gun ammo boxes and piled them at a safe distance from the helipad, then returned and man-handled the purification trailer down the ramp and into a muddy parking area. Back again, and all the medical supplies and the medics were into a waiting ambulance. Lastly they lugged the ordnance tool kits off to the side. Remphelmann gave a high sign to the Chinook loadmaster, who waved back and the machine chopped away. Another huey landed and began the same routine.

Ronnie pointed a hundred yards away. There was a clump of broken down vehicles, their mission. A Patton tank, three armored personnel carriers, five trucks and a howitzer. The mechanics swarmed over the machines, parts manuals in hand. Within thirty minutes, Ronnie had a complete listing of the repairs needed. At a dead run, he headed off to a signal corps tent which bristled with antennas, wondering how and where to transmit his needs. He fished in his fatigue pocket and came up with a crib note of radio connections that Sergeant Shortarm had scribbled.

Inside the radio shack, to his relief, sat a signal clerk, sitting in front of a huge transmitter, who beckoned him. Soon he was on the right frequency to Long Bien, barking out descriptions and part numbers. The good news was that all parts were in stock. The bad news was there could be no delivery until ten hundred hours the next morning. Remphelmann flew out of the signal hootch and bee-lined back to his men. Midway he realized his men lacked food and shelter. They hadn't thought to bring C-rations much less a tent. He saw the LZ commander waving off the last of the helicopters. He ran up to him, asking for advice.

"God blesses you rear echelon mother's abortions. The problem is solved. MAVC in town has taken over the Nuoc Lan Hotel as a billet. See that convoy forming up? Pile your men in one of those trucks and go to Da Lat and get the four star Michelin guide tour. The frigging grunts get to sleep in the mud and you ass-holes get a French hotel!"

Remphelmann did not pause to contemplate. He got his men and their personal gear, climbed in a truck and soon the ad hoc convoy had conveyed them ten kilometers up the valley, into Da Lat City and were dumped outside the second best hotel in town, the four story, four star pride of Da Lat, the Nuoc Lan.

The men lugged their gear into the hotel lobby. The marble accoutrements were much the worse for wear. Instead of a maitre'd hotel at the front desk there was an MP of decidedly less hospitable temperament. Remphelmann went to the room clerk and stated his case. The case was granted and room numbers issued. Four men to a room, army bunks included. The MP announced army chow in the grand dining room at 17:30 hours.

Boudreaux, ever the idiot's delight, exclaimed. "Ah gar-on-tee! I hain't never seen such. My Auntie Philomena, she say such exists in New Orleans, but I hain't ever seen! That reminds me of a story. Seems my Cousin Pierre and I decides to leave Grand Coulee for Baton Rouge and..."

Sergeant Gruntz barked. "Shut the shit up, Boudreaux." Gruntz turned to Remphelmann. "Lieutenant, I transferred from the infantry to the ordnance to get out of this kind of crap. You're holding on to my request for transfer. Have you signed it yet?"

Remphelmann turned to the mal-content. "Shut the shit up, Gruntz."

They went upstairs and found the rooms. The premises had been stripped of most civilian furniture. One room had six army bunks. Remphelmann counted off his junior men. Ronnie and Heimstaadt, being the senior NCO, claimed the other room. There was a French iron hoop double bed and an army bunk in the room, which faced onto the main street. The room had double swing French doors opening onto a small veranda. From their second story perch, the lieutenant and the kraut could see down the gorgeous valley views where the three rivers confluenced at a lake in a park. It was a view fit for royalty.

The men reassembled and they trooped down to the grand diner for dinner. At the usual army steel table smorgasbord steamed a seven-course French restaurant meal. Shit on a shingle, army bread, sheet iron fried potatoes, chicken stew with lead dumplings, oven baked hamburger patties, a simulacra of apple cobbler, and the piece de resistance, uncle sammie grease.

Remphelmann went back upstairs. The sun was setting. He opened the veranda doors to find three chairs tucked on the narrow balcony. He sat. Again, in the wondrous ways of sergeants since time immemorial, Heimstaadt appeared with an iced tub of '33' beer in the bottle. Gruntz soon joined them. The other enlisted men wandered in, snatched a brew, and went back to their own room.

Remphelmann contemplated in own young way as he gazed on the royal view, the royal food, the royal drink and the royal cool misty breeze. 'Is this not paradise?' He felt a million miles from Que Ell One.

Chapter Thirty-Eight

Lieutenant Remphelmann had no idea what an enlisted man's blowout was, but he was soon to experience such. He sat on the balcony of his room, the rattan chair squeaking beneath him, his boots propped on the wrought iron railing, as he admired the view down the Da Lat tri-river valley and the mountains beyond. Sergeants Gruntz and Heimstaadt did the same. Heimstaadt would fish into the tub of ice, and rescue three bottles of '33'. A church key was conveniently at hand around his neck on the same chain as his dog tags. The bottles were passed around. The three enlisted, Scheissenbrenner, Gonzales and Boudreaux, would wander into the room and be handed a beer. Soon a round robin affair developed. The privates would enter the room with handful of Pittsburgh Pilsner, real American brew in the steel can, with a steel helmet of fresh ice. Where they had scrounged the goods was not asked. Heimstaadt would shove the warm suds to the bottom, slop the ice on top and fish out a cold replacement for the junior men.

"I think I don't much like der '33', ja? It's not der dutch brew, but it's got der barley malt, it's got der hops, and it's got der alcohol, ja? Machts nicht. Skol!" Heimstaadt opened himself another.

"Lieutenant," offered Gruntz, "You know I transferred out of the infantry to the ordnance so I wouldn't have to do that straight-leg crap down in the valley there. Sitting here in a real hotel, quaffing brewskis, beats the crap out of lugging a sixty-pound pack through the boonies. But anyway, have you signed my request for transfer"?

Remphelmann emptied a beer and like magic another was in his hand. "Sergeant Gruntz, I am off-duty now, bring up the subject during company hours."

"Sir, yes sir."

Boudreaux and Scheissenbrenner re-appeared with more cans of beer and ice. Scheissenbrenner questioned Sergeant Gruntz. "Hey sarge, where the hell are the latrines around here? This beer is sitting on my bladder."

"Latrines, hell, Scheissie. We're in a four star hotel. Down the hall from our room is a real live flush toilet. But that isn't the half. Look here inside that door. Heimstaadt and the lieutenant got a real live American bathroom, tub, john, wash basin, plus an extra."

"With the lieutenant's permission?" Scheissenbrenner did not wait for a reply but exited into the toilet and closed the door. Soon he re-appeared, much relieved. "Damn, fellas, two things, first I actually had a door to close when I went, a private with privacy! What a luxury! Second, I never saw a private bathroom with its own urinal! Four star!"

Gruntz scoffed. "Damn it, Scheissie, urinal my ass. Did you just fall off of the turnip truck? That there is a bidet."

"A what? A bidet?"

Remphelmann rummaged another beer. "I quote the dictionary, Specialist Scheissenbrenner. A bidet is a 'low-mounted plumbing fixture or sink intended for washing the genitals or anus.' It is not there to piss into, it is there for you to pony straddle over and to lavage your crotch. It was invented by the French."

"I'll be damned," wondered Scheissenbrenner. "You mean it's a weenie washer, a peter pan?"

Gruntz had to add, "And French ladies use it to powder their noses."

Boudreaux peered into the bathroom at this wondrous device. "Swan my cajun heritage! My Uncle Fauntleroy told me such a thing existed, but I hain't never seen one till now. That reminds me of a story..."

Heimstaadt groaned. "TeJean, your stories never ever make sense, plus they never seem to bear on der subject at hand."

Boudreaux was un-dissuaded. "Seems my Cousin Pierre an' I gets in his pick-um-up truck and goes to Shreveport on business. On the way back, jus' as we passed the Terrabonne Parish line, we gets, boths of us, a hanker for a cold beer. So we stops at the Chien Rouge Saloon and goes in. We both short of cash and scrapes our pockets for change. But lucky us, ah gar-on-tee, we see that they's a sign about a cheap pitcher of beer on taps. So's we order up the taps of two pitchers and commences to drink the jugs. But all the time, ol' cousin Pierre, he's complaining, 'this here beer is tasting awful! It tastes like alligator piss.' But we'd paid our money so's we take our choice. Alla time, Cousin Pierre he's a griping, 'this here beer done taste like alligator piss'. But we guzzle it all. So we get back in the pick-um-up and goeses toward home. When we get to the bayou bridge, Cuz done stop middle of the bridge, gets out and starts apeein' over the bridge rail. Jus' then here come the parish sheriff and stops behind us. The cop done get out and yells at Pierre, 'Sha Pierre, you can't do that, public urination is again the law!' But Ol' Pierre, he say, 'Sheriff, I hain't doin' nothing but hippy-style ecology.' 'How dat?' says the cop. Pierre now done finished watering the dog and zips up. 'See here, mister cop, I was just down at the Chien Rouge honky-tonk afilling up on alligator piss beer, and now I'm recycling! I'm giving the alligator piss back to the alligators.'"

The assembled listeners were stunned. Boudreaux had told a coherent story. As if on cue Heimstaadt began to sing. No one had an inkling that the heinie could sing, but he did, in a clear soft light baritone. He wove his fingers like a symphony conductor and clearly annunciated first in German and then in his own English translation, the most beloved of World War Two soldier's songs, 'Lili Marleen."

All listened to the plaintive song about a soldier's girl waiting for her man, underneath the lamp light, outside the barracks gate.

Gruntz dissolved in beer tears. "You stinking heinie, you sleaze-ball god-damn kraut fascist, scum of the earth asshole, you aryan pseudo-superman! How can you sing a beautiful song like that, you nazi jackboot?"

Heimstaadt replied softly, "I vasn't a nazi, I was a vegetarian."

Gruntz persisted. "But you were a Luftwaffe gunner. You shot down allied planes."

"Ja, but it vas the war. I vas fifteen."

Ronnie was intrigued. "You were in the Luftwaffe? You shot down Americans?"

"Nein, mine under fuhrer. I vas on the day shift. I only shot down Englanders."

"Tell me more."

"You see, it's 1944 fall, und 1945 winter. All der men been drafted and sent to fight, some in Frankreich, against the Amis and der British, but most get shipped off to the east to deal with the Bolsheviks. That leaves nobody to man the anti-aircraft guns, the flak batteries in der homeland. So, Der Dicke, Hermann Goering, gets the smarter idea. He drafts all the high-school boys, fifteen, sixteen, seventeen, and trains them to run der anti-aircraft. Those days, you know, it's around the clock bombing, der Englanders during the nights and the Amerikaners during the days. So we high-school boys, it gets like this. We get up after dark, and we all march to the high school, ja, der hoch schule. We get der basics, reading, writing, arithmetic, until midnight. Then we march down to the cannon emplacements, der anti-aircraft guns. Den when der Englishmen bombers fly over we geshooten der British. Den we march home. Der other half of the schoolboys, they get half-day out of synchronicity. They get up at dawn, go to high school, march to der gun positions and they shoot the Amerikaner day bombers. This goes on a full year. But my heart is not in it, ja? I'm a bibel-forsher kid. Ja, mein father gets sent to the concentration camp because he is a bibel-forsher, ja? He gets kaput in der camp, ja? Typhus. Dead as a doornail."

"Bible Forcer?" Remphelmann asked.

"He was a Bible fanatic, you know. Jehovah's Witness. Contentious objector as we say in America. He refused to fight in the war, and resisted the draft. Not a good thing when the Gestapo is around. They round up my father and poof off to the camp. Poof, kaput. But I'm a swinehund, no proselytizing bible fanatic, ja? Off to Luftwaffe boy battalions. Geshooten Englanders, but I not geshooten Americans. Such is the war. Den my mama marry a G.I. after the war, we move to Venice, California, und I become a surfer boy! I got my Ford woody, catch the curl at Port Hueneme. Dazzle the bikini girls. I'm a kahuna board type, hang ten, dude. But I needed a job, so I enlisted in the U.S. of army."

Remphelmann was amazed at this beer confession. He turned to Gruntz. "And what about you?"

"It isn't any of your damned business, sir, all I care about is my request for transfer."

Then in the distance, far beyond the veranda view of the three, down in the valley so low, it erupted. The sun had barely set and in the gathering blackness, there was a red flash in Remphelmann's eyes, followed by dozens of others. Mean, dull vermilion smears of light highlighted themselves against the dusky fading terrain. After an interval the calm of the evening was rent with a horrendous roar of reverberating thunder. The flashes erupted again. Then the whole hotel reverberated underneath Ronnie's chair. It was a veritable earthquake.

"Right on time," Sergeant Gruntz remarked.

"Ja, der time is ripe," Heimstaadt seconded.

The self-same thundering came again. The sky lit up, the view lit up, the ground lifted up. The whole of the hotel shuddered. Horrid flashes of a thousand colors of red vomited out of the distance. First bright cherry, then dark vermilion, then dull rust and shimmers of pink. An incarnadine glow bounced off the thin monsoon clouds and back into their origin in the valley.

"What in god's name?" blurted Remphelmann.

"B-52 bomber strikes straight from Guam. Flying at 30,000 feet, nobody can see them fly. Nobody can hear them from the ground. But when they let loose with those thousand pound bombs! The poor suckers underneath hear the first bomb detonate, after that they're hamburger." Thus spoke Sergeant Gruntz.

"Ja, may god have mercy on der little godless commie souls," Heimstaadt added.

"How do you guys know all this and I don't?" Ronnie interrogated.

"That's because you are an officer and we are sergeants. Officers know nothing, sergeants know everything," Gruntz added.

"Ja," continued Heimstaadt. "Some of der bigger-wigglers know. They told the Arvin's and the American infantry to pull back at sundown. After that the whole mountain and valley where Charlie is gets the plaster. The wake-up and the lights out. Kaput. Poof."

Another wave of carpet-bombing slammed in the valley below. The flashes of light were at the speed of light, the paused rumble of sonic waves came after, and lastly the earth quaking heave of the ground underneath roiled toward the Nuoc Lan. Despite the dark, Remphelmann could see glass windows blowing out and red terra cotta roof tiles flipping and breaking on the houses in the distance. The whole palette of reds exhausted themselves. Burgundy, magenta, carmine, dark purples, blasted out in boils of flame and turned to dull clots of oxidized drying blood before fading into the dark. Remphelmann had a sickening thought. 'Stupid rice farmers, ignorant Charlie's, blown to bloody sausages, and why? Americans, South Vietnamese, Viet Cong, vaporized and why?'

The scene down the valley petered out. The B-52 bombers were gone. A massive silence descended on the little group of spectators. Boudreaux and Scheissenbrenner grasped the last of the beers from the ice tub and disappeared. Silently, Sergeant Gruntz went out the hotel room door and closed it. Heimstaadt skivvied down to his shorts. He located his duffle and got his big thick German language Bible from it. He located a passage. He knelt down at the edge of the bunk that was next to Remphelmann's French iron bed. He murmured something, some kind of a prayer in the German tongue, closed the book, and lay down, pulling a thin olive drab army blanket over himself and his eyes. Remphelmann gazed at the four star Michelin double bed in front of him with double-jointed alcohol eyes. He fell forward, fully clothed. His eyes were overwhelmed by a kaleidoscope of rufus tints, from blinding iron bright white to cherry heat to coagulated dark rose black. He slept.

Chapter Thirty-Nine

The sun also rose. Both Remphelmann and Heimstaadt were barely aware of it, not because of the festivities of the night before, but because the room was full of wall-to-wall quasi-luminescent fog.

"Good morning, Vietnam," a voice boomed through the white, "and a hearty good morning to you, Lieutenant Remphelmann of the ordnance. And, a hearty good morning to you, you frigging kraut!" It was the voice of Sergeant Peckerwood.

Ronnie sat stark upright in bed and his mind worked with an amazing clarity and celerity. Instantly he realized he was still in his fatigues, ensconced on a tattered Michelin four-star bed. Although he couldn't see through the fog he knew Heimstaadt was at arms length, and it was Peckerwood laughing through the white haze. Ronnie could not find his glasses. He fumbled his fingers around his pillow. "I can't see," he spurted.

"Ain't you got your coke bottle specs, Lieutenant Mister Peepers?"

Remphelmann found his eye prescriptions and put them on. He still couldn't see. The room was filled with the thickest fog he had ever experienced. He cast about and saw Peckerwood's grin, laughing disembodied in the doorframe, like a Cheshire cat's smile.

Peckerwood laughed again. "Damnedest pea-souper I've ever seen. But you left those French windows open and the fog has crept right up your crotch."

"But what are you doing here in Da Lat, sergeant? I thought you were out at Firebase Firefly."

"I thought I was too, sir. But then I get a radio-phonic. There's a dang M-48 Patton thereabouts in Da Lat, somebody says, with a punk electrical firing pin that's inoperative. Next thing I know I got a special laid on chopper, which picked me up. I went to Cam Ranh to pick up the part in the middle of the night, and I got the mechanism, all wrapped up in a Yankee carpetbag, and zing the same chopper comes here to Da Lat, wherever this is. The fog's so damn thick they can't land at the landing zone, so the chopper pilot lands on top of some hotel about a block from here, something called the Hotel Grande. The sarge on the roof says, 'go to this here other hotel, the Nuoc Lan, and hook up with the aforesaid Lieutenant Remphelmann of the ordnance. Soon as the fog lifts we have a convoy down the valley to FB Da Lat.' So here I am, in all my glory."

"Thank you for the update."

"Plus, I checked in with that fancy restaurant downstairs, what is now a mess hall at this so-called world famous Hotel Nuoc Lan, and the spatiality of the morning, the culinary pieced resistant, is shit on a shingle, reconstituted frozen eggs, and all the shit brown army coffee you can drink! Yahoo!"

The three wended their way down the stairs. Indeed, the only thing being served was chipped beef on toast, slathered with white flour gravy, and thawed frozen egg mix massacred on an iron griddle into a simulacrum of scrambled eggs. Also there was the famous army coffee, which legions of soldiers claim is filtered though the unwashed underwear of grunts.

When this repast was repasted, Sergeant Heimstaadt stood and began to sing again, oblivious of his performance the night before. His voice was a thin clear reedy baritone. His pitch was perfect, and his undulating finger kept perfect time:

"Mein Vater war ein Wandersmann
Und mir steckt's auch in Blut
D'rum wand're ich froh so lang ich kann
Und schwenke meinen Hut
Faleri falera, faleri falera
Ha ha ha, ha ha ha.'"

He repeated the performance in English:

"My father was a wanderer
It's also in my blood
So off I ramble happily
And twirl my hiking hat.
Val-de-ri, val-de-ra, val-de-ri, val-de-ra
Ha ha ha, ha ha ha."

Heimstaadt stopped abruptly at Peckerwood and Remphelmann, and then in an amazing display of clear English announced, "Lieutenant Remphelmann, sir, we are making up a small road convoy to leave here and go down the mountain to the airstrip. Me and you in a jeep, behind that a deuce and a half with food, water and the inimitable Sergeant Peckerwood, with his famous electrical breech mechanism for the Patton tank down there which is currently kaput, followed by another jeep. All of us will shuffle like a deck of cards into a larger road movement. Verstah'n, I mean, understand?"

"Ja wohl, feldwebel," Remphelmann said reflexively.

"And you, Herr Sergeant Peckerwood, you got your repair parts?

"Screw you, you frigging heine nazi, blond haired, blue eyed, jackboot jew toaster!"

"Danke shoen, thank you my fellow sergeant. I love you too. But I wasn't a nazi, I was a vegetarian."

Heimstaadt wandered off as he added an air to his previous song.

"Am der bergen mit der snee.

I hobo happily."

A surprising bored military policeman walked though the mess hall. "Convoy forming up for the landing zone. Estimated time of departure, five minutes."

The group of stalwarts went out the door of the Nuoc Lan. A convoy of trucks and jeeps had indeed assembled. An MP vehicle was first in line. Heimstaadt led them to the second jeep. To Ronnie's consternation, the driver of the jeep had the familiar form of Private Schweik. Schweik was in his usual clothing glory, which was filthy and rumpled.

"Schweik," said Remphelmann, "What are you doing here? I thought you were in Phan Thiet."

"Well, I don't rightly know how I got here myself, lieutenant, sir. There was a roust in bed, long about midnight, and here I am. I don't really understand, but this sure beats the crap out of burning shit on Que Ell One."

The convoy went into gear and began to stretch out of the town and onto the road that wound down the valley. They left the Nuoc Lan and went past the Hotel Grande, which was grander than the Nuoc Lan, and turned the corner at the city park where the three rivers emptied into the lake. At the park was a dispirited convoy of ARVN infantry waiting orders to move out.

Remphelmann tried to orient himself map-wise to the twisting terrain. He could not. Was he down east or down west or south? All he knew was that the road snaked down hill.

Schweik, exuding an odor of toasted diesel, turned to the officer, smiled and remarked. "I got to repeat, sir. I don't know how I got here, but I'm grinning from ear to ear like a possum eating defecation, cause I'd rather be here, driving this jeep, than be back in Bozo, frying feces."

The little convoy snaked around and went out of town, past the now dilapidated villas of long disappeared rubber barons, and glitzy French export merchants, down the zig zag road, that led to the temporary helipad and the artillery base. They first went through a grove of the famous Vietnamese pines, a rarity in Southeast Asia. There were workers carefully cutting grooves on the sides of the trees and attaching rusty gooey tin cans to collect the oozing sap. With this they made turpentine and pine resin. Then they passed though a grove of stately teak trees. Lumberjacks were sawing wood with old-fashioned broad bladed two man handsaws. They turned the corner of a bootlace and there was an Indian elephant replete with mahout behind the ears, astride the elephant's neck. The mahout was guiding the elephant as the pachyderm slid a massive log down a skid way to a landing spot next to the road.

Around the next corner Schweik deftly maneuvered the jeep around a most ancient snub nose log hauling truck. This little behemoth had a teak log ten feet in diameter and thirty feet long. The truck groaned under the weight of the log and a short steep grade. Like the little engine that could, it sounded 'I think I can, I think I can, I know I can' while blowing copious amounts of diesel smoke into the mountain air. Finally the log truck crested the grade and chugged easily downhill, while its radiator blew exposed steam in a happy relief of white water into another short valley.

Then there was another short vale. Nestled within was a tea plantation in full leaf. Teams of Vietnamese women, equipped with wicker baskets, were busily picking the choicest tealeaves off the bushes. Sergeant Heimstaadt took this opportunity to inform Remphelmann in clear English. "You notice how the women are picking the tea leaves? They can only do it in the early of the morning when the tea sap is full in the leaf. If they wait till mid morning and the heat of the day, the sap hides back in the stem and the leaf lacks the best tea juice."

Remphelmann nodded assent. Then he asked the German. "Why, of a sudden, can you speak perfect un-accented English?"

"Oh I studied English at Cal Poly, but it depends on my

mood, yes? Most of the soldiers expect the heinie kraut lingo, so that's what they get. Another thing, young sir. Notice how most of the women are picking bare breasted? It's a Viet thing we euros can't understand. But there is a local legend that if the ladies run around bare boob and pick tea leaf early in the day, that the tea is better. Get it? Bare breasted titty takes the best tea, like the mother's milk of the tea bush. Is that not picturesque?"

Remphelmann saw the women and indeed as the women worked their way thorough the tea field, they judicially pulled only the ripest and moistest tealeaves. They were bare breasted, their shoulder coverings tucked neatly and demurely about their waists. The line of trucks and jeeps turned down around the next bootlace.

"I hear," offered Schweik with his famous grin, "That this is where the Viet Cong tunnel city got hit by the B-52's last night."

At first Remphelmann saw nothing. And then he began to see that the hills had been struck. The vegetation at first began to wilt and then metamorphosed into knots of twisted fiber, first like string and then into blown out cotton-like bolls. They turned the next twist in the bootlace. There for a kilometer on the side of the road, black pajama bodies, wearing main force Viet Cong tunics, lay in the ditch. They passed a single body and then three, and then thirty. Discouraged ARVN soldiers were hauling bodies out of the jungle and onto the margin of the road. A sad group of the ARVN's had rigged up pulling straps of twisted cloth. They had attached the braids to the wrists and ankles of the dead Viet Cong and were bouncing the corpses out of the tunnel complex onto the side of the road. There they heaped the bodies into mounds, literally stacking them into cordwood piles. The foggy dew of morning and the rain had boiled off in the increasing heat. Gigantic purple bottle flies were swarming over the pyramids of dead.

"Look here, sarge. They are all black and blue, like one big bruise from head to toe, but there's not a mark on them, not even blood. Isn't that weird?"

"Over pressure," observed Sergeant Heimstaadt.

"Huh?" responded Schweik.

"Over pressure, concussion. When a gigantic B-52 bomb goes off the air pressure hits you and every blood vessel in your body, every capillary in your skin bursts. Your spleen turns to wet bloody tissue paper; your liver goes to oatmeal. Your kidneys explode. There is nothing inside your skin but a bloody mess of strawberry jell-o."

"Well I'll be damned!" said Schweik, "I remember from high school science that gas is compressible, but liquids aren't. So that means when those 1000 pound bombs went off on top of the tunnels the over pressure just water-hammered every drop of liquid in the Viet Congs bodies, and blew up in their guts. Hey sarge, do you know that the human body is 90 per cent water?"

Heimstaadt cocked a jaundiced eye at Schweik. "Schweik, you hast not enough brains between your ears to realize vat you just said."

"Maybe true, sarge, but his here sight sure beats the crap out of burning..."

"Oh shut up," the kraut cut him short.

Schweik lulled the jeep to a stop and gave a V for victory sign to the poor ARVN's who were tossing the bodies. The ARVN's ignored him. "I gotta count," said Schweik. He pointed his finger and counted, "One, two three...and twelve, thirteen and..." He finished his sums. "Twenty-nine in this pile alone. Dang, Lieutenant Remphelmann," the driver craned his neck to see Ronnie. "Twenty-nine slopes all in a row."

"Don't call them slopes," Remphelmann cautioned. "They were honorable soldiers, doing their best for a cause they thought right. At heart, rice farmers, nothing but rice farmers."

Heimstaadt also turned to Remphelmann. "Begging the under fuhrer's thanks, sir, I tend to agree mit you. Arvin, VC, all these little fellows are, or were about, is and was an attempt to make their little rice farmer lives a little less miserable. None of this peasant-like folk could even begin to talk about Marxist-Leninist socialism or capitalist crapola. They are thinking, or were thinking, about some way to make their crummy little lives a tad less burdensome. Den they got caught up in this geo-political silliness they don't now or ever will understand. I bet ve could come back in forty years and these farm folk won't have it any better off. They'll just get ripped by the same old power scum, commie or capital, and be just as miserable as before the kreig."

"Simple rice farmers, hoping to better their ways, going no place fast and slow," Remphelmann concluded.

Schweik suddenly brightened and said. "Hey lieutenant, I got my instamatic camera here in my breast pocket. If you want to crawl up on that cordwood stack of bodies, I'll snap a picture or two of you as a body count hero and send it to you after the war. Imagine, twenty-nine dead commies under your feet."

"I'll pass," Remphelmann sighed. "Twenty-nine farm boys."

"Verdamdt, Schweik," Heimstaadt swore, "get the damned jeep in gear." Schweik did as he was told. He eased down the bloody lane and within five minutes they came upon a branching mud track that led to the impromptu helipad, the artillery battery and the much-maligned Patton tank with its malfunctioning firing pin. The numerous men in the convoy spilled out of their carriages and went about their duties.

The workday devolved into the usual tedium of labor in the stifling heat. Work got done, repairs were made, and C-ration lunches were found and consumed. It was time to go back up the hill to Da Lat. Heimstaadt thought it convenient to stay at the landing zone. The convoy reassembled and wended a weary way back to the big city. They retraced their road march back over the bloody highway. It was almost routine.

It was routine to a point. As Remphelmann re-observed his way back up the mountain, he saw something he had not scouted before. Nestled in a manicured teak grove next to the tea plantation was a California split level house. There was a brick drive leading to the home that terminated in a circular turn-around. A new Buick and a Volkswagen van were parked in the yard. It was a magazine perfect scene of an upper class house in Marin County or perhaps the Hamptons. On the porch stood two oriental people, a well-dressed woman who was scowling mightily and an old gentleman who was openly weeping. On the lower stretches of the lawn a hundred civilian refugees from the bombing were gathered in spiritless knots about the pristine landscape.

Then the convoy made Da Lat, the Three Rivers park, and the switchback road back past the Hotel Grande and up to the Nuoc Lan. Exhausted, the men piled out. Tired, very tired, Remphelmann made it to his room and showered in the cold water that ran from the bath fixture. Peckerwood, Schweik and Gonzales-McGillicuddy showed up with beer again, and the small group sat on the balcony and watched the sun set.

═══ Chapter Forty ═══

Unbeknownst to the rear echelon mothers that sat on Remphelmann's veranda, another scenario was laying itself out only a block away. Helicopters were landing on the roof of the Hotel Grande. Grand dignitaries were whisked off the roof and down the only working elevator in the whole of Da Lat. One chopper landed that brilliant specimen of strategy and tactics, General Kegresse, on a short hop from Saigon. One of the other helicopters let off Colonel Slick and Chaplain Captain Champagne. A regular bevy of senior officers went down the elevator and were directed into the grand ballroom, grand bar and grand dining hall on the top floor of the Hotel Grande. A full party was in swing. The Vietnamese bartender, with his assistants, was in a hive of activity, slurping out old crow and tonic, beam and fizz and margaritas.

General Kegresse had staked out a table next to a large glass window, overlooking the three river valleys of Da Lat. His aide, Captain Lickspittle, was in a tizzy introducing officers and then dismissing them as Kegresse held court. The booze flowed, and underlings bootlicked into chairs, spoke their needs and desires to the squire and groveled out. It was a scene worthy of a third rate country club.

The poor grunt officers who were actually directing the fighting down the valley were given short shrift. The infantry and artillery situation, though dire, was actually under control. The ground commanders sought guidance. The only guidance they got was to return to the bar, where the liquor flowed. Colonel Slick and Captain Chaplain Champagne finally had their audience with the grand poo-bah. Lickspittle handed a memorandum to Kegresse, who read it and then turned to Slick.

"On the top of your agenda is the smuggling operation. The transit of high-grade heroin to our friends in Chicago. The goods, the first shipment, all sixty kilos, are here, actually in my private quarters. We only have to do the logistics of whipping the duffle bag of stuff from here to your point of departure in Cam Ranh. After that the ball is in your hands. Then, endless riches."

"Oh sir, yes sir, sir. We have all things arranged. We will lug the goods back into my return chopper for Surf City and all is as planned." Slick took out his comb and groomed his hair.

"And just why is my good whore-master, Captain Chaplain Champagne in tow?" Champagne had inexplicably outfitted himself with a huge pot-metal gilded crucifix and gold plated chain that dangled from his neck. Rather like a dagger to the sternum, he fingered it lasciviously.

"Oh sir, yes sir, sir. You know his astounding abilities to seek out the good, his knack for separating the wheat from the tares."

"Yes, yes. The Saigon sluts I have to thrash though are a pity. The chaplain will kindly provide. I want to screw the best hooker in town."

"Oh sir, yes sir, sir," The chaplain groveled. "My knack for nooky never fails. I shall prevail. Let us put our glory poles into the most choice glory holes in imitation of the comings of the lord."

Kegresse waved the two off. The chaplain immediately began

to work the room, the bartender, the maitre'd, the waiters and the bus boys, like a hound on the hunt. Slick scurried crabwise to a near by table and began to count his mental coin of Mammon.

Champagne soon hit pay dirt, or so he thought. He conferred with the bartender, who after a discrete conversation with a busboy, winked and said, "Wait".

Within five minutes an absolutely stunning lady appeared. She was twenty, lithe, cat-like and astounding for an oriental woman, endowed with a 36D chest pair and a slinky cocktail dress. She had a cleavage line that would challenge an engineer to design a suitable cantilever to hold up her mammary appendages. She was presented to the brigadier.

Kegresse, well known for his forthrightness and lack of small talk, cut to just the facts. "Hey bitch, let's screw."

The lady coyly replied. "Oh, GI, I like you, I like boom-boom very much. Especially with big strong general like you. Me very horny for you. You like boom-boom? Boom-boom now? Boom-boom later? Maybe I come back tomorrow?"

"Screw the preliminaries, damn it. Full speed ahead." He backed to his ever-ready aide, "Lickspittle, where's my key? In an instant, there was a key. An obsequious bellboy took the key and offered to lead the two to an adjoining suite.

Massively unsteady on his feet, Kegresse lurched up and draped himself unseemly on the woman's shoulder, while he peered wantonly down her cleavage. That she had to heave him right across her shoulder was an understatement.

The bellhop opened the locked door to the suite, gave the key to Kegresse and leered. "I hope Big Important General Man have a blast!"

"Damn straight. I'm going to blast her tush right though the mattress."

The lady of the 36D blushed. "Oh, GI general, I can't wait."

They entered the suite, which had a large four-poster bed, windows that looked down the Da Lat valley, and a complete French toilet room to one side. A nearby duffle bag hid the 60 kilos of heroin. There was also a massive teak door that led to an adjoining room, but Kegresse saw it not, as all he saw was his own lust.

The lady in black sensuously undressed Kegresse. Again coyly, she went to the window and adjusted the jalousie. "You so hot, you make room hot, I open window for cool breezes for to chill down hot General." Unbeknownst to her victim, she flicked the jalousie cord three times. "Oh, you make me so hot, I go to toilet, and cool my kitty with bidet. Big strong man like you, when I get GI general like water buffalo on top of me, oh, oh!"

"Water buffalo, hell, I'm a raging bull!"

Agent 36D went to the bathroom. She opened the bath window. One story below, on an adjoining rooftop, was an agent of the Viet Cong special sapper squad. He tilted up a ladder that reached the window. He clambered up and gave her a satchel charge full of explosives concealed in a straphanger leatherette purse. He also handed her a Viet Cong military tunic, which she draped on the windowsill. The lady agent deftly switched a timer on the plastique and returned to Kegresse. She placed the purse beneath the bed. She snuggled up to the putative general and stroked his anatomy.

"Let's do it, bitch, I'm going to mount you like Moses on Sinai." His eloquence was wonderful.

Agent 36D looked carefully at the inexpensive watch on her wrist. Even she was flustered for words, "Oh, two minute, no one minute, I got to go toilet one more time. But I promise to big important man. You get boom-boom like you never forget. Boom-boom, boom-boom-boom! Big general excuse me two minutes."

"Well damn it, hurry back," rejoined Kegresse. I'm at full mast and ready to salute!"

"Oh, one minute fifteen seconds, Big American, and you'll get the biggest boom of your whole military career." She sauntered sexily into the bathroom, closed the door and ran for the window. She flipped the military tunic on instantly. Below, her cohort was steadying the ladder. Ten rungs down, and the two scampered across the roof to a convenient stairwell. Waiting for them down at street level was an old Citroen sedan that made a slow get-away. She was counting on her watch, "Twenty, nineteen, eighteen, seventeen."

Kegresse was tossing on the Michelin bed and its Vietnamese sheets. "Hey bitch, where is my biggest boom-boom of all?"

In a Proustian aside, beyond the massive teak door that led to the adjoining room, somebody had been watching. The teak door had a discrete spyglass, a magnifying peephole installed in it. Behind it, peeping like Tom was Chaplain Captain Champagne. He was in a lather of voyeurism. Behind him the hallway door opened and Colonel Slick walked in. The chaplain did not budge from the keyhole.

"Champagne, what the hell are you doing?"

"For chrism' sake, Slick, the general is about to screw the whore I supplied! This door spyglass is giving me a 180 degree view!"

Slick protested. "You pervert! You peeping tom, you degenerate! Why are you hogging the telescope? Let me look!" Slick quickly combed his hair and changed places with the chaplain.

Then the bomb went off.

From Kegresse's perspective, there was none. He was not macerated, he was not obliterated, he was not severed, he was vaporized into a bloody humid mist along with the contents of the room. Along with him went the duffel of heroin.

On the far side of the Proustian peephole, a slight change of personnel had occurred. Chaplain Captain Champagne had yanked Slick from the spy hole to have a better look. When the blast hit the massive door, the pot metal crucifix about his neck flew up and down his gullet. The door slammed flat on the floor taking the erstwhile sky pilot with it. Lieutenant Colonel Slick, having been wrested from the view had turned slightly and his ass was peppered with a thousand fragments of splintered teak.

Smoke, concrete dust, tri-nitro gas, powdered opiate and wood projectiles filled the room. Slick was at a loss. All he could think to do was to try and lift the slab of the door off of Champagne. The chaplain lay lifeless, his cheap crucifix rammed down his throat. Colonel Slick, despite his butt pierced by a thousand points of toothpicks, took out his comb and stroked the smack from his hair.

═══ Chapter Forty-One ═══

Back on Remphelmann's veranda, it was again another of those meteorological oddities that only experienced military could understand. The explosion at the Hotel Grande was neither felt, nor heard, much less seen. All was quiet on the Nuoc Lan front.

The enlisted men had drifted away, leaving Sergeant Peckerwood and Lieutenant Remphelmann to their own private beer call.

Sergeant Peckerwood began a cryptic conversation. It began, "Say, lieutenant, it seems I've got a room down the hall all to myself. Nobody else, a lockable door."

"That's nice," said Ronnie.

"And you, since Heimstaadt elected to stay down at the FB, means you got a room all to your self. A lockable door."

"That's true," Remphelmann replied.

"So I thought I'd order up some pie, some pizza pie for myself, and thought seeing how I was going to call for delivery, maybe you might want a slice for yourself."

"I've lost your thread, sergeant. There's no pizza in Vietnam, not here or anyplace else, much less delivery."

"I hope you lost the thread. See, by pie, I mean nooky,

women, fur pie, a little diversion from the usual. You know?" Peckerwood opened a couple of more beers and handed one to Remphelmann.

Ronnie knew not.

"See, the military police downstairs have hooked up a phone line to the local cat house, 'Madame Nhu's.' So if a man hankers, all he has to do is ring 'Thunder Switch', then ask for Madame Nhu, and order up some entertainment. Soon enough, up the street, there appears a pimp on a motorbike, with a honey bunny on the back. You pay the pimp say three hundred piastres, and the lady in black is yours for the night."

Remphelmann was horrified, even if for a moment. "Sergeant, that's immoral. It's one thing for an enlisted man to sneak off post, and indulge a base desire. But to call a prostitute onto a military facility! And then attempt to involve a commissioned officer into the crime!" Nonetheless Ronnie took a deep sip on his beer.

Peckerwood saw his opportunity. "Look here, sir. I'm going to order up some pie, and all I can do is let you in on the delivery."

"But officers don't do that sort of thing."

"Sir, get off your high horse, what do you think is happening over at the Hotel Grande, a church social? They, those high rankers, are screwing the best hookers in town. And I suppose you have moral grounds?"

Actually, Remphelmann did have moral grounds. He, in his mind, went through a four part mathematical equation: moral rectitude, saving himself for marriage, the honor of officers, and the dim chance he might be found out. He contemplated this quadratic for ten seconds. Then he added two other factors, lust and the chance of adventure. The additive, subtractive and divisional rang bright in his young mind and answered, 'Why not!'

"Why not!"

Peckerwood was up in an instant. "Hey lieutenant, let me go downstairs, give Thunder Switch and Madame Nhu a ring. Ten minutes from now, come on down to the street and I'll give you first pick of the girls. I'm not picky."

Ten minutes later, Remphelmann was at the front drive of the Nuoc Lan. Despite the bombing, the streetlights of the town began to flicker on. Several streets down amongst the moldy stone villas, which alternated in the fading light between the monsoon showers and the moments of clear and the twilight's last gleaming, came three Japanese motorbikes. The operators of the three bikes were crafty young draft dodgers, sleazy young traffic dodging pimps. Three women were sitting primly sidesaddle in their slit pant dresses, holding onto the pimps with demure arms. The motorcyclists screeched to a halt in front of the hotel.

Remphelmann stood there, pretending not to notice. Peckerwood and another sergeant came out of the building and strode down the steps to the pimps. A negotiation began.

"O.K., so Madame Nhu delivers three girls. Fine, twelve bucks each." Peckerwood started.

"No, no, no," retorted the lead pimp, who had a case of skin outbreak. "300 dong, 300 piastres equal times three, twenty bucks real U.S. dollars, no Military Payment Certificate, so 900 piastres equal twenty dollar American time three, you give me sixty dollar American. Good deal, these girls, Madame Nhu's best. You give me sixty greenbacks, no MPC. Everything O.K., you three get all night boom-boom."

"Screw you, you pimply little slope pimp. The going rate is twelve a night, so I give twelve times three equal thirty-six."

No, no, no, Madame Nhu say twenty each girl. Times three equals sixty."

"Up your draft dodging ass, creep. Three time twelve equals thirty-six.

"O.K., O.K., G.I., I make capitalist counter-offer, fifteen each. Fifteen time three equal forty-five dollar American, American greenback, no MPC."

"Bite my hemorrhoids, low life. Fifteen a girl equal forty-five, but I got no greenback, all I got is MPC. Forty-five bucks MPC, or you can take the pizza back to the parlor."

"Oh, G.I. you drive hard Yankee bargain but I take. Madame Nhu not be happy.'

"Madame Nhu got syphilis up her snatch." Peckerwood forked over forty-five dollars in military payment certificates.

"OK," continued the pimply pimp. 'We be back tomorrow morning to pick up girls, eight o'clock military time, just before your convoy goes back down the road.

"Of course, you know our road movement, you slimy little commie spy."

"All business, G.I. All war is business. Another thing, you GI's, you not beat up girls. Understand, not beat up girl, damaged girl hard to sell tomorrow, Black eye, and bruise on arm, and damaged goods on kittycat no good. Damaged goods no sell tomorrow."

We aren't going to beat up your goddamn whores," Peckerwood swore.

The three pimps regained their motorbikes and roared down the hill. The three prostitutes huddled forlornly together in a thin knot, not knowing what was next, like cattle waiting to be cut out. The cull was short and brutal. The unknown sergeant compatriot of Peckerwood merely crooked a finger at one of the women, who timidly obeyed and followed him into the Nuoc Lan.

"That leaves two. Which do you want?"

"I, uh…" stammered Remphelmann.

"Well then, I'll take the young and juicy. That leaves you with the other, she's almost a mama-san, bet she's had kids." Peckerwood made an abrupt gesture to his chosen and was gone.

Remphelmann was at a total loss. He doffed his hat slightly. "You speakie the English?" He was immediately chagrined by his choice of words.

"Yes," came the surprising reply. I speak fluent French, je

parle Français, plus I can get along in English, Trung Uy, I mean lieutenant in English, your rank in American is lieutenant?

Yes," Remphelmann stumbled again, "American officer Remphelmann, Ronald. You can call me Ronnie."

"Oh, Ronnie, don't be mean to me."

"What's your name?"

"My name, Vietnamese is Tham Thi Tham, but Catholic, I have how you say, Mary Magdalene."

The sun was now at its last on the steps of Nuoc Lan Hotel. Remphelmann, embarrassed, stumbled verbally. "Well let me escort you to my room."

"Oh, Ronnie, Trung Uy, you are kind, not rough like other G.I."

Remphelmann motioned to the hotel doors. He opened it and motioned her in like a perfect gentleman. She entered first; he followed and led her up the staircase to his now empty room. He closed the door and locked the unfamiliar French style door lock. As he looked at her he felt an obvious erotic urge. However, the infinite sadness of demeanor that shone though her too obvious smile stopped him from advancing. The sun was now totally down and room was lit only by the flickering streetlamp below the window. What would Remphelmann say or do next? He knew not.

Actually that whole part of the evening was to put it mildly, anti-climactic. Remphelmann instinctively knew what to do. She knew what to do. It was simply the basic thing. As Shakespeare once quipped, making the beast with two backs was a country matter. They slept. It was the conversation the next morning that bothered Remphelmann as long as remembrance of things past remembered themselves.

It was the sound of sporadic artillery fire somewhere down the valley that awoke Remphelmann. He looked at his wristwatch. Its luminous hand pointed to five. He tried to look out the French windows of his room but even with the dim flicker of the streetlamps down below all he could see was a wall of fog plastering itself against window and wall. It was cold, cold for Vietnam. Only a single olive drab blanket draped him and Mary Magdalene. It was a source of delicious warmth. He looked over in the dimness and saw Mary. She was slightly curled away from him but with her back firmly in his side, as if she was attracted to his body heat or even his human presence. He again felt an earthy urge from his groin and easily, even daintily nudged her. He faced her beautiful fluttering opening eyes. They radiated the most immense sadness he had ever beheld. But as if on cue, she presented him with a wan smile. They make the twain backs again. Remphelmann could not think of lust or raw sex. Enjoyment was absent. After the biological coupling was done, they rolled slight apart and waited until their breaths subsided.

'Post coitum omne animal triste est,' the thought popped in his head. How true. Was it Ovid, or Virgil or Plutarch? The phrase tore at his sensibilities.

It was at this moment that the Magdalene said the most astounding thing. She said, "Do you want to see my family album?"

Chapter Forty-Two

"Huh?" Remphelmann was taken aback.

"My family pictures," Mary Magdalene repeated. She leaned over under the bed and retrieved a rather tatty plastic purse. From it she pulled a vinyl photo album. "O.K. Ronnie, I show you my family." She turned on a night stand lamp.

In black and white on page one was a rather formal portrait of a man about 45 years of age and his wife. Behind the patriarch was a twenty something young man dressed in a Vietnamese army dress uniform. On the lap of the parents were two girls, about six and eight.

"You see, Ronnie. This is my father, how you say, province engineer, he build roads and water things, O.K.? This my Mama. Behind, see, my number one brother, big brother. See. He Trung Uy in this picture, lieutenant just like you." She pointed at the two girls. "That's me and my baby sister. I number one daughter, she number two daughter. I look so cute when I little girl!" Mary Magdalene giggled girlishly.

Remphelmann looked her straight in the eye. Behind the laugh, behind the soft black eyes, he saw something fathomless.

The Magdalene turned the album page. "See, my wedding

picture." There was another overly formal photograph of newlyweds, a tall stern young man in an ill-fitting European suit, and a young oriental woman, replete with white wedding dress, bridal veil and a gold crucifix showing proudly from her neck. "You see," she said turning another page. There was Mary again, sitting next to her husband, now dressed in the uniform of a South Vietnam marine officer. They held two young girls in their laps. All four were smiling for the camera. "This my husband and me, and my two baby girls." The woman turned yet another page. This picture showed Magdalene sitting again, this time without her man. The two daughters were older now, four and six, with the beguiling smiles of children, but Mary was blank of emotion, vacant.

She started to turn the page again. Remphelmann softly put his hand on hers. "I really don't understand," he remarked. "Let's start your family album again."

She slowly closed the album. Then she reopened it to the first photograph. There again was the picture of the severe looking 45-year-old man, his wife, the standing son and two girls in the lap.

Remphelmann prompted. "Start again."

"This my father, mother, big brother, and me and my sister."

"And your big brother, where is he?"

"Oh, Ronnie, hard to explain. Parles-vous Français? I explain better."

"I don't speak French," Remphelmann sighed.

"I explain but my English is not good that."

"You speak English very well."

"Thank you, Ronnie."

"So explain the pictures."

"My big brother, Ronnie, I don't know how to explain, Vietnamese language best, second French, English not best. But I try. This picture 1954. Many Vietnamese think best way for Vietnam to stay friends with French. We don't like French but alternatives, Viet Minh, communist, you know? Viet Minh hate Catholic, you know. My family Catholic, you see."

"I see."

"My family co-labor with French, we Catholic, my family think that best for all Vietnam. My family co-laborer with French, co-labor."

"Collaborate," Remphelmann corrected grudgingly. "And your brother?"

"My brother die, Dien Bien Phu. Not Dien Bien Phu. Road to Dien Bien Phu, Highway 18, QL-18, big battle, Nonh Quat Tro, French and Vietnam loyalists all die in big battle to make trucks, to make road to Dien Bien. Big road battle with trucks."

"A convoy."

"Yes."

"So," Remphelmann flipped back the photographs, "The other people in the photos?"

"Pere, me papa? Parles-vous Français?"

"No," Ronnie repeated.

"Silly me, first I think in Vietnamese. Then translate in head to French, and then third time in English."

"You are doing just fine."

"So I don't know how explain political. Viet Minh win Dien Bien Phu, suddenly all over Vietnam north and south, execution people, death squads appear, kill many who oppose. They come to father's house, my house, I there, little sister, the mama, the daddy there. They take gun, say 'Papa, you bad, bad, bad. You reaction French, you make engineers with French, you die.' They shoot papa in head."

"And you were there?"

"My little sister, me big sister, there. Shoot papa in head, Blood, brains all over house. Then they shoot Mama, in you know, belly."

"Jesus."

"Yes, I love Jesus, Jesus friend of poor and meek."

Remphelmann stammered. "That isn't what I meant."

"They shoot Mama here," Mary pointed to her sternum, "shoot mama bullet go and stick in back spine. She alive, but she not walk now."

"You saw this with your own eyes?"

"These eyes see."

Remphelmann again took Magdalene's hand solidly in his and turned an album page. There was the wedding picture. A tall young man, turned out in a pin striped double-breasted European suit. Mary beamed out of the picture, a radiant young bride.

Remphelmann's hand smoothed over the picture. "And this?"

"Very hard to explain Viet society. Me young girl, no mama, no papa, big brother dead, maybe me end up as street labor. Maybe end up as, excuse me, as street whore. I got no money, papa dead, mama cripple, no good. But I'm lucky, I meet strong young man, good family, good people, Catholic religion. He, you say, money family, here in Da Lat, teak merchant family. Make teak, make plywood, manufacture furniture, good people. I lucky, I marry to save from street."

"And where is he now?"

"War start all over again, god damn war, you excuse my words, god damn war, all over again. My husband this time he go in marine, his regiment go north, way north to Hue. He gets killed. How I don't know, the government sent the notices, the letter, he dead up north, way up north."

"And in this picture, you and your brave young husband. He's dressed in fine style as Vietnamese marine officer, and your two daughters. Yet you're a nice Catholic girl. Now you are a prostitute, excuse me. How?"

Mary sighed as she returned the photo album to her purse. "Ronnie, you not understand Viet society. I widow, two daughters, family father in cemetery, no husband, I make no job. Sometimes, O.K.? I pick tea, sometimes, O.K.? I work in shirt factory, but war stop all work, no way for lumber factory to ship wood, send furniture, no send tea to Saigon, no send nuoc mam anywhere, plywood factory stops, no job, no money, no rice, no food. How in French, extremis?"

"So you have no money, no family, no means of support"

"Yes. So now, shame, shame. I whore. One night with G.I. more than whole month of no work, the government pension I not see. I hate this, against Catholic teaching, against moral thing, but I must support. Children, mother, terrible. What I do? No shirt factory, no wood machine shipping. VC cut road. I whore to feed my children."

"So you've got no money, no family, no means of support? But isn't there a means of support? I mean you are a war widow, with orphans, a widow's pension, child support?"

"Oh, yes widow and orphan pension, but you see, banks not work, postal system not work. So Saigon they got this way then, work like, the Viet National Assembly make money bill to send widow and orphan, but banks not can send money. So system work like this. I supposed get 3000 dong, 3000 piastres a month. But I pick up at local police station at local town hall. 3000 piastres leave Saigon, but politician big city take 300 piastres, then money go to province governor, he take 300 piastres, then money go to town mayor, he take 300 piastres, then money go to police chief, he takes 300 piastres, I go to town hall, get pension, they give me 300 piastres. I lucky 300, some time no piastres."

"So every crook takes their share all down the line."

"You bet, G.I.! Oh, I'm so sorry, Ronnie, you wrong name. You been Trung Uy, you always Ronnie. But same-same commie! Though north and south big commies take all the money all down road, real people get left-overs, in French, merde, shit stuff."

"I'm trying to figure this all out," said Remphelmann. "You are a decent woman, from a good family, with religious convictions, with a crippled mother and two little children to support and you are hooking for a living."

"It's all money. Follow this. Here Vietnam, it takes 600 piastres a month to have rent and rice. I can't depend on pension. I go to Madame Nhu, she pimp and take slice. I whore one night and I get food and rent for two weeks. I don't like what I do. But must, I must feed mama and babies, feed roof. You understand, I good woman, I believe God, I believe Catholic, but no money mean no money. I got to make food for family that left." She burst into tears. Remphelmann looked around. All he could find was a torn green tee shirt draped over a side chair. He offered it to her and she daubed her welling eyes. The sun had risen to such an extent that the fog against the French windows began to diffuse the room with a transcendent glow. The two huddled together, realizing their combined warmth thwarted the last chill of morning.

As they lay there, mutually morose, Remphelmann heard a nameless soldier turn on his eight-track tape recorder in the hallway. At first the song was garbled, but then the refrains of an old standard song was faintly heard. It was an lyric from the 1920's. A country and western singer had recently covered it. The timing was odd to Ronnie as it was sun up rather than the evening gloom that the song suggested. Nonetheless he took the words to heart as he lay nestled to the forlorn body of Mary Magdalene.

> Are you lonely today?
> Has your joy flown away,
> Since our love went sadly apart?
>
> Does that porch swing sway hollow,
> Do you wish I would follow,
> And cuddle alone with you there?
>
> It was a dark summer evening
> When I took my leaving.
> Love, are you lonely today?

As the refrain died out, there came the sound of three motorbikes buzzing to a stop beneath the Hotel Nuoc Lan windows. The pimps had re-arrived to retrieve their chattel.

A voice knocked at the hotel door. "Lieutenant Remphelmann, sir, the frigging god damn pimps are down on the street to pick up the left over pizza. Got your crumbs together?"

The Magdalene and the lieutenant got the hint. They gathered clothes, and hats, and tatty purses and plastic photo albums together and stumbled downstairs.

At the porch of the Nuoc Lan, the pimps re-gathered the whores with a snarl. Mary looked deeply at Remphelmann. With a flourish that even Ronnie could not imagine; he took her hand and reverently kissed it. The girls remounted the bikes. The pimps kick started the smelly two strokes and went down the hill. Mary looked back at Remphelmann and gave a knowing wave with her hand.

Remphelmann waved back.

PART THE FIFTH

Our Young Hero Meets His Dénouement

Chapter Forty-Three

How Da Lat had been left in detritus and dreams and forlorn longings, Remphelmann knew not. All he knew was that he was back in Phan Thiet. There was a certain strange familiarity to the place. His bunk in the BOQ was there, his work-a-day job was there, the cemetery across the wire had not moved. The Viet Cong still had command of the heights on Big Titty Mountain. Sergeant Shortarm was there, yelling his usual Texican obscenities.

"Holy frigging El Paso piss-ants, sir. They's a meeting over on the infantry side. Since Kegresse went up in smoke, they's another infantry commander in the loop, this time a west pointy type, a Brigadier Goodspeed. You all officers gots a meeting with the brass. Arrival time is thirty minutes from now. We sarges are out of skinny, maybe's you'll come back with the snoop, scoop and poop."

Soon enough Remphelmann, Duvalier, and Shinebaum were bouncing in a jeep to their new destiny. Along for the ride was Captain Manteca, huddled in back murmuring as usual about the collapse of his career and reputation. Major Dufuss was nowhere to be found. The group of officers filed into the meeting hall with the same mixture of resignation and disgust that preceded their earlier forays. A spare and serious general sat on a folding chair behind the podium, knocking down any attempts at military falderal as the officers came into view. On the stage with him was a South Vietnamese colonel, which the cognizant knew was the local ARVN honcho. This was a taking-aback. The new general had condescended to include his allies? Something was afoot.

Duvalier ran into a person he loathed. It was none other than the putative glory-seeker, Lieutenant Cervantes. "Rear echelon asshole, Duvalier, you dusky gear shifter, still hanging around, looking for your discharge on the ground?"

"I'm here to do duty, you dangerous man. Are you still seeking to put you men at risk to polish up your resume and your salad bar?"

"Bite my rosy-red. I'll have that Congressional before we meet again."

"God help your men."

"Hey, asshole, men are just stupid cannon-fodder, they are there to make me look good."

The briefing began in earnest.

Goodspeed did not seem different from his predecessors. He was different. He had a command of the situation, the real life and death situation, which had escaped his forebears. He opened gently in a methodical and geometrical pattern, as he took a pointer and jabbed at a large topographical map on the back wall. "The problem here is Que Ell One. That is the only real logistic lifeline from the coast here in Phan Thiet, to the northern reaches of the Saigon metropolitan area, Tan Son Nhut, Long Bien and so forth. The big problem is the famous cut off in the pass, that part of Que Ell One that snakes through the Le Hong Phong Forest, underneath Whiskey Mountain. For the last two years that has been the choke point. I make no empty promises about Que Ell One. The Americans, and our allies, the South Vietnamese, here represented by Colonel Han, have been trying mightily for years to clear the road. That unfortunately has not happened. The recent action in Da Lat, north of Que

Ell One, points to that. The Da Lat action was a tactical victory, but the main enemy logistic bases are still intact. Another push on clearing Que Ell One and driving the enemy beyond tactical range of the road is in the offing. My mission, as described to me, is to coordinate with our ally, here personified by Colonel Han, and to keep Que Ell One open and open for good. I realize that is what all of you, all of my honest troopers, and the ARVN soldiers have been attempting to do for a long time. The situation is not good. But orders are orders. I will re-open the road and keep it open, with the help of our friends." Brigadier Goodspeed nodded to Colonel Han. "I have nothing to offer but honest work, clean operational ideas, and the knowledge that many have died needlessly for this piece of road. However, I hope in my heart of hearts, that we will prevail."

The rest of the briefing went in a business-like and military-like manner that the denizens of Landing Zone Betty and LZ Bozo could only of dreamed a week before. There was a detailed analysis of the personnel and intelligence situation. The brigadier added a few words about the logistics, and even thanks, to the long-suffering rear echelon mothers for their attention to duty. A word of thanks to the rear in the gear types was unimaginable. Then Goodspeed addressed the assembled officers again. He thanked the infantry for their bravery and thanked the ARVN's for their valor. He added that the main force Viet Cong was planning a big push on the Le Hong Phong Forest the next day, and to stand aware. Colonel Han warned, in excellent English, that an attack on the LZ Bozo wire was rumored. The VC plan was to be a broad front infiltration followed by a sapper attack on the ammunition dump. The meeting came to a business-like end.

The three young officers, Shinebaum, Duvalier and Remphelmann, got back in their contrivance. The muttering corpse of Manteca joined them. They roaded back across the airfield to their digs.

Remphelmann went into the ordnance hootch to inform

Sergeant Shortarm. Shortarm was there. But also was the presence of a pasty-faced major. "Uh, Lieutenant Remphelmann," Shortarm coughed, "this here is Major Norbert Nosey, he's down for the day from Surf City to get acclimated to the situation on the ground around here."

In short order Remphelmann had Nosey in his jeep and showed him the sights of the LZ, especially a tour around the perimeter wire with a wonderful view of the cemetery and Whiskey Mountain lurking in the distance. Remphelmann found himself racing the jeep through the ruts.

"For god's sake, lieutenant, slow down, are you trying to get us killed?" Major Nosey was white knuckled, holding on to any protuberance the jeep had to offer.

"Well, Major, you see, this isn't Cam Ranh. There are snipers all about. See the cemetery in the distance? There's always at least four VC snipers over there, Moisin-Nagant bolt-action telescope precision rifles at their shoulders. They are just waiting for a good shot. Plus maybe the VC sappers have laid a bouncing betty bomb in one of pre-existing ruts on this track. Dark of the moon last night, you know? Really easy for a one man slither in and slither out, and plant a wake-up. They do it just for fun."

"Damn it, lieutenant, slow down! No don't! It's dangerous out here! When is my chopper back to Cam Ranh? Getting spattered on a road is not in my career path. I don't understand why Chaplain Captain Champagne and Colonel Slick even went to the that horrible combat zone up at Da Lat."

Remphelmann knew more than he let on. "Oh, the captain and the colonel? How are they?"

"Haven't you heard? There were in a horrible street-fighting situation in downtown Da Lat! A thousand pound car bomb went off while they were leading a counter-attack. General Kegresse, in a heroic act, was leading the assault, while he carried the Stars and Stripes into the breach. He was blown to smithereens. The chaplain, god bless him, was giving last rights to a wounded grunt. The explosion jammed his crucifix down his throat and he choked to death on his religious artifact. And then there were the amazing heroics of Colonel Slick. Although wounded by the first blast, he grabbed a machine gun and was advancing into the VC, firing deadly rounds, rallying his men, when another thousand pound bomb went off behind him and splintered his whole backside with teakwood fragments. He survived the assault and put himself in for the Silver Star or even the Congressional Medal of Honor."

"Is that so," Remphelmann said matter of factly.

"Slow down, damn it, lieutenant. I've spent 15 years in this man's army polishing my career. I'm 5 years from a sweet retirement, and I'm not willing to die in a road accident."

Ronnie looked at his watch as he turned around and headed for the helipad. "Never fear, Major Nosey, your chopper back to Surf City is departing in ten minutes."

"And not a damned minute too soon. It's dangerous out here. No career military man in his right mind would expose himself to a combat zone."

Nosey was soon flown out of harm's way. Remphelmann went on with his day. The day was routine, but with sundown, it was obvious the natives were restless.

It was scheduled for the rear echelon mothers to man the LZ Bozo wire. The sun set. There was guard call. The ordnance men got wire bunker number one, and Duvalier's men got bunker number two. The military police, under Shinebaum, were held as tactical reserve. Ronnie got his cohort into the bunker. They set up a M-60 machine gun with a field of fire though the narrow bunker slit, sighted on the cemetery. Private Einstein was designated gunner, with Scheissenbrenner as his assistant. Gonzales-McGillicuddy was issued a grenade launcher. Sergeant Gruntz and Boudreaux got the choice posting on top of the bunker so they could get an unobstructed view. Shortarm, Heimstaadt and Peckerwood and the rest of the men were held in reserve back at the ordnance hootch. Ronnie tested the field phone. Connection one was to Gruntz above and Shortarm out back. Connection two was to infantry operations. Connection two was the most important. Contrary to a Hollywood producer's scenario, military men never, never ever, open fire without orders. If tactical HQ rang and gave an explicit order to open fire, one fired, if there was no order, one sat pat. Even if a fire mission was called one had what was called a range card, a written instruction as to the compass degrees and distances one could shoot. All Ronnie could do in the meantime was to stay put and call if he saw any movement in the dark.

Then, as soldiers would have remarked during the American Civil War, the balloon went up. It was time to see the elephant.

It started with a horrific plastering of the LZ with mortar fire. Remphelmann could not keep count. There were at least a hundred in coming. The army four-deuce mortars replied. Dozens of flashes of red light erupted from the cemetery. This was followed by a series of parachute flares that lit up the whole scene as if it were a nighttime football stadium. Tracer bullets began to splatter, both outward to the graveyard, and inward towards the bunkers. Rounds smacked dully into the sandbags. Remphelmann rang connection one. "Gruntz, what do you see?"

Gruntz replied. "A platoon size infantry movement, sir. Maybe forty men, maybe more. They are leap-frogging. Bearing 270 degrees. Range six hundred meters.

Remphelmann switched to connection two and rang. "Enemy troops in the open, infantry, forty riflemen, bearing 270 degrees from bunker one, six hundred meters."

"We see them, get off the horn."

Einstein pulled back on the charging handle of the machine gun. "Sir, I see them, range card 270, 600 hundred meters. Sir, shall I open?"

"Negative", barked Remphelmann. "No firing without orders."

The elephant entered center ring. More four-deuce plastered into the cemetery. 105mm artillery from Firebase Firefly belched fire from their muzzles in the distance and were soon splattering red on the graves of the innocent. Overhead, a C-47 air force plane, a 'Puff the Magic Dragon' heavy gunship, droned into ear shot and circled. It streamed a long line of gatling gun bullets and tracers into the environs, like the long pee of some horrendous red giant pissing down onto a flat rock, the bloody urine hitting, splattering, bouncing off the ground again to drench the whole area, like a malevolent dog hosing a fire hydrant, oblivious of where its water went.

Suddenly Remphelmann heard a horrendous burp of M-16 fire just outside the bunker. He switched the field phone and yelled at Gruntz on the roof above. "Damn it, you have no orders to open fire!"

"Sir, it's not me! Major Dufuss is standing south of the bunker and is spraying and praying into the dark."

Remphelmann was out of the bunker in a flash. There, silhouetted by the illumining flares, was Major Dufuss. He had set up a folding TV tray. On it was his drink of choice, a bloody mary in a highball glass, and a dozen magazines of ammunition. He was engaged in firing off magazine after magazine towards the graveyard.

"Sir, pray God, sir! We have no orders to open fire."

"At ease, Mr. Remplestiltskin, I have the situation well in hand." He blasted another magazine at nothing in the black.

Out of the ghostly flickers of dark and stark flare light an infantry sergeant ran up. "God damn you, sir, cease fire! You have no orders to fire. We have a friendly patrol out there in no-mans-land about three hundred meters out. You could be shooting them in the back."

"I have met the enemy and he is us," Dufuss intoned. "The horrid atheistic communists and non-vodka and non-tomato juice drinkers are in my sights. Therefore I open fire." Dufuss loaded yet another magazine into his rifle and put it to his shoulder. "Rank hath its privileges, mere sergeant."

Just then an infantry major ran up out of the dark and stood

341

next to the grunt sergeant. Dufuss began to pull the trigger. The sergeant exploded, "I'll show you how rank hath its privileges," and with that made an expert round-house swing at the major and deftly cold-cocked him right in the left eye. Dufuss crumbled and his rifle went into the mud.

Dufuss lay idiotically on the ground. "Major, did you see that! A junior struck me. I shall prefer charges."

"Charges my ass," the infantry officer retorted. "If it had been me, I would have shot you between the eyes."

Dufuss regained his feet and his highball glass, but left his rifle in the mire. He shook his dignity and announced, "This is highly irregular." At that he dead marched off into the dark, hopefully towards his abode.

Just then elephant waved its trunk again. The ammo dump went up in a glorious explosion. Unfired artillery and mortar rounds came sailing out of the night sky. The two infantry types disappeared. Remphelmann gathered his wits. He yelled at Gruntz and Boudreaux. "Get the hell off the roof, get in the bunker!" The two were down and in without further prompting. The rear echelon mothers hunkered and waited. The ammunition dump fortunately did not go up in a Guy Fawkes but petered out. Somewhere in the distance a siren briefly wailed and wound out. It was a signal the attack was over.

After a decent interval, Boudreaux piped up. "This reminds me of a story. Seems Cousin Pierre and I..."

"Shut up," Remphelmann said.

"My Uncle Maurice de Broglie Einstein, the famous French physicist, remarking on the wave-particle duality, would have said on this occasion..." Einstein started.

"Shut up," Remphelmann said.

"This sure beats the shit out of burning shit," added Scheissenbrenner.

"Shut up." Remphelmann said.

"Sir, have you got my request for transfer?" Gruntz offered.

"Shut up," Remphelmann said.

Gonzales-McGillicuddy had to put in his two cents worth. "My cousin Hector, he wrote me a letter. Says he got a job for me as a body and fender man in Albuquerque, if I ever get out of here alive."

Remphelmann's final retort was, "That's the only sane thing I've heard all day."

Chapter Forty-Four

The stalwarts spent the rest of the night in wire bunker number one. They slept in two-hour shifts. The sun came up over the South China Sea. There was no rest for the weary. They dragged themselves back to their workstations and began to repair the trucks and armored carriers in the maintenance yard.

However, over at the ammunition dump, Viet Cong Sapper Sergeant Phuc Van Phuoc was in something of a quandary, a philosophical conundrum so to speak. His name, although sounding risqué to English speaking ears, is a beautiful one. It translates very roughly as 'Lucky Fortunate Cloud'. However he was feeling neither lucky nor fortunate. He had set off a demolition charge the night before, which had not gone quite as planned. The explosive had gone off a tad early, before he had time to crawl away. He was now buried beneath a pile of American ammunition. He had tried to extricate himself, only to find that he had blown his right leg off. He had not bothered to bleed to death the evening before, surely a breach of social etiquette. However, he reconsidered the invitation to the ball. He still had another charge of TNT explosive in a canvas bag. He found the glory of life ebbing away, and not wishing to miss an opportunity for a grand exit, decided to light off the satchel charge. Suicide was low on his priorities of life, but as the pain of his stump was rather annoying, and a taxi to the pure land was near at hand, he pushed the button. Off he went on the express, and off went the ammunition dump again.

The ammo went up in a fine mushroom cloud. Remphelmann and his men took the invitation and scurried off to the bunker behind the ordnance hootch. In a pile went Sergeant Heimstaadt, Sergeant Peckerwood, Specialist Scheissenbrenner, Privates Gonzales-McGillicuddy, Boudreaux, and Schweik plus the redoubtable Einstein. Remphelmann ducked back out again as exploding artillery shells sailed merrily about his head. First he went to the ordnance hootch, looking for Shortarm and Gruntz. No one was in attendance. Then he dodged the raining ammunition to the wire bunker number one. An infantry sergeant was there. He told Ronnie in no uncertain terms to get his rear echelon mother's ass out of Abilene. Remphelmann danced back to the ordnance bunker and flopped unceremoniously on the bunker floor.

"That reminds me of a story," Boudreaux started. No one had the energy to stop him. "Seems one day my Cousin Pierre and I decided to go noodling for catfish down on the river, but then we decided not to. So we stayed home."

"That reminds me of a story," Private Einstein continued. "Seems one day, my cousin Galileo Einstein had nothing to say."

"That reminds me of a story," Sergeant Heimstaadt chimed in. "It's got to do with my cousin Günter. Seems my cousin is from Alsace-Lorraine. Now Alsace-Lorraine is a nice peaceful set of mountain valleys sandwiched between France, Germany and Switzerland. They have der good wine in the valleys, grapes, ja? Grapes make wine."

Gonzales-McGillicuddy chimed in. "You mean to tell about an alsatian dog, one of them pit bulls or shepards?"

Remphelmann was exhausted. "Damn it, Gonzales, pipe down. A dog is a dog, and Alsace is a county in Europe."

Heimstaadt was in a story-telling mood. "Now my cousin Günter, see? Alsace-Lorraine has been fighting for two thousand years. First Charlemagne takes over from the Switzers, who took over from the Romans, and then the Froggies take over, und den the Bavarians, and then the Austrians, and then the French, and then the Germans. In 1871 Alsace was part of France. The Franco-Prussian war, it happened, the French lost und Deutschland got the place. After der First World War and the treaty of Versailles, the French got the place again. In 1940 the Germans invade France. Alsace-Lorraine, being over-run, went to the Prussians. In 1945, the Free French, they liberate, and Alsace went to France."

"Even I, with my brilliant logical mind, do not follow. Is this a Turing solution? Binary? Boolean?" Einstein queried.

Heimstaadt was unperturbed and continued. "So my cousin Günter was a vineyard keeper, who was fluent both in French and German. His grandfather was a draftee in the French army and fought in the Franco-Prussian against the Heinies. His father was a German draftee and fought in WWI against the Frogs. Günter he was born in 1917 as a German, but the next year was suddenly French. He grew up French. When the Second War started he was drafted into the French Army und fought briefly the Germans. Then things simmered down in 1940, the famous phony war, or sitzkreig. The French demobilized him and sent him home to wait orders. While tending the grapes, the nazis make der blitzkrieg and took most of France in weeks. Cousin Günter never got any re-mobilizing order, sat tight and was suddenly a German. The kraut draft authority came to town and told to him that he was a German. He gets drafted into the German Army. He gets shipped to the tail end of the frog fight and fought the French. Then off to the Eastern front where he fought the Russkies. He gets wounded, ja, at Stalingrad and got air lifted out just before the collapse. He was sent to hospital in Hamburg where he recovered. Then D-Day. Off from hospital, he fights the British. Bang, wounded next again! In the hospital, out again, he gets to fight the Americans. He gets the transfer, again he fights the Englanders. He got captured. Der Englanders, they got so many prisoners, und he gets to be American owned POW. Then comes De Gaulle's Free French Army goon squad, und tell him he was now Alsace French. He got re-drafted into der Frankreich Armee la Terre und closed out the krieg fighting the Germans. Ja, I make the recapitulation, ja?

First, he was a French fighting der Germans,

Then, he was a German fighting the French,

Den, He was a German fighting the Russkies,

Den, he was caught up fighting der Englanders.

Den, ja, he was an Alsatian kraut fighting the Amerikaners.

Den he was a Frenchman fighting der Germans!

You know he sent me a post-card, a letter here to Vietnam, because he's still alive, making the grapes in Lorraine, and you know what he say? 'Shit happens.'"

Remphelmann tried to stray out of the bunker for a look-see. The ammo dump was still doing its fireworks. A 105mm artillery shell, minus fuse, landed at his feet. He went back in the bunker.

"That reminds me of a story," said Gonzalez-McGillicuddy. "You'd think since how I was drafted out of New Mexico, the army would send me off to Fort Bliss, El Paso, Texas, for training, but no I end up at Fort Benning, Georgia. So I got leave and I hankered to see the ocean, which I'd never seen. I went to Charleston, South Carolina, and checked into the soldiers and sailors hostel. I want to see the ocean. 'Easy', somebody says, 'take the 44 bus to the beach'. I get on the bus, and I see that sign, 'Colored To The Rear, Please'. Now figuring I'm an Apache-Mexican-Irish I sit in the front. The bus goes along, but the bus driver picks up a microphone and says 'Hey you, soldier boy, get to the rear'. Now, I'm a lover not a fighter. I get up and go to the back of the bus and sit with the black folk. But here's a ruckus there too. Some old colored granny yells at me, 'you ain't no negro, get back to the front where you belong'. And some black dude chimes in, 'yeah that's right, we negroes ain't got much, but at least we got the back of the bus, and we don't cotton to you honkies crowding our space'. So, having got a C in high school math, I figured out a plan. There's twelve rows of seats in the bus, so I count back six rows from the driver, and six rows from the back, stand and hang on the overhead strap, midway between the whites and the coloreds. Then comes the driver on the intercom. 'Hey soldier boy, you trying to be some smart-ass uppity type'? He screeches the brakes; stops and pops open the door. 'Off', he says. I exited the bus and it goes away. I had to hoof it a mile and half to the beach, but what a fine sight it was! I'd had never seen the ocean before."

Remphelmann checked the weather outside the sandbags. It was raining unfired machine gun ammunition belts. He went back inside.

"That reminds me of a story", offered Sergeant Peckerwood. "Seems how we are talking about racial mis-relations, that puts West Rabbit Hutch on my mind. We got a definite series of pecking orders of peckerwoods, you will excuse the phrase. First there are the rich peckerwoods. You know there isn't any hereditary upper class in Tennessee, but they are characterized by their money. They can do any thing they want. They can buy the lawyers, they can buy the county judge, they buy the sheriff, they buy off everybody, so they can do whatever evil they want. Below them is the so-called middle class, you know the doctors and lawyers and Indian chiefs and schoolteachers and nurses and shopkeepers. Below them are the rednecks, like me. What we do is all the skilled and heavy tradesman work. I needn't but elaborate. Now beneath them is what we call in East or West Rabbit Hutch, the skaggs, or what you might call white trash, or what Marx called the lumpen proletariat. It's really hard to define a skagg, except that us rednecks not only don't want anything to do with them, because their behavior is so nasty, but also because most of us rednecks have at least two skaggs in the family. Mostly we find some way to send the men off to the state pen for twenty to life, and send their women folk off to Memphis to do the street walk. And well, some peckerwoods are even beneath the skaggs, god have mercy! You call a fellow southerner a redneck and you get a contemptuous response or even a joke, but if you call a white man a skagg or a peckerwood that there then is fighting words and you bought the farm! You see, after the civil war, or the 'War of Northern Aggression' as we call it, they freed the slaves, the colored folk. Good old boys being the polite sort they are, we stopped calling the black folk niggers, and started calling them blackbirds. Turn about being fair play the negroes started to call the white boys woodpeckers, cause a woodpecker has a red neck, see? Things being, the English talk being what it is, the blacks then in a turnabout of phrase, got to calling the skaggs, 'peckerwoods'. It's a black thing you wouldn't understand. Then things got worse. All of us white folk, from the hoity-toities, to the rednecks, the peckerwoods, and even the skaggs live north of the railroad track and all of the black folk crib south. But we've got this here 'separate but equal law' so I didn't know anything about the south side. And I don't know anything about black culture! The only time I interfaced with blacks is since I joined the army. They don't seem much different, excepting in one thing. I can't dance worth a hoot, but them colored got natural rhythm! As my daddy used to say, 'Ain't nobody make a fool out of Fred C. Dobbs'"

At this juncture Remphelmann again went out outside the bunker. The ammunition dump explosions were still in full flower. Sailing through the air came the body of Viet Cong Sapper Sergeant Phuc Van Phuoc, which landed with a thud at Remphelmann's feet. Remphelmann went back into the bunker.

"On second thought," offered Private Einstein, "That does remind me of a story. Seems people ask me why I'm on my second tour of Vietnam. After my first tour here in La-La Land I tried to go home. But all my relatives started asking me why I was acting so weird. I said, of course, that I'm not weird, you are, because a privileged observation space is a fundamental of time-space reality. So finally, my sister, my own sister, says to me, 'I don't know what happened to you in Vietnam, but you're not fit for polite society'. Now that cut to the quick. I was reminded of Hamlet, returning from England and running into Yorick the gravedigger who talked about Hamlet who was sent off to England, because he's loony and why because he's stark raving mad and it won't be noticed there in England because everyone's as mad as he. So promptly I re-upped, asked for Vietnam, and here I am. Doesn't my re-up story echo that of Sheissie's? I notice nobody laughed. I ponder, I lament, I scrutinize about my jest. Why is everybody in the war zone telling bad jokes? Bad jokes, meaning, they aren't even funny? The answer is, because war, like life, is a bad joke."

Remphelmann went back outside the bunker. The ammunition dump fireworks had fizzled into nothing. He thought the coast was clear. Instead the elephant had raised its tusks and was about to bellow again.

Ronnie went back into the bunker and surveyed his men with a practiced eye. "Scheissenbrenner, are you the only one at parade without a remind me story?"

Scheissenbrenner piped up. "That reminds me of Mad Magazine and its mascot, Alfred E. Neumann. You know the cartoon character with the idiotic smile and the missing tooth, and the comic line, 'What, Me Worry?' So, 'what, me worry?'"

═══ Chapter Forty-Five ═══

If the elephant had bellowed, now it shat. If the balloon went up, it was now far above the trees. Captain Manteca, the worst of the worst, looking like a wurst, appeared at the bunker door. "We are all going to die!"

Remphelmann was not impressed. What impressed him was the following information and order.

"General Goodspeed has sent a tactical order. The commies are pushing really hard against the Le Hong Phong Forest and Que Ell One. All of Goodspeed's troops are committed to that fight. But seems the VC are sending a left hook to envelop west Phan Thiet. Goodspeed has no reserves. So every breathing swinging richard in LZ Bozo has been ordered out to block the south side of Que Ell One to keep the VC from crossing the road into Phan Thiet City."

"And?" asked Remphelmann.

"Besides the fact that we are all going to sacrificed to Moloch, everybody from Bozo is told to convene on Ap Noi village on the south of the road and make a holding action. Any animate body has to grab a rifle or whatever and make a stand on the Ap Noi line. Grab anybody, everybody, any rifle, any ammo, and any

351

machine gun and set up a skirmish south of the road. What is a skirmish?"

Remphelmann pondered. "A skirmish line is a thin body of forward troops to act as a picket line or warning guard against the advance of the enemy."

"We are all going to die."

Nonetheless Remphelmann gathered his men. They had their M-16's. Sergeant Gruntz, appearing from nowhere, lugged in an M-60 machine gun. Sergeant Shortarm appeared with seven whole cases of machine gun ammunition and plopped three in Remphelmann's jeep and the other four in Manteca's. Sergeant Peckerwood ran up with a holstered 45 colt and web belt and tossed it to Ronnie, who strapped it on. Remphelmann piled his men into the 'Mudd Buck It' and a standby deuce and a half. They roared out of LZ Bozo to a hopeful line on the south side of Que Ell One. Manteca had his jeep bouncing behind, crammed with the ammo and as many quartermaster men as he could round up.

Ronnie was immensely relieved to find Porky Shinebaum at the location with his jeep and its radio and machine gun. Schlomo was yelling orders. Duvalier and his men were to Shinebaum's left. Shinebaum was trooping from left to right as the rear echelon ordnance men dismounted and came into walking distance. "What the hell am I supposed to do?" Remphelmann asked. "I can't even remember what they told me in OCS about deploying troops into an attack position."

"Screw the OCS, Get your men back on the south side of the road, string them out at ten yard intervals on the back side of the road hump, have them lock and load and sight in on that tree line across the rice paddy. Bearing one o'clock from the highway line, three hundred meters distance. Plus ditch your jeep and truck off the levee low enough where they can't be seen. I'm short an NCO for part of my line, can you loan me Heimstaadt?"

Remphelmann deployed his men thusly and parked his vehicles in the sheltering ditch, seeing that Duvalier had done the same some three football fields away. The kraut followed Porky and took leadership of some of Shinebaum's men.

Out of nowhere a huey appeared. No less than Colonel BeLay, the commander of the infantry battalion, jumped out and danced beneath the whirling rotors and ran up to Remphelmann. "Do you have your men in line?"

"Sir, yes sir."

"Do you have any boots on the ground leadership?"

"Sir, yes sir. Lieutenant Shinebaum, the military policeman, is a hundred meters over there and has a grasp of the ground. He's placing Lieutenant Duvalier's men as we speak. They are two hundred meters to his left."

"Fine, lieutenant, do you know what you are doing?"

"Frankly, Scarlet, I mean sir, I haven't the damnest idea."

"No matter, my fine young officer. Top down, listen to Officer Shinebaum, who is quite good. Also in your platoon, you've got Sergeant Gruntz. He's former infantry and knows the tactical ropes. Your basic mission is to spray and pray north across the road into that wood line out there three hundred meters. If you have to open fire, don't stint on the ammo. Just throw a hornet's nest of bullets that way. Have you seen Captain Manteca?"

"He's a hundred meters back, quivering in his jeep."

"Typical. You say Shinebaum is a football field to our left?"

"Sir, yes sir."

BeLay took off at a loping run in Shinebaum's direction. Remphelmann saw the two confer briefly. The infantry colonel scurried back to his helicopter and was gone, chopping into the misty tropical air.

Ronnie found Sergeant Gruntz. "Hey sarge, what do you think we should do?"

"For god's sake, sir lets belt buckle in the dirt and herky jerky on the safe side of the road cut. Charlie's is filling out that tree line three hundred distant, maybe 30 degrees east of north. I haven't got a compass. Let's say, as you look across the road, bearing on one o'clock, we will pour lead as needed. By the way sir, I transferred from the infantry to the ordnance to get out of shit like this. Did you sign my request for transfer?"

"It's in my in-box, awaiting signature."

"Too damned late for today. Oh my god, here it comes!"

A perfect hail of machine gun bullets and rifle fire sailed just over their heads. Gruntz glanced off to their left. Shinebaum was hand signaling to open fire. Gruntz added, "Sir, troop the line. Tell the men to go helmet up and spray the far wood line with everything they can jam in their rifles."

Remphelmann did as suggested. He scurried on elbows and knees, telling the men to peek up and unload on the tree line. They fired and fired. A sling of outrageous bullets came back in their direction. Remphelmann was slopped in the mud, but he felt as if he could actually see the angry enemy bullets drilling above his helmet. He was scared shitless. He was scared shitless not only for himself but also for the men under his command.

It suddenly occurred to him that he had lost track of Sergeant Peckerwood. He seemed to him, that in the absence of Captain Manteca, Peckerwood had slithered to the east to lead the quartermasters. A quartermaster clerk, now grunt, was firing across the road. "Have you seen Sarge Peckerwood?" Ronnie asked.

The clerk said, "Butcher blocked," and jerked his thumb. The body of Peckerwood, sans head, sans blood, sans life, lay nearby.

Remphelmann caught up with Sergeant Gruntz again. They slithered along the fire line. They met up with Sergeant Shortarm, who was feeding belts of ammunition into the M-60 gun, which was being manned by the redoubtable Private Boudreaux. In the mud behind them was Private Einstein who was handing up ammo belts from steel cans.

"Look here," Gruntz offered to Shortarm. "See how far that wood line is? It's nearly 300 meters away. The VC only got AK-47's and their effective range is only 400 yards. If a round should chance to hit you at this distance, it will only bounce off your helmet, or clunk your flak jacket. As any fool can plainly see, the rounds are looping in. Look at these rinky dinky bullets splatting harmlessly into the paddy water. Nothing but spit-wads." At this juncture, a burst of rifle fire was heard in the distance. Sergeant Gruntz dropped dead with a bullet hole neatly drilled though through his helmet into his brain.

And then in no particular order.

Remphelmann had done the decent thing. He dragged the brainy mess of Sergeant Gruntz off the parapet and flopped the body into the mud next to the 'Mudd Buck It'.

Out of nowhere an Air Force captain appeared. With him was a radio telephone operator or RTO, an airman with a huge backpack sized radio strapped on his shoulders. The air force type was obviously a Forward Air Control officer, or FAC. Attached to the radio was a telephone head set. The FAC was screaming commands into to the mike, which were incomprehensible to Ronnie. Out of the misty sky three jet aircraft swooped down on the tree line. These planes, Thunderchiefs, nicknamed 'thuds,' dropped napalm bombs along the road that paralleled the wood line. The bombs went up in oily, greasy, black yet orange plumes of flaming gasoline. The FAC kept yelling. The thuds did an amazing arc, rather like a ferris wheel, into the clouds and rolled over for another strafing run. Suddenly the mist on the ground met the clouds in the air and all ground visibility was lost. The FAC screamed, "Abort, abort, abort!" Two of the thuds did so, but the third could not fight the gravity force and splattered straight into the wood line. There was a horrendous crunch of airplane, bombs and ground. The FAC scurried away, still screaming into the RTO phone handle.

Then two hueys landed between Remphelmann's position and Shinebaum's. Out piled Lieutenant Cervantes and two fire teams of riflemen. Porky, P.T., and Ronnie converged on Cervantes. Cervantes pronounced, "My orders are to beef up the skirmish line, but by guts and glory, I'll attack."

Duvalier was beside himself. "Attack, hell!" You've got three hundred meters, three football fields of open flat rice paddy mud to traverse! Charlie's got machine guns emplaced. Traverse? Charlie's got the field of fire. You can't even get up the far side of the road without the VC getting a clear shot at your whole platoon."

"Screw you," Cervantes swore, "It's medal of honor time." With that he signaled his men up. They went twenty yards and a swath of bullet fire mowed them down. His men, knowing both discretion and valor, went back to the shelter of the berm. Cervantes, perhaps thinking of Custer's Last Stand, remained upright and shouted, "Death or dishonor!" Ten machine gun bullets stitched his torso.

Remphelmann had belt buckled in the asphalt crumbs behind the roadway, but reflexively crawled out and grabbed Cervantes by his achilles heel and muscled and dragged the glory hunter back behind the road ditch. Remphelmann knew not what to do. Cervantes was spurting blood in gushes. Red liquid pumped out of his abdomen, gurting from his guts. Remphelmann asked, "Are you alright?"

Cervantes cryptically remarked, "Ah, is this the end of Rico?" and died.

Ronnie had no time for time. From three hundred meters away Victor Charles was doing the bee's nest of lead swarms. He low crawled over to the ordnance men's M-60. Private Boudreaux was accurately laying down fire on the enemy position. Sergeant Shortarm and Einstein had been feeding belts of ammunition into the gun.

"Holy Winkler twinkies," Shortarm managed to swear to the lieutenant. "We done be done out of ammo. You gots any in the 'Mudd Buck It'?"

Ruefully, Remphelmann replied. "No."

"But sir, Captain Manteca is but a shy distance off. He done got another four cases in his jeep. Can's you fetch?"

Ronnie tried to fetch. He groveled through the rice water and found Manteca blubbering beneath his jeep. The captain did not even have a rifle but he did have a holstered 45 and a web belt slung uselessly over his shoulder. The belt was studded with canvas pouches filled with additional magazines.

"Look here, you worthless scrap of bacon grease! Get out from under there and hump those four cases of ammo up to the machine gun."

"What me? If I get killed, what about my career?"

"Career my ass, loser! Hump ammo or die."

Manteca screwed his fear to a rather greasy sticking point. He timidly crawled from the underside of the vehicle, took a can of ammo in hand and wheezed his way on his elbows to Boudreaux. Remphelmann was swearing and low crawling behind with another box. Lead was singing over their heads. Shortarm screamed to Einstein, who screamed to Boudreaux, "Loading, loaded, fire".

The M-60 spit. Remphelmann kicked Manteca. "Two more cans." They slithered snakelike back to the captain's jeep and fetched the last of the ammunition, each officer dragging a box. The two officers bellied the ammo up to Shortarm, who unlatched the ammunition cans and handed the belts on to Einstein, who fed the death material to Boudreaux's gun.

Out of nowhere a Viet Cong mortar landed. Shrapnel flew. Remphelmann looked about and everything seemed fine. Boudreaux, Shortarm and Einstein were at their post at the machine gun. However Manteca was writhing in the mud. Ronnie called out, "Manteca?"

"I'm not going to die, I'm dieing right now."

"Look, Lardy, stop this negative talk. Perhaps you should rise to the occasion and show a brave face to the troopers."

With that Manteca let out a scream. Remphelmann tried a quick examination and found that a piece of shrapnel had razor cut across Manteca's thighs and had at groin level snipped Manteca's membrem virile and testicles off and into the rice paddy.

Remphelmann found pause to attempt a diplomatic response. "Sir, it seems that the mortar round has sliced your joystick and walnuts off and blown them into the mud." He waited until the facts had set in, expecting a woeful response. Instead, Manteca made the following reply.

"Thank god."

"Sir?" Remphelmann had a field bandage at hand, with a huge gauze pad, stretch wrap and creamed antibiotic inside a foil packet, but could not fathom how to twirl the contents around such an ungainly mass of leg, groin and torso. "Sir, my goodness, sir, that shard of metal has cut your family jewels right off at the short and curly's. You are going to bleed to death."

"Thank god," Manteca repeated. "You see? I've lost my manhood! How wonderful. How glorious. Now I can get that sex change operation I always wanted. I can see myself now, Las Vegas, a showgirl in the chorus line. I know I'm going to make it! San Francisco, here I come. Hollywood will love me. I don't even have to think about being a transvestite. Even in the Big Easy I'll be part of the crowd."

Remphelmann as usual was at loss for words, but spoke anyway. "Captain, you are just having a post traumatic stress moment. Surely you know not of that which you speak. You have a short-term discombobulation. Look, I've found your penis in the mud. I'm stuffing it back in your shorts. Maybe the surgeon can sew it back on."

"Discombobulation, hell! I have been delivered."

The only thing that saved Remphelmann's mind at this moment was the arrival of a dust-off medivac chopper. Somehow amidst the chaos, eight wounded men, plus the bodies of Gruntz, Cervantes and the complaining mutilated Manteca were tossed aboard an overloaded huey. The VC machine gun fire splattered sporadically across the intervening space. Suddenly a medic crewman tossed Manteca head first out of the chopper.

"What are you doing?" Remphelmann yelled.

"He's meat, and we're overweight! Next trip!" With that the helicopter was gone.

Remphelmann belly-flopped next to the captain. He checked Manteca over. Manteca was indeed dead. He had gone to the great chorus line in the sky. Ronnie retrieved the holstered Colt and its ammunition belt from around the great man's neck and placed it around his own.

Despite the rather crowded affair, Remphelmann felt totally alone on Que Ell One.

Chapter Forty-Six

Both the elephant and balloon and Remphelmann's mind did what the old saying said, 'The three that I exalt the most, father, son, and holy ghost, took the last plane for the coast.' The next period of time was beyond Remphelmann's capacity to calculate. Did it happen in three minutes or thirty minutes, or thirty seconds, or thirty months? He could not fathom. The dreaded thousand yard stare had come to settle in behind his eyes and watch on his neurons.

A helicopter flew in and landed behind the 'Mudd Buck It'. To Remphelmann's amazement and astonishment, General Goodspeed stepped out and coolly approached Ronnie.

"Hello, lieutenant, how are things going here on the eastern part of the line?"

Remphelmann did his best to explain the situation. Stray bullets were singing about but Goodspeed was totally unconcerned. Goodspeed launched into an oration that was entirely too long, and to Remphelmann, who was hearing the charming song of bullets, too close for comfort.

"You see, I'm a West Point graduate, duty, honor, country and all that. I can see a decent officer when I see him, and you fit the bill. I'm old, you know, a WWII type. If peacetime had prevailed, I'd have been pensioned off as a full bull colonel, but as this war happened along, here I am. Why? Because I really do believe in a decent army and doing the right thing and giving a full measure of devotion to the profession. Sadly there are, at my level, far to many generals of the political stripe. What was Von Clauswitz's bon mot, 'war is the continuation of policy by other means'? I'm afraid I never cottoned much to the political end of things. Tactics, personal leadership, making sure the men troop the line and do the best they can, that's what I understand. I'm a nuts and bolts kind of guy. That sort of thing is sadly out of favor at the pentagon, at least amongst the higher brass."

"Why are you telling me this, sir?" Remphelmann enquired. "I'm not the rank or the type to hear such things from you. Especially while Charlie's looping lead into our position."

"Ah," said Goodspeed, "just the point. One of my main talents, I don't brag to tell it; it's a simple fact. I can size a man right off. You are too decent to be a lifer. You've got the sympathetic listener gene. You are the type of man folks naturally confide in. I bet you have heard more confessions than a Catholic priest. I bet you heard more sad tales than a Texas honky-tonk bar tender on a drunken Saturday night. After you get out of this stupidity, this insane excuse of a war, consider your god given talents."

Remphelmann, who thought he was beyond blushing, blushed. "Sir, you are trying to flatter me."

"Take the corncob out of your colon," the general laughed. "I look straight, I talk straight, and I shoot straight, that is what I am." Goodspeed paused, looked off for a long moment into the distant jungle edge from whence bullets flew. "Damn, I should have gotten killed, rather than wounded, when I crossed that damn wood line at the Hertgen Forest. My whole career after that has been anti-climactic."

Goodspeed got back in his chopper. As it bit air, a rocket-propelled grenade sailed out of the wood line and ran smack into the rotor root. The huey spun in a fiery mass into the rice paddy. Remphelmann looked for Goodspeed in the flaming wreckage, but there was nothing but meaningless bits of sizzling hamburger.

P.T. Duvalier appeared out of the sheltering road ditch. "For god's sake, Ronnie, I don't know how they did it but Charlie's managed to get a partial platoon, twenty men, up to that rice paddy dike not a hundred meters off of your right."

"Yes," Remphelmann managed to gasp in exasperation. "That's like the old joke, P.T., you know, Tonto and the Lone Ranger surrounded? As the Indians close in, Indians to the left, right and front, the Lone Ranger exclaims 'Hey Tonto, we are surrounded', and Tonto remarks, ' What do you mean we, pale face?'"

Duvalier laughed. "Just have your squad lower their fire, off the wood line into that paddy dike about a hundred yards out." P.T. was soon gone.

At that moment a horrendous yell came up from the near distance. "GI, GI, you die!" Remphelmann took the invitation personally. He realized that he had the two 45's, one strapped to his waist and the other looped about his neck. Doing a flourish that would have done Yosemite Sam proud, he yanked both of them from their holsters and announced, "Back off, ye heathen, back off," at which juncture he unloaded both pistols in the general if not specific direction of Mister Charles.

"Holy Alpine assholes, sir," said Sergeant Shortarm as he slithered up the ditch, "That there is a fine speech, but no pistol gonna carry a hundred. Lemme have Boudreaux lower his fire."

Remphelmann reloaded his pistols. "As usual, sergeant, you have good advice."

The selfsame cry came up again from their front, "GI, GI, you die!" and another blast of AK lead came their direction.

Remphelmann continued, "I don't think they like us."

Shortarm ducked into the mud. "Holy Toya turdballs, sir, I tend to agree with you."

Remphelmann stood again and emptied both magazines

of his pistols at the dug in VC. This time he bellowed, "Avast, ye pirates, back off." He got a dubious satisfaction from the gesture.

"Begging the lieutenant's pardon, sir," Shortarm observed. "Y'all only a wasting ammunition. Pluses that cartoon character done gots red handlebar mustachios. Y'all a tad short on the whiskers."

A withering fire arced over Remphelmann and his men. Bouncing up the ditch came Porky Shinebaum. "I don't know, Ronnie, how this story popped up in my mind. But did I ever tell you, how a nice Jewish boy like me got the nickname of Porky? By the way, tell your gunner to aim lower."

Remphelmann did so. Then out of the misty sky a Thunderchief came screaming down and unloaded a bomb on the tree line far away. However, the bomb bounced cockamamie, and exploded in the air sailing shrapnel any which way, and peppered the American troops in the ditch. Shinebaum fell. He had a wonderful splinter of jagged spiraling metal lodged in his upper body.

Remphelmann was on his P's and Q's. He low-crawled to Einstein and relieved him of his first aid pouch and snaked back to Shinebaum. Porky was flat on his back. The jagged piece of metal was sticking right through his flak jacket under his nipple. Ronnie ripped open Shinebaum's armored vest and fatigue blouse. Next to the shrapnel was a neat hole through the lung that was wheezing bloody froth with every breath Shinebaum took. It was a classic sucking chest wound. Remphelmann knew what to do. He ripped open the plastic first aid pouch and slapped the plastic over the open exhalations from the lung exit. Then he wrapped the stretch bandage around Porky's chest and cinched it tight. Remphelmann looked around. Bullets were screaming above his head. His men were doing yeoman duty. Porky was dieing beneath his hands.

"I didn't finish the story, Ron."

"I don't think it's time for stories, Porky. We need to get

our asses out of Abilene. Especially the wounded." With that Remphelmann stood in the ditch. He was at a distance from Duvalier who was obviously yelling into a radio microphone. Ronnie did not know any formal hand signals but attempted. He pointed to the sky, and then to his heart, and then made a pat down sign and then whirled his finger corkscrew into the clouds. Somehow Duvalier got the idea, and spoke into the radio. Another medivac helicopter would soon be on the way.

"You see, Ronnie, how a nice Jewish boy like me got the name Porky?"

"You really ought to save your breath."

"No, it's important. See my mother was a Sephardic Jewess, from Cuba and later from Puerto Rico. And my Dad, he was an Ashkenazi refugee from Danzig."

"Porky, relax, the next medivac will soon be here."

Shinebaum kept talking. "When I started to pop out of the womb, my mother was in a fog, a complete gaggle of anesthesia and birth pangs, and couldn't remember whether to speak Yid, or modern Hebrew, or Spanish or English, so she kept yelling through the final contractions, 'por que, por que'! See the joke?"

"No," said Remphelmann.

"'Por que, por que' in Spanish means 'why, why?' But in English it's 'Pork Kay, Pork Kay'."

"Shlomo, save your wind, you'll need it."

"Of course, when the nurse came out of the delivery room, to announce my happy and healthy birth, my father, ever the businessman, was on the long distance telephone to his broker in Chicago. He was wheeling and dealing copper futures at the time and doing well, I might add. So, he is on the phone yelling trade assignments, and the nurse comes in with the news of my successful birth and the 'por que, por que' punch line from my dear sweet mother. My father stops, has a brain fart and says to his broker, 'finalize the copper trade, but also buy a hundred pork belly contracts.' The guy on the other end screams to him. 'Abe, we're Jews, and you want me to contract pork bellies? What would the rabbi say, if he knew?' My dad says 'buy a hundred pork bellies and sell them, at precisely eight o'clock AM eight days out. The rabbi will be doing the foreskin deed thing at nine AM Havana time. Get the timing?' The broker says, 'Abe if anybody up here in Chicago gets wind of this, I'll be banned from temple for life.' 'Moe, buy on my account, sell on my account! Damn the torpedoes.' So to make a long story short, the belly trade went gangbusters, made my Dad a bundle, and happily ever after my Mom called me 'Por Que' and my Dad called me 'Porky'. See the joke?"

Remphelmann was rather worried about the lead spinning above his head and the bullets careening about his men. "No", he replied, "I don't see the joke."

Moise Aaron Shinebaum died.

The next medivac helicopter arrived and landed behind the 'Mudd Buck It'. There was a scramble to see who would fit. Shinebaum went in. Several other wounded from Cervantes's platoon went in. A medic hopped out and examined the wreckage of Goodspeed's chopper and came back waving 'no, no'. Nobody saw Manteca, whose corpse had sunk into the rice. Half-loaded the dust off blasted into the sky.

Pierre Toussaint Gustave Duvalier came loping across the intervening space. "Ronnie, evacuation orders from on high! Screw your jeep, screw the truck! When the next chopper lands, load your men and guns on the flight and di di mao. You got space for ten, fill it up."

"But P.T., what about you?"

"I got the same-o, same-o. I'm gone when you're gone. Time to clear the position. Charles is going to bulldoze the whole road." As Duvalier sprinted back to his position, a huey slicked in for a landing in the rice paddy behind the 'Mudd Buck It'.

Somehow Remphelmann managed to yell to his men, and they all, Einstein, Gonzalez, Scheissenbrenner, who knows who else and Shortarm, dropped everything except weapons and dashed for the chopper. The junior men piled in and Ronnie followed. Remphelmann signaled to the loadmaster to take off. Then he realized Sergeant Shortarm was still on the ground. "Wait, wait", he screamed.

Shortarm had a leg up on the landing strut and Ronnie grabbed his hand. Just then a stream of tracer fire blasted across the helicopter. The chopper pilot did the right thing. He pulled collective and the chopper went up. The river of machine gun fire went right through Shortarm's elbow and sliced it cleanly. Shortarm tumbled back into the paddy with only a stump of a bicep. Remphelmann was left handshaking Shortarm's fingers and forearm. He held onto it, and made a bloody scream. "Down, down, one on the ground!" No one listened and the air machine went up into the mist.

Sergeant Shortarm, falling away in the drizzle, falling backward into the rice water, cheerfully called out, "Holy Riceland horseshit, sir, ol' Shortarm done be short a arm!"

The helicopter twirled about and climbed out of the protective bar of the road. Machine gun bullets were slithering vapor trails through the air. Remphelmann still had Shortarm's handshake in his grasp. Que Ell One circled downward into the muggy air.

Chapter Forty-Seven

The sad flight of LZ Bozo's finest was choppered back home. The wounded were taken off first. Then the meat wagon came to take the dead. Remphelmann was still holding on to Shortarm's arm. A graves registration private pried it out of his hand and tossed it nonchalantly onto a stretcher. Disconsolation was not on Ronnie's mind. Nothing was on his mind. Another helicopter landed nearby. The gunner leaped out and began to yell for a certain "Lieutenant Remphelmann." Ronnie woodenly answered.

"Sir, a special chopper has been issued out of Cam Ranh, to take you personally to the 1369th battalion. Highest priority."

Remphelmann looked at his fatigues and his flak jacket. He was caked with dirt, mud, and the blood of Manteca, Shinebaum, Gruntz and Shortarm. "I need to change, I need to wash up, I need a clean uniform," he pleaded.

"No sir, highest priority, Cam Ranh."

Remphelmann was so shell shocked, so thousand yarded, that he blindly obeyed the orders. He tossed his 45's to one of his men. He got in the new helicopter and went to Cam Ranh Bay. The gorgeous scenery beneath him went by without notice. The helicopter, rather than landing at the usual helipad, squatted into a tight space next to the 1369th REMF Quonset. The loadmaster had to drag Remphelmann out and bodily point him to the headquarters door. Ronnie stumbled in. Private Zerk looked up.

"God, sir, you look like hell."

"Thank you, private, I feel like hell, but as things are well and all manner of things shall be well, so I am well."

"Sir, Colonel Slick, the heroic Colonel Slick, late of his glorious victory in the street-fighting of Da Lat is holding a battalion briefing inside the confines of his office. I was told that when you arrived, to not have you observe protocol but to go right in." The clerk pointed at the door. Remphelmann walked in, sweaty, caked with gore, a blind man going though a dark portal. He was immediately hit by a blast of cold refrigerated air. He had not felt air conditioning in months and the slam of the freezing temperature made him start back. He was instantly woozy.

Colonel Slick was at an easel. He had a pointer and was gesturing at a large graphical chart, which had numerous red and green and blue lines. Present were eight perfectly manicured, wonderfully starched, gloriously clean officers looking on in rapt, servile attention. He was finishing up some sort of lecture. "So you see, gentlemen. According to the best Harvard Business School protocols, the battalion, and I, I might add, is executing the most wonderful statistical achievements. The wonder of statistics is, that my job performance looks brilliant. The ratio of vehicular downtime to repair time to return to customer units is most excellent. I shall surely get the Legion of Merit for my brilliant leadership. The fact that these statistics bear no relationship to the facts in reality is irrelevant. Before I dismiss you fine officers, I must remind you that in addition the Legion of Merit, I have put myself in for the Medal of Honor, for my heroic stand in the Hotel Grande, I mean the Da Lat streets." He paused long enough to recognize the presence of Remphelmann. "Well, gentlemen, I see that we are graced with the appearance of my young stripling,

Rumpleskin of Bozo. As I have to have a private word with him, I now dismiss you all."

The attendant officers stood and filed out, only to have Captain Dunghill, ever the kiss-ass, mention viva voce, "Sir, What a wonderful leader you are, how thankful we are to grovel in your esteemed presence."

"You need not voice your thought, Captain Dunghill. I am well aware of my shining star in the firmament of outstanding officers."

Remphelmann was left alone in the presence of the great man. In his usual manner the colonel did not at first acknowledge Remphelmann. First he went to his preening side stand, took a currycomb and brushed his gray hair to his satisfaction. Then he unbuckled his trousers and fished in with his fist near his anus. With only a slight wince, he withdrew his hand and held up a toothpick-sized splinter of teakwood door. "Straight out of my heroic ham, you see, lieutenant? A mere reminder of my valiant fight against the enemy at Da Lat. The same action where his saintliness Chaplain Captain Champagne met his maker." Slick deposited the toothpick in a shot glass, no doubt as evidence of his heroism.

"Sir, I know more of the story than you think."

"But enough of my courageous life. I had you called in to discuss... damn it, lieutenant, what's wrong with your uniform? Unstarched, unkempt, wearing a flak jacket! What is that, mud? And what else is about you, that greasy gray slop on your shirt, that stinking black congealed crud on your pants?"

"Begging the colonel's perfumed nose, sir. I have had a bad day. I didn't have time to change. That gray slop, as you call it, is the brains of Sergeant Gruntz smeared on my blouse. The black crud is the dried blood of Lieutenant Shinebaum. Should I describe further?"

"Lieutenant, that is conduct unbecoming. Enough! If you are to be ushered into my presence I demand a scrupulous officer like appearance."

"All is well, and all manner of things shall be well," said Remphelmann. "But why did you call me in from the field?"

"Ah yes, the matter of the engine crate. The heroin, I mean heroic engine crate. There was to be a transfer of a engine box stuffed with, well, an engine that was to be sent to Rock Island Arsenal near Chicago that was stuffed with, well, information. Information of the highest monetary, I mean, military importance. It was being shipped from General Kegresse, of heroic memory, to me, for transshipment from Saigon here to Surf City for a priority flight to Illinois. However, the engine container somehow got lost. Between Kegresse's demise, the chaplain captain's needless death, and my heroic peppering with teak toothpicks..." At this Slick reached in his shorts and withdrew another splinter from his butt and plopped it into the shot glass. "And I was, what was I saying, the engine, the priority engine, went missing. One rumor is that it went to Bozo."

"Sir, I have just come off of the most horrible day on Que Ell One. I have had three of my men killed, and at least thirty other men totally slaughtered and I'm plucked away to answer about a missing engine?"

"Priorities are priorities, Rumpleskin. What is more important, men's lives or my heroin, err, herring, ah, engine?"

"Sir, I know nothing about your engine or its crate. All manner of things being well, all things are well."

Slick went forward. "Which reminds me of a missive I got in my in-box. About the retention of junior officers. It seems young officers such as yourself are not re-enlisting. Why, I don't understand. What a wonderful life this is! But the directive states that if you, Lieutenant Rumpleskin, re-enlist for two years, you'll soon get promoted to captain. Now, isn't that a fine thing, to be a captain?"

"Captain Manteca just got his nuts shot off in a paddy just off Que Ell One. Do you want to see his urine on my clothes? Do you think I want to be a captain?"

Slick had no ready answer. "Well, well, the reason you were

called in from the field was to locate that top secret engine canister."

"Engine crate? I don't need no stinking engine crate. It ain't at Bozo, it ain't at Betty, it ain't anywhere on Que Ell One. All is well and all manner of things shall be well."

"I perceive that you are being slightly cryptic. No matter. But my priority is the engine crate."

"Sir, I know nothing of any engine. But I hear the helicopter whirring its blades just outside the door. Can I return to my duties? May I return to my men?"

"Well, the heroin, I mean heroic cargo must be lost in transit, you have permission..."

Remphelmann took no heed of proprieties. He exited from the freezing room and into the helicopter. He said nothing to the loadmaster. He stuck his head into the pilot's cabin and announced, "Que Ell One."

Chapter Forty-Eight

The helicopter deposited Remphelmann back at his home. He felt infinitely alone. The 'Mudd Buck It' was not there. Sergeant Shortarm was not there. Sergeant Peckerwood was not there. Sergeant Gruntz was not there. Ronnie did not have the guts to go back to his officers BOQ, because neither Shinebaum nor Manteca, his hard-won friends, were there. He hit upon the idea of going to the platoon HQ, expecting a doleful and joyless emptiness. Instead, what he found was a wake. A real Irish wake, a tub of iced beer and all his enlisted men in attendance.

There was Sergeant Heimstaadt, his sole remaining NCO, Specialist Scheissenbrenner and Privates Einstein, Schweik, Gonzales-McGillicuddy, and Boudreaux. Ronnie relaxed. He sat behind Sergeant Shortarm's desk. "Men, I got called away to Surf City right at the tail of the fire-fight. What happened that I don't know?"

Heimstaadt started the details. "Ja, ja, so we got the evacuation orders with you, so we cleared the LZ with you, and..."

"What about Sergeant Shortarm?"

"Ja, herr lieutenant, ja, ja. Der Charlie's never carry through with the attack, they shrink back in the woods. They not attack the causeway. So another medivac, it goes in and brings out the corpse of Shortarm's und the others."

"So Shortarm is dead?"

"Ja, ja, mien kleine fuhrer. Shortarm kaput. Shortarm is in the graves registration cooler. Where you think we get the cold brew?"

"But everybody else is alive?"

"Ja, Gott willing. Except Gruntz und Peckerwood. They have been in the stiff cooler, yet. Ja? They make der body bag mit Shortarm. They are, zip, zip. For them the war is over."

Remphelmann looked around. He already had a third cold beer open with a handy church key and guzzled it. "So Boudreaux, how are you? You did fine duty with the machine gun."

"That done reminds me of story." Boudreaux started, "It seems my cousin Pierre and I were possum hunting down near Avery Island..." A collective groan went up and Boudreaux paused.

"And you, Schweik?"

"This is excellent sir! When we get home everybody is going to love us. We're regular ass flaming heroes. They're just going to love us for our heroics today. When we get home, the girl's, the women, are going to shower us with kisses. They are going to tell us what wonderful heroes we are, and every thing is going to be peachy keen. Every thing is going to remain the same at home, except we will come home heroes. Just like my Daddy from WWII. Do you believe that shit?"

"Scheissenbrenner?"

"Sir, I'm just a dumb ass from upstate New York. What do I know, no education, no brains. Canandaigua, Finger Lakes, concord grape pickers. But my family have always been good citizens and good part-time soldiers. My great great granddad was at Saratoga during the Revolution, my great granddad in the Civil War, 14th New York. Fought at Antietam. My granddad at Belleau Wood, and my dad at the Battle of the Bulge. So the stories pass down, sitting around the potbelly stove. Seems how seemingly ignorant country guys like us could discuss theological, philosophical and political things with the best of them, with reasoning and clear logic. Why? Because we folk are grounded in life and death and taxes and earning a living, dealing in wives and kids and local happenings. I don't know diddly about Thucicicides or John Locke. But there are certainties of life, the planting of corn, the ripening of grapes, the agony of women in childbirth. Got another beer?"

"Einstein?"

"Did you every notice about soldiers and what comedians they are? Comedians are the saddest people in the world. They are so overwhelmed by the grief of the human condition that their only defense is to keep making jokes, as if a funny response can stave off the hungry ravening dog of despair. The snarling teeth of a rabid hound. As my Uncle Darwin Einstein used to say, 'God started intelligent life off on the wrong foot. Instead of apes, turning into warlike, kill their own kind, so-called human beings, God could have began with a different basis, say like petunias or begonias, then we could just smile at one another under the sun, instead of doing this violent thing.'"

"I tend to agree," offered Remphelmann. "When I got here, I thought I was going to make changes, to make the world a better place. Like somebody promised, 'we can change the world.' I've found I can not change the world. I've found I can't even change myself." Remphelmann paused again to open another cold beer. "But Boudreaux, you were going to tell another one of your Cousin Pierre stories."

Boudreaux was fast asleep and quietly snoring. The snore was catching. After a horrendous day that had begun with dread and ended with horror, all had nodded off in the fading light, each with a beer still in hand. Only Sergeant Heimstaadt was still awake. He began to sing in his soft clear baritone,

"Heilige nacht,
Stille nacht,
All is calm.
All is bright."

The sun went down over Que Ell One.

═══ Chapter Forty-Nine ═══

The next morning, two sat disconsolate. Duvalier and Remphelmann slumped in the BOQ kitchen. Remphelmann had managed to boil up a small pot of c-ration powdered coffee with the electric heater. He had made too much. Neither Manteca nor Shinebaum was there to spoon non-dairy creamer or packets of army sugar. They sipped lightly.

Duvalier, made of sterner stuff, tried to broach a subject. "Well, Ronnie it was a tough day yesterday. Sorry to see General Goodspeed bite the dust. He had a grasp of the situation. Sorry to see you lose three of your best sergeants."

"Shut the shit up. Only ten months in country and I've lost it. Shut the shit up."

P.T. shut up.

Sergeant Ciezarowski knocked at the hootch screen and walked in. "Sorry to bother you two gentlemen."

Duvalier mollified, "It's alright."

"Gentlemen, sirs," the transportation NCO offered. "A bad day at black rock yesterday."

Neither lieutenant offered a reply.

"Especially for you Mister Remphelmann, you really got

Skip E. Lee

whacked. I mean Sergeants Shortarm and Peckerwood and Gruntz were my friends."

"Shut the shit up."

Ciezarowski shifted in his boots and addressed P.T. "Lieutenant, sir, it seems we got a new infantry brigadier, fresh off the boat. He's going to have a staff and officers briefing across the airstrip in twenty minutes. I can't find Major Dufuss. Captain Manteca is hanging out at the graves registration cooler. You two are the most senior now, so..."

"A new general, and what's his name, and what do the sergeants know?"

"Sir, I hesitate, but another brass hat kiss-ass from the pentagon. His specialty is golf courses and leisure trips, Nozzlesnott by name."

"Thank you, Sergeant Ciezarowski," Duvalier finished. "We'll be across the airstrip in a minute."

Remphelmann and Duvalier dragged their tired carcasses into P.T.'s jeep, went across LZ Betty and inserted themselves into the backmost pew of the assembly hall.

The true warriors, the true men, the officers and senior sergeants of the 999th filed in past them and slumped into the chairs nearer to the plywood podium. Leading them was Colonel BeLay, who looked like a cadaver. A call went up. "Attention." The exhausted men straggled to their feet.

General Nozzlesnott swept into the room, reminding some of a bad caricature of Claudius and Caligula combined. The brigadier limped slightly from a golf course ankle twisting and smirked as he gained the stage.

"Thank you so much for attending this tee off," Nozzlesnott announced. "As anybody knows, I am the army's greatest expert on golf course architecture, and therefore a prime candidate to solve this small time problem here on this insignificant piece of road, 'Square Ell Cubed'".

The long-suffering aide-de-camp behind him, Lickspittle,

tried to correct. "Sir, that is Que Ell One, Quoc Lo Mot, Highway One, the main highway in Vietnam."

"Thank you, my dear caddy, my little brownnoser, I stand corrected. This road is like the links at Arlington, it's the twelfth tee, a straight shot down the fairway and a short dogleg into the green, avoid the rough to the right. We merely need to mow the grass to the north-east and install a putting green on that insignificant hillock, Newly Tedium Mountain." The man behind him, the lack-luster Lickspittle, started to correct Nozzlesnott that it was Nui Ta Dom, but thought better and remained silent.

"So, again I survey the course. It is, as I was briefed in Saigon, it's all about clearing this crummy little piece of asphalt between Phan Thiet and Long Bien. It is no problem in my view. Actually it is an imposition on my time. My main assignment to oversee the construction of an eighteen hole set of links at Ton San Nhut."

A collective undertone of silent grief went through the hall. Grown men began to quietly weep. Remphelmann also found tears welling in his eyes. The tears began to drop over his downcast face and into the inside of his eyeglasses. He found a handkerchief, removed his spectacles and wiped them. Duvalier was alarmed. Remphelmann's eyes had glazed over and Ronnie was staring into the far, far distance. Remphelmann stood and said to no one in particular. "All things are well, and all manner of things shall be well."

None of the infantry officers or sergeants turned back to look. They knew that the thousand yard stare had claimed another victim.

Nozzlesnott, however, was puzzled. He pointed to the rear at the thin forlorn form of Remphelmann. "What is the meaning of this?"

Duvalier stood in Remphelmann's defense. "Oh, it's nothing, sir. Excuse the lieutenant. It's just another day on Que Ell One."

The End